I Give my Marriage a Year

HOLLY WAINWRIGHT

PAN
Pan Macmillan Australia

Pan Macmillan acknowledges the Traditional Custodians of country throughout Australia and their connections to lands, waters and communities. We pay our respect to Elders past and present and extend that respect to all Aboriginal and Torres Strait Islander peoples today. We honour more than sixty thousand years of storytelling, art and culture.

This is a work of fiction. Characters, institutions and organisations mentioned in this novel are either the product of the author's imagination or, if real, used fictitiously without any intent to describe actual conduct.

First published 2020 in Macmillan by Pan Macmillan Australia Pty Ltd
This Pan edition published 2021 by Pan Macmillan Australia Pty Ltd
1 Market Street, Sydney, New South Wales, Australia, 2000

A catalogue record for this book is available from the National Library of Australia

NATIONAL LIBRARY OF AUSTRALIA

Typeset in Adobe Garamond by Midland Typesetters, Australia
Printed by IVE

The author and the publisher have made every effort to contact copyright holders for material used in this book. Any person or organisation that may have been overlooked should contact the publisher.

The paper in this book is FSC® certified. FSC® promotes environmentally responsible, socially beneficial and economically viable management of the world's forests.

MIX
Paper from responsible sources
FSC® C018183

For my extraordinary friend, Penny.
This is not your story. That one's still being written.

Lou

The New Year, 2019

give my marriage a year.

Bold. Underlined.

I give my marriage a year.

Exhale.

Lou's hand didn't shake as she put her phone down on the bedside table.

She closed her eyes. It wasn't light yet, but she knew it was a matter of minutes, not hours, because the birds were beginning to jabber in the tree outside. The tree Josh wanted to cut right back, away from the house. The tree Lou used to love looking at as she lay here with him. Her head resting back on his shoulder. The smell of his skin. His arm tight around her.

She used to say it was her happy place. Here, in their bed, in their home. Safe. Loved. Spent.

How long ago was that? Lou opened her eyes. Stared into the lightening gloom for a moment. Rolled over. Listened for the steady breathing next to her. Rolled back, picked up the phone again.

Why don't I feel anything? she typed.

1

After all, this was a big decision. Twelve months to decide on fourteen years.

For at least ten of those fourteen years, Lou had told everyone who'd listen that Josh was the love of her life. Her person. He was the man she'd built her life around.

Deep breath. He was a good man, mostly. A great father, mostly, to their girls. Their crazy beautiful girls.

Now she was feeling something.

I'm going to try everything to save it, Lou tapped into her phone.

What did people do, when they'd made a decision like this? The cursor blinked yellow at her.

Most days, Lou couldn't decide what to have for lunch. Lately, her brain felt sludgy, like months and years of too many choices – both tiny and life-changing – were all still swimming around in there and she had to fight her way through them to any clear space where things could be sorted into 'yes' or 'no', 'do' or 'don't'.

But the clear space was where this sentence sat. *I give my marriage a year.*

Twelve months to decide whether to stay, or go.

Ballsy, Lou thought, and laughed softly to herself. I've decided to decide.

The people she knew, who'd been here, how did they decide?

She didn't know anyone who'd been here.

Oh, she knew plenty of people whose relationships hadn't worked. She and Josh had often talked about their divorcing friends and family with a confident kind of distance.

They'd nod and hug and provide the heartbroken with wine and shoulders to snot on. And then, when they were alone again, on the way to the car, or to bed, they'd find themselves holding hands. And one or the other of them would say, 'Thank God that's not us.'

What smug bastards we were, Lou thought.

Actually, now she considered it, they hadn't done that for ages. When Anika, Josh's sister, had turned up on their doorstep last year, sobbing so hard she couldn't speak, they hadn't done the holding-hands thing.

'Ed's leaving,' she'd said, and Lou had been incredulous. How do you decide to leave this whole life you've built, this family you've made, this home you've created? The secrets you've told, the fears you've shared . . . These children you've made. How do you decide to just leave?

Ed, you spineless quitter, Lou had thought. And said. What a despicable, scaredy-cat quitter.

But that night, when she and Josh had gone to bed, they hadn't even talked about it. Josh was angry, bristling. 'That fucking prick.'

'It's too awful,' Lou replied. And they'd gone to bed and she'd pretended to read and he'd fallen asleep, and all Lou could see was Anika lying alone in a bed on the other side of the city, still breathless.

I'm going to try everything to save it.

Bold. Underlined.

I'm going to try everything to save it.

I don't want to be a quitter.

Josh deserves better than that. So do I.

So do our girls.

Stella and Rita couldn't know. There was no need to upset them until it looked like it might be real. They were too little, and too happy. Too much in love with their daddy.

What would she say, if they did get to that moment? Lou let the thought squeeze in. The truth, she supposed. All those online experts would definitely say she should tell the truth.

'Mummy and Daddy don't make each other happy anymore.'

How long had it been since Lou had felt happy, in this bed, watching the sky lighten behind the branch of that old ash? How long since she'd felt lucky, the way she once had, before a million

3

dramas big and small had white-anted the solid base of the life she and Josh had built together?

Yes, this bed and Josh's shoulder had once been her happy place. But now, sometimes, Lou would just lie here next to her husband and cry. As the sun came up, it always crossed his side of the bed first, bathing him in that buttery yellow light that had made them buy the house in the first place.

Josh always slept like the dead. Like a man with a clean conscience.

Sometimes, he would roll over and throw an arm over her while she lay there, quietly sniffling. As if his instincts, even in the deepest sleep, were to comfort his miserable wife.

Humans are so weird, Lou thought. For years, she was physically obsessed with Josh, with inhaling him and touching him. And now just a comforting arm could make her flinch.

She used to play with his long, strong, blunt fingers. When they were out in public in the early days, they had a running joke that Lou would pick up Josh's hand and place it where she wanted it. On her thigh. On her chest. On her belly. It was a joke that would invariably lead to an urgent need for them to excuse themselves and go home. Even as that memory made her smile now, it felt like something other people used to do.

Now, those same fingers only had to brush against that same body for Lou to recoil. And even she knew that there were only so many times you could throw a 'Don't touch me' at your husband before he took you at your word.

How did desire turn to disgust? Was that just what happened after your body shifted from belonging to you to belonging to your children? Or was it what happened under a pile-up of disappointments, sleepless nights and towels left on the floor? If Lou was completely honest with herself, she knew there was a turning point, a moment when that changed. Could it be changed back?

I'm going to try everything I can to save my marriage, Lou wrote into her phone.

And if it doesn't work I'm going to let it go. Exhale.

But what did that mean? Lou, a teacher to her bones, knew it meant she needed a plan.

And they were going to start right there, with the bodies, she decided. And the hands. And that fucking extinguished fire.

1. We're going to start having sex again, she wrote. Smiled at the memory of some blog she'd once read and dismissed as lame, and added, *Every day for a month.*

There was a place to start.

Next to her, the steady breath broke. There was a stirring. A grunt.

Lou quickly put her phone back on the bedside table, face down, next to a necklace she would never wear.

And she looked out of the window at the tree branch one more time before she rolled over to the body next to her in their bed. She ran a finger down the smooth, dark spine and she leaned across and breathed in deeply. Then she pushed her hand flat into his muscular back.

'You'd better wake up,' she said. 'My husband's coming back today with the girls.'

Josh

The New Year, 2019

She looked like she'd been crying again.

Josh hadn't known what kind of welcome to expect from Lou as he fell through the kitchen door, arms full of bags – how much shit did two kids need for one night away? – but he hadn't expected her to ambush him with a bear hug.

He dropped the bags on the floor to return it, holding his wife tightly to him, smelling her freshly washed hair, feeling her breasts push against his chest. But when she pulled away and looked up at him, Josh could see that despite the grin, her face was pale and puffy.

'You okay?' he asked, still surprised by her enthusiastic greeting as the girls tumbled in behind him.

'Mumma!' Rita shrieked, wrapping herself tightly around her mother's legs, making her wobble. Lou stood there swaying, giggling, holding her daughter.

That was a good noise, that giggle.

'Hi, Mum.' Stella tried to slink past them, but Lou reached out an arm and pulled her older daughter to her, holding her tightly and kissing the top of her head.

'Oh, hello, hello, my beautifuls,' Lou said. 'You have a good time at Grandma's? On a scale of one to ten, how much did you miss me?'

'One hundred!' yelled Rita.

'Six and a half,' mumbled Stella from under Lou's arm.

Josh went back to the bags, and was surprised again when Lou lifted her eyes from the girls and asked, 'What about you? What's your number?'

'Number of what?'

Oh. Why was he such a dick? He knew what she was asking. 'TEN, obviously.' He smiled and winked, hoping that would make up for the cue he'd missed.

'Did you hear that, girls?' Lou said brightly. 'TEN! It's going to be a good year.'

Josh doubted that, if the last few had been anything to go by. But hey, if Lou was in a good mood, things were off to a better start.

'I'll just take the girls' shit up and come fill you in,' he said, heading towards the stairs.

The house was spotless. It often was if he left Lou alone for a day or so. She would say that was because he and the girls weren't there to trash it, but he also knew that spending a couple of days putting everything in its place made her feel calmer, helped her head. She'd probably spent the whole of New Year's Day cleaning up after the Christmas they'd had. Spent a wild night scrubbing the bathroom, most likely.

Personally, the show-home look made Josh itchy. Lou never used to give a shit about this kind of stuff. Neutral cushions in strategic spots and scrubbed-pine floors. The first few places they'd lived together had been full of clutter and colour and chaos. He kind of missed it. In this house, on a day like today, everything looked so much tidier than it was. It felt like bullshit to him. Not that he'd ever say so, of course.

Josh pushed open the door to the girls' room and threw the two bags inside. Then he went over to Stella's bed and lay down, stretching out his long legs so that his feet dangled off the end.

Twenty-four hours with the girls was knackering, even with his mum around. Lots of his mates said kids were much easier as they got older, but Josh wasn't sure. Stella and Rita had been impenetrable mysteries to him when they were babies, that was true, and now, at almost eight and almost five, they could tell him what they wanted. But also, now they never stopped telling him what they wanted.

Sometimes, he was overwhelmed at seeing them grow so full of life and energy and emotion. 'We *made* that,' he'd say to Lou, as he watched Stella cartwheel around the garden, or when Rita was using him as a jungle gym, climbing over his shoulders and dumping wet kisses in his ear. 'Would you look at this kid? She's *ours*.'

But all that energy and emotion was exhausting. There were endless demands and questions and instructions, and there were so many opportunities to disappoint them. And to disappoint Lou with how he handled them. So many women to let down daily.

Josh rubbed his temples. Driving up to Mum's yesterday with that New Year hangover was not one of his better ideas. What an idiot. Thank God he hardly ever drank like that anymore.

Still, he knew that Lou needed a break. Ever since Christmas Day she'd had this look about her like she might bite him if he came too close. And not in a good way.

He knew that look. They'd been there before. Best to clear out, if you could, even for one night. Might have worked, too. Despite the puffy eyes, she seemed a bit lighter.

Josh wiggled his toes, slipped his hands behind his head. How long could he get away with lying here? Five minutes or fifteen? He just needed a bit of peace.

Even as he thought that, he could hear Lou's voice in his head,

'*One day* with the kids and you're so tired you need a lie-down? Poor you, I have no idea how you do it.'

How is my own internal critic now Lou's voice? Josh found himself smiling at that. Could you know someone so well that not only could you hear their thoughts, but sometimes you got them mixed up with your own?

Not that Josh felt like he really knew Lou these days. He used to think he knew her better than he'd ever known anyone. But she'd begun to close off to him, bit by bit. Now he looked at her sometimes, the hard look around her eyes, the way her mouth slipped so easily into a tight line of disapproval, and he had no idea who she was, this woman in their house.

A lot of that's your fucking fault, mate, he thought. What did you think was going to happen?

'Daddeee!' It was Rita, yelling from downstairs. 'Dad-eeeeeee!'

So much of this had started after she was born, little Rita. It was ironic that she was such a sunny, smiley kid, when, really, her arrival had brought all kinds of shit with it.

All kinds of shit he hadn't handled very well.

'Josh!' Lou now. 'Are you coming? The girls say you've got to tell me the story about the stingray . . .'

She still sounded happy, despite the crying face. Maybe things were going to be alright.

'Coming!' he yelled.

Josh sat up, rubbed his belly and swung his legs so he was sitting on the edge of Stella's bed. Time to go back down. Have a coffee to get through the rest of the afternoon. Two more days of holidays until he was back in the relative peace of the workshop.

He'd been working on being better at home. Working on atonement, and forgiveness, and moving forward without anger. All that stuff he and Lou had talked about. And talked about.

Last night, after the kids were in bed, Josh and his mum had sat on her verandah, listening to the surf and watching the stars come out. Emma had moved two hours north last year, to a gated village of bland, blond-brick bungalows. It was boring, but pretty as hell.

'I think you're a bloody saint, Joshy,' she'd said to him, two glasses of white wine in as he nursed a lukewarm beer. 'I really do. Just promise me you don't let her have her way on everything. A man's got to have his pride.'

'Shut up, Mum,' he'd said, but he was smiling. He knew where she was coming from. He would do pretty much anything to ensure his kids had a childhood free from the toxic bullshit that had hung over his family homes like smog.

But his mum didn't know the half of it, really. She didn't know how deep it went with Lou, how she was the only woman he could love like this and how he knew, for sure, that she was too good for him. How he'd proved that over and over.

And his mum didn't know that if Josh wasn't such a screw-up, there would have been three little people asleep on the shell-patterned pull-out in her bungalow's spare room, not two.

Josh pushed his palms hard against his eyes for a moment, then pulled them away and shook his head from side to side, loosening that thought away.

Still, maybe this was going to be a good year. He stood up and stretched, slipped his thongs back on and started towards the bedroom door.

Tap-tap, tap-tap. Josh turned, looked at the window.

That bloody tree, it was going to smash into this place one day. He'd get on to cutting it back tomorrow.

Lou

Graduation Day
1 November, 2005

If Lou's parents mentioned her brother Rob's medical degree one more time, she was going to whip them with the tassel of her mortarboard.

'Is your brother a heart surgeon or something?' Gretchen hissed in her ear as Lou's mum, just a few feet away, told the bored-looking parent of another graduate that the teaching department's shindig was not a patch on the one over at the medical school.

'Better class of finger food, if I'm being honest,' Annabelle was saying, her English voice just one notch too loud for the setting – the glass annexe of the university's great hall. 'Not so . . . fried.' As she said this, her eyes were passing over the tray of mini spring rolls being offered to her by a stoned-looking undergrad in a greying white shirt.

'No,' Lou said. 'He's training to be a GP. My mum's never been so excited about anything. Ever.'

Lou's dad Brian was on Lou's other side, also talking about Rob, but with less focus on the canapés, more on the convenience of having a doctor in the family. He was telling Gretchen's dad, a crumpled-looking ex-rocker in a biker jacket and five days of stubble, that it was 'boys like my Robert' who were going to save them all.

'Cancer's going to get sixty per cent of us, you know, um . . .'

'Zeke,' said Gretchen's dad, looking past Brian's right ear as if searching for someone less depressing to talk to. 'I'm Zeke.'

Gretchen hissed at Lou, 'He's already had it. Throat. Too many ciggies. Speaking of which . . .' She started rummaging in the shoulder bag she was wearing over her black graduation gown.

Lou groaned. 'My parents are the most embarrassing people in the world. When will this fucking thing be finished?'

Gretchen widened her eyes and looked around with an exaggerated crane of her neck. '*Your* parents? Look around, love. This place is heaving with the people we've been hiding for four years. They're at peak embarrassing. Today's the validation of everything they've been bloody paying and praying for all our sorry little lives. We're finally qualified to do *something*.'

'Annabelle and Brian haven't been paying for anything, Gretch; Rob sucked up all of that gravy. Haven't you seen my student loans?' Lou put her head on her friend's shoulder and leaned a little, lifting one of her high-heeled feet off the floor. 'How do people walk in these, like, all day?'

'We'll never have to know, Lou-Lou, we're *teachers*.'

'Darling . . .' It was her mum, suddenly at her shoulder. 'Don't be showing everyone your stockinged feet. I think you can manage a proper pair of shoes for one day.'

Gretchen grimaced at Lou and began to move towards the door, waving her packet of cigarettes behind her back. Lou watched Zeke excuse himself from Brian's cancer lecture and follow his daughter outside.

Annabelle slipped her arm around Lou's waist, her fingers just a little too firm on the flesh above the waistband of Lou's long, flowy skirt. 'You feeling happy, BB?'

'Don't call me that, Mum.' BB was Lou's family nickname. Baby Bear. She hated it. Rob, of course, was Bear, the original. 'I think we can all agree that I'm not a baby anymore.'

I'm being a bitch, she thought. To my mum, on my graduation day.

'Oh dear.' Annabelle's arm tightened a little around Lou's waist. 'I've upset you again.'

'Can't do much right by you, can we?' said Brian, at Lou's other side now that his audience had fled.

The three of them stood together, looking around the room at all the other young women (and it was overwhelmingly women) in black, and all the family members holding drinks and eating the deep-fried spring rolls. For a moment, none of them spoke.

And then Annabelle said, 'I suppose this is it, really, isn't it?'

'It?' Brian wasn't following.

'Both of you, off. Gone into the world.' Annabelle's voice had dropped back to her 'real' English voice, not the one she'd been using on strangers, modelled on that of Princess Di.

The accent was all part of Annabelle's obsession with reinvention, something she still hadn't let go of in the almost three decades since she had left northern England in pursuit of sunshine and upward mobility. She'd worked hard to knock the flat northern vowels off her accent, to pick up her dropped H's. And now here she was, with two children who'd graduated uni.

'Mum, I've been living out of home for a year,' Lou pointed out, irritated.

'Yes, but now you'll get a proper job. Meet someone. Start a real life.'

I've already met someone, thought Lou. And I can't bloody wait to get away from this damn party to see him. Luca would be at the pub in an hour, waiting to see Lou in her cap and gown. He had some ideas about what he wanted to do with that, he'd told her. Luca said things like that. It made her blush. It was making her blush now, thinking about it.

'Maybe another teacher.' Brian was getting on board with Annabelle's vision.

'Or a deputy head,' Annabelle added, aiming high, as always.

'No, darling, they're a bit too old for –'

'Dad! Mum!' Lou interrupted. 'Can we not? I want to teach children; I'm not husband-hunting.' She lifted her heels out of her shoes again. 'This isn't really such a big deal, you know. In fact, if you want to leave . . .'

'Leave?' Annabelle's voice rose back up an octave. 'But we're taking you and Gretchen out for dinner! Rob's coming too.'

Shit. Lou had missed this arrangement somehow. 'But I've got plans. You know, with my *friends*.'

'You can have plans with your friends after dinner,' her dad said firmly. 'Your brother has changed *his* plans to be with us tonight, so it's the least you can do.'

Lou doubted that Luca was prepared to wait. In the three months they'd been seeing each other, she'd got the distinct impression that if she wasn't available at precisely the moment he summoned her to his side, she would be swapped out for the next available candidate. And tonight the pubs of Sydney's Newtown were going to be heaving with young women in the mood to cast off the shackles of parental expectation. Possibly in Luca's direction.

She pulled free of her mother's pincer grip and reached into the pocket of her gown for her Nokia. 'Okay. I've just got to make a call.'

As Lou tottered away from her parents she didn't miss Annabelle sighing to Brian, 'I told her to cut that fringe before today, didn't I?'

14

In the bathroom, Lou tapped away at the numbers on her phone until her SMS read:

Parent problem. Meet you 9.30?

She knew better than to expect an instant reply.

*

It was more like half past ten by the time Lou shoved her way through a thick soup of drinking, yelling twenty-somethings at the Bank Hotel. Her cap and gown were crushed into her canvas backpack, along with the heels she'd swapped for sparkly ballet flats.

'That's three hours of my life I'll never get back,' Gretchen was yelling into her ear as she was tugged through the crowd behind Lou. 'And your brother is *not hot*, you liar.'

'Had to get you there somehow!' Lou yelled back. 'Besides, from what he's told me lately, you're really not his type.' And she pushed on, tunnel vision focused at the back of the pub near the pool table, where Luca could usually be found.

His response to her SMS – *K* – had only arrived an hour ago and even to Lou's optimistic, and somewhat tipsy, mind it seemed like a tenuous arrangement.

'As soon as we find the bastard, I'm out of here.' Gretchen's voice was getting hoarser. 'I'm missing an actual old-school rave to make your graduation dreams come true tonight, friend. A rave with hot DJs.'

'Fine, I get it.' They were nearly at the back of the bar and Lou had seen no sign of Luca's signature bandana.

He was the kind of guy who had a few signatures. The tatty chequered rag tied around his close-cropped hair was one. His battered black mountain bike, which she was almost certain she had spied outside, was another. So was the ever-present Winfield Blue behind his ear or spinning in his fingers. And then there was his cunnilingus technique, which, to Lou at least, was a complete revelation.

Lou and Gretchen stopped by a crop of tall stools behind the pool tables and near the blue-lit entrance to the toilets. The group who'd been using them, sticky drinks in hand, graduation gowns now spun around as capes, were shouting loudly about where to go next.

'Where *is* he?' Lou's stomach was churning and she felt jittery. She wanted to see him. She wanted him to see her. This was supposed to be a great night. The greatest.

Gretchen hugged her. 'I'm going, babe. He's not here, and this' – she gestured to the heaving mass, pulled a shoe slightly off the sticky floor – 'isn't my idea of a good time. Why don't you come with me?'

'Nooooo . . . Just another five minutes, Gretch. He's here somewhere and if you leave then I'm just going to look desperate waiting on my own.'

'But you *are* desperate, Lou-Lou.' Gretchen laughed. 'Come with me to the ladies, then we'll have one more look around. But after that, I'm going to the doof.'

To Lou's frustration, the toilet queue was long, slow-moving and as raucous as the bar outside.

'This place is so sad-sack,' Gretchen was complaining. Always cooler than Lou, she had tired of student-filled beer barns just about the time Lou had started enjoying them, preferring obscure raves at deserted warehouses in suburbs too close to Lou's parents' house for comfort. But the two of them, tightly bonded from the first terrifying year of teacher training, tolerated each other's tastes. Up to a point.

Gretchen sighed. 'There are always some drunken fuckwits having sex in a cubicle.'

The door of one of the five cubicles had remained closed the whole time they'd been waiting. And as they got closer, it became clear that the shuffles and moans and bumps audible even over the churning guitar rock pounding from the bar were not the sounds of someone using the toilet for conventional purposes.

'We can hear you, you dickheads!' Gretchen shouted. She banged on the closed door. 'Go and screw out in the back alley like normal people! You're holding up the line. It's unsisterly!'

'Gretchen, shhh!' Lou snatched at Gretchen's arm. Awe and fear mingled in her stomach. 'They might come out and deck you.'

The door next to the sex toilet opened and the pink-haired girl who came out made a vomiting face at Lou, who was next in line. 'You might need earplugs,' she said, moving towards the basins.

Lou shrugged and motioned for Gretchen to go first, but her friend pulled a face and shook her head. 'I'll wait.'

The instant Lou slid the lock across the door, she knew who was in the sex toilet; she recognised the particular tenor of the gasps and groans. For a moment, she held her breath. Then she dropped to her haunches and, holding her long hair up and out of the way, peered through the gap between the cubicles.

She saw a pair of men's shoes facing the toilet. No women's feet, because, as Lou had already guessed, the girl was standing on the toilet seat. The shoes were beaten-up black Converse sneakers with *No Alibi* scrawled on them in white-out. Another of Luca's trademarks.

Lou straightened up, spun around and, still holding her hair back, vomited into the toilet.

When she was done, she wiped her mouth on the back of her hand and kicked the wall between her cubicle and the sex toilet with as much force as a ballet flat would allow, the crash immediately interrupting the moans next door. And then Lou burst out of the cubicle to gulp water straight from the tap. Seeing no sign of Gretchen, she shoved her way through the queue and back out into the bar. The only thing she could think, the only clear thought in her head at this moment, was that she must not see Luca – and he would be coming out of that bathroom door any minute.

She forced herself through the crowd, her breath coming in ragged gasps, her mouth sour and gritty, her face wet with what were certainly tears, even though she wasn't consciously aware that she was crying.

It seemed that the pub was even more crowded now, that all these people were here, between her and the front door, specifically to block her from leaving this place.

'Lou!' She heard Gretchen's voice calling above the racket. 'Lou! Stop!'

But she wasn't stopping, she had to keep going. It became clear that the only way to get through this mass of bodies was to throw herself at it. And so she did. She flung herself into the wall of sweaty people waiting at the bar. And bounced off, in a wave of indignant shouts and spilled drinks.

'Lou!' She turned and saw Gretchen, who was looking at her with wide eyes and mouthing, 'What the fuck?'

And then, just behind her friend, she saw Luca. Standing by the toilet door, he was reaching for the cigarette behind his ear and coolly looking around.

Lou dropped to the floor. It was the only thing she could think to do in that moment: to hide. Heads were turning, looking down now, at the tear-streaked woman with long wild hair trying to crouch in the middle of a crowd.

I want to disappear, Lou thought. I want to vanish. How do I do that?

There were legs all around her, like trees in a forest – if trees uniformly dressed in black skinny jeans. Still squatting, Lou began to waddle towards the bar, where the crowd was thickest.

But far from making her invisible, her duck-walk was attracting attention. 'What are you doing down there?' and 'What the fuck is your problem?' people were asking as they shuffled out of the way.

'LOU! Where are you?'

Among the knees and feet Lou could see Gretchen's blocky graduation heels coming towards her, and behind them the tell-tale black-and-white Converse. Her breath was coming quicker now; she thought she might hyperventilate if she couldn't disappear.

And then, suddenly, a pair of hands grabbed her shoulders. The grip was firm, but not painful. The hands were lifting her up, and all Lou could think was that any minute now she would be visible, facing the crowd, and she would be eye to eye with Luca, who for three months had been the only thing she could think about, but who had, three minutes previously, been bringing a girl who wasn't her to earth-shattering orgasm in a toilet cubicle.

The hands pulled her to standing. Lou found herself looking up into a man's face. He was tall. Pale blue eyes, an amused smile. 'Are you okay?' he asked her.

Lou could sense that, behind her, a pair of Converse approached.

So she reached up and put her arms around this stranger's neck. And she kissed him.

She kissed him like it was her last kiss.

Josh

1 November, 2005
11 p.m.

She smelled faintly of vomit, and her hair was in his mouth.

Josh pulled away from the stranger who was kissing him at the bar, and held her at arm's length.

She was small, this stranger, with a tangle of long brown hair falling across her face. Her eyes were ringed with smudged black make-up, the edge of her mouth was twitching a little. She glanced quickly over her left shoulder, then focused on his chest, his T-shirt. Well, it was vintage Ramones, who could blame her?

'What are you doing?' he asked her, still feeling the pressure of her kiss on his mouth.

'Hiding,' she said. And then she looked up into his face. Her eyes were wet, but she smiled.

'Hiding?'

Just as he asked that, another woman fell out of the crowd and landed on them. She was tall, with one of those interesting haircuts that was long and short at the same time. She was wearing a nose ring and a graduation gown. Students.

'Lou!' the woman shouted, because shouting was the only way. To Josh, reeling a little from the remarkable kiss he hadn't asked for from a woman he'd almost tripped over, the music was almost oppressively pushing on him now. Newtown was proving too confusing to him tonight. And he'd only had two beers.

'I thought you'd fallen down,' he said to the stranger, at a normal volume.

She shook her head.

'Lou!' the nose-ring woman was shouting. 'Why are you kissing this . . . T-shirt guy?' She looked at Josh as if he'd been doing the unsolicited kissing, not her friend. 'What the hell happened back there? Where's Luca?'

Josh saw the kisser flinch at the sound of this man's name. Jesus, he thought. Trouble. And he turned his body away from hers, back towards the bar. 'Nice to meet you,' he said, almost under his breath.

'And you,' she said quickly, quietly, just as the nose-ring friend pulled the kisser under one arm and away, into the crowd. He heard the tall woman say, 'Let's get out of this dump.'

Another strange night. Josh was getting sick of them. He'd only come out because his mate Mick had begged him to be his wingman on an internet date and Josh was curious to see how this new thing worked. It had been almost six months since Sinead, after all, and he was beginning to entertain the idea of what it might be like to be with someone else, for real. To talk to another girl for longer than a messy, drunken half-hour before sex. To kiss another girl, and feel something.

Well, he'd just felt something then, he thought, waving a ten-dollar note at the barman. But it was probably just surprise.

Mick and his date were playing pool, giggling and bumping into each other at every opportunity. Josh scanned the mass of bodies for other familiar faces, friends he'd spotted cruising the graduating class of 2005, who were getting drunk and sloppy all around him.

It was making him feel old. Ancient at twenty-seven.

This was his last drink, Josh decided. He needed to go home. Student piss-ups weren't really his scene. He was probably two beers away from texting Sinead. Again.

Mick came over, swaying slightly. 'We're going to go, mate. Thanks for coming, but we're good.' He looked back at his date, who was rummaging in her bag.

'No worries,' Josh said, summoning a smile that he hoped was encouraging. 'Godspeed, my friend.'

'You should try it, mate.' Mick leaned in, beery breath in Josh's ear. 'I know you're *tall* and everything, but even you could do with a bit of help meeting someone who isn't . . .' He trailed off, and Josh knew what the next word would be. 'Nuts,' Mick managed.

'Piss off,' Josh said, but he was still smiling at Mick, who nodded and turned back towards the rest of his evening.

Fuck this, Josh thought, I don't want to be the sad guy tonight, and he sculled half his beer before putting the glass on the bar, pushing his hands into his jacket pockets and heading for the door.

The night felt sticky for spring, and the street was almost as busy as the pub. Josh's house – or, rather, his room in someone else's house – was a ten-minute walk away, towards Redfern and the city. Josh liked the walk, especially at night. King Street was never boring, everything was open, all human life was here. Wide-eyed teenagers who'd doubtless told their parents they were somewhere else were standing outside pubs trying to talk their way past the bouncers. Couples were making out against graffiti-scrawled brick walls. Twitchy kids in tracksuits were outside the station asking everyone who passed for a dollar.

And tonight, there was a busker outside the kebab shop three doors down from the pub, playing a Coldplay song, an old one, one of the ones that didn't make Josh want to throw up.

The busker could sing. He looked young but worn out, and his feet were bare and dirty. Josh walked the few steps towards him to look at his guitar. *You can never walk past a guitar*, he heard Sinead saying in his head. *What's so bad about that?* he heard himself responding.

Then, just beyond the kebab queue and the guitar, he saw the stranger girl from the Bank.

She was talking to a man wearing a red rag around his head, and a long black coat that seemed too heavy for the weather. Even from here, Josh could tell the guy was pretty solid and good-looking, and even from here he could tell that the guy was a complete prick. There was the way that he was pointing at the girl with his cigarette, which he was holding between his thumb and forefinger like he was some kind of old-time gangster, not a wannabe with something written on his trainers in white-out.

Later, Josh wouldn't really be able to explain why he'd stayed there, several metres away, watching the way the man with the bandana was talking to the girl who'd kissed him at the bar. He didn't want a kebab. He didn't want a fight. He didn't really want to give the busker any money, since the kid had a better guitar than Josh did, shoes or no shoes. But still he'd stood there, watching this couple arguing. And they clearly were arguing, because the girl was crying, and the bandana dick was alternating between shouting and laughing.

So Josh was standing there watching, with his hands in his pockets, when the girl drew in a big gasping breath and looked up and past the bandana guy, straight at him. And Josh felt himself smiling at her.

This is the person she was hiding from, he realised, and I don't want her to go home with him. The thought shocked him, gave him a little jolt. What's that about?

Coldplay was over. The busker started singing something by Ben Lee. Josh had spent way too much time the past winter working through this album on the bed with his guitar, and obviously so had the busker.

'We're All in This Together'.

The girl kept looking at him. Bandana kept talking at her. And then she looked back at Bandana for a moment, raised both her hands – she had a little backpack on her back, and a silver charm bracelet on her wrist, Josh noticed – and pushed him away, gently but firmly, and walked past him.

She's walking towards me, Josh realised, as the girl passed the kebab queue and the busker and kept going, still looking at him. Shit. What now?

And then she was there, right in front of him, and Josh could see that her eyes were still wet and her nose was running, just a little. He was about to say something – he had no idea what – when she pushed her hair back from her face and said, 'Pretend I'm with you. Let's walk.'

He liked her voice; it was deeper than he'd expected.

The girl grabbed his arm, pulled it out of his pocket and grasped his hand. She gave him a tug. 'Let's go.'

'Okay.' As Josh closed his fingers around her hand and began to turn, he glanced back at Bandana, who was watching them, exhaling a cloud of smoke. The last thing Josh saw before he and the girl started walking away down King Street hand in hand was the bandana guy pulling his hand away from the cigarette in his mouth and giving them both the finger.

When the busker, the kebab shop and the angry middle finger were a couple of blocks behind them, the girl said to Josh, 'Nothing is going to happen. Between us, I mean. I just needed to get away from that guy.' She let go of his hand and wiped her nose on the sleeve of her black jacket.

'I know,' said Josh quickly. You were the one who kissed me, he thought but didn't say. Instead he said, 'I don't even know who you are.'

They stopped to cross the road and both looked back over their shoulders at the same moment, catching each other's eye for a fraction of a second as they did it. And Josh felt suddenly ridiculous, because he was being rejected by this girl before he had even decided he was interested in her, and why was that such a familiar feeling?

'Why don't I just get you a cab?' he suggested, turning towards her as a group of stumbling students fell past them into the road, crossing against the lights he was obediently waiting for.

'I don't live far away,' she said. 'I'll be fine.' Then she looked up at him and said, 'I'm Lou. I graduated today. I'm going to be a teacher.'

'Nice.' Josh wasn't sure what else to say, so he said, 'I'm Josh.' I'm a . . . what am I? A musician? A carpenter? Whatever.

'I just had a bad night,' she went on in her deep voice, and her eyes, even behind the rings of smudgy black crap around them, had something like a laugh in them. She raked her hands through her long dark hair and shifted a bit in her sparkly little shoes. 'And I just needed to get away from that guy. And I probably shouldn't have kissed you.'

'It's okay,' he said. 'I have weird nights too.'

She smiled at that.

The lights changed and they both stepped onto the road.

'I'll walk you home,' Josh offered. 'Make sure you're safe.'

Lou laughed, and her laugh had a little gravel in it. 'Look, that's nice and everything. But I don't know who you are either. I have no idea if I'm safe with you.'

'You are,' said Josh. 'I'm one of the good guys.'

And as he said it, he believed it, even as he hated himself for it, just a little. His mum's face suddenly came into his head, talking to him in the car on the way to every teenage party he'd ever gone to.

'Girls are people too, Joshy,' Emma would say. 'I'm a person, right? And your sisters, they're people, right? Don't forget that when your body's telling you girls are just things for you to take. Don't be your dad.' He could feel how much he'd wanted her to stop saying that. How it made his stomach clench and his teeth grind. Still, treating women like people had served him pretty well, as it turned out. They seemed to like it.

'That is exactly what a bad guy would say,' Lou said.

But she kept walking alongside him anyway.

Lou

JANUARY

Sex

Lou stood squinting into the sun, searching for Gretchen across a heaving mass of sandy, salty, barely clad bodies.

Rita was holding her hand and twisting forwards and backwards, straining Lou's wrist with every turn, and Stella was standing two feet away, sulking because her mother had enforced a hat-wearing policy.

'I'm taking it off the moment you stop looking at me,' she huffed.

'Then I won't stop looking at you,' Lou replied, her hand shading her eyes as she scanned the beach.

'You're not even looking at me now!'

'I'm always looking at you, I'm your mother.' Lou shot her a stern stare. 'Stop moaning and help me find Gretchen.'

'Will she be with JoJo?' asked Rita, still spinning.

I hope not, thought Lou. Gretchen had broken up with Johanna's father almost a year ago, but Barton still asked her to take his twelve-year-old daughter from a long-ago relationship for occasional weekends and holidays, and Gretchen, who loved the girl, was glad to oblige. Lou respected her friend's commitment, but the presence of JoJo, needy and at a deeply observant age, really impeded adult conversation.

'I don't know, darling. Can you stop twisting my arm off, please?'

It was hot. Finding a park had taken thirty nightmarish minutes, with the volume of the girls' complaints escalating in the back seat with every loop of the packed suburban blocks.

'I just want to go *swimming*!' Rita started twisting again.

'There she is, Mum!' Stella cried.

Lou's eyes followed her daughter's pointing finger and there was Gretchen, in a broad straw hat and a polka-dot one-piece, her sailors' tatts on full display under the shoulder straps and peeping from its boy-legs. She was leaning back on her arms surveying the beach, headphones in, nodding her head to a silent beat.

She's looking for us, too, thought Lou, and a surge of love for her friend welled up inside her. God, I'm happy to see you, she thought. And God, I need to talk to you.

'Come on!' Stella ran towards Gretchen as Lou hoisted her giant beach bag onto her shoulder and bent down for the sun umbrella at her feet, Rita still clinging to her.

By the time she'd picked her way through pinkish backpackers and toddlers wielding giant plastic dump trucks to Gretchen's tasteful palm-patterned towel, her friend and Stella were hugging.

'My favourite nieces!' Gretchen was shouting.

'Gretch, you have actual nieces,' Lou reminded her, as Rita let go of her mother to join the embrace.

'You know I like your girls better.' Gretchen looked up at Lou. 'Hello and happy new year to you too, lady.'

Lou smiled and started setting up camp. 'You alone?'

'For now, yes. JoJo is up the coast with her mother, so I'm off the hook until the weekend.'

The girls began peeling off their T-shirts and shorts to reveal their bright swimmers underneath.

'Can we go swimming with you, Aunty Gretch?' Stella was

pulling on Gretchen's hand and it touched Lou to see the excitement in her older daughter's face.

'Swimming? In this cossie? This is a posing cossie, Stell. This is an Instagram-only cossie . . .' But Gretchen was allowing herself to be pulled up and away by the will of Lou's daughters.

Twenty minutes later, the salty-sandy girls were digging a hole a few feet away, in sightline but out of earshot on the crowded beach, and Gretchen, her Instagram cossie dark and damp, was lying beside Lou, panting lightly.

'Those girls are dynamos,' she was saying. 'So much bloody vim.'

Lou laughed. 'Who says vim anymore?'

'I'm bringing it back,' Gretchen said. 'I'm hoping JoJo might catch some. Anyway, how the hell are you?'

Lou inhaled and raised herself onto her elbows to check where the girls were. They were piling sand on their legs, entirely involved. Stella's hat was off.

'I'm giving my marriage a year,' she said.

*

That morning, Lou and Josh had sat at the kitchen table with an iPad between them. On it was a contract she had written.

SEX CONTRACT

I, Louise Emily Winton, pledge to engage in energetic sexual activity with my husband, Joshua Mika Poole, every day for 30 days.

If, for any reason, unforeseen circumstances prevent the fulfilment of the terms of this agreement, the agreed amount of quality sexual intimacy will roll over to be claimed on a date agreeable to both parties.

'So we sign it,' Lou said when she'd finished reading it aloud. 'And we start.'

Josh had both hands around his coffee cup. It was an oversized white mug bearing the words: *I look like I'm listening, but in my head I'm playing guitar.* He rarely drank out of anything else. Stella had bought it for him, with Lou's help, for Father's Day a couple of years ago, and Lou had come to hate it because, well, it was mostly true.

'You want me to sign it?' he asked, raising an eyebrow at her.

'Don't do that,' Lou said, more sharply than she had intended. 'The eyebrow. Don't do that.'

The eyebrow went down. 'You want me to sign an iPad agreement about sex?'

'Yes, Josh, I do.'

'Where did you even get that?'

'I copied it from the internet.'

'A sex contract? With the word "energetic" in it?'

'Well, I might have edited just a little.'

He raised the eyebrow again, took a slug of coffee.

The annoying bastard is ageing well, Lou thought, looking at her husband looking at her. His curly dark hair was retreating a little, but in a symmetrical way that made him look intelligent and kind of rakish, somehow. It was Rita's hair too, now, which Lou tugged a brush through every morning to little effect.

The lines around his eyes made him look like he was laughing, and she'd always loved that his eyes were pale blue and, as her mum would say, 'twinkle like the devil's Christmas lights'. One of those northern English things she couldn't shake, clearly. They were Stella's eyes now.

Her husband was still attractive. Objectively, there was no doubt about that. Still tall and lean with only the slightest push of a beer belly against the old shirts he wore in the workshop. The other week she'd turned up to find him sanding a table wearing the now-grey and tattered Ramones T-shirt he'd been wearing the night they'd met. 'For God's sake,' she'd said. 'Don't you throw anything away?'

And he'd looked down at it, holes and all, shrugged and said, 'It's my favourite.'

But today his crinkle-twinkle eye thing was making her irritated rather than excited, which rather went against the spirit of this agreement.

'Yes,' she said, looking around to make sure the kids weren't close. 'I want you to sign the iPad sex agreement.' Lou pointed at the line at the bottom of the screen. 'You can do it with your finger.'

Josh looked at the screen, then up at her. Why was he looking at her like she was insane?

'It's going to be fun,' she said, tapping the screen.

'Contractually obligated fun?'

Lou let the iPad drop to the table and sighed. A rush of fury was surging into her chest.

I'm trying to fix things. I'm trying.

She stood up from the table and went over to the sink, where an eggy pan was sitting, soaking. Lou fished around in the tepid water for a scourer and started going at it.

After a few beats, Josh spoke, as she knew he would. He hated it when she went silent, always had.

'What's all this about, Lou?'

The girls were upstairs, supposedly getting their swimming things together for the beach, but Lou, unconsciously tuned in to wherever they were, could hear the telltale squeak and thunk of them jumping on Stella's bed.

'Stella!' she yelled, without moving from the sink. 'Stop jumping! You should know better!'

The faint noise stopped, then started again, more softly.

'And you, Rita!'

She pulled the pan out of the water, ran it under the cold tap, put it upside down on the draining board. Drying her hands on the tea towel, she turned around.

'It's about us getting –'

'Are you going to say "our spark back"?' Josh cut in, still sitting, still cradling his coffee, his face set in something like a sneer. For a second, she wanted to slap him.

'I was going to say "back in step".' Lou leaned against the sink. 'I know you'll roll your eyes, but we need to reconnect and I . . .'

'I know what happens when you're feeling disconnected.' Josh stood up, pushing his chair back with a scrape.

Lou flinched at the force of that comment, but she could sense what Josh was thinking right now; she knew him so well. He was silently debating whether to throw petrol on this fire or let it die down.

She hoped he couldn't read her mind quite so effectively. Because with 'disconnected' hanging in the air, Lou had a flash of a pair of firm hands on her hips, moving them slowly forwards and back again. Two nights ago.

She sighed, shook herself a little. 'Josh, I'm trying to stop us from fighting, not make things worse,' she said. 'So, please, humour me. Let's start this year differently. Let's try to shake things up.'

Josh brought his mug over to the sink. He stood right in front of her, close enough to kiss. 'I didn't know we needed to shake things up,' he said softly. 'I thought things were better.'

'So, then . . .' Lou decided to disarm. She looped her fingers into the waistband of his jeans and pulled him in to her. 'Why don't you want to have sex with your wife every damn day?'

Josh bowed his head into her neck. 'I do,' he whispered, 'you know I always do. I just don't like contracts.'

'Think of it like role-play,' she said, as her handsome husband kissed her neck and she felt nothing.

He was leaning into her now and her bottom was pushed up against the edge of the sink. As Josh sighed an 'okay' in her ear, she heard the clunking footsteps of Stella on the stairs and gave him a gentle shove.

'Sign it,' she said. 'And tonight, we'll pick things up right there.'

*

The beach noise filled the silence while Gretchen considered Lou's statement. Waves and yells and gulls and a distant pulsing beat from an Irishman's portable speaker.

And then Gretchen inhaled too, and she said, 'Why?'

'Things aren't . . . good.'

'Well, you've been there before, right? Worse than not good. You sorted it out.'

'Well, I don't know. I thought we did. Maybe we didn't.'

'What's changed?'

'I don't know.' Lou played with the sand next to her, letting it run through her fingers. 'Me? Christmas was . . . shit.'

'You should have called me!' Gretchen sat up now, and grabbed Lou's sandy hand. 'Why didn't you call me?'

'You were in Byron.' Lou twisted her finger around her friend's, gave it a little squeeze. 'Anyway. I'm giving it a year.'

Another pause. Lou's girls had abandoned their pit and were wrestling. Half of the sand on the beach was coming home with them, clearly.

'I hate to say it' – Gretchen always said it – 'but if you're back here again, if it keeps being not good, why wouldn't you just . . . leave?'

Lou looked around. Why did it look like everyone else on this beach – and there were hundreds of them – was having the summer of their life? That family over there, with the beautiful dark-skinned toddlers, everyone wearing tasteful neutrals and straw sunhats, the woman's blonde head thrown back in laughter, the man wrestling with his adorable sons.

Her girls. Just there. They were lying on their stomachs now, their arms back in their hole, burrowing out a tunnel.

'Them.' She nodded towards Stella and Rita. 'And history.'

Gretchen let out a little puff of air between her lips. 'History? History's bullshit. Donald Trump is making fucking history. History just happens, babe. It's the passing of time. It doesn't mean anything.'

'That's not true, Gretch,' Lou said. 'It means a lot. Look at us.'

'We're different. Being friends with me doesn't mean you're not allowed to be friends with anyone else, and' – as Gretchen spoke, Lou again had a flash of those hands on her hips – 'you don't have to live with me. If you did, I think you would have dumped me years ago.'

Lou knew her friend was about to go off on one of her diatribes about modern monogamy and how humans weren't meant for long-term cohabitation and why marriage was an institution that was good for men but terrible for women. But Lou, sympathetic to all of this in theory, couldn't bear to hear it again. Not today.

'Gretch, Josh isn't some guy I've been seeing,' she said. 'We've been together forever. He's my life. I'm his life. With the girls, we're each other's home. It's a lot. It's everything.'

'Still . . .' Gretchen took her hand back. 'Here we are again.'

'I'm not dumping Josh, Gretch,' Lou said, more decisively than she felt. 'Starting again feels like the end of the world. I want to fight for it.'

'I'd say you've been fighting for it for years.'

'I've got a plan.'

'Of course you have.' Gretchen let out a slightly snarky giggle, but she was smiling. 'What is it?'

'Right now, sex.'

A snort. 'Sex is not a plan. Sex is a given.'

'Said the woman who has never been in a relationship for longer than a year.' Lou pushed her friend's bare shoulder, her eyes still on the girls. 'Sex is a big deal when you've been with someone a long time. It can . . . go away.'

'I was with Gen for eighteen months,' Gretchen said, mock offended. 'And we still had sex.'

'With her and with other people,' Lou pointed out. 'Including Barton.'

'And Barton and I had sex every time we saw each other right up until he decided tantric sex was his destiny.' Gretchen blew a raspberry. 'Who's got time for tantra? It's so greedy.'

'This is not very useful, Gretch,' said Lou. 'I don't think tantra is on the menu. We need to start more vanilla.'

'Okay, so you tell me, married lady: when does the sex go away?'

Lou went back to playing with the sand. 'It wasn't our problem for the longest time,' she said. 'Much longer than a lot of other couples I know. We used to laugh about other people not having sex, when we were still . . .'

'Screwing.'

Lou suddenly felt an ache below her stomach that brought her hand there, pushing into her swimsuit. The word that came with the ache was empty. She was suddenly very aware of feeling empty.

'It's been a few years, I guess, since things changed,' she said. 'Two, three.'

Gretchen knew what had happened three years ago, but she also knew not to go there, not now. 'Maybe there are only a certain number of years you can actively remain attracted to one person, whoever they are. You ever think of that? Maybe you guys have just run out.'

'Again, Gretch, not helpful.' Lou took her hand away from her stomach, reset herself. 'Anyway, I give my marriage a year. My plan is that we're going to try all the things that people say you should try to save a relationship that's in trouble.'

'And you're starting with sex.'

'Sex with Josh.'

Gretchen suddenly sat up, took off her sunglasses and looked at Lou. 'Is there something you're not telling me?' she asked, and Lou knew that Gretchen was trying to get her to turn away from where Stella and Rita were now dumping double-handfuls of sand on top of each other's heads. 'You haven't gone back to . . .'

'Gretch, stop. I just need you to listen to me.' Suddenly Lou knew that this was what she needed. 'You know all kinds of things about relationships that I've never experienced, including bloody tantra. I want to try everything to stop my family from falling apart and I need your help.' She turned her head. 'I need your support. And your ideas about what to try next.'

Gretchen and Lou looked at each other for a long moment.

'So, are you going to keep score each month, like "this is the percentage I'm leaning towards staying or going"? Is that how it's going to work?'

'Well . . .' Lou hadn't really thought about that. 'Sort of, I guess. Like, how will I feel after the month of sex? Differently? The same?'

'And are we starting at fifty-fifty odds?'

Lou scrunched up her nose. Not really. But, sure. 'I guess so. That's the point.'

Gretchen put her sunnies back on and lay down. 'This is one of the crazier things you've done, Lou,' she said. 'Your marriage isn't a reality TV show. Or a blog. Like that woman who cooked a

Julia Childs recipe every day for a year even though she, like, couldn't cook and didn't have five hours to baste a ham.'

Lou laughed. 'Julia Childs didn't baste hams.'

'Whatever.'

Lou looked over at the neutral linens couple. He was taking pictures of her with his phone, the beautiful boys were building a sandcastle that was taking on epic proportions. The woman tilted her golden head back, looked at her husband like he was a delicious pie, and he lowered the phone and playfully began to crawl over the sand to where she was sitting.

'Do you think the sex will help us reconnect?' Lou asked.

Gretchen reached out a hand and squeezed Lou's thigh, which was covered by a sarong she'd draped across her lap. 'Can't hurt,' she said. 'But really, you have to want it. The connection, I mean. It's not going to turn up if you're not there for it. It's going to take more than fifty per cent.'

Lou nodded, still looking at the perfect couple, who were kissing now, as their sons worked on an improbably intricate sand turret. 'Wise words, my friend.'

'And there's something you haven't told me yet.'

Lou stiffened, knowing as she did that Gretchen's hand would be able to feel her tension.

'What?'

'Does Josh know about this? Does he know that his marriage, the whole fucking centre of his entire wood-whittling, guitar-twiddling, middle-aged life, is on borrowed time?'

Lou exhaled, loosened.

'Nope. Not yet.'

The girls came charging back at them, spraying sand.

'Can we have ice cream?' Rita yelled at a volume that made Lou flinch. She looked over at the destroyed hump of sand where they'd been digging and burying and dumping.

'Sure you can, it's the holidays,' Lou said, reaching out to brush sand off Rita's lips.

And Gretchen was looking at Lou again now, over her sunglasses, even as Stella was pulling at her to get up, get up, get up.

'Well, that's probably for the best, right?' she said to Lou.

'Yes, definitely for the best,' Lou answered.

And as she started rummaging in her cavernous beach bag for her wallet, Lou's phone, lying on top of towels and Tupperware snack-packs and squeezed-out sunscreens, started vibrating. It was flashing up a number she'd last called two nights ago.

Suddenly the heat felt unbearable on Lou's face. She grabbed the phone with a slightly shaky hand and quickly flipped it over.

'Ice creams!' she called to the girls. 'Let's go.'

Josh

JANUARY

Sex

Josh rested his head on the steering wheel of the van and closed his eyes, just for a second.

His head was heavy and the van was cool. He knew that out there in the timber yard a wave of inner-west heat was going to hit him like an iron to the face.

I want to be at home, he thought. All those lucky bastards having January off. I need to be at home with Lou and the girls, with my feet in that giant paddling pool they got for Christmas and a cold drink in my hand.

He knew better than to bitch to Lou about January. Living with a teacher for thirteen years had made him as defensive as she was when anyone commented enviously on the length of school holidays. He knew she'd be at the kitchen table right now with her computer open, hacking out the lesson plans for her new year one class while Stella splashed around out the back and Rita snoozed off a fever on the lounge.

Still, he'd rather be there than here.

But if he was, Lou might try to make him have 'energetic' sex again.

He lifted his head and hit it gently on the wheel. 'Shit,' he whispered.

'Hey, Jon Bon, are you coming?'

All the other chippies knew that Josh played guitar. He copped every rock'n'roll nickname there was, from Keef to Jimi to Slash, even though he'd never played a metal lick in his life. Now Jon Bon. Tradies – so very funny.

This was Tyler, one of his most regular partners in the jobs he'd been specialising in the last few years, restoring heritage buildings in Sydney's oldest and swankiest suburbs. They were both contractors, working for their old mate Mick, who had become something of a building tsar, much to everyone's surprise.

The days when Josh loved his job were the ones when he was in the shared workshop, focusing on details for one of the smaller, private projects he took on himself. His hands running over the wood, feeling his way. The satisfaction of standing back from a finished job – a frame or a table or an old chair that was going to sit in someone's home, quietly making life incrementally better just by being one proper, solid, beautiful thing that would last in the world.

Today was not one of those days.

Today was a day when he and Tyler had to sort through hundreds of old doors at this huge, chaotic mess of a place, trying to find six that were an exact match for a city hotel job that Mick had going on. And they'd have to haggle for them with Enzo, who was close to ninety and mean as hell.

Nope, this was a shitty, stinking-hot day and his heart was not in it.

'Mate, I'm getting sunstroke.' Tyler opened the door to the cab and Josh lifted his head and climbed out.

'Sorry. Knackered.'

'If you're already knackered in January, it's going to be a long year,' Tyler said, as they crossed the yard to Enzo's site office.

Why am I forty and still doing a job that I always swore was a stopgap?

This was a thought that Josh tried not to let settle for too long. It wasn't that the money was bad; it wasn't. The level he was working at now, the jobs Mick managed to pull him in on, he was doing alright by the family – a whole lot better than he had at other times. Times when he'd been trying to make music pay, for example. Lou was happier about that, surely.

But fuck, he felt too old to be clambering around a grumpy old man's timber yard on a thirty-degree morning.

'Lou at the beach?' Tyler asked, as they waited at Enzo's door. The old guy was on the phone, holding up a hand and shaking his head to stop them entering his air-conditioned shipping container.

'No, she's home with the girls. Probably working too,' said Josh.

Josh knew that Tyler had broken up with his wife more than two years ago now. That he barely saw his kids anymore. Josh knew this because there had been a night, about six months ago, when they'd gone out for a drink to celebrate one of the apprentices at the workshop getting his papers. Josh wasn't big on drinking with the boys. He told Lou it made him feel old, and like a walking cliché, but also it made him feel like he was truly part of this tribe, when he preferred to consider himself a visitor, an outsider passing through. But that evening, he'd gone to the pub with the others and he'd seen Tyler – who generally seemed sunny and confident – dissolve into a mess of a boy nursing a raw, open wound. Two hours in, he was slumped at the table in the too-bright sports bar, talking tearfully about how his son didn't want to come over to Tyler's new place, even though the agreement with his ex, Jodie, was that Tyler could see his kids every second Saturday night. How his little girl looked at him like he was a stranger and squirmed out of the hugs she used to fall into. It was all his own fucking fault, Tyler confessed. He'd been a shit husband who didn't pay attention, but he'd never meant for this to happen and he couldn't really blame Jodie, because she was just trying to have a good life, not one with a dropkick, you know what I mean?

Josh had been quietly horrified at Tyler's desperation and vulnerability. He'd slipped out while someone was getting another round in and gone home to find Lou curled up watching TV on the couch. 'I'm so glad you didn't leave me,' he told her. 'You know – when you could have.'

And Lou had looked at him for a long moment and then pulled her legs just a little bit to the side and Josh had folded his long and lanky self into the space on the lounge where he could still fit beside her.

The reaction of Josh's workmates told him that the same thing happened every Friday, after four or six or eight drinks, but he and Tyler had never talked about that night. Whenever Josh did ask him how his kids were, Tyler would shrug and say, 'You know.' Sometimes he'd mention that he'd been 'allowed' to go and watch a football game or rock up at a birthday party and he always made it sound like it was no big deal but Josh could tell by the way his mouth straightened at the edges when he said it that it was a big deal indeed.

'Let's just bloody get on with it,' he said, and pushed the door into Enzo's office open.

*

At home, he and Lou were more than two weeks into the sex contract. Last night had been a fairly typical example of how it was going – at first.

Lou had had to go to school for a few hours, so the girls had come to the workshop with him while he finished a job that had to be done before today's great door search.

By the time he got home he was exhausted from sanding in the heat while keeping Stella and Rita entertained and separated from saws and blades. He wanted to have a shower, get the kids' bath and bedtime out of the way and then go play his guitar for a couple of hours.

But Lou had other ideas.

She was already there, stirring something on the stove, when they entered the house. She looked great, glancing over her shoulder and smiling at him. 'Hey,' she said, as Rita flew to wrap herself around her mum's legs and Stella peered at what was in the pot. 'My people are home.'

Josh pretty much always thought that Lou looked great. One of the things he had always found so attractive about her was that, unlike almost every other woman he'd ever met, from his sisters onwards, she was not endlessly critiquing herself. At least not out loud, and not to him. She had an easiness about her appearance that, from the moment he'd picked her up from that grotty pub floor, he'd always found deeply sexy. The way her hair just fell like that, like it was doing now, over her shoulders and a little bit into her eyes. How she dressed simply, with her strong, runners' legs tanned from summer in her denim shorts and her T-shirt falling off her shoulder just a touch. They were both older now, of course, and they looked it, with lines appearing around eyes and waistlines shifting and expanding and the shock of the odd grey hair. But still, he would notice his wife in any crowd.

He leaned over the girls to kiss Lou's skin just where her T-shirt was slipping off her shoulder.

'Yuck,' said Stella, and it was unclear whether she meant the contents of the pan she'd been looking into or her parents' display of affection.

Josh felt Lou shudder just a tiny bit as he pulled back. 'Your people are all present and correct,' he said. 'I'm going to go and have a shower. Rita, come and wash up with me, you're covered in crap from the yard.'

His hand was on Lou's waist as he turned away, pushing Rita ahead of him just a little.

'Can you put off your shower?' Lou asked, not looking away from the stove. 'You know – till after dinner?'

Josh looked down at himself, his dusty T-shirt, his hands that were browner than they should be. 'I'm pretty gross,' he said.

'Daddy's gross! Daddy's gross!' Rita was pulling at him to move.

'You can just wash your hands and change your shirt,' said Lou. 'I thought' – and she turned from the pasta sauce to look up at him – 'we could maybe clean up together.'

Stella made a vomiting sound and headed for the door. 'You two are disgusting,' she said. 'I'm going upstairs. Call me when dinner's ready.'

Lou laughed and yelled after her, 'I have no idea what you're talking about! And I'll call you when it's time for you to lay the table!'

Josh had to stop himself from sighing. Lou wanted to have sex in the shower. After the kids were in bed.

In theory, this was exciting. Lou looked like she was in such a good mood, and she smelled great and he could feel himself getting hard as he watched her pad around the kitchen in her denim shorts and bare feet. But sustaining this enthusiasm through dinner and dishes and the kids' baths and bedtime stories? That was less exciting.

Imagine a world before children, Josh thought, where I could walk into the house and see my wife looking sexy and I could just pick her up and we could make love right here on the sturdy kitchen table that I made with my own hands. Not even make love. Something rawer.

That thought made him excited. The idea of what had to happen to get to the shower sex made him feel tired.

Still, a deal's a deal. 'Okay,' he said, and watched Lou smile back at him from the fridge. He grabbed Rita and threw her over his shoulder. 'Let's go and clean up just a little bit.'

But he'd been right. By the time he was cleaning the kitchen after dinner and the girls were finally asleep, Lou had a completely different look on her face as she came downstairs from bedtime stories.

She sat down at the table and rested her head on her hands. 'Bedtime makes *me* want to go to bed,' she said. 'Or just lie on the couch and mainline bad TV.'

'I know, babe,' Josh answered. 'Me too. Why don't you go and chill out on the couch and I'll go and hang out in the spare room for a while?' The 'spare room' was code for where Josh kept his music and his guitars. He was not allowed to call it the 'guitar room'; that would be tempting a re-evaluation of space allocation in their house. Something along the lines of: 'Oh, it must be nice to have an extra room of your own. We'd all like that, wouldn't we, girls?' That was to be avoided at all costs.

'We can't,' said Lou, lifting her head. 'We've got to go and have sex in the shower.'

Josh laughed a little. 'We don't *have* to.'

'But that's what we agreed.' Lou's voice was resigned. 'You know. Mixing things up.'

'Lou, this is stupid,' Josh said. 'I want to have sex with you when I want to have sex with you, not on some kind of enforced schedule.' He knew he'd said the wrong thing as soon as he'd said it.

'Well, how nice for you,' Lou said, pushing her chair back and standing up. 'Sex when *you* want it, never mind what I want? That's such a selfish, male thing to say.'

'Lou . . .' Josh softened his tone and leaned towards her. 'Be honest: do you want to have sex with me right now? Really? Do you?'

'No, I fucking don't,' she shout-whispered. He knew she was aware the kids' sleep was still at a tenuous stage. 'But you know how this works. Every night. And it can't be the same or it doesn't have the same effect. I've read loads about this. Even if you start off not wanting to, you never regret it afterwards . . .'

'Like a swim?' he asked, angling for a laugh.

'Or a workout.' She was almost smiling, he could tell.

'Lou, I'm knackered, you're knackered. Just watch telly – it's okay.'

But it wasn't okay. 'We are having sex in the shower, Josh,' Lou insisted, and she took his hand. 'We'll use the downstairs bathroom, so we don't wake the girls.'

Of course, it was fine. Great, even. The giggles at having to undress each other crammed into the tiny bathroom under the stairs had helped reset the mood. And he'd managed to recapture his earlier desire when he saw his wife lifting her T-shirt over her head and giving him the determined look he'd seen on her face at all the best moments in their relationship – like when she'd walked over to him outside the kebab shop, and when she'd told him that she was moving in with him, and when she'd told him that their next big adventure was having a baby.

He didn't regret it afterwards. It was, as he'd said, like a swim.

Well, he didn't regret it up until the moment he heard Stella calling out from upstairs. 'Daddy! Mummy! Rita's vomiting!'

Lou's face changed and she grimaced at him. 'I'll go,' she said, grabbing her shorts from the floor and a towel.

'Mu-u-um! It's everywhere!'

Josh wrapped the towel around his waist. 'I'll be right behind you.'

As Lou ran to the stairs Josh picked up his dirty clothes and headed back to the kitchen to fill a bowl or a bucket with water to salvage the girls' carpet.

Lou's phone was bleeping on the counter next to the sink. He didn't deliberately look at the WhatsApp message from Lou's friend Gretchen that flashed up on the locked screen as he bent down to the cupboard under the sink, but his eyes nevertheless took in the words.

How good is the sex with your husband? Still 50-50?

*

Enzo was the same kind of arsehole he always was, refusing to speculate on where exactly Tyler and Josh might find the bloody Edwardian doors. 'You find them and I'll give you a price,' he said with a shrug. 'But no bastard's done a sort-out for a while, so you've got Buckley's chances of finding them together.'

'We should split up, Jon Bon,' Tyler said to Josh as they left the office. 'Cover more ground.'

'Sure thing.'

Josh started walking towards one of the vast storage sheds that studded this sprawling, sun-blasted lot, then turned. He needed to ask his colleague a question that had come to him as they'd stood outside Enzo's crappy office.

'Tyler, how did you know Jodie was going to leave you?' he asked.

Under his Rabbitohs cap, Tyler's face creased in surprise. 'What did you say, mate?'

'Sorry, I know it's a bit random, but I've been thinking about it ever since we went for that drink. How did you know?'

'Fuck off, mate,' Tyler growled. 'I don't want to talk about that.' He walked off.

That was a dickhead thing to do, thought Josh, heading back towards the shed. Just as he reached the door, he heard Tyler shout, 'She hated rooting me! That was a big hint.'

As he walked into the dusty gloom of the warehouse, Josh could hear Tyler laughing his head off on the other side of the timber yard.

Lou

7 July, 2006

If this was a movie, Lou thought, he would not be late.

She was standing under the Central Station bridge at 6 am, and she was freezing. Her thin black coat was buttoned up to her chin, her bulging backpack was at her feet, and since it was still dark, her house keys – for a home more than a thousand kilometres west of here – were clenched between her fingers like baby claws.

'I should have called Dad,' Lou was muttering to herself when the ute pulled up.

It was not what she was expecting, this long, white, flat-back truck, but when the window whirred down and she saw Josh's smile, well.

'You're late!' she yelled, but she knew she was smiling, too. Beaming, possibly.

He jumped out, slammed the door and walked – too slowly for Lou's liking – around the back of the ute to stand in front of her. 'Welcome home,' said Josh. And he bent down, and he kissed her. And kissed her. And Lou dropped her keys.

Two months after the night Lou kissed the strange man in a Newtown pub, she'd left Sydney. For her first teaching placement, she was going west, where newly qualified teachers got extra points for taking a job at a 'high demand' rural school.

'There's no reason not to go,' she'd told Josh, as she'd put books in boxes in the bedroom of the Erskineville share house she, Gretchen and two other student teachers had been living in for more than a year. 'There's really nothing keeping me here now Gretch is going to Europe.'

Josh had been lying on her bed – really, just a mattress on the floor – with a guitar across his belly. If he was offended by this, he didn't show it.

'It'll be an adventure,' she'd said.

He'd nodded at her, played a few chords, then beckoned her to come back to bed.

They'd started dating pretty soon after that Newtown night – if you could call what they were doing dating, Lou thought now, as she bumped along in the ute's front seat next to Josh, her backpack in the tray behind them, driving to his new apartment. She hadn't been sure what to call it, and she still wasn't.

She hadn't gone home with him on the night she'd caught Luca having sex in the toilets. No, Josh had walked her home, just like he said he would, and he'd asked her for her number, which she laughed at because she hadn't been thinking, just an hour or so before, that her graduation night would be the night she gave her number to some guy who wasn't Luca and hoped that he was going to call her.

He did call her, but it had taken a few days. Days when Lou had remembered the feeling of this strange guy's hand in her hand walking down King Street, the particular weight of it.

'The last thing I need,' Lou said to Gretchen, as they sat on the floor of their living room surrounded by piles of placement applications, 'is to meet some other guy.'

But on day four, Josh did call. He asked Lou if she was okay, then told her that one of his band friends had something cool happening at the Hopetoun Hotel on Thursday and did she want to go? And Lou had pretended that going to gigs at edgy muso pubs like the Hopetoun was the kind of thing she did all the time and said yes.

'Just a distraction,' she told Gretchen.

When Lou saw Josh again – all tall and quiet and older than her (by a whole five years), with his lopsided closed-mouth smile and his sparkly eyes – she knew that yes was the right answer. And he hadn't made her feel stupid for not understanding the experimental music that shook the pub's walls, and afterwards they'd shared a bowl of Vietnamese noodles at midnight, and she told him she wanted a life of adventures, and he told her that was a noble ambition, and that night they had slept together, on her mattress on the floor. And it was incredible, and it chased away any memory of Luca and his world-class cunnilingus.

Afterwards she'd lain with her head in the crook of Josh's neck as he slept, and she walked her fingers across his collarbone and hoped they would do it again when he woke up.

They did.

And they'd just kind of kept doing it, right up until she left for Broken Hill.

*

'This is it,' Josh pushed open the front door of his unit with his hip, Lou's backpack in his arms.

His new unit was almost exactly how Josh had described it to Lou in his letters – the attic of an old Federation house, a bit dark and dingy, but with sloping ceilings and a skylight above the futon. Gretchen's eye-rolls over Josh's insistence on writing actual letters, with paper and pen, were all over her emails from Spain: *He's either a Luddite or a pretentious dick.*

But Lou liked the letters. She liked the wait for them, and the distance they had to physically travel to get to her and then hers back to him. She liked that, while she was discovering a whole new world in this strange, brown town in the middle of the desert, she was also discovering him, as Josh seemed more comfortable writing his stories than telling them. She understood that.

Also, she liked to think about him thinking about her while he made the time to sit down to write them.

He'd written about how sick he was getting of living in a room in his old friend Mick's terrace near Macdonaldtown station.

I'm 27, he wrote, *and the charm of share house life is fading fast. Last night I got home from a gig and Mick and three of his mates were playing strip Trivial Pursuit in the lounge room. I literally walked in the door to see Macca's bare arse wiggling around the coffee table because he didn't guess the capital of Australia. He thought it might be Melbourne. It's time to go. Or fumigate the sofa . . .*

His letters were funny, and honest. And sometimes ambiguous.

I've been meaning to write to you for three days, but I haven't been home. It feels good to be reunited with my guitar and my own bed and, yes, my notebook, so I can send a missive across country to this trainee teacher I know who needs a taste of city life . . .

And sometimes they made her tingle.

So the advantages of my new place are many, Lou. There's no Mick or Macca here, for starters. My guitar can hang out in the living room without fear someone's going to sit on it or use it as a cricket bat. And when you come back for the school holidays, there are four whole new rooms that we've never had sex in before. We can fix that. That includes the kitchen, by the way, which is kind of a cupboard, but you're small . . .

And here she was. Tomorrow she was heading out to Ryde and her parents' house – they were celebrating Rob's qualification as a GP – but today, and tonight, there was nowhere else to be, no-one else to see, other than her sort-of boyfriend in his very own boho Redfern attic flat.

'It's so weird to be back in the city,' she said, standing on tiptoes to look through the small, high window in the lounge room. 'It sounds different, it smells different.'

'Well, Redfern smells like demolition and gentrification right now,' Josh said, coming back from the bedroom where he'd put her backpack down. 'I can only afford this because there's a building site next door.'

'Oh, the serenity . . .' Lou suddenly felt very awkward. Their kiss at the train station felt very far away. Despite the letters, and the plan for Josh to come and get her today, right now she wasn't sure what was supposed to happen here. What she wanted to happen.

When the moment of silence had stretched a little too long, Josh said, 'I'll put the kettle on. You must be . . .'

'Knackered.' She nodded. 'Not a lot of sleeping on the sleeper train, as it turns out.'

She watched as Josh ducked his head a little to fold himself into the kitchen nook and fill the kettle under the tap. Tea? Really?

'So, what's it like out there?' he asked, stepping back into the lounge room.

It was a weird question, because he already knew. Lou had been writing letters too. She'd described how terrified she'd been walking into her classroom on day one, in this town where she knew no-one. How she couldn't quite believe that she was going to be allowed to stand here, on her own, and teach twenty six-year-olds. How, two terms in, she still couldn't believe it, but the fear was a little easier to live with. She'd told him how the air in Broken Hill was always a little bit gritty in your mouth from the dust, and how the weirdest thing about the place was that the last line of houses in town – ordinary, neat suburban homes, with gardens and Hills hoists and kids' scooters – back onto nothing: just desert. Endless red-brown nothingness, stretching out to a horizon that, on a hot day – and there were a lot of hot days – shimmered where the dirt met the sky, just like in a movie.

And she'd told him about her little room with a single bed in teachers' accommodation in town, with a big shared kitchen and a TV room, and an internet cafe downstairs. She'd met some great people, mostly young women like her, and on many nights their lesson-planning had devolved into swigging cask wine with *Australian Idol* blaring in the background. Some nights – Thursdays and Fridays, mostly – the young teachers would all go to the pub together (safety in numbers), where the female trainees were treated like fresh meat by the locals and the male student teachers were generally called poofters.

'It's wild,' Lou said. 'It's like I'm learning to be a teacher on Mars.'

Josh smiled. His hands were in his pockets. 'It's good to see you,' he said, shifting a little on his feet.

'Same. Thanks for picking me up.' Lou's stomach felt weird.

'I'll . . . do the tea.' Josh turned back to the kitchen, although the kettle hadn't whistled yet.

Had this been a mistake? Lou felt a bit sick now. What the fuck was she going to do if this wasn't right? Maybe the kiss at the train station hadn't felt the same from his side, and he was trying to work out how to ask her to leave.

Where could she go? Not to her parents' house; there would be too many questions. In her head, she began to run through a list of friends whose couch she could possibly sleep on tonight.

'This is weird, isn't it?' Josh had come out of the kitchen again. 'Are you feeling weird?' he asked.

'Yes,' she said. 'Maybe this was a bad idea.'

Josh's hands were still in his pockets. But he was looking right at her, and she had to tilt her head back to look up at him.

'I haven't seen you for six months,' he said.

'Maybe I should go,' Lou said. 'Too much pressure or something.'

He didn't ask her not to. He didn't say anything for a minute.

Then, 'Do you think you're going to move back?' Josh asked.

'To Sydney?'

'Yeah.'

Lou could hear the kettle bubbling now, and see the steam filling the tiny kitchen.

'I don't know,' she said. 'I don't know what's going to happen.'

Josh smiled that lopsided smile and shrugged his shoulders a little. 'Me neither.' And then he took his hands out of his pockets, put his arms around Lou's waist and he lifted her up so her feet left the swirl-patterned carpet.

'I think we should get this out of the way,' Josh said, before he kissed her again. 'Let's see if it still feels weird after the living room.'

And the kettle whistled its head off.

*

'Did you always want to be a teacher?' Josh was making eggs and asking questions.

The sex had done its job and cleansed the weirdness, at least for now. And Lou felt like maybe she had landed in that movie after all, because she was lying naked on the floor of Josh's living room, wrapped in a doona, with little piles of discarded clothes all around, and he was in the kitchen, naked, making her food.

'No,' she answered. 'I wanted to be a runner. Like, a Cathy Freeman kind of runner.'

'Really?' He looked back over his shoulder at her, an eyebrow up. 'Were you good?'

'I was great.' Lou laughed, laid on the sarcasm. 'Little Athletics had never seen anything like me. Right up until I was fourteen, when I did my knee and it never really got better. I peaked in my teens, Josh – it's a tragic but familiar tale.'

'Do you still run?'

'I do. I run most days.'

'I didn't know that,' Josh said, as she watched his bare bum and he reached up for plates. 'How do I not know that?'

'I don't go on about it. It's not very . . . cool.' It was true. 'Jocks aren't big in the inner west.'

'What about in the far west?' He was spooning scrambled eggs onto the plates.

'It's a bit hot in the Hill, but there's a gym. I can treadmill it if I have to.'

'I don't run,' Josh said. 'I'm a walker.' And he walked towards her with the plates in hand, still completely naked.

'Aren't you . . . cold?' Lou laughed again.

'Nope,' he said, and sat beside her on the doona. She sat up, took a plate, put it on her knee. 'I am far from cold.'

'Thank you.' Lou took big mouthful of eggs. 'You can cook.'

'Of course I can cook,' he said. 'I've been looking after myself for a long time.'

'So old, you are.' She smiled.

'So . . . teaching?'

'I didn't know what I wanted to do after I realised I wasn't going to be an athlete,' Lou said. 'I kind of messed around a lot in my last couple of years at school, much to my parents' horror. Then' – she picked up a piece of toast – 'a friend of mine talked me into volunteering at a youth program . . . here in Redfern, actually. And I loved it. So, I applied to do English and education at uni, and I escaped my evil parents in third year, moved in with Gretch, and the rest is . . . geography, maybe.'

Josh laughed. His laugh was low and gravelly. 'So your parents are evil?'

'Perhaps I exaggerate.'

'Really?'

'They're pretty . . . infuriating.'

'Everyone thinks that about their parents when they're your age,' Josh said, scraping the last of his eggs off his plate. 'You haven't learned to appreciate them yet.'

'Well that's the most patronising thing I've heard in a while.' Lou nudged him with her elbow. 'How the hell do you know?'

'Because I've only just started appreciating my own fucked-up family.' He put his plate down on the floor and lay back on the doona, hands behind his head. 'Well, my mum and my sisters. The less said about my dad the better.'

'Everyone thinks that about their dad at your age,' Lou told him. And she put down her own plate and lay down next to him, not sure if she should put her head on his shoulder.

'What have you been doing for the last six months?' Lou asked. She wasn't sure what she was asking him. Probably: What's between the lines of the letters?

Josh kept looking at the ceiling, but their thighs were touching. 'Well,' he said, 'I've been writing songs. I even sold a couple.'

'That's exciting!'

'Yes, it is.' He nodded. 'I've been writing letters to this teacher in Broken Hill,' he said. 'I think it's helped.'

Lou felt her face flush and her stomach ripple with excitement. 'Oh, really?'

'Yes. And I've been doing some cabinetwork for this big new store in Marrickville, which has helped pay the rent.'

'So, things have been good, then,' Lou said. And she nuzzled into his shoulder. She felt warm and happy. She was glad she was here. Glad he'd picked her up. This was the best kind of adventure.

Josh swallowed. 'And,' he said, his voice a little quieter, 'I've kind of been seeing my ex-girlfriend again.'

Lou stopped nuzzling. She heard herself say, 'Oh.'

'Sinead,' he said. 'She was away. She came back.'

'Oh.' Lou felt suddenly ridiculous. Eating eggs on the floor with no clothes on. Having sex with a guy she hadn't seen for six months just because he gave her a lift from the station. What the fuck was she thinking? 'You didn't mention that,' she managed. 'In your letters.'

'I know,' Josh said, still looking at the ceiling. 'I wasn't sure . . .'

'Me neither,' Lou said quickly. She felt a little sick. 'I think I was right the first time,' she said, rolling away. 'I'd better go.'

Now, of course, Josh looked at her. He seemed surprised. Which, Lou thought as she started picking up her clothes, must mean he really was an idiot.

'I thought you were staying,' he said.

'Yeah, well, you said it yourself. It's weird. I'm just going to . . .' Lou's arms were full of her clothes now, and she was walking backwards – why backwards? – to the bathroom. 'You know . . .'

'Lou,' Josh said, sitting up. 'You don't have to go.'

Lou shut the bathroom door. Rested her head on the tiles, which were remarkably clean for a man's apartment.

'Lou! I didn't know . . .' Josh was calling from the living room, but he wasn't finishing his sentences. 'I thought . . .'

'It's fine!' she yelled through the door. But she felt like crying, and that had not been in the plan. Lou filled the tiny sink with water, splashed her face and then quickly washed with her hands, under her arms, between her legs, before starting to pull her clothes on.

Where the fuck was she going to stay tonight?

'I didn't know if you were coming back,' Josh was saying now, sounding like he was right outside the door.

'Honestly, it's fine!' Lou yelled through the door. 'Completely fucking fine!'

And she buttoned up her coat and opened the door, pushing past Josh to the bedroom to grab her backpack.

'Lou . . .' Josh was still naked. Standing in front of the apartment door. 'I didn't . . .'

'You don't need to explain,' Lou half shouted, feeling a bit dizzy, but suddenly very awake. 'It's all cool. Totally cool. Bye!'

And she was out the door and running down the stairs, bumping her backpack behind her.

Josh

The next day

Josh looked at the house through the window of Mick's white ute.

It was a big, squat, red-brick bungalow on a street full of big, squat, red-brick bungalows. He looked at the piece of paper in his hand. This was the right address.

Josh hadn't grown up in a house like this. He'd grown up in a beachside weatherboard twelve hours from here, and then a variety of high-rise tower blocks forty minutes from here. Two childhoods: the one before, and the one after.

Women were the constant in both. Emma, his mother, trying to make things seem 'normal' wherever they were, always unpacking their toys and then their books, propping them up on shelves in poky bedrooms. 'Look, darlings, all your things are here. It must be home,' she'd say. And Anika and Maya and Josh all knew that it was Emma, really, who needed to believe that, so they'd nod and smile, and tell her it looked lovely, despite mould blooming on ceilings, or scary guys in corridors, or out-of-order lifts, or kitchen cupboards with doors hanging on hinges.

Nope, Josh didn't grow up in a house like this.

But this was probably the house where Lou had grown up. It had a long-established look about it, with well-tended flowerbeds in the front garden and sun-faded curtains on the big bay window.

Josh's hands were a bit sweaty, his mouth a bit dry.

'This sounds like a grand gesture,' Anika had said to him on his new mobile phone that morning. 'I like it a lot.'

'I just want to talk to her,' Josh said. And he did. He really did. 'And she won't answer the phone.'

'Don't be a stalker,' Maya had said, having prised the phone from her sister's ear. 'If she wants to talk to you, she'll talk to you.'

'It's just a misunderstanding,' Josh said. But he sounded defensive. He *was* defensive.

After Lou had left yesterday, Josh had sat on the floor, wrapped in the crumpled doona, for what seemed like a long time. She had only been in his apartment for two hours but suddenly it felt unbearably empty.

What was that about? The emptiness was one of the things he loved about this place. And, really, he hardly knew her. This teacher, this runner. This funny, messy woman. This Lou.

But he knew, as he'd watched her hurry down the stairs, that he wouldn't be writing her any more letters, and he didn't like that.

Treat women like they're people. He could hear his mother's voice in his head. And in his head he answered, *That's what I was doing. That's why I was honest with her.* *Yeah, no*, he knew his mother would say. *Go back a few steps.*

Sinead. Josh had written a lot of sad, terrible songs about Sinead in his early twenties. He'd met her at Sydney Uni on his doomed second attempt at getting a degree. She was the ethereal blonde he'd always imagined would break his heart, the kind he'd listened to music about his entire life. And for a while there, they were a couple – Josh and Sinead, Sinead and Josh – and at first he could hardly believe his luck.

She was studying art, because of course she was. And she was from a big old-money sandstone mansion in the eastern suburbs, and she found everything about Josh's gritty inner-city student life fascinating. The bedsits and the roll-ups. The milk-crate bedside tables. The novelty of meeting him at the end of a late-night pub shift – 'I told my friends I had to leave the party because my boyfriend's finishing *work*,' she'd say, delighted, as he, stinking of beer after a sweaty night behind the bar of the Oxford, got a sharp thrill from seeing her waiting for him at the door, wrapped in an oversized fisherman's sweater, long blonde hair hanging down, eyes wide.

Sinead liked to party. That was the euphemism everyone used then for taking a lot of drugs. Josh didn't – he'd been surrounded by the chaos caused by drugs for much of his childhood – but he knew plenty of people who did. So he got used to being the watchful one who gathered up his girlfriend and brought her home when things got too messy. And he got used to wild fights and sudden absences. He got used to panicked calls from her father, who hated him, and tearful calls from her mother, who thought he would be the one to rescue her. He sent himself broke following Sinead on a backpacking trip to Europe to spend three months fighting in museums and picturesque piazzas. They had an abortion. She had intense flings. For a while there, they split up almost weekly.

It was exciting. And then it was exhausting. And then it was just sad.

It had finally ended a year ago – she had moved to Melbourne with a guy who was happy to bankroll a new start – and, honestly, it had been a relief. Five years of high drama had left Josh tired, bruised, wary. He'd needed it done.

And it had been. Right up until a few weeks ago, when she'd called him.

'How do you know,' she'd asked, 'whether something's destiny or just a bad habit?'

He'd laughed at her line, and she'd laughed too, and said she was back in Sydney for a weekend and would love to see him – you know, just to see how he was doing.

And Josh had a head full of letters to Broken Hill, but also overwhelming curiosity about what it would be like to see Sinead after their longest-ever time apart.

'Dangerous,' Mick had told him, panting as he helped Josh carry a second-hand lounge up the stairs to his attic. 'Very, very dangerous. You've finally cleaned that shit off your shoe; why would you step back in it?'

'That is not a cool analogy,' Josh panted back, 'for an actual human.'

'I'm not talking about the human,' Mick had replied. 'I'm talking about your fucked-up, co-dependent relationship.'

And it turned out, of course, that life in Melbourne with the new guy wasn't so shiny anymore. Sinead was staying with her sister in Mosman, working out what the universe was trying to tell her. Really, she wondered, was it trying to tell her that still, after all this time, her destiny was here, in Redfern, in Josh's attic?

'Don't we owe it to ourselves,' she'd said, when a quick 'hello' drink had led to the front door of his building, and the bottom of the stairs to his flat, 'to test that theory?'

It was three weeks until Lou's holiday visit. And Sinead looked frail, like her pale skin was pulled tighter across her features, and the skin under her eyes looked purplish, and her voice had a shake in it that wasn't there before. Josh had felt protective. And nostalgic. And like somehow he was always going to say, 'Yes, come up.'

But now he was here, outside Lou's house. And he was fucking furious with himself. Because he didn't have to say that. The moment

Sinead was back in his bed, he knew that he'd been right a year ago. He needed this done. It *was* done. She and he had their old scripts that they could run through over and over, in bed and in the kitchen and outside some seedy pub that he was trying to pull her out of, but the motivation was gone. So why was he still going through the motions?

He wasn't treating Sinead like a person. He was treating her like a memory he revisited to make himself feel strong. Yeah, Mum, I got it.

Josh looked at himself in the rear-view mirror. Maybe Anika was right, and this was a grand gesture like in *Say Anything*, that John Cusack movie. Or maybe Maya was right, and he was a creepy stalker who was about to get kicked out on his arse. Either way, it was time to change something.

As he was looking in the mirror, trying to flatten his hair with his hands, he saw a red car pull up behind the ute. A man about his age, but with something of Lou about him, climbed out of the car and walked around to the passenger side to open the door. Another man got out, younger, taller. The look the two men gave each other when he stood up, the way the first guy reached out and straightened the second guy's collar, instantly told Josh that they were a couple.

This must be Lou's brother. He was a doctor, she'd told him in her letters. He was fairly certain she'd said today had something to do with that.

Josh opened his door, climbed out of the cabin and called – he hoped it wasn't a shout – 'Hey! Excuse me!' to the man who resembled Lou.

Lou's brother turned around. 'Yes,' he said, surprised.

'I'm Josh. I'm a friend of Lou's.'

'Oh.' The brother exchanged a quick look with the other man. 'Hi. I'm Rob, Lou's brother. And this is Peter.' He nodded at the man beside him. 'Come in.'

'Thanks.' And Josh walked with them towards the gate of the red-brick bungalow. He noticed that Peter was carrying a foil-topped bottle and suddenly his hands felt very empty.

'I didn't know Lou was bringing someone,' Rob was saying. 'Are you a Broken Hill friend?'

Josh looked down at his black jeans and what he hoped was a decent shirt – checked, done up to the top button. 'Oh no,' he said. 'Sydney friend.'

'Oh.' When they got to the front door of the house Rob pressed the doorbell, and turned to look at Josh again. 'Well, it's Peter's first time here, too. So, you know . . . good luck.' And the twitch at Rob's mouth let Josh know that this was a joke, but also not.

Josh remembered what Lou had said about her parents the day before. *They're pretty . . . infuriating.*

'Ha, got it.'

'Rob!' The woman who opened the door was clearly Rob and Lou's mother. Fiftyish, taller than her daughter and shorter than her son, with dark hair cut into one of those neat shoulder-length styles with a fringe, good posture and wearing what Josh's mum would call a tea dress. 'You're only a little bit late.'

The woman's eyes had rested solely on her son for the first seconds of the encounter, genuinely excited to see him. And then they slid to the left, to Peter. 'And you brought your friend Peter,' she said, her accent obviously English. To Josh's ears it sounded a little bit forced, like it was a bit posher than it should be, but what did he know?

'Yes, Mum, although you know Peter's not my friend . . .'

'And who's this?' Her eyes had settled on Josh, standing behind the two men at the door. 'Another friend? I do hope we have enough steak, darling.'

'No.' Rob looked momentarily confused. 'This is Lou's friend, Josh.'

'Lou's friend?' Lou's mother's eyebrows met in a tiny frown. 'Oh, well I didn't know we were having Lou's friends too.'

'She is . . . here, right?' Josh heard himself ask, then he shook himself. Rude. 'Sorry, yes, I'm Josh, Mrs Winton.'

'You can call me Annabelle,' she said, and she took his proffered hand and shook it lightly. 'Yes, she's here. Come in.' She turned back inside and called in the direction of a closed door down the hall, 'Louise! We have company!'

Josh's palms were really sweating now. He rubbed them together and again wondered why he'd come empty-handed for this grand gesture. John Cusack would have something. Wildflowers, a mix CD, something.

As Rob and Peter-the-Not-Friend followed Annabelle down the hallway, Josh stayed standing, two feet over the front step, focusing on the door where Lou's mum had directed her shout.

It felt like a long moment before the handle turned and Lou came out. She saw Josh immediately and, even in his nervous state, her double-take made him smile. She was wearing baggy tracksuit pants and a T-shirt with a half-peeled banana on it, and her hair was in a messy pile on top of her head. And of course, when she settled on what she was looking at, she said to him, 'What the fuck are you doing here?'

'I wanted to talk to you,' he said.

Lou suddenly touched the top of her head, as if checking that her hair was still there, looked down at herself, and then over her shoulder to where Rob, Peter and Annabelle were disappearing through a door. 'This is my parents' house,' she hiss-whispered.

'I know.'

'How did you find it?'

'Gretchen.'

'Gretchen? No way. She wouldn't have done that. Not without telling me.'

Josh took a step forward. 'I had to write the email of my life to get it from her,' he said.

Lou almost smiled. 'You wrote an *email*?'

'What can I say?' Josh thought it could be time for levity. 'I'm growing as a person.'

'Louise!' Annabelle's voice, loud enough to carry down the hallway. 'Are you and your . . . friend coming?'

'Hold on, Mum!' Lou called back. 'I'm getting changed.' Josh looked down at her trackpants and Lou pulled a face at him.

'Then send him down here for a drink, darling.' Annabelle appeared in the doorway at the end of the hall. 'Now he's here, we don't want to be rude.' She disappeared again.

'So what are you doing here?' Lou repeated.

Josh knew that this moment was the one he had to get right. Not a man familiar with the grand gesture, he considered that it was time to do justice to whatever had pushed him to hunt down Gretchen's email address, beg her to tell him where Lou's parents lived, get his sisters' advice, and stand here in an almost-stranger's house filled with actual strangers that he would now, likely, have to make small talk with.

'I screwed up yesterday,' he said. 'When I said that about Sin– . . . my ex.'

'When you said you'd just started seeing her again?' Lou's eyes were on his, and they were not friendly. Not friendly at all.

'Um. Yes.' Josh wiped his palms on the front of his jeans. 'I didn't mean it.'

'Which bit?' Lou asked. 'Which bit didn't you mean?'

'The bit when I made it sound serious. Like we were back together.' He flinched a little at that phrase. 'I was trying to be honest with you about what's been happening while you've been gone, and I didn't know . . .'

'If I was going to care about that?'

'Well, yes, I guess.'

'We had just finished' – Lou looked over her shoulder down the hall – 'having sex. You made me eggs. It shouldn't have been difficult to guess that I might care.' She crossed her arms over the banana. 'And if you're surprised that I did, your emotional intelligence is not very high.'

Emotional intelligence? That was what his mother always said about his dad. 'The emotional intelligence of a slug,' was her favourite way to put it.

'I misread things,' Josh admitted. 'Not my best day.' *Say what you mean* – his mum's voice again. 'Although, to be honest, right up until then, it had been one of my very best days. Really, pretty up there.'

'Louise!' Annabelle's voice was coming closer again.

'COMING, Mum!' Lou yelled, and then turned back to him. 'So you've come here to apologise and . . . what?'

The what was the hard part, Josh knew. Being wrong was the easy bit. But then what? Again: *Say what you mean.*

'I'd like to see you while you're here,' he said. 'As much as you want to.'

'I'm here for nine days,' Lou said.

'And I wasted one.' Josh stepped towards her. 'Can I kiss you? And can we rewind?'

'No,' Lou said. But she was smiling. 'You can go down there and chit-chat with my evil parents and my brother and his boyfriend while I get changed.'

Josh felt dizzy. Actually dizzy. She was saying yes. 'I don't think your brother is allowed to have a boyfriend,' he said softly. 'Just a vibe I'm getting from your mum.'

'I told you,' Lou said. 'They're the worst. And you have to go and talk to them, explain why you're here, and who you are, and where you live . . . I'll probably be ages.'

He laughed. She laughed. Then she spun him around and pushed him gently down the hall. 'Go,' she said.

And he went.

Brian, Lou's dad, offered him a beer as soon as he walked out to the backyard. 'Come and help me with the barbecue, son,' he said after Annabelle had introduced him, eyebrows still raised, as a friend of Lou's. 'My son's a doctor, you know; he's not good with the practical stuff.'

So Josh turned steak and Brian poked around with coals while Rob and Peter sat at the patio table with Annabelle, who told them about what was happening at the dentist's surgery where she worked part-time. 'They're getting younger and younger with the fillings,' Josh heard her say. 'I think their mothers are putting Coca-Cola in their sippy cups.'

When the steaks were done, and Lou came out from the house wearing a loose black dress, with her hair down and her trainers on, they all sat down together and Josh had to tell them about how he was doing a bit of carpentry, but only until the whole music thing took off, and then that would be his focus. He saw Annabelle and Brian exchange a look about that.

Then Rob complimented the steak and said to his dad, 'I could have helped you with these, you know. Peter and I cook steaks all the time. The way to test if they're done is to push them with the heel of your hand and –'

Brian interrupted. 'Not your strength, son. Leave the barbecue to the non-doctors, I think, don't you?' And this time Lou and Josh exchanged a look, while Rob sighed and took a swig of his beer.

Lou's parents weren't that bad, he decided. They were just trying to stick to a script that had been torn up long ago, and they weren't at all sure that they liked where the rewrites were going.

*

That night Josh and Lou lay on the futon, under the skylight. The skylight was the reason he'd liked the attic in the first place.

Josh could feel Lou's breath on his neck. His arm was around her and her body was pressed into his side. Her head was on his shoulder, tilted up just a little. When he looked at the skylight he knew that somewhere, in his subconscious maybe, this was what he'd imagined when he'd seen it. It felt more right than he could ever explain in words. Even in a letter. Even in a song.

Josh heard his phone ring. He looked across to his mobile on the bedside table. Sinead's name was flashing on the screen.

Lou stirred under his arm. She opened her eyes, just a little, and closed them again.

The phone kept buzzing.

Josh pulled his arm out from under Lou's head; she moaned and opened her eyes again. 'Hold on,' he said to her.

He reached for the phone. Lay back down. Answered the call.

He felt Lou stiffen beside him as he said, 'Sinead.'

'What are you doing?' Sinead was somewhere loud.

He didn't say anything.

'Can I come over?' Sinead asked, her voice a little drowsy, close to the receiver.

'No,' Josh said immediately. 'You can't. I'm sorry. But you can't anymore.'

'What?'

'I've got to go,' Josh said. And he looked at Lou, who had rolled over to face him, her cheek resting on her hand, watching. 'I'm with someone.'

'Who is it?' Sinead sounded more curious than upset. 'It's not serious, is it?'

Josh took a breath. He was still looking at Lou, and she was smiling at him now. He wanted her to smile at him for a long time. 'Actually,' he said into the phone, 'I think it is serious.'

The noise of wherever Sinead was, a party or a bar, swelled as if she was holding the phone away from her ear, and then her voice came back close to the receiver and she said, 'But destiny, Josh. Destiny.'

'Goodbye, Sinead. Take care of yourself.'

And he ended the call.

Lou

FEBRUARY
Fun

I give my marriage 11 months, Lou tapped into her phone.

She was sitting in her year one classroom, in one of the kids' chairs, her knees up near her chest. For the last week, it had been Ryan Harcourt's seat, but he was already proving a frenetic handful who needed to be closer to her and further from the other kids who cast around the room looking for an excuse to lose focus.

So Lou was meant to be rearranging the name tags on the desks. She should have known she had sticky-taped them down too soon.

Assessment of success of sex contract experiment: undecided, she typed.

She looked around the classroom. She'd spent the final days of the holidays in here getting it ready for her new class. She'd folded triangular paper flags of the world over rustic brown string to loop around the walls. Found a beautifully illustrated giant world map on Etsy back when she was doing the Christmas shopping, and now it was tacked to a big felt board in the corner. This year, she wanted to open her suburban kids' minds to the scale of what lay beyond their little lives. *Be kind*, she'd written in giant letters, then googled the same phrase in twenty languages and spent a night in front of

72

the TV copying it and copying it. *Be kind, Etre gentil, Budi ljubazan, Dayaalu hon, Sei freundlich* . . .

She'd tried to enlist Stella's help drawing some Chinese characters, but her elder daughter had rolled her eyes. 'They're year one, Mum,' she'd said, with all the wisdom of someone in year three. 'You're going over the top. They don't care.'

Lou had let Stella off the hook but she knew her daughter was wrong. They do care, Lou thought. You do. You might not know that you do, but you do. Every year it got harder to summon the enthusiasm to throw everything into a fresh start for a new class, but Lou knew the difference between when she did and when she didn't. Lately there had been a few years when she didn't.

She certainly hoped that Rita's kindy teacher had put this kind of attention into her first few days of classroom life. Stella and Rita didn't go to the school Lou taught at, which was by design. The moment Stella was born and she held her, she knew that despite all the love she'd felt over the years for the kids who'd passed through her classes, whose problems she'd taken on as her own, whose parents she'd reassured and cajoled, whose messes she'd cleaned up and whose tears she'd wiped away, she could never pretend that this little peachy bundle was just another one of them. And she'd suddenly understood the intensity in some of the parents who'd stood in front of her over the years, their eyes full of fear.

So Stella, and now Rita, went to the local public school, while Lou was in her fourth year teaching at a smaller school two suburbs over. The travel was a bugger but the separation was worth it.

'It's nice of you though, Mummy,' Stella had said. '*You're* kind.'

'Thank you, honey,' she'd said. But she knew that wasn't true, either.

Target exceeded, she tapped into her phone at Ryan Harcourt's old desk.

Gap not closed.
I give my marriage 11 months.

*

That morning, Lou had set the alarm on her phone fifteen minutes earlier than usual to roll over in bed and stir Josh. She knew she'd be late home after tonight's teachers' meeting, and she'd be tired and he'd be hiding in his guitar room. So she'd reached for him this morning, and he'd enthusiastically reached back.

'This is February sex, so strictly it's out of contract,' she'd told him afterwards, when she was lying back on the edge of Josh's shoulder, looking at the green-gold leaves of the tree outside the window as the morning brightened.

'Well, that doesn't have to mean anything, does it?' Josh had said. 'I mean, the contract wasn't *real*, Lou.'

At first she hadn't said anything, because she knew that it was, that it had been a test. A connection test, a chemistry test.

'I'm getting up,' she said instead. 'The girls need to eat a proper breakfast this morning.'

Josh hadn't tried to stop her. 'I'm going to cut the tree back this weekend,' he said, looking out of the window. 'Sorry it's taken me so long to get around to it. The chainsaw's been at the workshop and I keep forgetting to bring it home.'

'Please don't,' said Lou, halfway to the door, a towel wrapped around her. 'I love that tree.'

'One decent storm, and that tree is going to come crashing through the window. Or the girls' window.'

'Oh, come on,' Lou said. 'We've lived here for seven years and it hasn't happened yet.'

'Trees *grow*, Lou,' Josh said, his tone impatient. 'Seven years ago it wasn't a threat.'

Threat was a big word, Lou thought as she walked out of the bedroom and headed towards the girls' room.

There had been days, in the Month of Sex, when Lou had felt that maybe everything really could come back. Maybe this was all we needed, she thought, this daily session of skin and sweat, to bind us back together somehow. Some days she'd felt, in her husband's arms, a lightening, a gurgle of joy, something worth crying out about. Other days, she'd felt nothing much at all, found her mind wandering as she moved through familiar motions. Running through the list of things that must be done – *I've got to find Stella's library bag; that chicken needs to come out of the freezer; it's Gretchen's birthday next week; I need some brown paper bags for the sandwiches since the bloody plastic ban* – and feigned a whimper of satisfaction at a moment that seemed appropriate to wrap things up. Fourteen years and you'd hope my husband can tell when I'm faking it, she thought, although she was relieved that he didn't seem to.

What was the difference between the days when it worked and the days when it didn't? Sometimes, she knew, it was entirely down to her state of mind. How harried she felt about the lesson plans that hadn't yet been written. How infuriating the kids had been at bedtime. What time she'd made it home from work. What time Josh had.

Sometimes it was how long her other list was – the one she and plenty of her married friends kept in their heads: the list of disappointments she could pin on Josh. Frustrations about who he was and who he wasn't. Things he hadn't done lately. How freshly she could conjure up the things she'd said to him and he to her on New Year's Eve. On days when those memories were sharply in focus, the sex was something to seethe through. I'm doing this, she'd think, because I'm a good person, trying to save my family.

And other times, the difference was her phone. Everything was in there. It was constantly buzzing at her, nudging her with its whispers of dissatisfaction and promises of simple solutions. And, of course, its potholes of risk.

Like the time when Lou was lying on the couch with a sick Rita on her chest. It was a blisteringly hot day and everything Lou had tried to bring her daughter's temperature down was failing, so they'd given in to TV and icy poles under the fan and Lou being a bed for her sick daughter.

Lou's phone was still resting in her free hand when a message popped onto the screen while her daughter's sweaty little head rested on her breasts. It said, *Up for a fuck?*

Lou had immediately jolted and Rita, disturbed by the sudden movement, had started to cry.

Lou threw the phone across the room with as much force as a woman pinned under a sick child could muster.

'Mummy,' Rita whimpered. 'What's happening?'

'Nothing, baby,' Lou said, stroking Rita's hair. 'Mummy's phone was making her hot. You go to sleep. Just let me get you comfy.' Lou had eased herself out from under her daughter as gently as she could, stroking Rita's head until she nuzzled back into a cushion.

By the time Lou had crossed the room to pick up the phone from the floor the message had been joined by three more. There was a googly-eyed emoji, presumably to add levity to the first.

Then: *I miss you.*

And: *I'm horny.*

Lou madly scrolled through her phone's settings until she found Block Number, and tapped it with force.

'*Mum*, I think I'm going to be sick again,' Rita moaned from the couch.

'I'll be there in a second, baby,' Lou said, moving towards the kitchen for another plastic bowl, and typing with the other hand. *You'd better come home soon*, she wrote to Josh. *Enzo's doors can wait, I need you here.* After a pause she added, *Rita's really sick.*

Her hand holding the phone dropped to her side, and she held on to the kitchen doorframe, feeling unsteady on her feet, her head almost bursting with heat. What the hell was she doing?

And she heard Rita behind her, quietly vomiting onto the couch.

*

In the classroom, perched on her tiny chair, Lou scrolled back through her notes app.

I'm going to try everything I can to save it, she read.

And if it doesn't work I'm going to let it go.

The next project should be something that lifted them out of the grind of school pick-ups and sick kids, she knew. Something that would make them laugh together again, rather than just communicate via exchanged to-do lists.

2. Fun, she wrote. *We need to remember how to have some. Find a joint purpose or project that's not at all practical.*

What the hell was that going to be?

'Excuse me, miss?'

Lou looked up to see Theo, the school's deputy head, filling the doorway. He was smiling at her, like he always did, his arms full of colour-coded files.

'Oh, hi, Theo.' Lou jumped up from the low seat. 'I was just . . .'

'Wondering what to do with Ryan Harcourt?'

'Exactly.' Lou looked at the phone in her hand. 'And, you know, daydreaming it's still the holidays.'

'Oh, the holidays are long gone,' Theo said, still smiling. He looked down at the files. 'You all revved up for the staff meeting, first of many?'

'Of course. I'm coming.' Lou looked around for her bag, threw her phone in it. 'Wouldn't miss it. They're always so *fun*.'

They exchanged a look. Even for the deputy head, staff meetings were not fun. Not even for the head, Gabbie Scott, most likely, since she had to be the one to convince a mob of cynical, underpaid and tired teachers that the year's new strategies were worth trying. That the structures they had to implement this year were going to somehow fix the stresses of having too many kids in too few classrooms with a whole mountain of standardised tests bearing down on them.

'So, how *was* January?' Theo asked, as Lou looked around the classroom to decide where to stick Ryan's name down before they left. 'There,' he added, pointing to the spare seat next to the tag for Andrea Frick, the best-behaved girl in the class.

'Oh, yes, great idea – thanks.' Lou pushed the tag down onto the desk, even though she knew Ryan would make Andrea cry by nine fifteen tomorrow morning and there was no way that was where he was going to sit. 'Look, January was . . . an interesting time. You?'

'It had its moments,' Theo said, still smiling, and then he turned and started down the hall.

'Yes, it did.' Lou flicked off the light switch and followed him out.

This is ridiculous, Lou wrote in her head. *We need to try something else.*

Her phone buzzed in her bag. She quickly checked it as Theo led the way to the staffroom.

The text was from Josh. *I picked the girls up. Cooking dinner. I've signed us up for something fun. Think you'll love it.*

A joint project. Josh was ahead of her.

WTF? she typed back.

He replied with a shrugging emoji and a laughing face. Which suggested the girls were in on this, because Josh had no idea how to send emojis.

Well, maybe it was time to let Josh take the lead, she thought, sliding the phone back into the pocket of her bag and continuing up the hall.

Theo was holding the door to the staffroom open for her. He beamed. 'Welcome to another year in paradise,' he said, a little too loudly, as she walked through.

Josh

FEBRUARY
Fun

'**W**hat about "Born to Run"?'

'Very funny. Nope.'

'What about "Creep"?'

'No!'

'Okay. What about "Shake it Off"?'

'Are you *kidding* me?'

Josh was trying to find a song that Lou would be happy to sing with him at the school fundraiser. He'd signed them up to join the parents' covers band, an institution at the girls' school that they had so far resisted, in the hope that Lou would think the idea of them doing a duet together was romantic. But buy-in was proving tricky.

They were sitting in Lou's car, the family station wagon, waiting for the girls to finish their karate class. The radio was discussing Meghan Markle's 'on point' pregnancy style and he and Lou had just knocked off the giant monthly grocery shop. Lou had pointed out that this had to be the height of long-married Valentine's Day romance – sharing an evening supermarket trip.

'Well, you didn't want me to take you out to dinner,' Josh had reminded her, heaving a bulk box of washing powder into their trolley.

'How do you know?'

'Because you said, "I don't want to go out for dinner and sit there with all the couples who have nothing to say to each other anymore."'

Lou pulled an 'oops' face.

'I thought that was harsh, but you were obviously feeling it at the time.'

'So instead I wanted you to whisk me away to Aldi?'

'Well, it is one of your favourite places,' Josh said. He'd thought he was being charming. Apparently, his timing was off.

Now they were sitting side by side in the car outside the church hall where the girls had once done ballet, which had morphed into hip-hop dancing and now martial arts. It was an evolution Josh and Lou appreciated, not least because karate meant no more sitting through interminable dance concerts where parents had to pretend to care about all the tip-tapping children who weren't their own.

'I thought it would be cool for us to do something together that didn't involve the kids,' Josh said, his hands gripping the steering wheel. 'I'm sure you've said that to me more than once.'

'You thought it would be cool for you to be able to play the guitar in public and not feel guilty that you weren't including me,' Lou snapped back, flicking off the radio. 'This is about *you*. Not us.'

Fuck you, thought Josh, and he released the steering wheel and slammed his hands against it. 'Screw you,' he said to Lou quietly. And he opened the car door and got out.

Once outside, Josh suddenly felt ridiculous. That was a pointless gesture. Where was he going, exactly? He walked around the back of the car and over to the open door of the hall.

Seriously. Fuck Lou.

It took a lot to get Josh angry. At least, it used to take a lot to get Josh angry. He had been raised by his mum and his sisters to 'work through' those roiling waves of fury that had begun to hit him in adolescence. He had been conditioned, he could see now, to consider angry outbursts a weakness, not a show of strength, by a woman who'd had to tolerate living with a man – his father – who thought the opposite.

But really, he was just trying to give Lou what she wanted, right? This wasn't about him and his guitar. This was about 'mixing things up', a project she'd seemed to be set on since the beginning of the year. He'd thought he was taking the initiative, prioritising them doing something together. Lou was always telling him to do that. That he needed to *show* her he was thinking about her, about them.

Mind you, the first couple of rehearsals with the school parents' band had felt great. The guitar in his hands. The band behind him. The other parents in the group telling him he was definitely one of the most talented musos they'd had up there so far . . .

Josh looked in through the door of the church hall. There was Rita, looking tiny in her oversized white karate uniform, the rolled-up legs dragging on the floor behind her, getting greyer by the minute. Still, she had her fists up, good defensive stance.

Stella was closer to the front of the group, kicking and spinning like a yellow-belted ballerina. She caught sight of him, mid-turn, and offered a tiny secret wave of her fingers. Josh waved back, offered her a karate chop motion. She shook her head, just a little, as she turned, but she was smiling.

Josh glanced back towards the car. He could see Lou, hunched over her phone in the passenger seat. Since the end of what she'd started to refer to as 'Sex Month', they had barely touched each other.

'Fuck,' he whispered under his breath.

'Josh?' A woman stepped in front of him. He had no idea where she'd come from. Was she coming in or going out of the karate hall?

'It's Dana,' she said helpfully, clearly registering the blank expression on his face. 'From the band. Keyboards. "Don't Stop Believin'".'

'Oh, yes, of course!' In truth, Josh had barely noticed the other parents playing in the band, unless they were praising him. Apart from the other guitar player, of course. He'd sized him up, decided he was worthy competition. But the others? They were a blur – his back-up band. Was that *bad*?

'My son's in Stella's class,' Dana went on, and nodded through the open doorway towards one of the boys; Josh couldn't tell which one. 'Umbert.'

'Umbert?' Josh wasn't sure if he'd heard that right.

'Yes.' Dana rolled her shoulders back a little. It was clearly not the first time she'd had to explain. 'It's Italian. My husband's Italian. Our daughter's called Aurora.'

Oh. Josh could have sworn he'd never heard the name Umbert come out of Stella's mouth. Or Lou's. Still, now they were here, he and Umbert's mum, apparently bonded by rock music, while Lou sat in the car.

He reached around for small talk. No-one tells you this about school life, Josh thought. That you're going to have to spend all this waiting time with people you don't know. That all the friends you've chosen over the years because you liked each other and had things in common are going to be superseded by people who'd had sex at roughly the same time as you did and decided not to abort.

This was the kind of thought he used to share with Lou. Once, she would have laughed if he said that out loud to her. Looking towards the car, Josh could tell by the set of her shoulders that she would choose not to find that funny these days. Especially not right now.

He turned back to Dana. 'Karate's great for the kids,' he said, gesturing vaguely towards the class. 'Confidence and all that.'

'I wanted Umbert to learn self-defence,' Dana said. 'His father is a weakling.'

Josh wasn't sure if he'd heard her right. The woman was standing right beside him, her arms crossed. She looked completely normal, in her leggings and T-shirt; she looked like all the mums did – like she was on her way to or from the gym. She had a yellow ponytail, some make-up on her face. She looked normal, but that was not a normal thing to say. Josh waited to see if Dana was going to laugh. She didn't.

He looked back towards the car again. He needed to tell Lou about this.

'I'm sure he isn't,' he found himself saying, keeping the tone what he hoped was upbeat. 'Umbert looks . . .' Josh had no idea which kid was Umbert. 'Tough!'

Dana looked at Josh again, this time as if he was crazy. 'You don't have to stick up for all men, you know,' she said. 'His father *is* a weakling. And he doesn't have a musical bone in his body. Umbert' – she nodded again, and Josh desperately tried to follow the exact direction of her head, to pinpoint which kid she meant – 'is going to be different.'

'Okay.' Josh decided to stop talking to Dana. Surely the class would be over any minute. He couldn't go back to the car without the kids. He'd just have to be the rude prick standing here in silence, refusing to engage.

*

Joining the band hadn't been all Josh's idea.

How good is the sex with your husband? Still 50-50?

He had been trying to forget the text message he'd seen the night he and Lou had had sex in the shower and Rita had vomited all over the bedroom.

The fact that Gretchen clearly knew about Sex Month was unsurprising. Josh was used to her being more across Lou's thoughts and movements than he was; he was even quietly grateful for it, at times, knowing that her friend could offer his wife a level of emotional support that he couldn't. But the fact that Lou had appeared to give him such a stinging sexual review? That was brutal. Surely things weren't that bad? He'd genuinely thought that Sex Month was going well. After that, though, the rest of the experiment had bordered on grim. Lou had been determined that not a day of the contract could be missed, that there would be no reneging, no renegotiation – but enjoyment didn't seem to come into it. There was no longer anything playful about what was going on between them. There was no space for joy.

Josh didn't have a Gretchen to confide in. He couldn't picture himself talking to Mick or Tyler about the fact that his wife was making him have sex with her every day, even though she seemed to hate it. He couldn't tell them how it felt to be above or below her – this woman he adored but was scared of now – willing himself to be enough. No, that was not a conversation for Tyler.

Nor Anika. And not even Maya. Josh's sisters had been his chorus of Lou-related wisdom since the beginning of their relationship, but over the last few years everyone's lives had grown more complicated and crowded. Space for impartial advice had been gradually bumped out by grudges and tiny, tangled resentments.

Anika was in the middle of what she called her post-divorce 'relaunch'. She was training to be a yoga teacher, a life choice of such staggering predictability that Josh had to refrain from rolling his eyes every time she spoke about it. He watched as she and her boys tried to find a rhythm in a new world of two homes, two suburbs, scheduled days here, borrowed nights there . . . and he just wanted to kill Ed, her husband, for forcing his indomitable big sister into this bullshit situation of having to remake herself in her mid-forties. She had already become who she was, you dick, Josh thought. And you were never good enough for her anyway.

The only pertinent piece of advice Anika had given him about marriage since hers went to shit was to 'stay in the room', to never give up.

'I thought I had stayed in the room,' she'd told him once, in one of the wine-fuelled sessions that had followed Ed's abrupt departure. 'But it turns out I was there on my own. He'd already left.'

No. Anika had enough on her plate.

And Maya was away, as she always was. 'My little gypsy,' his mother had called Maya since she was a tiny, adventurous child. Perhaps his mum had always wanted one of her girls to live a life she might have chosen if everything had been different. Perhaps she had always seen the restlessness in her second daughter. Whatever the case, Maya lived up to her label. She was entirely untethered. In her early forties now, Maya would still arrive on his doorstep unexpectedly, a single suitcase in hand, stopping in on a trip from the Territory to Bali or from Bali to New Zealand, chasing a new plan, a new job, a new relationship. Sometimes she sent epic emails full of wisdom and insight; sometimes Josh wouldn't hear from her for months. Either way, she was not available for real-time relationship counselling, which, let's be honest, was never her strong suit anyway.

The night after the text message from Gretchen, Josh had turned to Google. That day, Lou had called him at the timber yard and asked him to come home urgently. He'd found her tearful but nevertheless insistent that they fuck in the laundry immediately. She was distraught, almost delirious with sleep deprivation from being up all night with a sick Rita, and the whole encounter left Josh feeling panicked.

Later, when Lou had finally passed out on their bed and the girls were gently snoring side by side in their room, Josh had found himself in the spare room – the guitar room – in the dark, at his old laptop, searching, literally, for 'marriage advice'.

He was immediately confronted by his husbandly shortcomings. There were listicles filled with trite soundbites from long-married couples compiled, he suspected, by uncoupled twenty-one-year-old interns: 'We never wanted to get divorced at the same time.' 'He makes me a cup of coffee every single morning.' 'Never try to win an argument for the sake of winning.' 'Do something every day that lets her know you appreciate her.'

Then Josh found Eva Bernard.

She was, according to her bio, the 'guru of long-term love,' and that night, despite being a man deeply cynical of gurus, despite being a man who had spent years teasing Lou about her interest in the shallow pleasures of social media and its stars, he clicked. And he watched. And he read.

Bernard was what Josh's mum would call 'a woman of a certain age', her appearance polished and put-together in a non-intimidating way, and she had a beguiling non-specific European accent and a list of letters after her name. Her qualifications made him comfortable, the sheer number of followers on her YouTube channel gave him confidence. He sat back with his guitar across his knee, headphones on, and watched her talk directly to the camera with gentle certainty. Each short video he watched was aimed at a different, eerily specific problem he could identify but not solve in his wife. This is *interesting*, he thought.

That night Josh watched twelve of Bernard's 'Mini Marriage Masterclasses' videos. The next night he watched them again.

Eva never broke eye contact with him, even when she was delivering bad news. She just sat in her pastel-toned office and spoke into the camera about everything he was afraid of. And it felt soothing.

'You must find the space in your love, in your life, for play,' she said to the camera matter-of-factly. 'Playing together really is a very big part of staying together. Most of us have forgotten how to do this.' (The way she said 'this', with the hint of a 'z', was quickly becoming Josh's favourite thing.) 'And this is crucial. *Crucial*. A love without play is like a kite without a breath of wind. Lifeless, lying on the floor, looking pretty, going nowhere.'

It was Eva who urged Josh to find a joint project for he and Lou to enjoy together. She suggested tennis, or dance classes, or running a marathon, or even taking a course, and this was what led him to the school band, which was playing an evening of cover duets at the next fundraiser and needed volunteers. That's us, he'd thought. That's exactly how I picture us being: community-minded but still cool. Not dead yet, he'd thought. We're not dead yet.

If Lou was curious about why Josh was suddenly making plans for them, after more than a decade of her being the one who made social arrangements, organised 'date nights' and controlled their calendar, she didn't say so. She was mostly just irritated with him for doing it, which Eva had discussed in a different video – how change made people unsettled but was essential for growth.

Yes, Eva would be proud of Josh's proactivity, right up to the point where he'd told Lou to screw herself and slammed the car door.

*

The sky was darkening over the suburban streetscape of red roofs and jacaranda trees and karate was finishing.

The girls were lining up to thank their teacher. Lou was still in the car.

'It's Valentine's Day,' Dana said. 'Remember when that meant something?'

Why does this woman keeps saying this shit? Josh wondered. What does she think is going on with me? He was trying to remember the band rehearsals, whether he could remember Dana being there, what he might have said. He'd definitely said 'my wife and I' when he mentioned the song they were going to sing together, hadn't he?

He searched for a standard response. Something that wasn't rude but that didn't encourage further sharing. 'Oh, it's all commercial nonsense, right?' he managed. 'Invented by greetings card companies.'

That's what people said, wasn't it?

A little boy with dark hair, dark eyes and a slightly awkward air about him burst from the hall and ran at Dana. 'Mama!' he cried, wrapping his arms around her waist, burying his head in her sweat top. Umbert.

Stella was walking towards Josh, a smile on her lips at having earned an extra sticky-taped stripe on her belt, which she was swinging lightly so that he would notice it. Proud. Rita was doing handstands against the wall with another girl, hair swinging.

'Romance isn't nonsense,' Dana said before Stella reached them. 'Married people have just convinced themselves it's frivolous when, really, it's everything.'

Josh smiled what he hoped was a polite smile at Dana and, turning away, beckoned Stella into a one-armed embrace. His mum would say that the universe was trying to send him a message today, and it was not a very subtle one.

He called Rita over and he and the girls walked back to the car, where Lou was still occupied with her phone.

At the sound of the car door opening, she looked up. 'Hello, my little valentines,' she said, and Josh flinched; Guru Eva would not approve of him failing to make his wife feel special on this bullshit day. 'How was karate? Kick some butt?'

They drove the short distance home, darkness closing in.

'I met this woman from the band outside the hall,' Josh said. 'She's Umbert's mum.' He caught his daughter's eye in the rear-view mirror. 'He's in your class.'

'No he's not,' Stella said. 'There's no-one called *Umbert* in my class.'

'Maybe he has a nickname?' Josh suggested.

'I don't think I know them,' said Lou.

Josh frowned. 'Maybe they're new? She said he was in Stella's class.'

'Nope, we don't have any new kids.'

'Weird.'

Josh turned into their drive, pulling up under the old tree in front of their house. 'Another reason to chop this thing back,' he muttered at the deep scattering of leaves carpeting the car space, although he kept his tone quiet, since he still hadn't remembered to bring the bloody chainsaw home.

'I've thought of a song we can sing at the concert,' Lou said suddenly as they climbed out of the car and the girls ran towards the front door.

'Oh, really?' Great, thought Josh. She's coming around. Maybe Eva's plan is working. 'Tell me.'

Lou looked at him levelly over the roof of their old Subaru. '"I Still Haven't Found What I'm Looking For".'

Lou

20 November, 2008

Getting married at twenty-six had not been in Lou's plan.

That's what she knew for sure the day she sat on the edge of Gretchen's bathtub, smoking a cigarette, her hair in rollers and a white dress hanging on the back of the bathroom door.

'Come on, babe,' Gretchen was shouting from outside. 'My landlord will kill me if you keep smoking inside.'

'I don't smoke!' Lou called back.

'Of course you don't. But that's the third one you've had this morning. Come the fuck on.'

'I don't know what's the matter with me,' Lou shouted. 'I'm terrified.'

It wasn't Josh. For more than two years now, Josh had been the best thing about everything.

The attic flat in Redfern with the sloping roof had become their first home together.

Lou had gone back to Broken Hill, back to her teachers' accommodation, but she and Josh were never apart for that long again. He'd drive the twelve hours to see her more often than was sensible, and they'd pay for a room above a raucous pub just to get away from all her jeering teacher mates. They'd stay there for two days, leaving bed only to venture downstairs for cold frothy beers and hot chips with chicken salt, or to take the occasional drive out to watch the light glow and fade across the desert.

And in the school holidays Lou would come back to the city and drop her backpack on the bed of the attic apartment and they'd play house – he'd cook for her and she'd shop for him while he was at work, and they'd go for drinks with each other's friends and he'd take her to gigs and she'd take him to plays and they'd sit as close together as two people could sit, always touching, stroking, sniffing. Their friends rolled their eyes and made vomiting noises, but everyone was always smiling when they did it, including Josh and Lou.

She'd told him she loved him for the first time outside the gate of her Broken Hill school at eight o'clock on a Monday morning. He was going to start the long drive back to Sydney, she was going to go and stand up in front of her twenty six-year-olds, and they weren't going to see each other for a month or so.

'You've got to go,' he said to her in the front seat of the ute, after they'd kissed again, and again. She'd made as if she was going to open the passenger door what seemed like a dozen times, but somehow she was still sitting there. 'You're going to be late.'

'I actually feel sad,' Lou said. 'I should feel so happy, but I'm sad. I think I might cry in front of the kids. And if I've learned anything . . .'

'. . . it's don't show any fear in front of the six-year-olds,' Josh finished. He smiled at her, and Lou loved it when he smiled at her.

'It feels like,' she started, but she looked out the window as she said it. 'It feels like . . . how I've heard this stuff is meant to feel. You know – when you . . .'

'Lou,' Josh said, 'I don't want to drive home.'

'Then don't.'

'Come on, I have to.'

And she'd kissed him again and just bloody said it. 'I love you.'

And the best thing was that he didn't pull away, not from the kiss and not from the words. He just said it back and they kissed in the ute for so long that the students started arriving and Lou caught sight of the head teacher's car pulling up ahead of them and she pushed Josh's away and said, 'This is not a good look, I've got to go.'

And he said it again, 'I love you, Lou.' And, 'Four weeks isn't that long.'

Which wasn't true, because when you were as completely infatuated as Lou was right then, twelve hours might as well have been a year and four weeks might as well have been a decade. But fuck, it felt great to miss someone so much and know they were missing you, too. To call them just to hear their voice, and to shudder with a little charge of excitement when they called you. To count the days to seeing them again. To dream about a time when you wouldn't have to miss them anymore, and for that dream to be perfection, untouchable, like a glittery snow globe of a tatty Redfern attic filled with laughter and love and sex and stories.

And then it was real, because Broken Hill was over, she'd done her year and didn't want to do another. And they decided she'd move in with him when she got back because, really, life was too short for them ever to be apart again.

She didn't have a placement at a Sydney school yet, so she registered to be a relief teacher, and spent the summer holidays running around Prince Alfred Park every day. And she'd meet Josh there at the outdoor pool when he'd finish work for the builder he'd started odd-jobbing for, and he'd be hot and have dusty smears on his face and they'd swim and then walk back to *their* flat holding hands.

They'd cook dinner and eat on the floor because they didn't have a table and they'd drink beers out of the bottle, and watch *The West Wing* and sleep on the futon.

They decided that they were going to spend six months travelling in South America because life was an adventure, right? Lou started relief teaching, which was terrible, and Josh hadn't sold any songs for ages so he went back to pub shifts on the weekends, which meant he was working days *and* nights. But it was still romantic, because they'd lie in bed and look at maps and talk about tango and Machu Picchu and how they weren't going to do all the touristy things that everyone else did, they were too grown-up for that.

And they'd gone and it had been incredible, just this overwhelming rush of difference everywhere they went, and she felt protected by him but also like she was in charge, because she had the language. They stayed in terrible little hostels and also in beautiful old hotels with mosquito nets over the beds and they did all the touristy things that they said they wouldn't and they got into one screaming fight one night after too much booze when a man had touched Lou in a way that scared her and Josh had laughed it off. They ate strange food and they met a hundred other Australians doing what they were doing and they got super-lean and brown and they found some perfect beaches and they stayed there longer than they should have, reading passed-around books and drinking sour, limey drinks until they remembered they were there for a cultural adventure and pulled out their guidebooks again.

When they'd come back of course the Redfern flat was gone, so they moved in with Josh's mum just for a month while they found somewhere new. That was the worst, because Emma liked everything just how she liked it. But Josh promised they'd be out of there soon enough and they were, and now they lived in the ground-floor apartment of an old terrace in Erskineville and Lou had a proper teaching

job at Newtown Public and Josh was getting his ticket to special-
ise in heritage renovation and they had a cat called Pocket and the
backpacks were high on top of the wardrobe where they couldn't
reach them. And she was still happy to hear him moving around
the kitchen when she came home from school every day, and she
still always had a hand on him when they went out for dinner with
family or to the pub with mates or sat watching TV on their new
second-hand lounge. And they were getting married.

So no, it wasn't Josh that terrified her.

Lou opened the door to the bathroom and Gretchen almost fell
in, snatching the cigarette out of Lou's hand and throwing it in the
toilet.

'What is wrong with you?' Gretchen asked. 'You want to do this.
You've been telling me for months how much you want to do this.'

'I know.' Lou looked at the dress on the back of the door. It was
vintage – 'You mean second-hand,' her mum had said – and simple,
and exactly what she wanted. 'I guess I'm just thinking . . . Why are
we doing this? Things are fine exactly as they are.'

'Well, it's a good question,' Gretchen answered, hustling Lou
out into her bedroom. 'But one that you should have considered a
bit earlier than two hours before every single person you know is
turning up at the park to see you do it.'

Gretchen was Lou's maid of honour, of course. And she was
wearing black. Since her time in Europe, she'd been going through
what she called her sophisticate phase, and she was wearing her hair
in a severe, black geometric bob. For today's big occasion, a pretty
good impersonation of a diamond was glittering in her nose, and a
heavy jet necklace was around her neck. The cigarettes of hers that
Lou had been nervously pilfering were Gitanes, naturally.

'This is like every crappy rom-com ever made,' Gretchen was
saying, as she pushed Lou's shoulders to sit her in front of her big

Art Deco mirror and started unravelling the rollers. 'Will they, won't they? Well, I won't let you be a cliché, Lou-Lou: they fucking *will*.'

'I'm twenty-six,' Lou said to her reflection in the mirror. 'Is that too young?'

'Well, obviously *I* think so.' Gretchen was pulling out the rollers one by one and throwing them onto her bed. At this point, Lou thought that the version of herself in the mirror looked like a shocked clown. 'But, again, you've been telling me for months that it's not.'

Lou stared at her chaotic reflection and let her mind go to all the places she'd been pulling it back from. What if she and Josh got bored with each other? What if they had kids and moved to the suburbs and became exactly like all the sniping couples they'd never wanted to be? What if they stopped having sex? What if they became . . . her parents?

Lou thought about what Josh would be doing right now. If he was all ready and in his suit, Mick would be encouraging him to have a beer, but Josh would be too nervous to drink. He would probably be feeling exactly like Lou – terrified, uncertain, questioning. She could almost feel his anxiety rising in the same surge as hers.

'I want to go talk to Josh,' Lou told Gretchen in the mirror. 'I really need to see him. It's the only thing that will stop me feeling sick.'

'Well, that's stupid,' said Gretchen. 'I don't give a shit about tradition, but logistically it's a problem. Mick's place is on the other side of the park.'

'I don't care, Gretch – I need to.'

'But your mum and his sisters are going to be here in about twenty minutes to pick you up.' Gretchen almost sounded stressed. Clearly, she was taking her duties seriously.

'We'll tell them to meet us at the park.' Lou was standing up. Her hair was still all over the place.

'I haven't even done your face . . .'

'Fuck it. Come on, Gretch, let's order a cab.'

Everything about marrying Josh was right apart from actually doing it. The world was changing. This month, she'd been teaching her class about the first African American president of the United States, who'd just been elected. Earlier in the year, they'd been studying the National Apology to Australia's Indigenous people. The world was modernising, progressing, shifting. And here was Lou, waiting to be 'given away' to a man by her dad. She was too young and these traditions were too old.

So Lou threw her dress over her arm and in her tracksuit pants and trainers with her hair all over the place, she climbed into a taxi with Gretchen – carrying shoes and a bottle of champagne – right behind her. In the car she put her head between her legs while Gretchen stroked her back and called everyone, and Lou took deep, gulping breaths. Her heart was smashing against her ribcage as she heard her best friend tell her mum, 'I know, Annabelle, but she just needs a bit of chill time.'

Lou could hear the response to that three feet from the phone.

Bizarrely, when the cab arrived at Mick's place in Surry Hills, Josh and Mick were sitting out on the front wall in their suits, looking for all the world like they had nothing else to do that day. Josh was fiddling with a guitar and Mick was smoking what looked like a joint.

Lou saw a look of absolute shock pass across Josh's face as he clocked her tumbling out of the car, her arms full of the lacy white dress. And then his face crumpled into a smile. And then a laugh. And Lou felt her breath slow down for the first time that day.

'What the hell are you doing here?' Mick asked, stubbing out his smoke and stepping towards them.

Gretchen looked at Josh and shrugged. 'Apparently, she's not sure why you guys are getting married.'

Lou saw Josh's smile fade and he just looked at her, confused. 'What?'

Lou shoved the dress at Mick and ran to Josh, who put down the guitar and let her fall into his arms. 'What's going on?' he asked, his mouth in her hair as she burrowed into his neck.

'I'm scared,' Lou said. 'I'm really scared. And I knew you would be too. I thought we'd be less scared together.'

'Lou,' Josh said, 'I'm not scared.'

He pushed her away a little, so he was looking at her. Mick and Gretchen started backing away into the house. 'I've never been more sure of a decision.'

'Really?'

'Really.'

'You don't think we're too young?'

'We made this call together, right? For lots of very good reasons.' He pulled her into his arms again. 'And' – he was talking into her messy hair – '*I'm* not that young.'

Lou laughed, stood back and wiped her face with her sleeve. Josh, she noticed, looked good in his suit. 'I want to go with you to the wedding,' she said. 'I want us to go together.'

'Of course,' Josh said. 'Why not?'

'Um, because my mum, your mum, your sisters, our friends. There are all these rules . . .' Lou was beginning to feel a bit silly. Like she'd made this big fuss about nothing, and now phone calls were pinging around Sydney's inner west like there was some kind of crisis. When everything was going to be fine.

'Fuck the rules,' said Josh. 'I think that's what young people are meant to do.'

Lou and Josh looked at each other for a minute, and Lou thought she felt a moment of real fear when she thought about what they were asking each other to do: stand by each other no matter what came, when neither one of them had the imagination or experience to know what that actually meant.

'I'd better go and get dressed,' said Lou. 'Why the hell are you out here anyway? Shouldn't you be inside playing Xbox or drinking down the pub or something?'

'Nah.' Josh looked down at his hands. 'I'm waiting for my dad.'

'Your *dad* is coming?'

Lou had never met Josh's dad. Not in the two (and a half, depending on when you start your count, she always said) years they'd been together. She didn't even know where he lived.

She'd heard about him, of course. From Josh, in those early days when they'd been pouring out their stories to each other, to be picked up and held to the light and examined like clues. And from Emma after a couple of wines. And from Josh's sisters, when she'd asked. And what she'd heard was that he was terrible. Mean. Abusive, even. That he'd blown up the family and left them with nothing. That Emma would have been a whole lot of things if he'd never fucked everything up. Partly, the insinuation went, by fucking everything.

'Why is he coming?' Lou asked Josh. Behind him, she could see Gretchen in the front window of Mick's house, beckoning to her madly and waving the wedding dress.

Josh shrugged, looked at the ground. 'I invited him.'

'But your mum . . .'

'. . . is going to lose it.' Josh had seemed so relaxed just a couple of minutes ago, while she was hyperventilating, but now he looked twitchy.

'This seems like something we should have talked about,' Lou said.

Josh nodded, put his hands in his pockets. 'I didn't think he'd come,' he said. 'Turns out he's a *romantic*.' And the word came out of Josh's mouth sounding sour, like limey South American drinks.

Josh

The same day

Josh had never proposed, as such.

After South America, he and Lou talked about another trip, but even as they did, roots began to unfurl beneath them.

Their place, the one they'd moved into together – putting tatty bits of furniture here, hanging framed postcard pictures there – felt as much like home as anywhere he had ever lived. Josh's work started early and finished early, and he loved being home and hearing Lou's key turn in the lock. She always kind of fell into the house, with stories spilling out alongside her school books and folders – what this kid had done or that kid had said, what a parent had complained about, the idiotic decision that the head had made. She was a whirlwind of energy in his quieter existence, and it worked.

The whole wedding thing had come up because of Lou's mum. Annabelle didn't really approve of Josh, even when it became clear that he was sticking around. It was his work that appeared to be the problem. A musician-tradie hybrid was not what she had in mind for her daughter.

Every question asked at their first Christmas as a couple hinted at this, with Annabelle coming at Josh from slightly shifting angles under the cover of a sunshade in the baking-hot backyard.

'So, Josh, do you have any big career plans this year?'

'Does anyone really make money out of music? I hear it's heart-breakingly competitive.'

'Is carpentry really a profession, though? Or is it a trade?'

'Have you ever thought of starting your own business?'

Josh could tell that Annabelle was making him over in her head: trimming his hair, exchanging his T-shirt for a polo shirt, his jeans for trousers. She wanted Lou to have a boyfriend who would talk about his career ladder and house prices and where her imaginary grandchildren should go to school. Growing up as he did, Josh knew what a woman's disappointment looked like and it was written all over Annabelle's face.

He and Lou had only been back in the country for two weeks when they attended a family dinner at an inner-west club that Annabelle deemed acceptable. Rob and Peter were travelling over from Kirribilli, where they'd recently bought a small apartment with a water view. Josh and Lou had discussed the fact that if Peter were a woman, this development in the family – a harbourside home! – would be the subject of much pride and celebration; instead, it was something to be rushed past with a hasty, 'How nice,' and a vague reference to the number of bedrooms.

Annabelle had seemed upset that evening. Happy to have Lou back safe from a part of the world she considered a dangerous hellhole, but clearly unsettled by the way her family life was turning out. There was no solicitor or accountant or deputy head on the horizon for Lou, nor a picket fence in sight for either of her children. She was taking out her dissatisfaction on the club's wait staff, who didn't know where the fish of the day had been caught and insisted that drinks had to be ordered at the bar.

'I'll go,' Josh volunteered.

'This is not meant to be a *pub*,' Annabelle was saying. 'We are not eating dinner in a pub.'

'Well, we kind of are, Mum,' Lou said, gesturing to the beer-laden tables and the screens silently showing football matches, horseracing and Keno. 'And it's fine. The steak here's meant to be great.'

'You must have eaten some great steak in South America,' Peter offered, trying to redirect the conversation.

'What would you like to drink, Annabelle?' Josh asked, rising from his seat.

'I wouldn't trust the meat in South America – would you, Brian?' Annabelle asked, ignoring Josh.

Lou's dad, who was looking defeated, said, 'I'll have a pale ale, please, son.'

'Son?' Annabelle repeated. 'That's optimistic.'

'Mum!' Lou put her face in her hands. Her wrists and hands, Josh noticed, were still tanned from the trip, and she was wearing a frayed friendship bracelet that they'd been given by kids in Peru.

There was a tense beat before Josh said, 'I'd be lucky to be.' He was still looking at Lou, who lifted her head from her hands when he said it. And then, to the table of confused faces, he added, 'Your son-in-law, I mean.'

Annabelle started talking very loudly and quickly, and Brian was shaking his head, but Lou just kept looking at him over her hands. She was smiling.

If this was commitment, if this was what it took to convince the people around your person that you could be counted on, that you were a serious adult human, able to step up – well, here he was.

Lou, he knew, didn't wish he was someone else, like her mother did. He'd never been more sure of anything as he was in that crappy club with the sticky carpet and the bleeping slot machines and the winner of the meat raffle being announced over loudspeaker.

And Josh was still certain now, as he sat on the low wall outside Mick's impeccably renovated Surry Hills terrace on his wedding day and waited for his father to turn up.

He was hot in his suit, and his neck itched as a drop of sweat snaked down from his hair.

It was springtime in Sydney and the jasmine was out. Even the houses on Mick's street that hadn't yet fallen to gentrification, the ones that still had sheets hanging in windows and sagging couches out the front, were dripping with the tiny white flowers. It was a beautiful day for a wedding.

Josh picked at Mick's guitar. The first couple of bars of 'Here Comes the Sun'.

Lou was inside now, getting changed, with Gretchen at her side. Mick was on the phone – to the girl he was seeing, from the sound of it – convincing her she should definitely come to this wedding party tonight, it was going to be sick.

Where the fuck was his old man? Wouldn't it be typical of him to say he was coming, against all odds, and then not show up? And why the hell hadn't he told his mother about this impulsive invitation?

Josh had been eleven when Emma had finally put the three kids in the old family Bluebird and driven away from the weatherboard house on the coast. By Josh's count, it was overdue by about three years of unexplained absences and constant bickering and nights of unnerving silence punctuated by screaming outbursts. His dad, Lenny, unimpressed by Emma's desertion, for a while insisted on seeing the children every second weekend, in keeping with the custody arrangements. This was hellish for everyone, including Lenny, who really had no interest in or aptitude for fatherhood. Josh and his sisters would be driven up to the Central Coast in Len's smoke-filled, battered Beemer to spend hours watching TV at the homes of women he was 'seeing', usually in the company of the children of the house, who were unimpressed by the interlopers and let them know it. Or they were dropped off at a park or beach and told to 'entertain yourselves' for a few hours while he headed off to 'see a man about a dog' and came back smelling of beer and Winnie Reds.

Some weekends, the three kids sat outside whichever house or unit they were living in with Emma, waiting for the Beemer to pull up, but it never came. Josh would be listening to his CD Walkman, his most prized possession. Anika would have found neighbourhood kids to hang out with and Maya would have her head in a book as they let an hour tick past before heading back upstairs to Mum. 'No Dad?' she'd say, in as even a tone as she could manage. 'No Dad,' they'd reply, and pull their pyjamas and swimmers out of their backpacks. The feeling, then, was a kind of toxic swirl of relief and guilt and anger. It was the sensation that Josh associated with Saturday mornings throughout his teens.

Josh began to feel a twinge of that same anxiety as he sat on Mick's wall.

And then, just as Mick emerged from the house saying, 'Gretch reckons fifteen minutes to go-time, mate,' a silver taxi pulled up.

Josh stood, carefully rested the guitar on the wall and straightened his jacket.

His father climbed out of the front passenger side of the cab, and then walked around to the back door without looking up. He opened it and a woman in a flowery dress and a yellow hat with a ribbon stepped out. She was fiftyish, and smiling. Len reached into the back seat to fetch a small, tired-looking leather holdall. Then he took the woman's arm and turned towards Josh. 'Hello, son.'

'Thanks so much for inviting us,' the woman said in a broad Irish accent. 'I'm Christine.'

And Josh had no idea what to say. His dad looked old. He looked like an old man. In his head, his dad was lean and sharp. He had edges that didn't invite close contact. This guy's lines were much blurrier, his stomach pushing against his thin blue shirt, his jacket undone, his jaw loose. His suit had a slight sheen and looked like it probably wouldn't button. His hair – thick and black like Josh's – had been oiled down and forward, as if to disguise a retreat. But when he finally met his son's eyes, the recognition was unmistakable. This was his father's steady gaze, the one that had scared him witless as a kid.

When was the last time they'd seen each other? It had been years – maybe Maya's eighteenth? Shit. What had Josh been thinking when he'd called to invite him? And who the hell was Christine? This was going to be like rolling a grenade into a garden party. The familiar panic was back, popping in the pit of his stomach.

'Hello, Dad.' Nothing about his dad's demeanour suggested a hug, so Josh offered his hand.

'Hello, Mr Poole,' Mick said, stepping forward. 'I'm Mick. Best man.'

They just stood there, four figures in the blistering, fragrant afternoon, with no idea how to proceed.

And then Lou walked out of the front door in her wedding dress.

'Is that the bride?' asked Christine, looking from Lou to Josh to Lou. 'Well, how unusual.'

Lou didn't respond to that. She just walked into the centre of the four frozen figures, stood in front of Len, and held her arms out as if for a hug.

'Hello, you must be Josh's dad.'

And Lenny clearly had no idea what to do other than to hug her, this lovely young woman in a white lacy dress, her wavy hair dusted with jasmine flowers.

'I'm Lou,' she said, separating herself from the embrace and stepping sideways to stand next to Josh and take his hand. 'It's so nice to meet you. And on a day like this!'

Josh looked at the woman next to him. The woman he was marrying. The one who, less than an hour ago, was shaking with fear and clinging to his neck for reassurance. She looked now, for all the world, like the calmest, most self-assured bride who had ever pulled on a frock. And he knew she was doing it for him. And he knew all over again, in that moment, that this was what was supposed to happen. That you found someone who could help you to be strong in the face of the shit that made you weak.

Lou looked at him and smiled, almost as if she were amused by how strange this day was becoming. Josh squeezed her hand hard.

'Dad, I just want to tell you how lucky I am,' Josh said. 'To be marrying a woman who's as strong and loving as my own mum.'

He didn't know where those words came from. It wasn't like him, that was for sure, to be so direct, and so emotional. But there was something about the day, and the suit, and the jasmine, and Lou holding his hand, that made him tell the truth.

His dad flinched a little at this, gave a slight chuckle, looked sideways at Christine. 'Well, then . . .'

'And Lou and I would love for you to come today, that's why we asked you,' Josh rushed on, giving Lou's hand an extra squeeze on the 'we', because there had been no 'we' about it and they both knew that. 'But, honestly, I don't think it's going to be appropriate for you to bring Christine, because . . . I don't want anyone to be upset today. Least of all my mum and my sisters.'

Lou looked up at him quickly, surprised, and he could see she was proud of him. It was a good feeling.

Len's steady gaze settled back on his son. 'Well, then,' he repeated, and then seemed to direct his words to Lou. 'That's a bit . . . We've come down from Newcastle, you know, to be here today.'

'When I called you,' Josh interrupted, 'you didn't mention a guest.'

'I'm sorry, Christine,' Lou said to the woman, who was now looking a little shocked under her yellow hat. 'I know you've gone to a lot of trouble, but Josh is right, it's not appropriate.'

'This is bullshit,' Josh's dad said, his shocked face twisting into something more like a sneer. 'You invited us. We came all the way down from the fucking coast, son. Where did all this come from? Your mum get in your ear, did she?'

Christine was opening and closing her mouth, confused. 'The bride's not even supposed to be here,' she said. 'Before the wedding. I don't know how you do things here, but this is all upside down. Telling your own father what he can and can't do . . .'

'I'm not telling him what he can do,' Josh said, as evenly as he could manage. 'My father can do what he likes. I'm just spelling out the rules for coming to our wedding.'

'Rules!' Len looked angry but also, Josh could see, upset. A flustered old man, trying to take on the shape of the threatening force he had once been to a little boy.

'Well, I'm glad we came all this way to meet your bride on the street,' Len said, nodding at Lou, his voice gruff but a little shaky now. 'But you're kidding yourself, mate.' His eyes were now back on Josh. 'You think you're your mother's son, but you're not. You've got more of me in you than you'd like to admit.'

For Josh, who had lived through years of Emma telling him not to be like his father, it was an insult that stung. He gulped. 'I don't think so, Dad.'

'You invited me here to embarrass me, didn't you?'

'I . . .' Did he? Was that what he'd done? Had he really wanted to punish Len? The heat and the suit felt suffocating now, and his most pressing urge was to leave this messy scene. To run away with Lou, to a place where their families' tentacles didn't reach. Where was that? Back to South America? 'That's not why I invited you, Dad. It just . . . seemed like something you should witness.'

Again, Len's face folded into something of a sneer.

'You two have a chat and decide what you'd like to do,' Lou said to the couple. 'Josh and I are going inside to have a cold drink while we wait for the cars.'

And she just pulled his hand gently and started walking back to Mick's door. Mick was still standing nearby, looking at the ground, shifting uncomfortably. Gretchen was standing in the doorway, a bottle of champagne in her hand.

'Who even are you?' Josh whispered to Lou as they walked up the path. 'That was amazing.'

'I'm your wife,' she said. 'And I don't like your dad much.'

He kissed the top of her flower-scented head as they followed Gretchen into the house.

'Cars will be here in five!' Mick shouted after them, phone in hand.

As Lou grabbed a glass from Gretchen and took a big gulp of champagne, Josh stood at the door watching as his dad picked up the holdall and he and Christine started walking off down the road together.

'Well,' said Josh. 'That was a pretty terrible idea.'

'You should really run all your terrible ideas past me,' Lou said.

'Oh, I will,' he said. And as the stomach popping began to subside, Josh suddenly had another urge. 'Let's go and get married. Are you in?'

'I am so in,' Lou replied. 'Clearly you need me more than I thought you did.'

Josh pulled Lou and her glass into his arms and held her tight. 'You have never been more right about anything.' And he kissed her champagne-y mouth, and felt the bubbles on her tongue.

Lou

MARCH
Therapy

'**T**he hard part,' Lou was saying, her hand shielding her eyes from the blast of afternoon sun that seemed to be beaming directly into her face, 'is that everything in the world seems so bleak right now. It's hard to stay positive about us.'

'Everything?' asked Josh. 'Our kids? I wouldn't describe them as –'

'You know what I mean,' Lou said, a little too quickly and harshly for the setting probably. 'Don't be such a Pollyanna.'

'Lou, try not to be aggressive or labelling in your responses,' Sara, the therapist, chided gently.

Lou couldn't help but think that some slatted blinds might really help people to relax in this office. The sun was brutal and the couch was hard on her bum. Didn't Sara want people to be comfortable?

'I sometimes feel,' she said, 'like the planet's on the brink of catastrophe, lunatics are in charge, and tinkering around with each other's little foibles is . . . pointless. We're all on our own, really, aren't we?'

'Wow,' said Josh. 'You're really fucking nihilistic today. I had no idea you were gripped by so much existential angst.' His voice was dripping with sarcasm.

'You sound like your father right now,' Lou snapped, turning her head to look right at Josh, sitting next to her on the rock-hard couch.

'Nice.'

'Lou, Josh, again' – Sara's voice was calm and smooth like cocoa; it made Lou want to punch her in the nose – 'I have to remind you that trading insults is not what we are here for. It's really not going to help.'

In a different moment, Josh and Lou would have laughed together at Sara's meditative tone, her use of psych speak and her attempts to keep them playing nice, but looking over at him now, it was very clear this was not that moment.

Lou had rarely seen Josh look as awkward as he did right now, sitting on the blue couch in his jeans and his collared flannel shirt, like he'd made some effort but not too much. His long legs meant his knees were just a little too high, and he looked like a forty-year-old man who was waiting to see the headmaster. She also knew he would be mortified that he'd just lost his cool in front of the therapist and said 'fucking'.

And why was she trying so hard to impress Sara? Presumably the couples' therapist was not going to think she was petty for talking about her relationship at relationship counselling. But as soon as they'd walked in, and Lou had seen how smart and accomplished the therapist appeared in her sheath dress and heels, she'd wanted Sara to like her.

'Sorry,' Lou mumbled.

'Are you apologising to me?' asked Sara. 'Or to Josh?'

Now Lou felt like she was being reprimanded by the headmaster. 'Both,' she muttered, looking down at her fingernails.

'The idea is that you don't insult each other in here,' Sara said. 'You're here to listen.'

'I'm listening,' said Lou.

Josh nodded. He was listening, too.

'So, let's go back to what brought you here,' Sara suggested, sitting back in her chair. 'Lou, why do you think you're here?'

*

I give my marriage 10 months . . .

This countdown is feeling depressing.

On 4 March, Lou had typed that into her phone and then flicked over to her settings and unblocked a number. She texted, *Are you free right now?* Right now was important, because she knew she was going to change her mind if the text wasn't returned almost immediately.

But it was.

Yes. Where?

Not my house.

My house then.

Lou didn't know where '*my house*' was. She had never been there before. Oh, she thought. A roadblock. That's good. Maybe I'll just cancel. But her thumb hovered just a moment too long and another message came quickly.

You can follow me home. See u in the car park.

You can still cancel, she told herself.

But she didn't.

The day before, she and Josh had been at a rehearsal for their duet in the hall at the girls' school. Lou felt absolutely ridiculous, and also like she spent way too much of her life in school halls.

She'd sat simmering with resentment at the trestle table that had been set up in front of the stage. Other parents had brought cheese and wine, and they came and went as the rehearsal dragged on, talking between songs, applauding each other as they took their turns on stage. Kids were playing at the back of the hall or running around outside in the playground, rushing in every few minutes to cringe at the music and beg for some chips.

Why can't I enjoy this? Lou had asked herself. It's fun. What's wrong with me?

She sat there and watched people she knew – some well, some only by sight – push through terrible versions of Lady Gaga's 'Bad Romance', Toto's 'Africa' and Lizzo's 'Truth Hurts'. And she'd made tortured small talk with one of the mums she didn't know, the one from the P&C who was always asking her to volunteer for things. Right now, it was helping with the winter carnival, which was a few months away and, apparently, chronically under-supported.

'I know you get a lot of this at work,' said the P&C mum, 'but I did think' – and she put a hand on Lou's arm – 'that as a teacher yourself, you'd really understand the value of parents being involved in their child's education.'

Lou looked at Josh up on the stage, fiddling with his guitar and laughing with the blonde woman on keyboards. She could almost taste the irritation in her own mouth at the whole situation, at being here in this stuffy hall on a Sunday afternoon, at indulging Josh's rock star fantasy and having to talk to this woman.

'Oh, I do,' she said, scanning her brain for the woman's name and coming up blank. 'But as a teacher, when I'm not working I prefer to spend as much time as I can with my own kids, as I'm sure you'd understand.'

The woman took her hand off Lou's arm and gave a little shrug. 'Well, I always say, if everyone did just a little bit . . .' and she turned away to focus on the stage.

Lou got up and walked outside. She saw her girls swinging on the monkey bars and suppressed the urge to shout at them to get down – monkey bars and broken arms went together like teachers and wine, in her experience. Instead, she pulled out her phone.

What did we do to avoid awkward social interactions before phones? she wondered, opening Instagram and starting to scroll. One of her friends was in Europe, smiling on a boat. Another was posting every stage of her kitchen renovation, and Lou was trying to think of something supportive to comment about a splashback choice when she felt a hand on her waist and heard Josh ask, 'What are you doing out here?'

The music had stopped, she realised.

'I was avoiding that woman who's always trying to get me to "join in",' said Lou, nodding through the open door of the hall towards the one-woman volunteer press-gang, who had moved on to another mother. 'I don't want to join in.'

'Well, bad luck, babe, because we're up in a minute,' Josh said. He was happy, she could tell, being here, playing music. And seeing him happy made her feel like she wanted to say something horrible, which was not a good sign. Don't. Don't. Don't.

'And that's Lyndall,' Josh said. 'She's the president of the P&C. I thought you knew that?'

'I forgot,' Lou replied. Which was true. 'Well, she's scaring off more volunteers than she's encouraging.'

Josh pulled the face he pulled when he didn't agree, mouth down, eyes narrowing. 'I think maybe that's just you. I've been talking to her about starting a music therapy workshop . . .'

'Oh, shut up, Josh.' Uh-oh.

Her husband's face changed.

I'm going to say it, I'm going to say it.

'You've never given a shit about volunteering until you figured out there was an opportunity for you to feel like a real musician again. I can't believe that you're making me do something I don't have the time to do and pretending it's about us when, really, it's about you not facing up to your failures.'

'Are you guys ready?'

Lou knew they were inexcusable, these harsh words she'd just thrown at Josh in a rushed, hissed whisper, surely loud enough for others to hear.

Now she turned quickly to the voice of the interrupter, a guy from the band. Lou didn't know him, but thought maybe he was married to Abigail, one of the yoga mums. Whatever, he clearly hadn't yet sensed the tension in the air.

'Yes, we're ready,' Lou said brightly, as Josh stared at her. 'Let's do it.'

And she turned and entered the hall, her hands shaking. I can never speak to my husband like that again, she thought. There is no justification for being cruel. There is no excuse for how I'm feeling. I need to do something, or we're not even going to make it to the end-of-year deadline.

She turned to see if Josh was following her. He wasn't. He was standing near the door, looking at her. His face – his eyebrows, his mouth – suggested that he was, understandably, furious.

'Come on, babe!' she called brightly, in front of the dozen or so adults in the hall. 'Let's get it over with.' And she laughed a little too loudly, to show that she was only joking and, really, she was delighted to be here making her husband's dreams come true and raising money for the school's new tech suite while she was at it.

Josh began to walk towards her slowly. Behind her, she heard the band play the opening chords to their song. U2 had been deemed too bleak. They were doing 'Walking on Sunshine'.

That night Josh hadn't spoken to her at all, and after what she'd said to him at school Lou wasn't surprised. But they'd gone through the motions of dinner and bath time and bedtime books for the girls, passing each other wordlessly as they moved through the hundred little tasks that had to be done between them – toothpaste squeezed out for Rita so it didn't go all over the tiles, clean pyjamas dug out of drawers, lost books found, stories, hugs, silly bedtime songs – before the house was quiet. And then Josh had gone to his guitar room and closed the door, and Lou had gone to the living room and looked at her phone, and then she'd folded some washing and made the kids' lunches for the next day and gone to bed, where she lay looking at the outline of the tree in darkness until she woke up and it was morning and Josh was lying next to her, sleeping, and the curtain was drawn, so she couldn't see the tree anymore.

And now, with her text answered, here she was rummaging through her bag for her keys and walking towards her car.

Then sitting in it and looking at the red sedan over by the gate of the car park, blinker on, turning right.

She looked at the outline of the head visible in the driver's seat. And she knew he was looking at her in his rear-view mirror, waiting for her to move, to put her family wagon – strewn with icy-pole wrappers and sand and miscellaneous teeny-tiny plastic toys – into drive and follow.

She turned the key in the ignition and put her blinker on to indicate she was pulling out of her car space. As she did, she saw the man in the red car move his head slightly, in what looked like a short, pleased nod.

Lou put both palms up to her face, pushed the heels of her hands into her eyes and sat there for a moment, just like that.

And then she flicked off the indicator. Turned off the ignition. Opened the car door. She didn't look back at the red car as she turned the other way and retraced her steps through the crowded lunchtime playground towards her classroom.

There, she sat on one of the tiny chairs and texted: *I can't treat you like that anymore. I'm making an appointment with a therapist. For both of us. We need it.*

She saw the little bubbles on her iPhone that meant Josh was typing. And they were there for the longest time, like he was composing an epic response. And it was a few minutes of that before Josh sent back: *OK.*

And she flipped to her notes. *3. Therapy*, she wrote. *We're going to call in the experts and do whatever they tell us to do.*

*

'I think we're here because, for a few years now, we've been damaged,' Lou said to the therapist.

'Damaged?' Sara queried.

'There are some things that have happened between us that I . . . I've struggled to come back from.' Lou realised that in the white light of this office, she was saying this out loud for the first time.

'We've been together fourteen years,' Josh said. He wasn't looking at her. 'Every couple has stuff after fourteen years.'

'Well, over the course of these sessions,' Sara said, leaning forward from her straight-backed chair, where she sat with a notebook resting on her crossed knee, 'we can begin to unpack some of that "stuff", and how it's impacting you as a couple and as individuals.'

'I don't think Josh thinks we should be here,' Lou said. 'Doesn't therapy only work if you want to be here?'

'I'd like to hear that from Josh,' Sara said, and turned to look at him. Lou approved of this shift in focus. 'Do you think you need to be here?'

Josh didn't say anything.

I know you so well, Lou thought. I know how much you are hating this, being asked to talk about us. I know that right now your stomach will be in a knot and anger will be scratching in your throat and you're just wishing you were in your guitar room, with your vinyl records and your three old six-strings and your garage band. And I'm glad. I'm glad you're feeling uncomfortable about it, because I feel like I'm looking at our relationship up close all the time, and maybe it's right that now you have to do the same.

Josh rubbed his forehead and cleared his throat. 'I don't want our marriage to end,' he said finally. 'So if I need to be here to stop that from happening, I'll be here.'

Lou looked at the therapist. 'Is that good enough?' she asked. She desperately wanted Sara to say no, it wasn't. She wanted Sara to say all the things to Josh that she wanted to say herself, but couldn't. She wanted the therapist to tell him off.

'It's a good enough place to start,' Sara said. And she reached around to her desk and picked up a piece of paper. 'Here's something I would really like you both to do.'

She was going to email them a questionnaire, she said, and on it was a list of values. Words like *Fun. Security. Family.*

'I want you each to rank these values into a top ten. It will give me a sense of what's important to each of you, and what shared foundation we have to work with here.' She looked at them both in turn. 'It's crucial that you're honest.'

Lou felt herself flinch, just a little.

'And there's one more thing I want you to think about over the next week.'

Josh's leg was shuddering now, jiggling up and down ever so slightly. His hands were resting on his knees and his fingers were gently tapping.

'The "stuff" you're talking about . . .' Sara made little quote marks in the air around 'stuff'. She had a very neat, neutral manicure, Lou noticed. She must be a very organised person. I wonder if she has

117

kids? 'You're right, Josh – there's stuff that every couple does have. But there's also stuff that shouldn't be dismissed. Significant stuff. In this room, in this hour, there's no point in playing down the things that matter.'

'I don't know if I can tell what matters anymore,' Josh muttered. 'Little things are big things and big things barely get a mention.'

Lou looked at him.

'That's what I'm talking about,' Sara said. 'Think about what matters. The milestones that have brought you two here. For example –' and she began to count things off on her shiny-tipped fingers – 'some couples have a trauma they can't move past, an event of grief.'

Josh looked down at his rapping fingers.

'Or' – second finger – 'there's been a significant breakdown in communication linked to a particular event. Or there's been a significant breach of trust.' Three fingers up. 'That could be, but is not necessarily, an infidelity.'

Lou looked down at her own hands. Her nails were a mess. Broken, short, bitten.

'Has there been an infidelity?'

Lou could feel Josh looking at her now. She knew that Sara would be taking this moment in, reading their faces, watching how Josh was looking at Lou. She took a breath in, as if she was about to speak, but she couldn't. Lou's mouth was suddenly so dry that her tongue felt heavy, unwieldy.

Sara spoke first.

'Those are the kind of things I want you to think about that we can unpack over our eight sessions together.'

The therapist gently slapped her hands on her knees and stood up. 'Please fill out the values sheet before our next session. And in the meantime, try to listen to each other, try not to blame.'

Lou knew this was the signal for them to leave. Josh stood up, but he didn't offer her a hand, which was what he always used to do, once.

'There was –' Lou began.

'Next time, Lou,' Josh said firmly, cutting her off. 'We've got to go pick up the kids.'

The therapist didn't say anything, but Lou could feel Sara's eyes on them as she got up and followed Josh to the door.

Josh

MARCH
Therapy

Josh wanted to put *Creativity* and *Love* at the top of his 'values' chart, but he knew Creativity would really piss Lou off, and he was stumped on the Love part because it was broken in two: *Loved* and *Loving*.

Did he value feeling loved more than he valued giving love?

Didn't everyone?

Josh was sitting in the guitar room (don't call it the guitar room), at his old laptop, staring at the exercise from the therapist.

It was Sunday night. The kids were asleep and he could hear Lou moving around downstairs, putting things in order for the week ahead of them. Tomorrow, they were going back to the therapist to look at their rankings. Josh felt like he was preparing for a test and almost all of the answers seemed wrong.

World peace was on the list, for God's sake. If he didn't put that in the top ten, what kind of person was he? But, then, he'd been deeply irritated when Lou had tried to bring the depressing state of the universe into their therapy session last week. The world might be going to hell in a handbasket, as his mum would say, but that wasn't what was wrong with their corner of it.

There was a song in this, Josh thought, if he even wrote songs anymore. In all these words in front of him and how to place them in an order that made them say something profound about him and his life and his family.

He'd wondered if Eva Bernard used the 'values' ranking method. When Lou had sent him the text that day about therapy, it was the idea of Eva Bernard that kept him from resisting.

The last time Lou had suggested counselling, two years ago, he had said no – even though, on some level, he'd known they really needed it. Every fibre of his being was screaming against being held to account by a stranger. He'd been so full of shame and anger that he hadn't wanted to give Lou the satisfaction of seeing him fall apart and knowing she was right to bring him here, and bring him down.

That was how he'd seen it then. But now, his fear of what might happen in that room seemed petty in the face of Lou's wild frustration. In fourteen years, she had never spoken to him the way she had at the rehearsal a week ago. He had realised, in that moment, just how bad things were. She was right: they needed help.

So here he was, filling in his survey, uncharacteristically doing as he was told.

Maybe it was all the late-night Eva videos he'd been studying.

Maybe he was just tired.

Maybe the concert last night and its aftermath had drained him of fucks to give.

He looked at the values he'd ticked.

Simplicity – To live life simply, with minimal needs
Hope – To maintain a positive and optimistic outlook
Acceptance – To be accepted as I am
Family – To have a happy, loving family

I sound so boring, he thought, and pressed reset on his answers.

*

The previous night's school fundraiser was held in the cavernous hall at the local leagues club, a place devoid of charm even with several hours spent on homemade decorations – pictures of the rock stars whose tunes were being played tonight had been hurriedly printed from home PCs and pasted to cardboard table-toppers and posters on the walls.

Josh had arrived early to rehearse and help set up, and Lou had come later, having been relieved at home by a babysitter, one of the many teenagers in their suburb doing very well tonight.

Parents were beginning to stream in, excited to be out, ordering fizzy wine by the bottle and jugs of frothy beer and plates of soggy schnitzels from the bar.

Josh saw Lou instantly when he came out from the dressing room – really just a hastily constructed partition – in his outfit of black jeans, black T-shirt, leather jacket, biker boots. Skinny jeans at forty felt like a faintly ridiculous place to be, but Lou's eyes, that steady look she gave him when she approved, told him he was pulling it off.

'You look great,' he said to her, and she did, in a black dress that tied around the back of her neck and showed her strong shoulders.

The important thing was that she was here. Lou was wrong about why he was doing this, he told her and himself – she was wrong. And even though she might not want to be doing this, she was here. She had turned up for him. And Eva Bernard would say that was half the battle.

'You do too,' she said.

They stood there for a second, smiling at each other.

Then Dana had appeared, waving a jar of some kind of hair cream. 'Let me slick it back, Josh!' she said loudly. 'It will make you look seventy-eight per cent cooler.'

Josh saw Lou's face flash with irritation, but she gave him a little nod before she turned back to the bar and Dana grabbed his hand to pull him backstage again.

He hadn't managed to avoid Dana the Strangely Straightforward, as he thought of her, over the last few weeks of rehearsals. He'd asked her if she was sure Umbert was in Stella's class, after his daughter had come up blank about him, and Dana said no, she wasn't really sure, she'd just thought it was a good icebreaker. Actually, a top-line investigation by Lou had uncovered the truth – Umbert was in the year below, and at school he was simply called Bert, or Bertie.

When he'd presented this to Dana, she just shrugged and said, 'Sure,' leaving Josh to suggest to his wife that maybe Dana was a bit on the loopy side.

'There's no such thing as loopy,' Lou had said. 'She must want something.' But Lou hadn't seemed particularly troubled by what it might be.

Backstage, Dana pushed Josh down onto a steel-framed chair. The noise was building in the room as the crowd grew, and band members dashed in and out, getting ready for the opening songs. Dana took big, globby handfuls of hair cream and slapped it on Josh's head, raking her fingers through his curly hair to make it sit flat. It felt good. Josh was excited about getting up there and playing, excited to be singing with his wife later. The blue couch of couple's therapy and their mountain of 'stuff' seemed very far away at that moment.

'Your wife's really going to appreciate this hair,' Dana said, smoothing her handiwork down with the palm of one hand. 'It might make her less shitty about singing with you.'

'Oh,' – Josh shook his head – 'she's not that shitty. I think she's secretly enjoying it.'

'I don't,' said Dana, putting her hands on his shoulders. 'There, finished. But it's nice for people to do things for each other.'

Josh got up quickly. 'I'll see you out there,' he said to Dana, who had her blonde hair tied back in a high ponytail with a bow and wore a scarf around her neck, like she was in *Grease* or something. She waved, and he headed to the bar, where he saw Lou talking to a group of mum-friends, as she called them, standing around a high table with a cardboard Robert Smith from The Cure stuck on top of it, all wild hair and smudged eyeliner. Lou was laughing.

Josh headed straight over to the table, but just before he got there a tall, broad man stepped into the circle of women and leaned in to talk to Lou. He looked familiar, but Josh couldn't place him. He must be another teacher, he thought, or possibly the husband of one of the other mums.

As he got closer, though, just a few steps from Robert Smith's cardboard head, something about the way this guy was talking to Lou made Josh stop. His lips were just a little closer to her ear than Josh's would be if he were talking to one of the other women at the table. And, it was hard to tell from this angle, but it was possible one of the man's hands was on the small of Lou's back.

Two more steps. 'Hey,' he said, over the pumping sound of 'Praise You'. 'Lou.'

The second she looked up and saw him, Josh knew that this wasn't one of the other women's husbands. For a start, Lou stepped away from the man immediately, almost bumping into Yoga Sal as she did.

And then Josh got a look at the guy. He was tall, as tall as Josh, but broad, a big guy. His eyes registered surprise at seeing Josh, as if he knew who Josh was, but didn't expect to see him.

He looked like a man who usually wore a suit but was in a polo shirt tonight because that's what guys who usually wore a suit wore when it was 'smart casual' night.

'Josh,' Lou said, but her mouth exaggerated the word, because the music was loud. And she gave him a smile broader than any she had been offering him lately. 'Your hair!'

The guy nodded at Josh, waved at Lou and the other women and walked away.

Josh was aware of the three other women at the table as a kind of blur, all of them commenting on his hair and his leather jacket and how much they were looking forward to seeing Lou's performance. 'My husband would never sing with me,' one of them was shouting over Fat Boy Slim. 'You're so lucky, Lou!'

'I hardly think so!' Lou laughed. 'It's Josh who made me do it.'

'Well, I think it's romantic,' said Yoga Sal. 'Break a leg.'

Josh took one more step forward and took Lou's hand, and the women cooed again as he and Lou turned and he led her to the hallway where the music wasn't quite so deafening. 'Who was that?'

'What?'

'That guy you were talking to. Who was he?' Josh let go of Lou's hand now they were just outside the hall and no longer a picture of romance. They were two middle-aged parents in borderline ridiculous clothes, squaring off.

'It's just someone I work with,' Lou said. 'He's here for a big fortieth in the other bar. Came to say hello.'

'How did he know you were here?'

'Because I've been bitching about the fact my husband's making me do a duet at the school fundraiser for weeks,' Lou said, and she looked half annoyed, half amused. Maybe this was okay after all. 'What do you think?' she asked him, and her eyes were challenging him.

'I think he likes you,' Josh said, and he crossed the space between them and put his mouth up to Lou's ear. 'The way he was leaning into you like this.'

Lou's eyes went wide as Josh put his arm around her waist and his hand in the small of her back and whispered, 'Like this.'

'Fucking hell,' Lou said. 'You're crazy.' Then she looked up at him. 'It's kind of hot though.'

She turned her face to kiss his neck, ever so quickly, as people walked past. 'Is that how Loopy Dana talks to you?'

He laughed, feeling better. And then it was time for the band to go on, and soon he was up there playing, and he saw Lou in the crowd of parents getting progressively drunker and more appreciative as the covers played on.

And then Lou came up and they sang 'Walking on Sunshine' together. And even though he kind of hated that song, they smiled at each other while they were doing it, and pulled off some cheesy dance moves that a cringing Stella had choreographed for them. When they came offstage, panting and sweating, so many women came over to tell him that they wished their husbands would sing with them, and he and Lou laughed and made vomiting faces, but they felt light, right.

And then Josh had some drinks and danced, as much as he ever danced, which was really just shaking his shoulders up and down on the spot, and he didn't think about the polo shirt man again. At least, not until he was packing up his guitar at the end of the night, as the band milled about congratulating each other, collecting instruments and rolling up cables.

Dana came to give him a hug. 'You two were great,' she said, stepping away, ponytail swinging.

'You were great, too,' Josh said, and then, probably because of the beers, he asked, 'Where's your Italian husband tonight, anyway? Doesn't he like to see you play?'

'Oh, Marco would never come to anything like this,' Dana said. 'He has no sense of joy.'

Why the hell are you married to this guy? Josh thought, but didn't say.

'He's at a fortieth tonight, anyway,' she went on. 'I think they're going to the casino, God help them.'

'There's a fortieth in the bar next door,' Josh said, picking up his guitar and slinging it over his shoulder. 'He's not at that one?'

'There's no fortieth next door,' Dana said, looking irritated. 'We're the only function here tonight. I had to argue with the club about the bar. They weren't going to put on as many staff as I knew we'd need. You know parents when they get drinking . . .'

'Yes, I do,' Josh said. He looked at Dana for a moment, and then leaned in to give her a quick kiss on the cheek. 'I'm going to find my wife.'

He found Lou in the crowd of tipsy people hugging each other goodbye just outside.

He'd given back the leather jacket and the biker boots to whichever band member – cooler than he – had loaned them to him. Now he was just Josh again, in his old Stones T-shirt and his denim jacket.

'I was wrong about that,' Lou said to him as they stood out the front of the club together, with his guitar, waiting for their Uber. 'It was actually great fun. I genuinely enjoyed myself.'

'I'm glad,' Josh said. 'That's what I hoped would happen.'

'Well, you were right.'

'Wow.'

Lou punched him in the arm. 'We need to get home,' she said. 'I have these stupid stick-on chicken-fillet things under my dress. I keep thinking they're going to come unstuck and my old boobs will go completely rogue.'

Josh watched Lou, her phone in one hand, the other down her dress, hiking at her stick-on bra. He knew that he had a choice. He could push her about the polo shirt man and send the evening in one direction, or he could stay quiet and trust her in that moment, and keep things where they were right now, in a rare place of non-irritation.

'How much is the babysitter going to be?' he asked, making the decision.

'Too much,' Lou replied. 'I'll have to do a transfer; I have no cash on me.'

'Worth it, though,' Josh said. 'To have some fun together.'

She looked at him and smiled. 'Sure.'

He lifted up an arm. Lou looked at him like she was considering something, and then stepped towards him, accepting his hug.

He'd stood outside the leagues club with his arm around his wife, with people stepping around them, calling to each other and waving. And he'd known that this minute of everything being alright wasn't real. But it was enough, right then, not to ruin it. A moment's peace.

*

Why isn't *Trust* on this list? Josh wondered, scrolling through the values. Seems like an obvious one to me.

I value *Trust*.

Monogamy was, but that seemed a bit heavy-handed, somehow, when you could only choose ten words.

Eva Bernard would say that his insecurity right now was less about the idea of his grown-up wife talking to a man in a bar and more to do with his own unfulfilled desires. Eva would say that couples project their own stuff onto each other and it's important to know the difference.

Josh clicked on *Forgiveness* – to be forgiving of others.

And *Passion* – to have deep feelings about ideas, activities, or people.

He felt a sense of dread welling up about tomorrow. After dinner, before bath time, Josh had gone over and put his hands on Lou's hips as she stacked the dishwasher. 'Thank you,' he said. 'For the concert.'

Lou had quickly stepped out of his attempted embrace. 'I'm glad it made you happy,' she said, without looking at him. 'But it's not the answer, you know.'

One of the big changes in Lou recently was that she wasn't going to pretend things were okay in the hope of the pretence becoming reality. She had shifted, ever so slightly, into a determined position of opposition. Well, maybe he should do the same.

He looked at his list again. Be honest, he heard Sara the therapist and guru Eva Bernard say.

He clicked on *Monogamy*. Screw it. She needed to know.

Lou

24 December, 2008

On Christmas Eve, 2008, Lou had the orgasm of her life.

Honeymoons, Josh and Lou decided, were for ordinary people.

After their wedding under the tree in Camperdown Park, they waited for the summer holidays then went camping. Along with many thousands of ordinary people.

They agreed about the romance of road trips versus resorts; agreed that sleeping under the stars was sexy, and that counter meals in country pubs were the kind of Aussie kitsch they approved of.

By Christmas they were at Pebbly Beach, home to tourist-plagued, tame kangaroos on the sand, raucous flocks of iridescent lorikeets and gums soaring against the bluest of skies. It was, Josh said, just the right side of cheesy for their first holiday as married people.

They had a double swag, and that night they broke the campground rules and smuggled it down to the beach in the pitch-black and made love. And that was the right term for it: it really was making love.

I will never forget this moment, Lou had thought. I will bring it to me whenever I need to conjure calm. This night, in this swag with Josh, with the sound of the waves and the sparkle-studded sky above us. I will remember it as being as close to perfection as we're ever lucky enough to get.

Of course, in reality, it wasn't quite perfect. There were sandflies, and the canvas of the swag was too heavy for high summer, and the bottle of champagne they'd brought with them was cheap, warm and flat. But the sex *was* mind-bogglingly good. She felt that thing teenagers felt when they first discovered orgasms – what, you mean I can do this *whenever I want to*? And she lay back on the swag and laughed out loud at the sheer joy of it.

She lay on top of Josh on that swag, sand in every crevice, sweaty and exhausted, her chin resting on her hands resting on his chest, and the two of them made promises to each other that they had never made before.

'I promise you,' Lou said, her voice thick and heavy, 'that we will never be boring.'

'I promise you,' Josh said, 'to always tell you if you say something stupid.'

'But I never say anything stupid.'

'That's why it's a great promise.'

Lou kissed him.

'I promise,' she said, 'never to break your heart.'

'And I promise,' he said, 'never to break *your* heart.'

The sky began to lighten over the ocean, the darkness slowly lifting, the stars gently fading.

Their sandfly bites began to itch, a chill edged the air, and Josh and Lou rolled up the double swag and went to meet Christmas morning, with the kangaroos and the lorikeets and all the other ordinary people.

Josh

31 December, 2008

Two-minute noodles for Christmas lunch. Warm beer and mozzie bites in unspeakable places. Tent sex. River sex. Beach sex.

This honeymoon road trip really was the best of times.

'Maybe we should just keep going,' Josh said to Lou on New Year's Eve, as he picked bits of grass out of her hair after an evening swim. They had reached the Snowy Mountains and were camping at Thredbo. They'd wanted to see the new year in sitting by the river, their feet dangling next to their beer bottles in the cool water as the campground buzzed quietly around them.

'Keep going?' Lou rested her head back on Josh's shoulder.

'Never go home,' he said. 'Make life a road trip. One long adventure.'

'I don't think the Newtown principal would like that much,' said Lou. 'But then again, screw the boss – I'm in.' She laughed.

'I'm serious,' said Josh, realising in that moment that he was. 'We've always said we want life to be an adventure, well, here's our chance.'

Lou pulled her head back and looked at him. After two weeks on the road, she had a broad sprinkle of freckles across her tanned face. She wore not a smudge of make-up, her hair was always drying from a swim, a singlet and cut-off shorts were her constant uniform. Bare feet. Perfection.

'We can't,' she said. 'We have two more weeks before we have to go back to being normal.'

'Why do we?' asked Josh, warming to his point. 'We're both employable wherever we go. Imagine if we just kept driving. Decided to hop over to Tassie for a while, head up north, whatever . . .'

'You've got honeymoon fever,' Lou said. 'Life won't be like this forever. You'll need other people soon.'

Josh flung out an arm to the campsite behind them. 'There are other people everywhere if we want them.' And he leaned forward to kiss her. 'I don't.'

'Now you don't,' Lou said, smiling into his eyes. 'Because we're sex-drunk, and we've escaped our families and our jobs and all the drama of the wedding. Right now' – she kissed him back – 'we're unbearably into each other.'

'And we shall stay that way, I just know it,' Josh said, in a mock-serious voice. 'I can't imagine anyone else I'd rather talk with, eat with, sleep with, drive with, sing with . . .'

'Argue with.'

'Sure, sometimes.'

'Well, me neither. But we have the flat, and Pocket . . .'

'Gretchen will keep Pocket.'

'Are you kidding? She didn't want to look after her this time. She says an animal is more of a commitment than she's ready for.'

'My dreams cannot be thwarted by a cat,' Josh said. 'We have gypsy blood – we must push on!'

'*You* have gypsy blood,' Lou said, laughing. 'My blood is stubbornly suburban, and I'm in constant battle with it.'

Josh lay back on the grassy edge of the river, looked at the black outlines of the trees against the navy sky, breathed in the cooling air. 'Two thousand and nine,' he said, 'should be our year less ordinary. We can go anywhere, do anything.'

Lou lay next to him, her head in the crook of his neck. 'I love it here,' she said. 'But I feel like I love it anywhere you are.'

And they stayed there, talking about all the versions of the future they could imagine. The one in which it was only a matter of time before they had to move to New York, or London, or LA, because Josh sold his songs to big stars. The one in which they travelled to a remote community in Arnhem Land where Lou taught in the local school and the children also learned from the elders. The one in which Josh built them a beautiful wooden home in a tropical rainforest and they raised a gaggle of wild-haired, barefoot children. The one in which Lou ran marathons and wrote plays while Josh stayed home and played guitar. The one in which Josh became a session musician and toured with rock stars and Lou jetted out to see him play in front of screaming fans in Japan and Scandinavia.

And then they began to hear their fellow campers cheering and clinking glasses, and it was 2009.

'Happy New Year, Lou,' said Josh, kissing his wife deeply. 'Thank you for marrying me.'

'We are entirely insufferable right now,' said Lou.

'And I love it,' said Josh.

Lou

1 March, 2011

My baby looks like Len.

She's a tiny, hours-old girl who looks like my arsehole father-in-law wrapped in a pink-and-blue-striped blanket.

That's what Lou was thinking in the surreal small hours of the first day, lying in the half-dark of the maternity ward, with the background soundtrack of shuffling feet and whimpering newborns, beeping machines and the occasional muffled sob of a shell-shocked woman.

Little Len. Look at you.

How typical that the most troublesome member of the family also apparently had the strongest genes.

Josh had gone home an hour before and Lou was on the semi-elevated hospital bed, trying to lie on her side so she could watch this new baby sleeping and snuffling in a see-through plastic crib next to her head.

Moving wasn't easy. Lou's body felt like it had been pulled inside out, everything was aching, she appeared to be wearing a giant nappy and exhaustion felt like a literal weight on her shoulders, pushing her down. And still, she couldn't sleep, which was what the midwife had advised her to do 'while you can'.

How strange this was, that this helpless little person was 'hers' – or, rather, theirs. And that, eventually, she and Josh would be taking her home, back to the Erskineville unit, to sleep in a basket next to their bed. This tiny little thing who would literally die without them. It barely seemed legal.

They couldn't agree on a name. Lou wanted Stella, just because it was a name that she had always loved. Josh wanted Rose, because Rose had been his nan, his mum's mum, and she was a woman who'd always been there for Josh when he was a confused little boy.

Lou thought that was all very nice but not a good enough reason for a namesake.

They'd decided to wait and see what she looked like – not that they'd known their baby was a she. They both agreed they liked surprises and Lou had also enjoyed being at the ultrasound check-ups and telling the sonographer that neither of them wanted to know. *Look how compatible we are.*

But this morning a baby girl had fought her way out of Lou, looking like Len, not Rose, but certainly a tangible being of her own with round brown eyes. And still they didn't know what to call her. She was here, with no name. The midwives and doctors were calling her 'Baby' and Lou 'Mum'.

'How's Mum?' and 'If Mum would just like to turn over . . .' and 'Does Mum need any more pain relief?'

'I'm Lou,' Lou had said three times today.

And the midwives had smiled, and called her 'Mum' again.

Baby opened her eyes a crack and let out a panting little mewl, and Lou's stomach flipped. What was wrong?

Lou pulled herself into a more upright sitting position – *ouch, ouch* – and peered over the edge of the crib.

Another mewl, a little arm moving.

Lou looked around. There was another bed in the room, but there was no-one in it. The sliding door to the wider ward was half open; the corridor looked quiet.

Was she allowed to just *pick her daughter up*?

Lou's head felt like it was full of thick, murky slime. Thoughts had to wade through the sludgy mess to make it to clarity. She was allowed to pick her baby up, right? And try to feed her like the nurses had shown her?

Baby inhaled and let out a big, squawking wail. And another. Uh-oh. Lou suddenly felt fear. There was something wrong. And she didn't know what to do. Of course she didn't.

She looked around for the button to press when you needed someone to come. She could just reach it without having to twist. Lou kept her thumb on it for a while, as Baby wailed beside her, until a young midwife appeared at the sliding door.

'My baby's crying!' said Lou. It came out more like a plea.

Lou could have sworn the midwife stifled a smile as she came over to the bed. 'Let's have a look at Baby, shall we?' she said brightly.

And she scooped up Lou's daughter with palpable confidence, tucked her blanket back around her and looked up at Lou. 'Are you comfortable, Mum?' the young woman asked her. 'Might be time to have another try with the feeding.'

Then the young midwife passed Baby to Lou, whose mind went completely blank. What was she was meant to do with her? The baby was yelling as loudly as a tiny baby could and her face was scrunched up in fury.

'Just try to put her on,' said the midwife, who was nodding at Lou's chest at the same time as shoving a pillow under her arm for support, and pushing another one into the small of her back. *Ouch, ouch.*

'It's going to take a while to get used to,' the midwife added, as Lou struggled to free a boob from her pyjama top with both hands full of Baby. 'That's totally normal.'

'But is she . . . starving?' Lou asked as the angry little mouth tried to close around Lou's suddenly enormous-seeming nipple. *Ouch, ouch.*

'No.' The midwife smiled, manhandling Lou into position. 'Just move that arm a bit under there to support her . . . yes, that's right.'

Lou's baby had been out in the world for less than twelve hours and Lou could have sworn that every midwife who came past had told her a different way to breastfeed.

'Is she getting anything?' Lou asked.

'Your milk won't come in for a while,' the midwife said. 'But she's getting colostrum, and that's liquid gold. The milk is probably three days away.'

Three days?

'Just let her suck. As long as the position is right, it's going to help bring the milk in. But if the position's wrong, well, your nipples are going to shred.'

Shred?

'I'll leave you to it,' the midwife said, and tucked the now-flapping wrap under Baby again and turned to leave.

'Wait!' Lou was suddenly terrified again. 'What do I do next? How do I know when she's finished?'

'She'll let you know,' the midwife said. 'And then just try to get her to have a little sleep. New babies are sleepy. And you could do with the rest, too.'

So Lou's first night as a mother was spent crying, sporadically pushing the button – 'She's got hiccups, is that normal?' – texting Josh, who didn't reply, and being gripped by a kind of seismic dread that what people said was true: she really was never going to sleep again.

The clock crept around from three to four to five, with Lou falling off the edge of consciousness every so often only to be yanked back by a whimper from the crib. She'd try to pull herself up to sitting, swing her legs around to the side of the bed – *ouch, ouch* – to pick Baby up. She'd try to get her to latch on to a giant nipple for a while and then pat her and lay her back down. She did it again, and again, and again. The midwives changed shifts. The young woman was replaced by an older one who didn't smile much. Her tactic for breastfeeding was different again. 'Just shove it in any old way you can get her to take it,' the woman said. 'It's the sucking that's important.'

It did feel very important to get this right.

The exhaustion had moved to her head and was now crushing it like a vice. It was 7 a.m. when she called Josh. Still no answer.

'You need to come,' she said to his voicemail. Was he . . . asleep? 'I need you to hold the baby while I get some rest then wake me up to try to feed so my boobs learn what to do and my nipples don't shred.'

*

Being pregnant had felt like an invasion. Lou hadn't felt like herself anymore, not even a little bit.

She'd looked at her swollen feet and didn't recognise them. Her puffy lips, her thickened neck. Her breasts were complete strangers, thick with veins, nipples the colour of cocoa. Even her hair was like someone else's hair – someone who had twice as much but was simultaneously losing it in fistfuls.

'The baby's taking everything,' her mum had said, as if this was meant to comfort her. 'I lost a tooth when I was having you. You sucked all the calcium out of me.'

Annabelle never missed an opportunity to point out to Lou how much of herself she'd sacrificed for her family, even if in the next breath she was making it clear that becoming a mother and raising respectable children was the pinnacle of a woman's achievement. The take-home message seemed to be: This is the only thing worth doing, but it's also the worst thing that can happen to you.

And sometimes, as Lou's body swelled and pulsed, that seemed terrifyingly true. One month before her due date, Lou had been watching the little invader travel under her skin, rippling across her body in some strange, unguided movement. She and Josh were lying together on their bed in their apartment's only bedroom, too hot for covers, his hand on her naked stomach, tracing the baby's journey.

'You're witnessing the traditional migration of the as-yet-unnamed Baby Poole,' Josh was narrating, in a pretty ordinary impersonation of David Attenborough. 'From one side of their mother's tummy to the other, in search of a more comfortable spot from which to stick their foot right between her ribs . . .'

Lou laughed and pushed his hand away. 'Help me up, sir,' she said, holding out an arm.

'But of course.' Josh jumped up, hauled Lou off the bed. 'Where are you going? It's Sunday. We don't have to be anywhere for ages.'

'I can't lie around, feeling like a blob,' Lou said. 'I want to go for a walk. Get some breakfast.'

The truth was, as hard as it was becoming to move around, to sit up and stand up and lie down, if Lou stayed in one place for too long, contemplating what was happening to her, and what was about to happen to them, she began to panic. Ever since she'd seen the double lines on the pee-stick, she'd been very prone to panic.

'I'm going to call Gretch, see if she'll meet us.'

'Gretchen won't be out of bed, Lou,' Josh called after her as she closed the bathroom door, her new iPhone in hand. 'She probably won't even be home.'

Lou sat down on the toilet seat, looked at her alien ankles. The giddy feeling that had just made her laugh at Josh's lame dad jokes was draining away.

This is all happening too quickly, she thought. And she sent Gretchen a message saying the same thing, and sat there looking at her phone for a reply.

Nothing. Maybe Josh had been right, and Gretchen was sleeping something off or still out dancing. Maybe she and Gretch were destined to grow apart now, with the baby coming. Maybe all her friends were going to find her so boring with her bulging veins and, soon, her crying baby. Maybe they wouldn't ever return her text messages again, and no-one would invite her to anything anymore, because who would want a *mum* around? Then Josh would wake up from this dreamy state he seemed to be in and he'd realise that the woman he loved had turned into a tired old hag. And she would probably lose her job, because she'd seen women return to school from maternity leave. They arrived late and left early and the head started talking about them differently and, before you knew it, they were telling you it just hadn't worked out and they wanted to spend more time with their kids, so, you know . . .

Everything was going to change.

Tears were dripping onto her phone and Lou bent over her belly and stifled a sob, but clearly not very well, because almost instantly Josh was knocking on the door.

'Lou, are you okay? What's wrong?'

'Everything's wrong!' she shouted back. 'Nothing will be alright again.'

She heard him laugh and she sprang up from the toilet seat as fast as she could physically move and threw open the door. 'Fuck off, Josh!' she yelled into his face. 'You have no idea what this is like.'

Lou had caught sight of herself in the bedroom mirror behind her husband. She was a big, naked, pregnant woman with hair across her face and snot around her nose.

'Hey, hey,' Josh said, taking hold of the arms she was holding out to push him back from the door. 'It's okay, Lou.'

And Lou had kept on crying and she knew she was becoming just a badly drawn stereotype of a pregnant woman, complete with drastic mood swings, being tolerated and whispered about by those around her. '*Hormones*, man,' Josh was probably saying to Mick when he caught up with him for a beer after a job. And yes, Lou knew it probably *was* hormones, but how was that helpful? This had become her life. Her reality. Her body.

Her phone had pinged and she pushed Josh away to look at it. Gretchen: *I'm sure it feels that way, babe. I've been at bloody boxing. Go me. Brekkie?*

'See,' Lou said to Josh, waving the phone in his face. 'Gretch *does* want to have breakfast. My friends don't think I'm boring.'

'I didn't say . . .' But she could see him deciding to abort that sentence. 'Of course she wants to,' he said instead. 'Why wouldn't she? You're her favourite person.'

And Lou smiled through her snotty tears because she knew he was trying to make her feel better, and that was a role he had played often over the last few months.

It wasn't like they hadn't wanted this. They had *really* wanted this. Lou had never considered herself maternal when she was younger, but after her first years of teaching, and of learning to live with Josh, she had changed her opinion about that. They both had, slowly. She had told him she didn't want to be a mother like her mother, whose constant state of disappointment she felt so keenly, and Josh said he didn't want to be a father like his father, because he was awful, and they'd agreed that they would be completely different, their own people. Build a family their way.

So she'd gone off the pill and they agreed to 'see what happened'. They didn't tell anyone. Lou knew her mother would say they weren't financially secure, which was true, and Gretchen would say that there was still too much fun to be had, which was questionable, but what they were whispering to each other was that this was their next great adventure. That having a baby wouldn't change anything in their lives; Lou would still teach and Josh would keep plugging away at his music until his luck changed and they'd still travel and go to parties and all of that, just with a baby in tow.

They certainly weren't going to move to the suburbs. That would never happen. Babies were small, their apartment was great.

But as the big change approached, Lou had worried that the way she saw Josh was shifting.

It sounded ridiculous, she knew, but she felt like she was doing all of *this* – and what was he doing?

Her body was plotting and scheming so hard, knitting fingernails and building brain cells and forming feet, and his was doing what it had always done. Eating and sleeping and going to work.

And God forbid we should talk about Josh's work, thought Lou. About the fact that just a few short years ago the path he saw himself on was one where he was writing songs and soundtracks and jingles, and that from being a sideline it would grow into a business; he'd be doing something he loved, something that made him feel whole. They would talk for ages about the best way for him to achieve that, discussing who was doing it well, the connections he'd made through some of the small successes he'd had – selling a song to a soap opera, scoring the theme to an old friend's play – and what things would look like for them when, as was inevitable, success came calling and they'd have to pack up and move. Lou had always told him that she would travel for him, support that dream for a time, because she could do what she loved to do, teaching, almost anywhere. Until they had kids, at least.

That was the conversation they'd been having for years, as they snuggled up in bed, or walked through a park on the way to meet friends at a pub, or sat around a campfire on a camping trip.

But not lately. Lately he had been taking on more and more building jobs with Mick. Lou knew she should be thankful for that; it was regular money and they were facing some time where that's all they would be living on – which would be difficult, but doable if they were careful.

But Josh didn't love carpentry the way he loved his guitar. He didn't love building a staircase like he loved writing a song. They'd stopped talking about what was going to happen when his big break-through came. Josh had taken on jobs on weekends when he might have otherwise gigged. She knew he was being responsible, but she worried he was losing himself in the process.

That Sunday morning, standing at the bathroom door with her big naked belly, she'd looked at Josh and felt, for the first time she could remember, frustration. Was this going to be it for him? Despite all their talk of a baby not changing them, pregnancy was already changing her. Was Josh's change going to be that he settled comfortably into his second-choice life? Was that going to be her fault? Would they be happy being 'just' the teacher and the carpenter? Should she feel guilty about how that made her see him a little differently?

Hormones, she thought. This is all just hormones.

'Let's go for breakfast,' she'd said, taking his hands. 'We won't be able to afford to soon – and anyway, you can't fit a pram in that hipster place with the good coffee.'

*

When Josh returned her call, Lou was crying.

'I'm on my way,' he said. 'I'm picking you up a coffee.'

'I can't drink coffee,' Lou sobbed. 'I'm trying to make milk.'

'Then I'll bring you a muffin.'

'Just. Come. Now.'

'Are you okay?'

'Do I' – sob – 'sound okay?'

By the time he made it in to the hospital, with a muffin, Baby was twenty-four hours old and Lou had made a decision.

'I'm calling her Stella,' she said to Josh. 'I love it, and I'm the one with the broken vagina and the soon-to-be-shredded boobs.'

Josh was standing over the plastic crib, where Baby was finally sleeping. He bent over and sniffed her noisily. 'Well . . .'

'What did you do last night?' Lou asked him.

He looked at her blankly.

'What did you do last night?'

'I left here and had a drink with Mick,' he said, looking up from the crib. 'She's perfect, isn't she?'

'She looks like your dad, but yes, she is.'

Lou saw Josh look harder at his little daughter. 'You think?'

'Yes. But you went for a drink with Mick?'

'Yes. To be honest, after everything that happened yesterday, I was pretty wiped out. It was . . . emotional.'

'Hmmmmm.'

'So we just had a couple to wet the baby's head, as they say.' He touched Baby's head with his finger; she stirred and Lou's stomach clenched. *Ouch*. 'And then I went home and crashed out.'

Lou thought about her night. About the delirium of the seemingly endless stretch of time, of the fear and the worry and the whimpering and the pain and all the instructions she was trying to make sense of while being unable to hold a thought in her head, and the changing faces of the people who were telling her what to do with her baby, and how to hold her, and how not to feed her and how to shush her and how to wrap her. And she realised that her night was still going on, that it would probably still be going for a while yet, because babies, she'd been told, didn't know night from day and they just needed feeding and changing and patting whenever, always, twenty-four seven.

Lou took a bite of her muffin. She was ravenous, but it felt like sawdust in her mouth.

'There have to be some perks in all of this,' and she motioned to herself, from her face to her mid-section. 'There has to be an upside. And I think it's naming rights.'

'Oh, come *on*,' Josh said, but he wasn't really listening, it seemed to her. He was still staring into the cot. What she wondered, through the veil of exhaustion and overwhelm, was whether he would ever focus entirely on her again. 'That's how we're going to do this?'

'Stella Rose,' she said. 'It's my final offer.'

Josh

Later that month

J osh was hiding.

He was standing outside a pub in Newcastle's red-brick heart of Hunter Street, wearing his wedding suit and wishing he smoked cigarettes.

He felt a sharp pang of guilt about the fact Lou was inside, with tiny Stella wrapped close to her body, talking to all these people she'd never met before and probably wouldn't again while Josh hid in the alleyway.

Josh had been a dad for two weeks when his father died.

Just four days ago, the call. He and Lou had just begun to find a groove at home with everything different. *Really* everything.

It felt like they'd walked back in the door from the hospital, their three-day-old bundle in a baby capsule – the practical gift they'd requested from Annabelle and Brian – and looked at their lives and thought, Well, that's not going to work, is it?

From the size and layout of their unit, where there was nowhere to hide from a crying baby and nowhere for a crying baby to hide from them, to the entirely impractical vintage furniture they'd furnished their place with, which was all but impossible to wipe down or clean up from vomit, poo and tears. To the neighbours, who had always had parties but seemed to ramp up their late-night noise in defiance of having to share a wall with anything as ordinary as a *family*.

When his phone rang, Josh was in the middle of hauling a big, beloved, felt-covered armchair to his ute and then the tip.

Lou had been inside, trying to nap on the bed in the weak afternoon sun as Stella (finally) slept beside her, wrapped so tightly in her little starry cloth she looked for all the world like a chubby little caterpillar busting out of its cocoon.

As he was lugging the chair, he'd been thinking about that wrap, in a sleep-deprived way, and how Lou had become so good at that so quickly, while he was incapable of replicating the secure folds and twists, and only succeeded in making Stella look like a particularly cute bundle of rags. Was that a gender-specific skill? When his phone rang in his pocket, he put down the chair and reached for it. Seeing Anika's name, he answered the call.

'Hello, sis,' he'd said, with as much energy as he could muster. He didn't need his sister's pity or concern.

But her voice had instantly told him she wasn't calling to check on Stella's progress.

'It's Dad.'

'What's Dad?' Josh didn't understand.

'He's been in an accident.'

There was a car parked in front of Josh's ute with one of those big red noses attached to the radiator, making it look like a clown, for charity or whatever. That's what Josh was looking at, for some reason, when she said, 'He's not going to . . . make it.'

That's what people said in movies when someone was going to die.

Why was this car wearing a red nose? Josh wondered. It wasn't Red Nose Day, was it? When was that, anyway?

'Where is he?' he thought to ask.

'Newy.'

'What happened?'

'It's not very clear. But a car. He got hit by a car.'

Josh stared at the red nose. Well.

'Josh?'

'Yes?'

'We need to get up there.'

Oh. Josh turned, looked from the red nose back towards his open front door. Just behind that blind in the window was Lou, exhausted, furious Lou, and little Stella. Little Stella sleeping.

'I just saw him,' he said to Anika. 'He came to see the baby.'

'I know, mate, he told me.'

'He did?'

'He did.' Anika's voice sounded muffled for a moment, like she was wiping her nose and had covered her mouth. 'He told me Stella was beautiful.'

'She is,' Josh said automatically.

'Yes, she is, Josh. That's what I said to him: "What did you expect?"'

'Ha.' Josh said the word, but he wasn't laughing.

To say Josh had been surprised to see his dad at the door the day after they'd brought Stella home would be an understatement. Josh hadn't seen Len since he'd watched his father walk away down Mick's street on his wedding day. There had been a few awkward phone calls, and information passed along via Josh's sisters about how 'ropeable' Len remained about what had happened that day, and Josh had decided just to let it lie. Len had never been much of a dad anyway, he told himself. No great loss.

But he'd found himself calling his dad on that night after Stella was born, home from the pub, full of conflicting emotions. And a few days later, Len had just appeared at the front door of their flat, clutching a pink teddy bear with the price tag still on it in both hands, a battered-looking old Beemer parked behind him in the street.

It had been surreal for Josh to see Len standing in the middle of his living room, surrounded by baby paraphernalia, wraps draped over chair arms, the portable bassinet on the dining table. A dazed Lou had brought Stella out from the bedroom and passed the tiny baby from her arms to Len's, and he stood there, this tall, tired-looking man in faded slacks and vinyl trainers, looking down at his granddaughter's brand-new face.

'You've done well,' he said, after a moment. 'She's beautiful.'

Lou made a cup of tea and Len handed the baby back to Josh and took a look around the flat. 'You'll be outgrowing this place soon, hey?' And he thanked an exhausted Lou for the tea and asked if he could go outside for a smoke, and Josh gave Stella back to Lou and joined his dad out the front.

'Any advice for me, Dad?' he asked, as they stood out on the pavement. And he was only half joking.

'I made a bit of a mess of all this,' Len said, pulling on his roll-up, his other hand wrapped around his tea mug. 'I know that, son.'

'Well . . .' Josh didn't know what to say, so he just looked down at his feet.

'But you love your kids,' said Len, 'you always do. You know that now. How you feel, it's how I felt.'

Felt. Josh, a man in his thirties now, tried not to feel hurt by his dad's use of the past tense.

As Len stubbed out his ciggie and handed Josh his empty mug, he said, 'I'd like to see more of you and Lou and the baby.'

'Yes,' said Josh. 'We'd like that too.'

'You realise how much family matters when you've got bugger-all else.'

'Is everything okay, Dad?'

'Josh, everything has never been okay, has it?' Len replied with a dry laugh. 'But it's a little bit better now I've seen my son with his daughter.'

Josh looked up at his dad, but Len was on his way to the car. 'Tell Lou goodbye,' he said. 'Babies are hard on women.'

And Josh called out, 'I'll call you, we'll come up,' as his dad folded himself into the Beemer. Two tries of the ignition, a quick wave, and the car had pulled out from the kerb, right where Josh was standing at this moment.

'Josh, I'm going to come and get you,' Anika was saying. 'Ed can deal with Henry for the night. You need to tell Lou.'

'Anika . . .'

'You have to come, Josh. Go and tell Lou now.'

'And Maya?'

'Our sister's in fucking Sumatra. I've tried, but . . .' Anika sounded muffled again. 'I'll be there in an hour.'

'Anika, I don't know if I can leave –'

'Josh, we have to. There's no other option – not one you're going to want to live with, anyway. I'm coming, go and tell Lou.'

He did. He'd hung up the phone and left the big red chair right there on the pavement and went back inside and lay down next to Lou on the bed. He didn't want to wake her, she looked so exhausted, even when she was sleeping. She was wearing the giant black shirt of his that she'd been wearing non-stop since they came home. She could undo it quickly for feeding, when the feeding was going well, and it had little white smears on it – breast milk? Baby cream? He didn't really know.

He was going to have to wake her, but he didn't want to. He wanted to lie here with his wife sleeping as she should be and his baby girl sleeping as she should be and not have to get into a car with his sister and try not to talk about their dad for the two-and-a-half hours it took to drive north to Newcastle.

He didn't imagine Lou would want to hear it, but she smelled beautiful like this, her scent a mixture of baby milk and light sweat and her shampoo from the five minutes she'd found in which to wash her hair with him home this morning. Josh inched a bit closer to her on the bed, breathed her in, and then he whispered in her ear. 'Wake up, Lou.'

Her eyes snapped open instantly, and she looked at him as if he'd shoved a knife under her ribs. 'What . . . are you doing?' Her voice was a loud whisper, instinctive already. Stella was sleeping and no loud noises were allowed. 'Why would you . . .'

'It's my dad.'

'What's your dad? Why are you waking me up?'

'I have to go,' and Josh told Lou what Anika had said to him. Lou put a hand out to him, touched his arm, his shoulder.

'Josh, we'll come with you,' she said.

'No! No, you can't come. You've got . . .' and he motioned at the bassinet, where Stella was snuffling.

'*We* have that,' Lou said, 'And we'll be with you.'

In Newcastle, only hours later, the hospital was awful. Honestly, he couldn't bear to think about it.

It seemed so ridiculous that only two weeks before, Josh had been at a different hospital, watching his daughter being born. Lou had gone early – only by a week, but it had been enough to surprise them, as everyone kept saying that due dates were only a guess and all first babies were late.

Not Stella. She was in an enormous hurry, and by the time Josh had driven them to the hospital and they were on their way up to the birthing suite in the lift, Lou was doubled over, holding on to his clothes and bellowing, 'I want to push!' When the nurse who was with them in the elevator said, 'No, not yet,' Lou told her to get fucked.

Josh thought then that he'd never been so afraid in his life. What was happening to the woman he loved seemed terrible, frankly. Life-threatening. It was like the Lou he knew had been replaced with this roaring, pain-soaked beast. It must be where stories of demonic possession came from, he thought, as, with a new wave of contractions, Lou's face contorted into a shape he'd never even considered before.

He'd watched her push Stella out, one gargantuan effort at a time, and he'd still been terrified, but also in awe. How did Lou know how to do that? How did she know she wasn't going to die from this pain that seemed literally unbearable? After what seemed like a long time, but was in reality only three hours, Stella came tumbling out of his wife, slick and yelling. The midwife told Josh to cut the cord and he did, and then he took the little ball of baby and laid it on Lou's chest, as if he was presenting her with the prize she deserved for what she had just done. And he was still shaking. Because he had no idea that people could survive that sort of thing, and he really didn't know if he could have.

They had both looked at the baby, completely baffled. And then Lou had laughed, and he had too. And then he cried and cried, like so many new fathers do.

I wonder if Len cried when I was born? Josh thought as he and Anika waited outside the intensive care ward to see their dad.

He doubted it. In fact, he seemed to remember that Emma told him Len hadn't been there for any of their births. Maybe in the waiting room for Anika, the first.

Josh recognised Christine, the woman he'd met on the street on his wedding day, coming out of the ICU. He hadn't seen her since, and he was embarrassed that he didn't even know she was still around. When Len had come to visit Stella, only a week before, he hadn't mentioned her at all. Though Josh hadn't asked.

Christine walked straight up to him and Anika, who was standing beside him. 'They've told us he's going today,' she said. She looked destroyed, this woman in a pink tracksuit, her face a mask of faded, smudged make-up. 'I think you two should go in.'

'What . . . happened?' Josh asked.

Anika put a hand on his arm as if to warn him against asking that, but Christine didn't blink.

'He walked in front of a car,' she said. She just said it like that. 'Bloody idiot.'

'On . . . purpose?' Josh couldn't help it, and he suddenly felt cold.

'Oh, no.' Christine shook her head. 'I shouldn't think so. Showing off. Had a few drinks, we'd had a row, he was trying to prove a point, I think . . .'

Josh's dad was in his sixties. Too old to be drunk and messing around on a highway. Too young to die.

'I need to hear . . .' but Anika pulled him away.

'Thank you, Christine,' she said. 'We'll go and talk to our Dad.'

'He's not talking, dear,' Christine said. 'It will be a one-way conversation.'

Josh wanted Lou. But she was waiting in a cafe; she couldn't bring the baby in here, they'd realised when they arrived at the hospital. There was way too much sickness and sorrow.

He and Anika went in, stood next to the bed and looked at the man who was their dad, in all his disappointing glory. His face on one side was bruised and mangled and his head was bandaged, but the rest of him looked almost normal.

Anika said, 'What shall we say to him?'

Josh didn't know. It was suddenly too much, this whole thing. Josh's chest felt tight, his heart racing. 'I'm going to find Lou,' he said to his sister. 'You say your stuff, then come and find us.' And he went and found his wife and daughter at the cafe.

'How is he?' Lou asked, and he shook his head at her.

An hour later, she was standing next to him at his father's bedside, while Anika wheeled Stella up and down the street outside. Lou held his hand, and he held his father's hand, and for the second time in a month, he stood by a hospital bed and cried and cried and cried.

*

Now he was hiding.

From Christine, and his mum, and all his dad's old piss-head mates.

Josh peered through the pub window. He saw Lou, one hand on Stella's pram, rolling it forwards and back, forwards and back, talking to Maya, who'd arrived home yesterday.

He wanted to run away from this ugly place, from this whole ordeal. He'd had to listen to so many people telling him what a great bloke his father was. A larrikin, sure, but salt of the earth, would do anything for anyone. A generous person with a big heart, his mates insisted. Was that just what people said about dead people, or was that who Len really was – for everyone but his family? Because Josh was trying really hard to think of anything generous and selfless and kind his version of Len had done for him or for the girls.

'You need to stop being so tortured about this,' someone said, and it was his mum, Emma, standing next to him in the alleyway.

'Mum.'

'I know you've got a lot going on right now,' Emma said, putting her hand on his suited arm. 'But if I can forgive him enough to be here today to see him off, you can too.'

'Mum.' Josh was having trouble saying anything else. If this was a movie, he thought, his mum would recall something his father had done for his children that revealed this other side to him that everyone else spoke of so warmly.

'I didn't get to talk to him before he died,' Josh said. 'I just . . . cried.'

'Well, that's okay, isn't it?'

'I wanted to tell him about Stella,' Josh said, leaning back against the wall.

'I heard he met Stella,' Emma said. 'Came all the way down to see her. That surprised me a bit, I must admit.'

Josh shrugged. 'Maybe he was in town seeing a man about a dog.'

'Maybe.' Emma nodded.

'Anyway, I wanted to tell him something else about Stella,' Josh said. Anika had suggested that he speak at the funeral today, but he had said no, he couldn't think of anything he wanted to say. But it turned out there was something.

'I wanted to tell him that Stella's only three weeks old, but I know already that I would never, ever leave her sitting somewhere, waiting for me, and not show up.' He coughed; something in his throat. 'I would just never do that. I can't imagine how you could . . .'

'Stop it, Josh,' his mum said. 'You don't have to say that out loud. Everyone who knows you knows it's true.'

'It's changed everything. Stella – she's changed everything.'

His mum took his hand. 'Let's get back inside,' she said.

He nodded, and let himself be led.

'It's supposed to change everything, Josh,' his mum said to him, putting her arm around his waist as they walked through the pub door. 'If you're doing it right.'

Lou

APRIL
Quality time

'I give my marriage nine months,' Lou told Gretchen. 'We've tried sex and we're trying therapy. Josh has tried rock'n'roll. So far, I'm no closer to clarity.'

'I don't believe you're naive enough to think that therapy works after two sessions,' Gretchen said. 'Can you pass me that hair tie?'

JoJo, Gretchen's stepdaughter of sorts, was staying for the weekend, and that evening she was going to a schoolmate's party that had a nineties theme. While Gretchen and Lou sectioned and twisted her hair into a 'Scary Spice' confection of many different little buns, JoJo kept her headphones on and her eyes on her screens of choice – an iPad and an iPhone, interchangeably – letting herself be gently yanked from side to side, in a world of her own.

'There's another problem.' Lou didn't look up as she said it. 'You know . . . *him?*'

'Him?' Gretchen kept twisting, and then paused, 'Oh, *him?*'

'Yes. Well, things – things have . . .' Lou searched for the word. She was rarely lost for words, but she just didn't know if there was one for what was happening here. 'Resurfaced.'

'Are you kidding me?' Gretchen let go of JoJo's mini bun, leaving the hair to unravel from its knot and the twelve-year-old to look up in irritation. 'When?'

'Back at the beginning of the year,' Lou said, in a whisper now. She looked up at her friend, who was staring at her, wide-eyed. 'Don't be mad with me. You're not allowed to lose it.'

Gretchen and Lou had been each other's safety net for almost two decades.

Lou had collected other friends, of course, colleagues, parents from the girls' school, people from her old running club. But none of them would know the things she and Gretch knew about each other, from the intricate tangle of insecurities their very different families had left them with, to their romantic (or otherwise) relationship histories. They'd seen each other through health crises and melt-downs, heartbreak and grief. To anyone else in her orbit, Gretchen appeared to bounce through life landing on her toes, constantly changing course but always sure of every step. But Lou knew what went into that façade. And how scary it was for Gretch every time she felt a sure-thing fall away.

There was very little she didn't tell Gretch. But sometimes, the timing was key.

'I am not losing it, Lou,' Gretchen said in a voice Lou knew meant she disapproved, just a little. 'But holy fuck, you haven't been telling me the full story on you and Josh if that's back in the mix.'

JoJo's hair was done.

'Gretchen, can I go and look in your wardrobe for the rest of my outfit?' JoJo asked, as Gretch stared at Lou. 'I bet I find something nineties in there.'

'You rude little bugger,' Gretchen said, but she was laughing. 'Go! But don't look in any of my drawers, please! And no TikTok-ing my clothes for LOLs.'

'Wow.' Lou rolled her eyes at Gretch as JoJo and her screens scrambled out of the room and down the corridor. 'You speak Young Person now.'

'I still am a young person,' Gretchen said. 'Sit down. We need to talk. Wine or tea?'

Lou looked at the time on her phone. 'Still tea.'

It was a Saturday afternoon, and Josh was at home with the kids. Things had been tense between them since the last counselling session, when he had all but told Sara the therapist that Lou was a cheater.

'I want to hear about what's really going on,' Gretchen said, heading to the big open-plan kitchen to put the kettle on. 'I can't believe I tell you everything and you've been banging on about this whole "I give my marriage a year" experiment without including a very important data point.'

'I guess I don't want to you to think one of those things has anything to do with the other,' Lou said, sitting down at the kitchen bench and drawing a finger across the white marble top. 'What's a data point, anyway?'

'Something important to note that affects all that comes after,' Gretch said. 'Like fucking someone else before you start questioning your fourteen-year relationship.'

'Shush!'

'Oh, JoJo's not listening. She'll be filming herself in my thigh-high boots right about now.'

'Still, shush. It sounds awful when you say it like that.'

'It's not the way I say it that makes it awful. It's the fact that it happened. Again.'

'Jesus, Gretch.' Lou put her head in her hands. 'That's not very supportive.'

'I would support you if you decided to cut Josh's head off,' Gretchen said, pouring hot water into two cups. 'But it doesn't mean I wouldn't tell you it was murder.'

'Stop it with the trademark brutality, okay? I get it. You don't approve.'

'It's muddying your thinking.' Gretchen brought the cups to the bench and perched next to Lou on a high stool. 'It nearly destroyed your relationship last time. If Josh knew . . .'

'I think maybe he does.'

'How?'

'At the therapist's, he made a big deal of saying how important monogamy is to him.'

'Well,' Gretch blew on her tea, 'not my thing, but hardly a controversial thing to say in couples counselling.'

'And also . . . at the concert . . . *he* was *there*.' Lou turned her cup. Her English nana had always told her to turn her tea three times; she had no idea why, but she always did it.

'Why was he there?'

'To see me.'

'Whoa. That sounds like risk-taking behaviour, Lou. He's trying to force your hand.'

It was true, Lou knew. Turning up that night had been an escalation she hadn't seen coming, and it had been keeping her awake.

JoJo strutted back into the kitchen. Gretchen was right; the girl was wearing her old thigh-high boots, a silver crop top and a pair of what were probably hot pants but on twelve-year-old JoJo looked like rugby shorts.

'How do I look?' asked JoJo, holding up her phone to film their reaction.

'Like a hot mess,' said Gretchen.

Lou said nothing, only shook her head.

'So can I wear it to the party?'

Lou said no and Gretchen said yes at the same time.

*

Josh had started writing songs again, these last few weeks. Lou had heard him, through the spare room door, as she padded past and back again with the washing and the sheets and the uniforms after the girls were in bed. She'd heard him playing the same section of a tune over and over, and murmured words snaked out from the gap under the door. She couldn't make them out, even though she had paused there, straining.

'Are you writing?' she asked him, in what she hoped was a casual tone, downstairs in the kitchen the Monday morning after Gretchen's while they grabbed toast and cereal for the kids. 'I thought I heard . . .'

'Just messing around,' Josh said, too quickly.

He had started coming to bed later and later, when she was already asleep. She felt like they were exchanging about a hundred words a day.

'I think it's great if you are,' she said, bending down to the dishwasher. 'I really do.'

Josh hadn't said anything, just taken his *in my head I'm playing guitar* mug to the table.

Lou changed the subject. 'Camping's next week, you know.'

School holidays were coming up, and they were going away. They always did at Easter. Sometimes with other families, sometimes just them. It was a standing arrangement, an annual booking at a beachy, bushy campsite on the south coast.

This year it was just them. And the idea of that seemed improbable. She and Josh sitting up when the girls had gone to bed, like they had in years past, drinking red wine and playing Cards Against Humanity?

'Should we . . . cancel?' Lou asked, looking at Josh, who was looking at his coffee.

'Why would we do that?' Josh asked.

Because you can barely look at me, thought Lou. 'I just . . .'

He kept his eyes on his mug. 'What? We can't cancel. The girls love it.'

That was true. The highlight was setting their little suburban girls free in the bush for a couple of days. Rita was just getting old enough to have some more independence to roam around the campsite with the other kids, and city parents got to feel smug at seeing their children with dirt on their faces and sticks rather than iPads in their hands, if only during daylight hours.

'Okay.' Lou turned back to the sink. Maybe it will be cleansing, she thought, and looked around for her phone.

4. *Quality time, in nature*, she would type. *We'll get away from all the daily grind bullshit and see what's there.*

There was a moment, and then Josh said, 'Dana and her lot are at that same campsite next weekend.'

'Really?' Lou pushed her hands into the warm soapy water where the pan from warming milk for Rita's Weet-Bix and Josh's very particular coffee was soaking. 'That's weird.'

'Well, not really.' As Josh said this, Rita chased Stella into the kitchen. Stella was in her school uniform, but Rita was only in her pants, screaming at her sister. 'Half the school's down there for Easter weekend.'

'Hmmm.' Lou caught Rita on her second run past and grabbed her hand. 'Let's go get your uniform on, Reet,' she said, and led her out of the kitchen and to the stairs.

Up in the girls' room, she pulled a polo shirt onto her squirming daughter. So far, Rita was loving her first year of school. Lou felt such a mingling of teacherly and parental pride seeing her marching away towards the school gate with her giant backpack on. Well, she did on the days she could be there to see it. She was on playground duty today and was due at her own school in half an hour.

'Go brush your teeth, Reet,' she said, and the little girl, still protesting about something Stella had done, headed to the bathroom.

Lou went to the window and looked at the tree. Its leaves were turning, their dark green beginning to fade, and the yellow flowers of summer were all gone. One of the big branches on the other side to the house had snapped, she saw, and it was hanging tenuously by a strip of bark. Josh was all talk, Lou thought. She didn't want the tree cut back but, still, he'd been insisting how dangerous it was, how urgently it needed to be trimmed, yet nothing had happened, and now one of the branches was going to fall on someone's head.

Irritated, she heard Rita calling her to the bathroom, because of course a nearly five-year-old can't brush their teeth without company. 'Coming!' she shouted back, and turned to go.

But as she passed the guitar room's open door, she stopped and looked in. Why did Lou feel like it was trespassing to walk into this room? It wasn't actually Josh's space – it was the third bedroom, the reason that they'd bought this house in the first place. It was meant to be for Stella.

But the room had such Josh energy about it now, it would be hard to imagine a girl's single bed in there. There were three guitars – two propped up on stands and one lying on the floor. They were all old, bought and inherited over more than a decade. IKEA bookcases were filled with vinyl records, old books and tapes. There was his stereo and fancy speakers – the most expensive thing he owned.

And on the walls, gig posters that he'd framed himself: some of them from shows they'd been to together (the Scissor Sisters at the Opera House); some from his youth (Red Hot Chili Peppers at the Big Day Out); some from his fantasies (Nirvana at Selena's).

'Muuuuummm!'

Lou saw Josh's phone lying on the couch and she instinctively grabbed it to take downstairs to him.

There was a piece of paper underneath it, a note in Josh's hand-written scrawl. The words were written one under the other as if it were a list. But it wasn't a list.

Dana – Campsite – cancellation – Two nights – site 17 – confirm.

What the fuck? Lou felt her face getting hot. Hadn't Josh told her that 'Dana's lot' just happened to be coming?

'Muuuuum!'

This was different. This was new.

She heard Sara's voice in her head – 'Have there been any infidelities?' – and her stomach clenched in the same way it had in the therapist's office. And she recalled the look Josh had shot her in that moment – accusing, angry, hurt.

With Josh's phone still in her hand, she walked to the bathroom and found Rita with toothpaste dripping down her wrist. She wrestled the messy toothbrush from her. 'You're getting it all over your school uniform, silly,' she said. Putting the phone down next to the sink, she touched the home button to see if it was locked. It was.

*

Later that afternoon, when the playground had emptied, Lou was standing outside the deputy head's office, some files under one arm, a hand on the door, taking deep breaths.

Come on, she urged herself silently. Come on.

'Hi, Lou. You okay?' said a voice behind her. It was Diane, 1G's teacher.

'Oh yeah.' Lou turned to look at her, found a smile. 'Just, you know, end of term.'

'You here to see Theo?' Diane asked.

Lou shook her head, but immediately regretted it, because Diane looked appropriately confused.

'Thought I needed to,' Lou said. 'But just remembered I'm meant to be somewhere else.'

'Sure you're okay?' Diane asked. 'There's a lot going on, isn't there?'

'There really is.' Lou smiled again and began to walk away. 'I'll see you later.'

As she moved quickly down the corridor towards her own classroom, she pulled her phone out and dialled Gretchen.

'Think I'm losing it,' she said, when her friend picked up.

'Me too,' said Gretchen. 'Kim has posted that we're Insta official. I was not ready for that.'

Lou rolled her eyes inwardly. Gretchen was currently dating a younger woman who worked as a 'lifestyle influencer'. Lou had met her once, only to find herself appearing on Kim's Instagram Stories with the caption *Finally met Bae's Bestie* with a heart-shaped eyes emoji, which had made Lou feel smug and old at the same time.

'Gretch, if I ask you for a really big favour, will you do it?'

Gretchen sighed. 'What a stupid question. How am I supposed to answer that question?'

'You say yes,' said Lou.

'But . . .'

'You just do.' Lou was at the door of her classroom now. It was strewn with paper Easter eggs, scissors and glue. She would usually have packed all this up the minute the kids were gone – in fact, way before – but the end-of-day bell had caught her by surprise.

'Go on, ask,' Gretchen said.

'Will you come camping with us next weekend?'

'Are you fucking high?' Gretchen asked. 'I don't go camping.'

'Please.'

'And I'm busy.'

'Please.'

'Kim wants me to go to Byron with her. It's an Easter autumnal harvest thing, something to do with Bluesfest. Gratitude something.'

'Well, then. It's sorted. You don't want to go to that.'

'And the alternative is *camping*? With *children*?'

'With your best friend who's having a breakdown.'

'Sounding even more enticing.'

'And the woman I think Josh might be sleeping with.'

There was a pause. Gretchen exhaled.

'Please,' Lou repeated. 'I can't go without you.'

'Well, that sounds a little bit more interesting, although I'm sure you're wrong.'

'Then why did he invite her?'

Pause.

'Please?' Lou jammed the phone between her ear and her shoulder and began to sweep paper scraps into the bin, probably losing a few lovingly made eggs on the way.

'Is the man you've been sleeping with coming too?'

'Gretch, please.' And Lou knocked over a pot of craft glue whose lid was loose, spilling the white sticky muck onto the table and her shoes.

'You do sound pretty shocking.'

Lou exhaled. 'Thank you.'

Josh

APRIL
Quality time

Easter Sunday morning and it was raining. Josh was lying on the blow-up mattress with his arse on the floor. Overnight, every bit of air had slowly hissed out of it. Not that Josh had noticed.

He was alone in the tent, he realised. Lou wasn't beside him and the other mattress, shared by the girls, was sagging under a pile of blankets in the far corner.

Josh watched the rainwater forming a dark line in the seam above him. He knew it was only a matter of time before it began to drip. There was no way he had pegged the fly out tight enough to stop it.

Last night. Oh.

The texture of his tongue and the acrid taste at the back of his throat stirred a feeling of toxic unease he hadn't felt since New Year's Day.

A close-up view of Dana's mouth flashed into his head. Lips, tongue.

Where was Lou? He couldn't hear anyone outside the tent and it was Easter. By now he should have been roused by children jumping on him and yelling about an egg hunt.

Shit.

Josh rolled sideways and off the mattress and felt some relief to see he'd been wearing boxer shorts under the unzipped sleeping bag.

He pushed his head out of the tent flap. There was no-one around, despite the steady drizzle. There was evidence that breakfast had happened here under the tarp – plastic plates still on the table, a half-loaf of bread still out with a butter knife balancing on it. But no Lou, no kids, no Gretchen, no Dana. No Marco.

He turned his head. No cars, either.

Ah. They'd gone somewhere to escape the weather.

Josh pulled a slightly damp pair of jeans from the floor of the tent and dragged them on. Everything on the tent floor was a little bit wet now, and likely to stay that way.

He was outside in the rain, pulling out the guide ropes and hammering in the pegs to try to keep the tent dry, when another image came back to him.

'If you want to, why don't you?' Lou was saying. 'Maybe that's exactly what you need.'

Her face had been close to his ear, her breath hot, her face twisted into something like a smile, but there was no lightness in her eyes.

'Stop it, you two.' Gretchen's voice, forceful. 'You are not cut out for this shit.'

*

Eva Bernard wasn't helping. Josh felt like he'd failed an important maturity test when he used the recent therapy session with Sara to provoke Lou. Eva, in her low, calm voice, always emphasised the importance of remaining neutral in counselling. You should refrain from trying to persuade the professional to take your side, because of course everyone wanted that, the validation of the marriage counsellor saying, 'Yes, you're right, *they're* the problem, not *you*.' Therapists don't do that, Eva said.

And it was true, Sara had not done that. When he'd launched into his values speech about Monogamy and Security, she had just looked at him with a direct, unwavering stare as Lou squirmed in her seat, and he had the uncomfortable feeling that Sara might assume he was projecting. 'No,' he wanted to say, 'you don't understand. *She's* the one who's . . .'

He'd walked out of the therapist's office that day feeling irritated with himself and the way he was handling this.

That night, instead of watching more Eva videos as he waited out the evening in the guitar room, he started to write a song.

It had been Dana who suggested he started writing again. After the concert, rehearsals had stopped. But on the days when he collected the girls from school, he'd see Dana the Strangely Straightforward in the playground, and she'd told him it wouldn't be good for his soul or his marriage to put down the guitar again.

'We could jam,' she'd said in the schoolyard one afternoon. 'Why not? We both have partners who don't care about music. It will help.'

Josh had suspected that Eva Bernard would consider this a dangerous invitation. That there was a high level of risk involved in embarking on a new friendship with a woman at exactly the moment your wife was questioning your relationship.

He knew that, in theory. But also, he just wanted to.

He liked how he felt when he was playing. He liked how he felt when this woman told him he sounded good, that this was his talent. He liked that she was encouraging him to do more, rather than Lou, who, it felt, was always trying to make him go away.

What? Was he supposed to just be miserable?

So these last couple of weeks, Josh had been working on something in the guitar room, and he'd send Dana the file, and she'd send back notes. Notes like, 'Love the opening, lots of heart, maybe bring the first chord in a beat sooner . . .' and Josh had felt listened to; he had felt heard.

The invitation to come camping had been a weird one. He'd been waiting for Stella to finish her violin lesson on a Wednesday afternoon, listening to her murder 'Three Blind Mice' note by note (she had no passion for the fiddle, but Lou insisted that she choose an instrument, and that was the one she'd picked this year) when Dana had appeared next to him, as she seemed to do quite a bit lately. She'd asked him about Easter, and he'd told her about camping, how they always went to the same campground, booked the same spot. How often another family or two would join them, but this time none of the others could make it . . . Dana said that was strange, because she and Marco had planned to take Umbert and Aurora to that very same campsite, but she'd only just realised that her husband hadn't actually called to make the booking, and now the kids were devastated, because they'd set their hearts on camping by the beach. And somehow Josh had found himself saying that he knew the guy who ran the place, after a few years of going, and sometimes there were late cancellations – he could give him a call.

And that's how they'd got to this strange situation of arriving at their allotted spot on Good Friday to discover that Dana and Marco were right next door, set up already. Lou had looked like she might explode. She and Gretchen – who'd somehow managed to book a late-cancellation cabin – had taken the kids off for a swim as he put up the tent and pondered how the hell he'd let this happen.

The first day had been fine, really. The four kids formed a fast alliance, and roamed the campsite's attractions – a jumping pillow, a playground, a ping-pong table, a giant foam Jenga – falling in and out of gangs, occasionally returning to their parents to get fed or register a complaint or show off a scraped knee. Gretchen and Lou went for long walks while Josh sat under the tarp outside the tent with his guitar.

Marco didn't look like the 'weakling' Dana had described. He looked like a short, stocky man whose irritation with life – and his wife – was close to the surface, roiling just under his tanned skin. He wore a button-up shirt with a collar (camping!) but with the sleeves rolled to his elbows and said hardly anything to anyone. He was into fishing, so he was either away doing it – no invitation extended to Josh – or was endlessly fiddling with his rods and lines, tightening, loosening, hooking things to other things. It was an all-consuming hobby, clearly, and Josh knew Lou would be looking at Marco and comparing him instantly to Josh and his guitar.

Last night, they'd all decided to cook together.

First, the kids and their sausages, and then, when the four small mouths had been fed and banished to tents with torches and movies playing on their iPads, the adults sat down to eat their meal – steaks and salad, and a lot of red wine.

It wasn't too weird at first. An advantage to taking Gretchen anywhere was that she was gregarious company in any awkward social situation, always ready with a story, a self-deprecating joke, the suggestion of a game.

Josh sat back and said as little as he could get away with as he drank the wine and avoided Marco's glare. Marco didn't drink the communal red. He had a bottle of Johnnie Walker Blue Label, and after the steaks he sipped it from a tin camping mug, no ice, and offered it to no-one else.

'Marco, what do you do?' Gretchen asked, stretching out her legs to spray them with RID.

He winced at the smell of the insect repellent. 'I work for a data company,' he said. 'I make systems work.'

It was the kind of answer that meant absolutely nothing to Josh. Yeah, mate, he said in his head, but what do you *do*? Like, all day?

Gretchen seemed to get it, though. 'I'm a corporate coach,' she told him, which was another job Josh didn't get. 'I work with people like you.'

'No you don't,' Marco said quite quickly.

Josh had never heard anyone be rude to Gretchen before – other than himself, on occasion – so he looked over at her, wondering how she'd react, and whether he was expected to come to her defence. She was kind of a third sister in his eyes after all these years, someone he was duty-bound to side with.

Lou was carrying a tub full of plates back from the shared kitchen area, and missed the moment. Dana was checking on the kids.

Gretchen, to Josh's surprise, smiled. 'Oh, I do,' she said. 'Little big guys like you, all the time.'

'Hey, hey, let's change the subject.' Josh's interruption was half-hearted, and clearly Marco could tell, because he spoke over him.

'I don't need any coaching,' he said. And he reached under his seat. 'Who would like some whisky?'

The evening turned right then, on the uncapping of the Johnnie Walker Blue.

Josh could remember all that, and he could remember Lou and Dana coming back, and everyone having some whisky. He remembered a crumpled-looking Stella coming out of the tent at some point and telling all the 'grown-ups' to be quiet, she couldn't sleep, and Josh had taken her back to bed and lay down on the girls' mattress for a bit, boozily singing them a camping lullaby.

He should have stayed there. Fallen asleep right then. Because after that, everything went weird.

When he came back out, Marco poured him another drink and Dana told Josh to play the song he was writing.

Lou said, 'How does *she* know you're writing a song?'

Before Josh could say anything, Marco did. From his giant camp chair, whiskey in hand, he'd said, 'Because she wants to fuck your husband.'

Gretchen laughed. A big, mad laugh. But Lou wasn't laughing. And Josh couldn't remember every word, but he remembered Lou not shouting, but hissing. Things like: 'Go right ahead, I think the feeling's mutual,' and, 'Well, I'm glad somebody does,' and, 'Stroke his ego for a minute and he's all yours.'

Dana was strangely quiet. Josh remembered trying to say, 'Hey, hey, it's not true. It's not like that. Everyone. Calm down.'

But the weirdest thing, as Gretchen went over to Lou and Josh sat frozen, like he was stuck to this stupid fold-out chair, was that Dana did not correct her husband, even when Marco said, 'Why else do you think we're here?'

And then things got really blurry, because as Gretchen yelled out, 'They're fucking *swingers*, this is excellent!' and Dana started to say, 'No, no,' Rita had cried out.

Lou rushed to her daughter in the tent. As Josh stood up – to follow, he was certain – Dana lurched towards him, all tangled blonde hair and this big, wet mouth, and tried to kiss him. Josh stood there a beat too long, her mouth on his mouth, her tongue pushing between his lips. He could hear Marco laughing and Rita crying. Then he pushed her away.

But Lou was there, holding Rita, and she said, 'If you want to, why don't you?'

And Josh was shaking his head at her. 'No, I don't want to.'

Marco's voice. 'You don't know what you want. You're as bad as *her*.' Nodding at his wife.

And Lou: 'Maybe we should all just get this out of the way.'

But little Rita was still there, and Josh took her, and he stumbled off towards the toilet block with her, and that's when he heard Gretchen telling Lou that they weren't cut out for this shit.

When they got to the toilet block, Rita wasn't crying anymore, but she needed a wee. I'm hiding in here, he thought, sitting on the floor with his back to the cubicle door, his five-year-old daughter on the loo inside. I'm always fucking hiding.

And when she was finished, he carried his little girl back towards the tent, her head nodding drowsily on his shoulder. He stopped just before he hit the circle of light cast by the lantern hanging above the table.

Dana was sitting in a camp chair, her head in her hands, Marco beside her, using a torch to examine something important in the fishing box at his feet. Really? Josh thought. Now's the time to sort your tackle?

He could hear Lou and Gretchen talking quietly, urgently, but he didn't know where. And Josh had carried his sleeping daughter past the oblivious couple and into the tent, put her to bed, and then collapsed onto the leaking blow-up mattress.

*

Josh was sitting under the tarp in the rain alone, drinking bad coffee from a plastic mug, when one car came back to camp. It was Marco and Dana with Bertie and Aurora.

Marco got out first. He was wearing an expensive-looking rain jacket, the collar up. He gave Josh a brusque nod.

Then Dana and the kids emerged, their arms full of chocolate eggs.

'Good haul,' Josh said to them, trying to act normal in an abnormal moment, but they just looked at him and disappeared into their tent.

'Your family is gone,' Marco said to him.

Josh frowned. 'What do you mean?'

'Are you surprised?' Marco asked. 'After you two made such fools of yourselves last night?'

As he said that, Marco gave Dana the kind of look you might give a misbehaving dog. What an awful prick you are, thought Josh. How did I get here, tangled up with these two?

'They've driven back to Sydney,' Dana said. She came and crouched next to Josh, put a hand on his arm. She looked different this morning. Her hair was back in its ponytail. Her mouth seemed to have shrunk to a normal size.

'But . . .' Josh felt furious. He looked at the tent. All the stuff inside it. The rain. 'What do you mean?'

'They said' – Marco smiled slightly – 'you could pack up and get the train home.'

'Mate . . .' Josh stood up, found himself squaring up to Marco. 'There's no need to look so happy about it. In my memory, you started all this' – he looked around for kids' ears, saw none – '*shit* last night.'

Marco stepped forward, smirking. 'Yes,' he said, his voice dripping with sarcasm. 'The problems in your marriage are definitely *my* fault.'

'My marriage? You said what you said about *your* wife, mate.'

'Stop it,' Dana said, again putting her hand on Josh's arm; he had to resist the urge to brush it off. 'We were all drinking, things just got away from us. We *are* sorry. I feel just terrible about all this . . . mess.'

'You *should* feel terrible,' Josh's anger was rising to the pulsing pain in his head. 'None of it should have happened.'

He looked around at the other campsites that surrounded them, their guide ropes were all tapped in nice and tight, plenty of distance between the tent and the fly. No leakage.

He thought about Lou and Gretchen getting in the car and leaving him. What would they have told the kids? Fuck, he needed to talk to Lou.

'You don't have to go,' said Dana. 'You can stay another night. We'll give you a lift back tomorrow.'

'I think that is a terrible idea,' Josh said, picking up his rain jacket from a camp chair.

'Easter Sunday, friend,' Marco pointed out bluntly. 'Hard to get a train.'

'I'll manage,' Josh said. And he shook Dana's hand off his arm, drained his tin mug, and walked towards his soggy tent.

Inside, he found his phone and called Lou.

No answer.

He called Gretchen.

No answer.

He called again.

'Josh, come on,' Gretchen said as she picked up the phone.

'Come on?' He looked at the phone for a moment. 'Where are you? Can you come back and get me? Put Lou on.'

'She's angry, Josh, and she's driving.' Gretchen's voice was calm, resigned. 'She thinks a bit of clear air is for the best.'

He could hear the bleep-bleep of one of the girls' games in the back seat. He also really doubted Lou was driving. Josh felt like throwing his phone.

'Gretch,' he said, 'what am I meant to do?'

He heard Gretchen sigh.

'Make your own way back!' It was Lou's voice, calling from somewhere else in the car. 'Sort out your own mess.'

'Josh, I'm hanging up,' Gretchen said. And she did.

'Fuck!' Josh looked at his phone in his hand for a moment, feeling the frustration building to an unbearable pulse in his head. 'Fuck!' And he threw the phone across the tent, watching it plop into rainwater that had been drip-drip-dripping into a murky shallow pool right next to the sagging blow-up mattress.

'Fuck.'

Lou

18 April, 2012

When Lou saw the tree outside the house in Botany, she knew immediately that they were leaving the inner west.

She hadn't told Josh she was coming here today.

The place was everything she had said she never wanted. A multi-storey townhouse near the airport, not close to anything in particular, not old, not 'character-filled', not within walking distance of a cafe or a pub or a supermarket. It was one of a complex of ten, all identical, built just five years before.

Josh was going to hate it.

But the tree. The tree might get him over the line. A beautiful, spreading yellow ash; the developer must have had to wrap that trunk in cotton wool to preserve it as the complex went up all around. And here it stood, in the front garden of the first house in the block, the only one that faced the street. It gave the house a feeling of privacy and the front rooms something pretty to look at. And the house was for sale.

Lou looked down at Stella sitting in the pushchair, shoving a banana into her face, her hands covered in mush. Stella looked up at her, giggled through a mouthful of goo.

'You like it, right?' Lou said to Stella. 'This is the kind of place we can get messy.'

'Mmmm,' Stella answered. 'Yayayaya.'

'We're going to have to talk to Daddy.'

'Dada.' Stella had just begun making sounds that could be mistaken for words. Lou, home all day with her daughter, had been coaching her to say 'Mama' for weeks.

'Don't be saying his name first, now, Stella,' Lou warned her. 'That would just be cruel.'

'Dadadada.'

*

To say a baby changes things is the understatement of a lifetime, Lou decided.

If pregnancy had made her feel like a stranger in her own body, the first year of motherhood had made her feel like a stranger in her own life.

Her world had expanded and contracted at the same time. It had expanded to include all these things she had never even thought about before, like: What kind of bullshit design flaw makes breast-feeding so hard? Was she ever going to be by herself ever again? How was it possible for even your hair to feel tired?

Every week and month brought a new cluster of baffling, banal conundrums. If Stella sleeps for an extra hour in the afternoon, will that mean a later bedtime or an earlier wake-up? If I don't look her in the eye when I go to settle her, will she go straight back down? Why have I spent a day googling whether the pram should now face in or face out? Why do I suddenly feel that Pocket the cat is a menace who has to go? Why is it when I leave Stella with Uncle Rob for an hour she's an angel, but as soon as I turn up she cries?

And so on. And so on. And so on.

But as all these new questions crowded in, her world had contracted to the four walls of her home, and the specific streets of her suburb.

Suddenly, the only other people she saw were essentially strangers: other mothers with babies who weren't at work during the day. They'd huddle together in any coffee shop that would welcome them, as no-one's home was big enough to hold them all with their prams and their huge bags stuffed with essential accessories.

Parks and playgrounds, previously only for pounding around in her trainers, tucking kilometres under her belt as she calmed her mind, were now essential escapes from her ever-shrinking home. She was there even in the cold, even in the heat, early, desperate to get out of the house. She hadn't pulled on her running shoes for eighteen months.

Conversations revolved around poo and food and sleep. Even more alarmingly, these were now topics that Lou had opinions on. She actually spent time thinking about them. Quite a lot of time.

But maybe the change that surprised her the most was the one between her and Josh. Because it felt as if from the moment they walked in the door with newborn Stella, their roles began to shift.

Lou had never aspired to be a homemaker. In fact, she'd spent a large chunk of her life dismissing her own mother's preoccupation with domestic matters; Annabelle's very identity was tied up in having a nice Australian home and well-turned-out children. In all the time they'd been together, Josh and Lou had both been busy working – Lou more so, to be honest. Ever since she'd moved into Josh's place in Redfern, they'd shared the household jobs. If she cooked dinner, he would wash up, and vice versa. They both cleaned, they both paid bills. It had never occurred to her that this might change, and when friends complained that their partners weren't pulling their weight, she would tell them that the bonus of living with a man who'd been looking after himself for years was that he wasn't looking for a second mum, someone to do his washing. Josh had always done his own washing.

At least, he *used* to do his own washing.

It would be churlish, since this year she'd mostly been home all day with the baby, *not* to do Josh's washing along with hers and the never-ending mountain of Stella's tiny clothes. And it would seem petty not to fold it up and put it away.

But slowly, over the course of the year, she'd noticed that Josh no longer went near the washing machine at all, and sometimes he'd say things like, 'Do you know if my black jeans are clean?' And she'd say things like, 'Oh, I haven't done darks. I'll get them done this afternoon.' And he would nod, rather than say thank you.

It was the same with food. Because he'd always finished work before she was home from school, Josh had almost always cooked the dinner. But now, she was home, and he was taking on any extra hours he could find, so again it seemed reasonable that she should be the one to decide what they were eating, take Stella out in the pram to shop for it, and then cook it, often with a squawking baby under her arm.

At first, Josh had been all, 'Don't do that, you don't need to do that, you've got enough going on.'

But now? Now he was much more likely to ask, 'What's for dinner?' when he called her in the middle of the day to check in. Occasionally he even appeared disappointed with the answer.

And then there was Stella. Josh adored her. Every day, when he got home from work, he'd take her from Lou to whisper and giggle and play with his little Stella star, his sunshiny Stell-Stell. Often, he'd take her out for a walk or, later, to the playground, to give Lou 'time to yourself', but she was the keeper of all Stella knowledge.

It was Lou who knew that if she slept for an extra half-hour for her afternoon nap, it'd take two hours longer to get her down to bed that evening.

It was Lou who knew what number of zeroes were on the labels of Stella's clothes at any given time.

It was Lou who knew their baby liked apple, but only if you peeled it, and pear, but only if you didn't.

How did all that just happen?

'I'm sure that will change when I go back to work,' she'd say to other women, who would just smile and shake their heads.

'You used to be equals,' said one of the mothers' group mums. 'Now you're just Mum.'

Fuck that, thought Lou.

But she also realised that she and Josh, consumed with each other as they were in the years before Stella, had never had a conversation about the time when it wasn't just the two of them anymore. About how it would work. About who would do what. Was that a mistake?

*

'We can't afford it,' Josh said, the minute Lou told him about the house with the tree.

Which was exactly what she'd known he'd say. She was prepared.

'Don't dismiss it without even looking.' They were sitting at their tiny dining table in the kitchen of their tiny unit. Stella had just gone down, and the dinner that Lou had cooked that afternoon – a Moroccan tagine, if you don't mind – was ready to be served. 'You don't know that for sure.'

'I do know that for sure, Lou,' Josh said, reaching for the rice. The recipe had said to serve the dish with couscous, but they didn't have any couscous, and Lou wasn't about to go through the hassle of leaving the house with Stella and all her paraphernalia just for a grain swap. 'It's been a while since a chippie and a teacher could afford a house in any bit of Sydney worth living in.'

That was the first time Lou had heard Josh refer to himself as a chippie. She didn't like it; it embarrassed her, somehow. 'You're not just a chippie,' she said. 'You're a craftsman. And a musician.'

Josh had looked up at her in that moment, and there was something like surprise on his face, and Lou suddenly felt guilty. 'Well, great, but there's no shame in being a chippie,' he said. 'People need chippies.' He went back to his food.

'I was thinking that we could . . .' Lou took a breath, preparing herself. 'I was thinking we could ask my parents for some help with the deposit.'

He looked up at her again. 'We can't do that.'

'Why not?' Lou busied herself with the chicken, very keen to act as if this wasn't the big deal that she knew it was. 'Lots of people do. And if we don't . . . well, then we really can't afford it.'

Josh put down his knife and fork. He raked his fingers through his hair. 'Lou,' he said, and she'd always loved when he said her name, but not in this moment, not in this tone. 'I really don't want us to do that.'

Lou was trying to read what, exactly, was the worst part for Josh. Pride? The idea of moving out of the neighbourhood he'd always considered part of his identity? Stress about the money? All of the above?

Judging by his face, it was all of the above.

'Josh,' Lou said, 'it's not such a big deal.'

'It's a very big deal,' Josh replied. 'To be honest, I'm surprised you're even asking me to do this.'

'I'm not asking you,' Lou said. 'I don't need to ask. I'm not a child.'

Lou really wasn't asking. She'd already done it. She thought about the conversation she'd had with her mum. The one Josh must never know about, because he would be devastated to think she'd talked to Annabelle and Brian about their lives, their money and the gap between what she wanted and what she had.

Lou knew it was a betrayal. And even as she sat there with tagine on her fork, she knew this was a line she had crossed that hadn't been crossed before – the first time she and he were not on the same team. That she and he were not *the* team.

'Of course you're not, Lou, but we've tried so hard to –'

'To what? Keep on living in a shoebox? With neighbours upstairs, downstairs, across from us? In a place where I feel trapped, all day?'

'You'll be back at work soon.'

'And meanwhile we'll live in a place where Stella has no room to run about?'

'Well, of course we're going to move eventually,' Josh said. He put a piece of chicken in his mouth and chewed, and for the very first time, Lou noticed how when he chewed his food, his lips never really met. She could just make out the yellowish chicken turning in his teeth, a tiny speck of fat on his lower lip. Why had she never noticed before that her husband chewed with his mouth open?

'How is that the end of your sentence?'

'What do you mean?' Josh spoke, but he hadn't fully swallowed all the chicken.

'We're going to move eventually . . . Where to, and how? If we want things to happen, we have to *make* them happen.'

'Well, now you just sound like a bad greeting card, Lou.' He swallowed. 'Is that your inspirational quote of the day?'

She stood up. Went to the sink and ran the tap. Passed her finger through the stream to check it was cold, then grabbed a glass from the drainer and filled it almost to the top.

'Lou?'

'Josh.'

'We can't afford it.'

She took two big gulps of water, looked at the kitchen clock. It was seven thirty. She needed to be in bed by nine. Stella still woke up at least once in the night, usually more like twice, and Lou was trying to work out a way to push her through. It was less than two weeks until the end of the Easter break and after that Lou was going back to work. Suddenly a full night's sleep felt urgent.

'Josh, my parents will lend us the money to add to our savings to get the deposit.'

He leaned back in his seat and looked at her. 'How do you know they've got that kind of money?'

She turned, her glass still in her hand. 'I just do.'

Josh seemed to think about this for a minute. He knows, Lou thought. He knows I've already asked.

'They'd be borrowing it,' Josh said, still watching her closely. 'Surely.'

Lou shrugged, took another gulp.

'It's humiliating,' Josh said. 'For grown-up people like us to be begging from your folks.'

'No it isn't.'

'How isn't it?'

'It's practical, Josh. It's how people get ahead.'

'Well, isn't the world *fair*?' Josh's tone was sneering.

'Josh, I'm not putting that complaint ahead of my kids . . .'

'Kids? Plural? Is there something I don't know?'

'We can't keep living in this very moment, Josh.' Lou's voice was rising to a shout, but she felt a sense of desperation she hadn't before; her heart was beating faster, her hand with the glass in it was shaking a little. 'We might have another baby. People do.'

'Let's stop talking about "people", Lou, and talk about us.'

This is a proper fight, thought Lou, putting her glass down. They never did this.

'We – me and you – have always talked about how every family doesn't have to need a quarter-acre block . . .'

'We're not talking about a quarter-acre block, Josh. We're talking about a townhouse with a concrete garden.'

'But it's got a tree?' He rolled his eyes, and Lou noticed he still had a tiny piece of chicken on his chin. Her hand twitched with the urge to slap it off.

'Yes, out the front.' She took a deep breath. 'I know we always said we weren't house-in-the-suburbs people. And we're not, I promise we're not. But there's a reason why families move out of tiny units in the city . . .'

'Not all families! There are lots of kids around here.'

'There's a reason,' she repeated.

He sighed. 'Okay, I'll bite. What is it?'

'It's so they don't kill each other, Josh.'

She saw him smile, in spite of himself.

'I can have a bit more room, Stella has space to grow. *If* we decide to have another baby . . .'

'Which we haven't even talked about.'

'And there'd be space for other things.' Lou returned to the table and sat down again, across from Josh. 'There could be space for music. Maybe even a little workshop in the garage . . .' Lou knew she was being manipulative now, and the way Josh just flicked his eyes at her told her he knew it, too. 'You'd have more space to be you.'

This was a moment, Lou could feel it. Like the one when she'd told him she was pregnant. Things were really changing between them. Here, in the kitchen, sitting at the tiny table, with the chicken congealing between them and Stella making a quiet grunting noise from their bedroom.

'Even if your folks would help us with the deposit,' Josh said, and Lou knew it was happening, 'even then, the mortgage repayments would kill us.'

'No, they wouldn't,' Lou said. 'I did some maths. I can show it all to you. It would be tight, but if I go back to five days sooner than we'd planned, and we get Stell into that community day care and not the private one, and you keep doing those extra jobs for Mick . . .'

Lou stopped talking, and it should have been a silent moment, the big decision in the quiet kitchen. But there were footsteps on the ceiling, and the clink of beer bottles from a backyard two houses down, and the soft but relentless thrum of the techno music that next door was playing, and would be playing until midnight.

'I'll come and look at it,' said Josh.

Lou reached across the table and took his hands. But as relieved as she was, she could also see her mother's face in her head. The particular expression Annabelle had worn, her mouth a thin line, her eyes twinkling with something like pleasure, as she'd said, 'I always knew that we'd never stop supporting you if you married him.'

And Lou had just thanked her mother for her generosity, and carried Stella back down the hallway of her family home, past her old bedroom, and out through the front door where Josh had once turned up out of the blue to ask her to be with him.

Josh

23 April, 2012

'**A**nd this is where our children will study to become Nobel Prize winners,' Lou was saying, spinning in the alcove off the living room where she was, apparently, picturing a 'study space' for her, their one-year-old and any hypothetical further offspring. She was thinking a desk, she told him, something distressed maybe, painted off-white.

Josh looked at thirteen-month-old Stella and raised an eyebrow. She was spinning on the spot. She stopped, wobbled, and plonked down on her bum. 'Dizz!' she yelled, then threw her head back and laughed.

'Genius material, certainly,' Josh said to Lou, who nudged him back towards the kitchen, which was big and open plan and had doors that opened onto a concrete yard.

'You could build us a deck, put down some grass . . .'

'On concrete?'

'Whatever.' Lou pushed on. She was trying so hard. He knew that she knew he'd agreed to the house in theory, that his feelings about borrowing large sums of money had been largely overruled, that his opinions about a townhouse far from the inner west had been mostly discounted, but now she needed him to be happy about it. To want it.

And he just couldn't, not yet.

The possibility of this house felt like the end of something he wasn't ready to end. And the beginning of something he wasn't ready to start.

Resentment was shooting out of him in uncharacteristic ways. 'You do know,' he'd said to her this morning, as they were in the middle of the now-familiar hundred-step process of leaving the house with a toddler, 'that if we buy this house it's officially the end of my music career.'

And Lou had looked at him sideways as she was trying to wrestle a pair of shoes onto a wriggling Stella. 'What are you talking about?'

'Mortgage payments, Lou. I'm talking mortgage payments. I'm never going to be able to turn down a Mick job for a muso gig with the bank breathing down our necks, am I?'

He'd been rummaging through their seemingly bottomless pile of clean washing as he said this, trying to find his Rage Against the Machine T-shirt. It suited his mood and signalled what he wanted to say to the real estate agent who was going to be guessing at Josh's take-home pay from their first interaction, no doubt gauging how much to jack up the price.

'When was the last time you did that?' Lou asked. 'Turned down a job for a gig?'

Josh tried to think. Not lately, it was true. But. 'If I didn't have to grab every job that came my way I'd have more time to write and get things moving,' he said, pulling out the T-shirt with a feeling of triumph.

'And we seem to manage to pay the rent every month . . .' Lou looked up from Stella's now-shod feet. 'No,' she said. 'Please don't wear that.'

It was the first time Josh could remember Lou ever saying such a thing. 'Don't be ridiculous,' he said, as Stella jumped up and started to stomp in her shoes. 'I'm not dressing up for a real estate agent.'

'Oh, but you *are*,' he heard Lou say under her breath as she moved past him towards the door.

And now here he was, feeling a little bit silly, if he was honest, in his T-shirt and jeans, as the shiny house guy showed them around Lou's dream home.

It was nice enough, this place, but it didn't feel like *them*, to him. Not his vision of them, at least. But clearly it was Lou's.

'Look,' she was calling from upstairs as he stared out of the open door at the front garden and the road outside. Stella was bumping down the bottom few steps on her bum while the real estate guy looked at his phone in the kitchen. 'The spare room can be your music room for a while. You know, until we need it. Come and see, Josh, I think you'll love it!'

He turned to lift Stella into his arms and take her with him. 'Stairs are very dangerous for a toddler, Lou,' he called. 'That's not a problem we have right now.'

But Lou was at the top of the stairs, giving him a look. 'We can get safety gates,' she said slowly, as if he was very stupid. 'I don't think we should be afraid of stairs.'

There were three bedrooms, two bathrooms, windows in two of the rooms that overlooked the tree and the street. Josh dragged his feet a little, walking over to see the view. You're trying to find faults, he thought. You know it, she knows it.

Lou stood behind him as he looked. Stella lay down on the carpeted floor – only floorboards and rugs in their flat – and moved her arms up and down, as if she was making snow angels.

'Soft, isn't it, Stell?' Lou said.

'So what does he say, Mr Suit downstairs, about the price?' Josh asked.

'He says seven-fifty.' Lou put her arms around his waist, pressed her face into his back.

'Which means eight.'

'Don't be negative,' Lou said, but she kept her tone light. 'He seems nice.'

Josh knew Lou knew the real estate guy wasn't nice. Well, he might very well be nice to his mates and his mum, but he was trying to sell them a house. *Nice* didn't come into it. 'Come on, Lou.'

She tightened her arms around him. 'It will be fine,' she said. 'I've done the maths.'

'So you keep saying. It's just *so* much money.' But Josh was getting sick of himself. It was what it was, and Lou needed him to be on board.

He just wasn't used to feeling like he and Lou were on different sides. And over the past year, since they had Stella, that's what he was feeling more and more.

They used to talk about everything, the two of them, lying in bed. It was his favourite place to be in the world, on his side, looking at Lou, listening to her talk. He liked to play with her hair while she told him stories about the kids she was teaching, about her friends, about the news, and politics (a female prime minister!). He used to love reaching for her, mid-sentence, and kissing her, feeling her soften in arms even as she kept talking to him, whispering right into his ear as he pushed inside her and they moved together.

He had never felt more himself than at those moments.

But those moments never came anymore. There were no slow nights and lazy mornings. There was always Stella – brilliant, heart-lifting, all-consuming Stella – and all the things she needed daily, hourly, by the minute, filling the time that used to be theirs.

He wouldn't change it, he kept saying – to Mick, to Anika, to whoever was asking. But he missed Lou. The Lou who wasn't always preoccupied, and tired.

Josh was achingly aware that he wasn't as attuned to his daughter's needs as Lou was. But it did feel sometimes – often – that he wasn't invited to be. Whenever he tried to take ownership of even the smallest Stella-related project, he got it wrong. Lou was constantly irritated by his inability to understand the tiny nuances of how to make his daughter happy, to convince her to stop crying, to persuade her to cooperate.

And he knew Lou struggled with her new role, the one women were supposed to settle into effortlessly but which, as far as he could see, required her to give up on many of the things that had made her Lou. She was home all the time, and she had never loved that. She didn't have time to run. She had taken on all these household tasks he didn't even know existed, and she clearly hated doing them. It felt like his role now was a supporting one, both literally and figuratively. And it weighed on him in ways that made him itch.

Yes, having babies changed everything, just like his mum had said.

'You know I love you,' Lou was saying to him, arms still around his waist, head still at his back. 'But you're being a real pain in the arse about this.'

She stepped away, turned him around and took his hands. 'Look at the possibilities,' she said. 'Think about how happy we could be here.'

'Here, here, here,' said Stella, still rolling around on the floor. 'I heeeeeeeere.'

'It's still just me and you,' Lou said to him. 'We're the same people, just on a different set. One with some space to breathe.' And she widened her eyes and smiled at Josh as she mimed taking in some deep breaths.

He looked at her, with all her energy, her positivity, her ability to look at this blank room and paint a picture of a happy home.

'No more than seven-seventy,' he said, and he smiled, and she let go of his hands and turned in a tiny victory circle, pumping her fists like a champion boxer.

'Hear that, Stell?' Lou said, beaming. 'Your daddy's choosing happiness.'

'Happiness and debt,' corrected Josh, as he bent and swept Stella up in a hug.

And for a moment, he saw them through the real estate agent's eyes. *Think I sold it to a young family*, Josh imagined him saying when he got back to the office today. And his colleagues would all nod, because the city was full of young families who were taking on big loans to buy small houses with the optimistic hope of living happy, ordinary lives in them.

Why did he think they were special enough to be any different?

Lou

MAY

Honesty

'I'm giving our marriage seven months,' Lou said to Josh, loudly, clearly, directly. 'We can't keep going like this.'

It felt like those words had been stuck in her throat for weeks now, and saying them out loud, to Josh, was like expelling them with an almighty, cleansing cough.

But *I should have chosen this moment better,* she thought, as she held on tight to the base of the ladder. Josh was at the top, high among the branches of their tree, safety goggles on and a chainsaw in his hand. He peered down at her. 'Pardon?'

'I decided in January, Josh,' she called up to him, 'that this is the year of make or break.'

'Make or break?' He pushed the goggles back on his head with one hand, the other still clutching the saw.

'Us,' Lou said, her face turned up to him. 'One year to decide if we should stay together or not.'

Josh didn't say anything. Lou held on tight to the legs of the ladder. A minute passed. Lou looked up to see that Josh's goggles were back on. She heard the chainsaw start up.

Against the noise, she yelled up into the leaves, 'Don't take too much! Just a trim!'

*

The month since the camping trip had been . . . fraught was the word that Lou was using. She'd been in the house with the girls when Josh arrived back that Easter Sunday, climbing out of an Uber from Central Station, weighed down by backpack and tent, still damp and darkly furious.

'I had to leave a lot of stuff there with . . . them,' he'd said as he came into the kitchen, where she was sitting at the table, reading news about a terrible bombing in Sri Lanka on her phone. The kids were already in bed, full of chocolate. It had been a long day.

'How could you just take off like that?' he asked. She could hear the anger in his voice. His hands were shaking as he planted them on the table and leaned towards her. 'How could you just leave me? What did you tell the kids? All the way home I've just been trying to think of why you would leave me there . . . with them.'

Lou looked at Josh then, her tall and handsome husband, bedraggled and confused. 'You thought about it for three hours on a train and you still couldn't work it out?' she asked. 'Really?'

'Explain it to me. Because I bet that what you think happened last night and what actually happened are not the same.'

'This isn't just about last night, Josh,' Lou said. 'I think you know that.'

'Lou, I *don't* know that!' Josh walked around to stand next to her. She looked down at his muddy, battered Blundstone boots. He still wore those, always. This pair was now coated with mud and leaving smears on the kitchen floor. 'I need you to tell me what the fuck is going on,' he said.

'I'd tell you, but I have no idea.' Lou looked back at her phone and kept scrolling. 'I think you're the one with the answers.'

Josh was going to shout. It took a long time for him to get to that. What Lou knew and Josh's mum Emma knew was that Josh pushed his anger down and down and down, afraid of being that man he'd known from childhood. The kind of man who punched holes in plaster and shouted into faces and made everyone around him feel they were always, always standing on a fault line that could fracture at any moment.

But there was a tipping point. She'd seen it once or twice, over the last few years. There came a point at which Josh couldn't pretend to be the opposite of an angry man anymore. She hated seeing him reach it, because after fourteen years together, his feelings were entwined with her feelings, and the disappointment and disgust he would be soaking in for days after an explosion would make the whole house toxic. Still, she wasn't going to defuse him. Not this time.

Josh hadn't yelled yet. Lou could feel him wrestling with it. She could feel the frustration and confusion rolling off him in waves, his energy crashing into hers. But, for some reason, Lou was finding it easy to stay calm in this chair, in this spot, in this kitchen, right now.

And then Josh roared, a big, ugly noise from deep in his chest, and slammed his hands onto the table. 'You think I slept with Dana. I didn't fucking sleep with Dana! I don't want to. That is not what I want. I want you. I want our family. I want our home. I want you to stop treating me like I'm the world's worst person, because I'm not.'

Lou didn't feel anything as Josh's words poured over her. She knew that she should, she knew that leaving Josh at a rainy campsite on Easter Sunday was something to feel guilty about, but she didn't. She just felt tired.

I promised I'd give it a year, she thought. I promised a year, for Stella and for Rita and for all the years we've passed through together and all the ones ahead.

Josh collapsed into the seat next to her, and put his head on his arms, and cried.

And still, Lou sat, just numb.

*

She and Gretchen and the girls had driven back to Sydney in almost silence. She had spent the night in Gretchen's cabin, the two of them lying on narrow bunks, and they'd done all their talking then.

Lou was shaken and teary. Gretchen thought the whole scene with Dana and Marco was hilarious, and a little pathetic.

'Josh is out of his depth,' she said. 'I think he's casting around for something to make you notice him, and he's fallen into something he didn't expect.'

'Make me *notice* him?' Lou almost laughed. 'I don't think that's it.'

'I do,' said Gretchen. 'He doesn't know what's happening to his life. Lou, you have to admit some fault there, friend.'

I do, Lou nodded. I do.

'I know you're struggling, but Josh looks lost to me.' Gretch looked like she was taking a deep breath, like she was about to say something important. 'I don't think he deserves it. I think he's a good man. And deep down, so do you.'

'I just saw him kissing another woman on our family holiday!' Lou argued, but even as she said it, she didn't really believe it herself.

'He was *being* kissed, Lou,' Gretchen said. 'You know it. And, really . . .' She trailed off, but Lou knew exactly what her friend was thinking. *Glass houses.*

'I should go and see to the girls,' Lou said half-heartedly. She didn't want to go back out there.

'They're with Josh, they're fine,' Gretchen said. 'Let it all cool down.'

'Fine? They could be witnessing an orgy.'

'No chance. Josh will be snoring his head off. If we're quiet, we can probably hear him.' Gretchen laughed.

She was right, of course. As soon as it was light, Lou had tiptoed out to the tent. The girls were tangled up on one mattress, Josh was alone on theirs. Everyone was snoring. Storm clouds were rolling in.

Lou couldn't face any of them. Not Josh, and not Dana and Marco. She just wanted to get her girls and go home, and that's what she did. She shook Stella awake, pulled Rita into her arms, and took them back to Gretchen's cabin just as the birds were beginning to shout. She lied to her daughters about rain cutting the holiday short, the Easter Bunny delivering directly to the car and Daddy staying behind to pack up.

All the way back to Sydney, Lou had looked out of the window and told herself it was time to unpick all this mess.

'Take it all to the therapist,' Gretchen said, looking sideways at her as they barrelled down the highway. 'And for fuck's sake, you've got to talk to Josh about what's really going on.'

Lou knew she was right. *I'm going to try everything to save it*, she had promised herself in January. *And if it doesn't work I'm going to let it go.*

But only then.

5. *Honesty*, she wrote into her phone. *What happens if I'm not counting down alone?*

She watched the tops of pale green gums flash past against the blue sky as they left the south coast behind. But the thought of having the conversation made her feel nauseous.

She still hadn't been ready that night at the kitchen table, after

Josh cried, when she eventually reached out a hand and put it on his head.

'It's okay,' she said. 'It's going to be okay, one way or another.'

And she hadn't been ready in the weeks since, when they'd fallen back into the routine of school and home and dinners and sport and backyard catch-ups with neighbours on a Sunday and doing the big shop on a Saturday afternoon and Josh writing in his guitar room, and Lou fighting the urge to follow the red car.

And Josh hadn't mentioned Dana and Marco again since the camping weekend. Lou hadn't either. Josh had attempted to make a joke when they saw Dana from a distance at the school gate, and Lou had tried to laugh, but it came out hollow. And they'd had sex maybe twice, in the bed, Lou looking at the leaves as her husband's mouth was up here and down there, but she couldn't feel much of anything. And most days Gretchen would message to ask if there had been 'progress' and Lou would reply 'soon'.

But nothing actually happened until the tree came through the window while Rita was sleeping.

*

The scream was louder than the smash, louder than the wind that had been whipping the house all night. And when Lou and Josh reached the kids' bedroom door and flicked on the light, Rita was still screaming, her covers over her head, her pink and blue *Frozen* doona sprinkled with terrifying shards of broken glass.

Lou ran to the bed and sank down next to her daughter's pillow, tiny spikes pushing into her knees.

She was aware of Josh at Stella's bed, lifting her in his arms. She was crying too, and over at the window, a tree branch was swaying through the jagged edges of the broken window, like an arm reaching in.

'For fuck's sake!' yelled Josh, over the wailing and the wind. 'That tree!'

Lou was trying to peel back the cover from Rita's head, 'Come on, baby, are you okay?' she asked. 'Let me see, sweetie. Let me see . . .'

And in that moment Lou did what people in movies did. She started making deals in her head. If Rita's okay, I'm going to start living my life without lies . . . Her daughter whimpered. If Rita's okay, I'm never following the red car again. If Rita's okay, I'm going to tell Josh what's been going on.

'Come on, Reets,' she pleaded. 'Let me look.'

Josh was suddenly next to her, seeming not to notice the shards of glass cutting into his bare feet. 'You need to move away from here, Lou,' he was saying. 'I'll lift Rita out, but we need to get away from the glass.'

It must have been a powerful blast of wind that had smashed the tree branch through the glass at just the right angle to shatter the pane. Looking at what was left of the window, Lou could see there were big spikes still sitting in the frame; another gust of wind and they might fall onto Rita's bed under the window.

'Come on, Reets,' Lou whispered close to the cover. 'We need to get you out. Come on, darling . . .'

And suddenly Josh was lifting Lou by her shoulders, moving her away from the bed, and in spite of her fear, Lou was instantly, instinctively reminded of the other time he'd lifted her like that, on the night they'd met, when he'd pulled her from the floor she was cowering on and she'd kissed him, just like that.

And then Lou became aware of the spikes of pain in her knees and looked down to see blood running in thin lines down her legs. And now she was out of the way, Josh bent down and in one decisive move, yanked off the duvet and swept down to gather Rita and carry her in his arms to the other side of the room.

Lou got to look at Rita, and she was fine. There was no blood anywhere that Lou could see.

'Muuummy!' Rita was calling out now, from the safety of her father's arms. '*Muuummy!*'

And Josh and Lou's eyes met over Rita's head. And they shared a smile of relief for a moment before Lou cupped her daughter's little face in her hands and kissed it.

And that branch was still reaching in, flailing about for something, and the whole family stood there looking at it for a few moments before they cleaned up to go and sleep in the other room, all of them together.

*

So Josh was up the tree with the chainsaw when Lou finally blurted out the truth about her marriage experiment.

Rita and Stella were on a play date a few doors down with a neighbour's kids. This is exactly how I pictured it, Lou thought. Living here, in the house with the tree. I imagined that the kids would be able to play in each other's back gardens. I imagined that we'd have enough room to invite people over. I imagined that we'd plant a garden together, talking about important things that didn't always revolve around the kids. And the tree would grow with our family.

'Watch out down there!' Josh called over the buzz of the saw. 'Branches are going to fall.'

'Not too many!'

'Lou!'

And she jumped a little to the side, still holding on to the ladder, and small branches did fall, whizzing past her ears. I didn't picture this part, she thought. The temporary board on the window.

The kids' bikes overturned on the too-long grass. The angry husband at the top of the ladder. The guilt and frustration in my gut.

'That's too many!' she called as another branch fell.

'This tree nearly killed your daughter!' Josh shouted, loud enough to be heard over the saw. Loud enough to be heard by Ahmed, who was washing his car across the street.

'Not on purpose,' Lou replied. She knew how ridiculous that sounded.

The tree was the reason she'd loved the house in the first place. The reason she was able to talk Josh into it.

More leaves fell.

'Get out of the way,' Josh yelled. 'This is a big one.'

Lou let go of the ladder and stepped back.

It was the branch that had smashed Rita's window, heavy and knobbly with the weird-looking 'hand'.

It crashed to the lawn next to Lou's feet. She looked up at the tree without it. It was still there, lopsided, uneven, all cut back on the house side, the yellowy leaves still spreading out over the pavement.

Josh climbed down the ladder slowly, the chainsaw in one hand, leaves in his hair, dust all over his goggles and his old, ripped Ramones T-shirt.

'I'll go and get the green bin,' Lou said, 'and a rake.'

Josh pushed the goggles up on his head. 'Seven months?' he asked.

'That's what we're up to,' Lou said. 'Since January.'

Lou watched Josh's face as he took the goggles off and lifted both his hands to shake the tree out of his hair. His expression was hard to read.

He dropped the goggles to the lawn and wiped his hands on his jeans.

'Fuck me,' said Josh. 'And I thought I was going mad.'

Josh

MAY

Honesty

Tree Day, Josh decided, was a blessing and a curse.

A curse, because it was the day he found out that his worst fears were real. And a blessing, because now so many mysterious things made sense.

Sex Month. Camping. Couples therapy.

But now it had been two weeks, and he couldn't sleep and he felt physically sick almost all the time.

On Tree Day, Lou had stopped hiding and said what she really meant. She meant: *Leaving you is a live possibility. I am actively considering it every day. In fact, I am keeping a running score of your ability to make me want to stay with you. Just so you know.*

'What am I supposed to do with that?' Josh asked the only person he felt he could talk to about it. 'The pressure is ridiculous.'

'Josh, I can't discuss this with you,' Gretchen said to him.

'But you've known us both longer than anyone,' Josh said. 'You know what we've been through. You were there when we *met*, for God's sake.'

He was on the phone in the guitar room, hiding. Still.

'Yes,' said Gretchen. Her voice was faint. It sounded like she was at an outside bar, chill techno music pulsing in the background and young voices squawking as loudly as the seagulls. 'But you know where my loyalties lie.'

He did. Of course he did. But he wanted to feel close to his wife, who was pushing him away, and Gretchen was closer to her than anyone.

A moment went by. He could hear a ferry horn in her background.

'Is she going to leave me, Gretch?' Josh asked. He knew he sounded desperate.

'I don't know,' Gretchen said, and paused. 'I don't want her to, Josh, I'll tell you that for free. You two are as good together as any other couple I know. But . . .'

He held his breath, wondering what the 'but' was going to be.

'She's looking at the next half of her life. And just like men have done forever, she's asking, *Is this it? Is this enough?*'

Josh almost laughed. 'Are you saying Lou's having a midlife crisis?'

Gretchen actually did laugh, a little. 'Why is that so ridiculous? We all have choices, Josh. Used to just be you guys, now it's all of us.'

'Gretch . . .' He didn't really know what he wanted her to say, but he knew he wanted to stay on the phone with her. Gretchen was a link. A clue. 'Is this about . . . anything else?' He couldn't bring himself to say *anyone.*

Gretchen didn't speak for a moment, and in that moment, Josh's stomach dropped to his shoes. 'I think Lou's just trying to find her "why" again,' she said eventually.

'Her "why"?'

'*Why* have you two been together forever? *Why should* you be together forever?'

Josh could immediately think of ten reasons. 'That shouldn't be so hard,' he said. Also, he thought, that wasn't a no. When he'd asked Lou's best friend if all this was about *anything else*, she hadn't said no.

Gretchen sighed. Harbour noises. Seagull sounds.

'I've got to go.' Her voice had changed, like she was smiling at someone near the phone. 'I'm meant to be with people.'

'What am I supposed to do with this information?' Josh asked. He was pacing around the room now.

'Hey, you called me,' Gretchen said. 'Look, just don't lose it, Josh. Staying cool has always been one of your most endearing qualities.'

Josh was trying to stay cool. But it wasn't easy.

Sometimes he was overcome with sadness at the thought of his girls experiencing a childhood similar to his own. Sometimes he just felt disgusted with himself for not being able, after all these years, to keep the woman he loved happy. And sometimes he wondered whether it was possible for anyone, any couple, to unchain themselves from their history.

Josh had seen Dana two days ago.

He was working on a new private job – a heritage renovation in the inner west. A music producer had bought a warehouse in Camperdown and wanted to turn it into a state-of-the-art home that still had traditional touches. He and Tyler were doing a staircase, a mezzanine, an internal pool deck, all with rich, dark, knotty recycled timber. It was bloody beautiful, if he said so himself.

But Josh was finding that every day he went to that job he got a little angrier. Driving north into his old neighbourhoods, fighting choking traffic on narrow roads at 6 a.m., he'd tick off reasons in his head why he wasn't a music industry professional about to move into a converted warehouse.

Because I've had a family to support for nine years now.

Because I don't know all the right people.

Because I'm not an arsehole.

He was clinging, he knew, to his deep-held belief that people successful in a field he would quite fancy being successful in himself must be dickheads. So when he briefly met Pearl Hass – a Kiwi woman in her thirties with a pregnant girlfriend and a bouncing kelpie – and she was lovely, it almost irritated him more.

Mostly, he and Tyler dealt with the architect, who *was* a bit of a dickhead, really, and who on this particular day had ordered the project manager to send the chippies home early because the French tiler was coming and needed peace in which to make some big decisions.

So Josh dropped Tyler at the pub and sulked his way back through the traffic to collect the girls from school on the dot of 3 p.m. and take them to the park for a kick-around. He knew Lou was up to her ears in marking and would appreciate two knackered kids who'd fall asleep easily after dinner.

He was trying to be helpful.

But as soon as he pulled the ute up to the park – the girls crammed illegally but thrillingly (for them) into his passenger side – he saw Dana with Bertie over near the goalposts, exactly where he was planning to take Stella and Rita.

His irritation, building since this morning, when he'd seen the techies loading in the home-studio kit at the warehouse conversion, was almost overwhelming. He sat at the ute's wheel, gripping it tightly and cursing under his breath.

'What are you doing, Daddy? Aren't we getting out?' Rita was asking from the passenger side.

Dana had spotted the car and started waving. Since the Easter camping disaster, Josh had felt so foolish about the whole thing that he'd tried to erase it from his memory and his world. He'd been with Lou once when they'd seen Dana at school pick-up and he'd tried to make a joke about it – 'Shall we swing over there . . .?' – and Lou's laugh had been so sad, so humourless, that he knew it was a mistake.

He had stopped messaging Dana about music, about anything. Had ignored her texts, had tried his best to avoid places where he thought she might be. But here he was, on this annoying autumn day, having told his girls they were getting a kick-about with Daddy, and he had to deliver.

'Come on, girls,' he said, opening the door. 'Let's go over this way.' And he motioned in the opposite direction to the other side of the park, but by this time Dana was almost at the car, dragging Bertie by the hand.

'Josh!' she was calling. 'Josh!'

Josh kept walking, but Stella and Rita had stopped.

'Dad,' Stella said. 'She's calling you. That lady from camping.'

'Bertie's mum,' added Rita.

Bugger bugger bugger.

When Josh turned, he was horrified to see that Dana was crying. 'Josh,' she said again. 'Josh, please.'

Stella and Rita just stood there, staring at the crying blonde woman in her leggings and fleece as she came to a stop in front of them. Bertie, clinging to his mum's hand, looked mortified.

'Josh, I'm so sorry,' she said, her voice crackly and wet. 'I'm so sorry. Please . . .'

Josh looked at his girls – pointedly, he hoped – but she kept going. 'I really miss you.'

Stella looked at him sharply, and Josh immediately tossed her the AFL ball he'd brought out of the car. 'Stell, take Rita and Bertie for a kick. I'll be there in a minute.'

Stella looked like she was going to refuse, but Josh's eye contact didn't break and soon she started towards the oval with a dramatic, 'Come on, then,' to Rita and Bert.

'Dana,' Josh said, his insides roiling with anger, 'this is really inappropriate.'

'You've got it all wrong,' Dana said, stepping closer to him. 'Honestly, I've been needing to talk to you ever since Easter – it's really not what you think.'

'Dana, I just think the whole thing was a big –'

'Misunderstanding. It was a big misunderstanding.'

Josh remembered Dana's lips pushing determinedly into his. Her husband's words.

'I just think we should all move on,' he said.

'We were just drunk, Josh.' Dana took another step, and she reached out her hands as if he might take them. 'Marco shouldn't drink. That's the truth. Things between us aren't good. We're not . . . *happy*.'

Josh kept his hands by his side. He looked over to the kids. They weren't kicking the football. They were a hundred metres away, the girls staring at him and Dana, Bertie looking at the ground.

'I miss you, Josh,' Dana went on, her hands out flat now, as if she was pleading. 'I miss our friendship, the music . . .'

'Dana, please. It's all caused enough trouble already. And' – he nodded towards the children, and Dana looked quickly too, but didn't seem perturbed – 'I've got to go.'

'Trouble? With Lou? I'm really so sorry.'

'Dana . . .' Josh was so fucking angry. Why was this woman still talking to him? His girls were watching, his wife needed no excuse to kick him out, he was still speckled with sawdust from working on someone else's dream house. 'Just leave it. Really. I don't want to talk about it, and especially not with you.'

Dana looked surprised, but at last her hands dropped to her side in something like defeat. 'I see.' And then she just looked sad.

Josh started walking away towards the girls. He was holding his breath, he realised.

'Josh!' Dana called after him. 'Maybe I can talk to Lou, explain everything. Tell her our bond's about the music.'

And Josh turned. 'Don't,' he shouted loudly.

As he resumed walking, Bertie ran past him towards his mother. When he drew level, the boy delivered a quick kick to Josh's ankle, sending a shot of pain up through his leg.

'Fuck!' Josh exclaimed, and stumbled a little.

Stella and Rita looked shocked as their dad hobbled towards them.

'It's all okay, girls,' he called. 'I'm fine.'

Just keep walking, he told himself. Just keep right on limping forward.

Lou

18 May, 2014

'**M**ocktails are bullshit,' Lou said to Gretchen down the phone. 'I miss vodka.'

'The science is in,' said Gretchen. 'You are *not* on the vodkas.'

'Sigh,' said Lou, who was lying on her bed in her underwear, tracing the thick dark line that now ran from her bellybutton and arced over her pregnant belly and into her pants. 'I guess I'll still come.'

'I'll meet you there at eight.'

'Eight? Are you insane? Six thirty.'

'The place will not even be open at six thirty, Lou.' Gretchen was laughing.

'I'm a pregnant woman with a preschooler and a job. Being in bed by nine is my religion. I will sacrifice all before it.'

'Fine, I'll meet the others at nine. You and me six thirty. Can I go and get on with my shallow, selfish, late-night life now?'

'If you must,' said Lou. 'But don't be having any sex. It's gross. That's official.'

'Definitely not official. See you Saturday, Lou-Lou.'

It was Sunday. Lou had two more weeks of work before her mat leave started. She was so tired that the idea of getting off this bed and going downstairs to see if Stell had fallen into their construction site of a backyard seemed all too much. Josh would have yelled up if she had, right?

The window was open and the tree was blowing the yellowing leaves around outside in a pleasant autumn breeze. Lou closed her eyes, felt the cool air on her bump. She'd been right about this room, right about this house, right about this tree. It was well and truly home now.

For a while it had looked like it would slip through their fingers as the owners decided on a nerve-shredding auction, and then there was seemingly endless paperwork, money-moving dramas and hidden costs of this and that. Every time, Lou was convinced Josh's cold feet would turn to ice blocks and she wouldn't be able to shift him.

And then there was her mother. When Lou had brought her mum to a viewing to actually see the house that she and Brian were helping them buy, Annabelle said they were aiming too low. 'This isn't a forever home, BB,' she'd said, standing in the empty kitchen and looking out at the concrete yard. 'You can do better.'

'I don't want to do better, Mum,' Lou had said. 'This is almost manageable. We can be happy here.'

The way Annabelle tightened her lips as her eyes swept the medium-sized rooms and the bland white kitchen and the tiny strip of front garden told Lou that her mother doubted that.

'Mum, honestly – to me, this place is perfect.'

'I want you to have everything you deserve,' her mother said. 'And a lovely big house is part of that. It's what your husband should want to give you.'

'This isn't the fifties, Mum; Josh isn't giving me anything,' Lou said, looking nervously at the other people who were there for the open-house inspection. 'We're a partnership.' She knew Annabelle was looking at the others too, and had somehow decided they weren't the right kind of competition. She clearly thought Lou should be in a different contest.

'The fifties! How old do you think I am?' Annabelle said loudly, with a laugh, and then she pulled Lou closer to her and lowered her voice. 'When I met your father, I knew he could offer me a better life. That's what's supposed to happen, Lou: you're supposed to get a step up for your family, and they for theirs, and so on . . .'

'I've heard this story before, Mum.'

And she had. It was her mother's origin story. The legend went that Annabelle had never felt at home in the small northern English town where she was born and raised, with its working men's clubs and its narrow range of life choices for a girl. But Brian, a young apprentice engineer from Sydney whose family had ties in the region, made the then-bold choice to do his training in Leeds. Annabelle always joked she met the only Australian in northern England on the day he walked into the uninspiring cafe where Annabelle was waitressing and the rest, while not quite worthy of history, was nevertheless passed on to Rob and Lou as if it were a fairytale.

Now Annabelle, who had graduated from a worker's terrace in a bleak English town to a semi-detached (and then a detached, mind you) house in the bleached blandness of Australia's sprawling suburbs, ran a finger down the wall of the Botany townhouse as if judging its cleanliness. 'I suppose this can be a stepping-stone house.'

Now they'd been living here for eighteen months, and Josh had stopped grumbling and they were handling the monthly repayments – just – and Stella was growing bigger and louder and more energetic by the day, and soon she would have a deck and a little turfed garden to play in, and then there would be another little Josh or Lou, and she wouldn't be bringing them from hospital to a little bit of someone else's home, but to her own. And she felt pride in that. Yes, it turned out she was her mother's daughter.

Josh appeared at the bedroom door, looked at Lou lying on the bed in her knickers looking at her phone, and smiled. He was dusty, dirty from the deck.

'What are you smiling about?' she asked him.

'You look beautiful,' he said, 'lying there like that.'

'I look like a blimp,' she said. 'But thanks. Where's Stell?'

'*In the Night Garden*.' Stella was obsessed with the surreal English kids' TV program. 'It's like she's fixated on someone else's acid trip.'

'Then I look more like the Pinky Ponk,' Lou said, thinking of the green, spotty airship in the show. 'It's a weird time for her to be watching TV.'

'Yeah, she kept trying to play with the nail gun, so I had to distract her.'

'I hope you're joking.'

'Kind of. Can I lie down with you for a while?' The way Josh was looking at Lou, smiling at Lou, she knew exactly where this was meant to be leading.

'Only if you want to look at my Pinterest boards of deck doors,' she said, holding out her phone. Lou had read the stories about impossibly horny pregnant women; women who had never felt more sensual, more powerful. She could safely say that, this pregnancy, she did not feel the goddess moving within her. Just a lot of gas.

'I can think of better things . . .' Josh started taking off his dusty T-shirt. He dropped it on the floor, began to unbutton his jeans.

'You're not leaving that there, are you?' Lou said instinctively.

Josh looked confused for a moment, then at his T-shirt on the floor. 'Only for a moment,' he said. 'The briefest of moments, I promise.'

Lou squirmed. The effort of even that felt like a lot. 'Josh . . .'

'Okay!' He picked the T-shirt up and threw it across the room, where it landed in the washing basket, but not without hitting the white wall, leaving a tiny, dusty plume.

For fuck's sake, Lou thought, irritated at herself. This is who I am now. I'm the woman who's turned off by dust.

'Seriously, Josh,' she said. 'Come and look at deck porn with me. It might get you off.'

He stopped undoing his pants, looked for a moment like he might sulk. But then he shrugged. '*Night Garden*'s not long enough for one of my epic performances anyway,' he said, and came over to lie beside her, dirty jeans and all, and held out his hand for the phone.

The thing was, Lou thought, as she pointed out blistering paint finishes and weather-proof fairy-light streamers, she just couldn't *see* Josh right now. She could see this baby, and the one downstairs, and she could see what needed doing at work on Monday, and she could see the before-birth to-do list sitting in her computer. Lying on her side, she pushed her big belly into Josh, and he smiled and put his hand on it. 'Hello, bump,' he said, his voice thick with warmth.

You'll come back, she thought. You'll come back into focus, when I have some space to see the sky through the trees. Can you hold on till then?

Josh

A few days later

Josh unwrapped the tea towel from around his middle finger and watched a bright stream of blood pour into the kitchen sink.

'Lou,' he called over his shoulder, 'I think it needs a stitch. I'm going to have to go.'

'Fuck,' Lou called from the next room. 'Gretchen's picking me up in an hour.'

'I know, babe, but . . .' Josh peeked under the tea towel again. 'A bandaid's not going to fix it.'

'Daddy! Let me seeeeeeee.'

Stella came rushing into the kitchen, practically skidding on the tiles, all knees and elbows and dark hair flying.

Lou followed her in. Walking slowly – Josh wouldn't dream of saying waddling, even in his head – a towel wrapped around her, her belly pushing at the thinning blue cotton.

'I haven't been out in forever,' she was saying. 'This is typical.' And then she saw the blood on the draining board, and she went white. 'Oh.'

Josh bashed up his fingers at work often enough to be able to judge when bleeding was going to stop, and he knew this wasn't going to be stopping any time soon.

'I'll be as quick as emergency will let me be,' he said, pulling the tea towel bandage as tight as he could. 'Promise.'

'Give me a second to get dressed,' Lou said, turning back to the door. 'You can't drive, you idiot.'

Idiot was a bit rich, Josh thought. The deck he was trying to build was Lou's dream, after all. And a one-man project of that size was always going to result in injuries; it was inevitable.

He'd been 'saving' spare boards from his jobs for months, ever since they'd moved into the new house, to get the outside area Lou was picturing underway. And over the Easter break, he'd been trying to get a proper start on it, but that was hard with Stella wanting to be involved in everything these days, and Lou so tired all the time.

'I can drive with a sore finger, Lou,' he said. 'I've done it before.'

'That's a bit more than sore,' Lou called from halfway up the stairs.

'That's *big* ouchy, Daddy,' said Stella.

'Get your shoes on, Stella!' Lou shouted.

'Shoes, shoes, shoes,' Stella echoed, and started turning in circles. Like a puppy, thought Josh.

His finger was beginning to throb. Fuck fuck fuck. This was the last thing he needed.

He tried to mop up some of the blood from the floor, his injured hand in the air, crouching and swiping at the scarlet mess with a dishcloth in his good hand. Blood so stark against the newness of the white floor lino.

Everything in this house was so fucking shiny.

'Yuck, Daddy.' Stella was watching him. 'Yuck.'

'Go find your shoes, Stell,' Josh said. 'They're near the front door.'

'Door, door, door,' Stella carolled as she wandered out of the kitchen. 'Knock, knock, knock.'

Josh knew there was zero chance of going out into the hallway and finding their two-year-old daughter waiting patiently by the door with her coat and shoes on. He really wanted to drive himself to the hospital; it would be so much easier on every front.

But the tea towel was turning red and he was beginning to feel a bit dizzy. Shit.

He heard Lou coming back down the stairs and headed towards her. She'd pulled on what she referred to as one of her 'tent dresses' to cover her bump, and her wet hair was hanging around her shoulders. 'If we can wait for Gretch she could sit with . . .' she was saying, but she stopped when she saw Josh's face. 'Don't worry, let's go.'

It took another five minutes to cajole Stella out to the car and persuade her to be strapped into her seat. Fifteen from there to the hospital. Lou was grim-faced; Josh, holding on to his smashed finger with his good hand, didn't have the will to be cheery.

'That fucking deck,' he moaned, head against the window.

'Fucking fucking fucking,' chorused Stella in the back.

'Well done, Josh,' Lou said, and called, 'Bad word, Stell,' into the rear-view mirror.

'Well, it's going to kill me,' he said. 'It's too big a job for me to do on my own.'

'I never asked you to do it,' Lou said quickly. 'And certainly not on your own.'

'Oh no, you never asked me.' Josh's chest was tight. Actually, he couldn't remember the last time it wasn't. 'You just mentioned about a thousand times how much better the house would be if we could use the garden more, had somewhere to sit outside.'

'Well, it would.'

'Right.'

They'd been in the house almost eighteen months and Josh was still waiting for the day when he felt at home there. The day when he didn't pull up in his ute and feel like he'd arrived at someone else's house, somewhere they were house-sitting, maybe. A place that belonged to a cousin-made-good, or to a high school friend turned accountant.

He didn't understand Lou in that house. That's what it felt like. As if she wasn't the same person there. She was suddenly cleaning all the time, and spent chunks of her evening on eBay trying to 'win' homewares that she somehow understood were a bargain but he couldn't see a possible need for.

A planter on legs. Matching distressed bedside tables. A ladder that was really a towel rack.

How were these things that Lou knew about now?

*

The day they'd moved into the new house had been, for Josh, one of the most disorientating of his life.

His mother had come over. Annabelle and Brian too, of course, with a bottle of champagne. Even Rob.

They congratulated Lou and Josh as they stood among boxes – far too few for the amount of space they had to fill – and Stella toddled from room to room, uncovering life-threatening hazards as she went.

Bump. Into the doorframe. *Waa.* Down the step to the kitchen. Eek, onto the edge of the staircase.

Josh didn't know what they were celebrating. Everyone there knew that they would never have been able to buy the house without Lou's parents, so it hardly represented an achievement: to have asked for money and, with it, tethered themselves to a debt so enormous it made the soles of Josh's feet sweat if he thought too much about it.

He'd said as much to Lou that night, as they went to bed for the first time in their new bedroom. Which was, he had to admit, an improvement on Erskineville – big and light and empty. And the yellow tree in the window cast a pleasing, dappled shadow. But, still.

'Why is everyone congratulating us?' Josh asked. 'We didn't do anything.'

'We *picked* something,' Lou said, turning onto her side and looking at him, her hands under her head. 'We picked something, and now we have a plan.'

Josh looked at Lou – the woman he adored, the force of nature, the one he had always thought of as charging towards adventure – and he saw in her face that she really was happy that they'd picked something. She wasn't panicking about the mortgage and the debt and the monotony of the payments and what that meant for any choice they might make from here to eternity. She looked genuinely excited.

'Is this your idea of adventure now?' he asked. As soon as he did, he regretted it. It sounded patronising. Mean, even.

But she allowed him that little dig.

'Well, sure,' she said. 'We're here anyway, right? We've got Stell. No running off to the circus for us.'

And he nodded. But he felt, inexplicably, teary.

His mother knew it. All that day she'd been looking at him sideways as she and Lou unpacked things and tried to keep Stella alive while he built beds and tables with Rob, and Brian and Annabelle sat out in the garden on a couple of folding chairs, surveying what they had helped pay for.

'You okay, Josh?' she'd asked, appearing at the bedroom door as he unrolled the bed slats across the base.

'Of course,' he said, and looked up to give her what he hoped was a reassuring smile.

'Don't let all this get to you,' she said. 'It's only a house, it's only stuff. It doesn't really change anything.'

And Josh knew she was thinking about his dad. As he had been. Sometimes he felt like he and everyone close to him were just waiting for that guy to come bursting out of Josh's chest like the alien in that film. For Josh to show his true colours – the stripes of a selfish arsehole who couldn't see when he had it good.

'I know, Mum,' he said, and turned back to the bed.

'And it's only money, too,' she added. 'Don't let it colour things.'

'Can you go and check Stella's not fallen down the stairs again, please, Mum?' he asked, as kindly as he could, and she left the room.

The truth was, he thought about his dad more now he was gone than when he'd only been a couple of hours' drive away. Josh becoming a father at almost the exact same time he'd lost his own seemed like a strange coincidence to him. He knew his sister Maya believed it wasn't a coincidence at all. That the universe was removing a barrier for him, an example he didn't need. 'You're free to be the dad *you* want to be, Josh. History won't repeat with you,' his sister had said at the funeral, pulling him into a hug.

And Josh had squeezed her back but said nothing. Because it felt disloyal in the worst way to suggest that his own dad had to die for Josh to be able to be a good father. His old man might have been a dick, but Josh was capable of recognising that and choosing a different path, wasn't he? Len could have stuck around for that.

It had become clear that sticking around wasn't much of an option for Len, those last few years. He was deep in debt and his relationship with alcohol was growing more abusive by the week. He and Christine were pretty much homeless, crashing with her relatives and his dodgy friends, or staying in the kind of hotels you wouldn't find on lastminute.com. Josh realised that a part of him had always romanticised the old man's unconventional post-divorce lifestyle.

Even while hating him for never being present for his children, he had nonetheless felt a grudging admiration for his dad's ability to live life on his own terms, not caring enough what anyone thought to change. Not even caring what his own children thought.

Exactly what had happened on the night Len was hit by a car was still not clear. Christine's version of events varied with each telling. The cops had clearly washed their hands of it and the driver of the car had been cleared of any wrongdoing. So what did that mean? That Len had stepped out in front of the car? On purpose?

Why was he thinking about this now? Josh had thought, with a surge of irritation at himself. Just when he was moving into this fancy new house with his incredible wife and their amazing little girl, such a ball of whirring energy. Why was he still thinking about his dad?

*

Josh's head was still against the window of the station wagon. They were almost at the hospital, and Lou was talking.

'Four weeks isn't very long, Josh, and I feel like we're not at all ready,' she said. 'I'm freaking out a bit, aren't you?'

'Hmmmm.' Josh nodded, but he wasn't really listening.

'What about?' Lou asked. 'What are you worried about?'

'Oh . . .' Josh quickly flicked through a list of generic concerns in his head. Pick one; pick one quickly so it seems like you're listening. This was interesting, he noticed: even with his hand throbbing and blood trickling down his arm, his desire not to upset Lou was paramount. 'Money.'

'Money.' Lou flicked on the indicator to turn left into the hospital, and Josh could have sworn that the tick-tick of the turn signal was mirroring the tsk-tsking in her head, her irritation at Josh's answer.

'Money will be okay, Josh. We'll go interest-only on the loan for a while. And I'm only taking six months' leave with the baby this time.'

'Uh-huh,' said Josh, still holding up his hand.

'Uh-huh, uh-huh, uh-huh,' sang Stella in the back. 'Baby, baby, baby.'

'That's right, Stell-stell, a new baby's coming!' Lou sang out. 'How's the hand feeling, Josh?'

'Like I almost cut my finger off.'

'How did you do it, anyway?' Lou asked. 'If you can tell me with little ears here,' she added, tilting her head in Stella's direction.

Josh thought about the moment before he drove the nail through his forefinger. He'd been thinking about how little he was feeling these days. How since they'd moved into the new house, he'd opted out of expressing his opinions on a whole range of things that he and Lou used to talk about all the time.

He moved through the shiny rooms in the new house like a visitor, trying not to upset things – order, routine, rows of ornamental owls – and it was one of the things he'd been thinking about today, as he stomped the boards down: was this what all men felt when children came? Was this what his dad had felt? Silenced? Was that where his rages had come from?

Josh had crouched down to nail the stomped board into place, as he had twenty times already that afternoon. He was hot, and a film of dust and grime from the wood had settled into his sweat. He felt coated in crap.

When Lou's mum had heard that he was building the deck, she'd scoffed at the idea of Josh 'making himself useful', and although Lou had loyally scolded her for the comment, Josh couldn't help but feel that was all they thought he was useful for, now: odd jobs and heavy lifting. And there was another baby coming. He had no idea if he could love this child as much as he loved Stella, but he was feeling more and more determined that he was going to change the way they did things with this one. He didn't want to be on the sidelines anymore. He was here now, feeling like a stranger in his own house, but wanting to feel like he belonged again. To Lou, to his family, to this place.

Josh sized up the board and, just before he raised the hammer, he was hyper-aware of the weight in his chest, the sensation of feeling like he was moving slightly underwater, separated from what was happening right in front of him.

And the hammer had hit the nail, but the angle was wrong, and instead of pounding into the wood, the metal spike was driven into his flesh, and he'd pulled his hand back so quickly it had kind of ripped out of his finger, leaving an ugly gash. Josh hadn't yelled out straight away, he'd stayed squatting on his haunches, staring at this jagged break in his skin, quickly filling and overflowing with blood. Oh, he thought. I can feel *that*.

'My hand just slipped,' he said to Lou in the car, as they pulled up outside the emergency department. 'Stupid mistake. I must be tired.'

Lou let out a breath between pursed lips. '*You're* tired,' she said.

Josh felt a snap of fury. It frightened him. He had to get his shit together. 'You can leave me here,' he said. 'I'll get a cab home.'

He didn't think Lou would go for it, but she did.

She turned to the back seat where Stella was beginning to droop a little. 'Okay,' she said. 'Call me if anything serious is happening.' She didn't really look at Josh as he pushed the handle down with his good hand and got out of the car.

'See you, Stell,' he said, bending into the back. 'Be a good girl for Mummy. I'll see you later.'

'Later, later, Daddy.' Stella blew him a big kiss.

I can feel that, he thought.

Lou flashed him an impatient half-smile and signalled for him to close the door. 'Better go before I get moved on,' she said. 'Good luck.'

Josh closed the car door and, bloody tea towel–covered hand still raised, he watched as the station wagon pulled out and drove away.

Don't think it, don't think it, he told himself. But it was hard to ignore. There was zero chance that Lou would have left him at emergency on his own a couple of years ago, grown man that he was. She would have taken control, gone up to talk to the triage nurses, tried to make him laugh while they waited, emptied the vending machine of salt-and-vinegar chips and called his mum to update her. He didn't need all that, he knew, but it had been pretty wonderful to have it.

Stop whining, Josh told himself; she's about to have a baby. And the thought of that caught in his throat as he turned to walk through the automatic door to get a stitch.

Lou

JUNE
Stay positive

Lou was running again. Treading the neighbourhood at a medium plod in the winter mornings, nodding at dog-walking neighbours and boomers doing tai chi in the park. With every footstep, every morning, she felt a little more herself.

She was glad she'd told Josh the truth about the year. She felt lighter. Less like she was carrying around an enormous secret. Josh, however, clearly thought what she was carrying around was an enormous ledger, ticking off pros and cons, keeping a running tally.

That morning, when she'd arrived home from her run at seven o'clock, panting, she found him ready to leave for work. To her surprise, the girls were not only up and out of bed but already in their school uniforms. Bowls and a cereal packet were on the kitchen table, and a coffee pod was ready and waiting in the coffee machine.

'What's going on?' she asked, holding her elbow in an overhead stretch. Stella and Rita were sliding into their chairs at the table, smiling at her in a slightly frozen, unfamiliar way. Rita even looked like she'd attempted to brush her own hair.

'It's the beginning of your birthday week,' said Josh, smiling at her. 'And I think I could do a bit more to make your mornings easier, yes?'

'How was your run, Mummy?' asked Stella, pouring some Milo loops into her bowl, with something like a seventy per cent accuracy rate.

'Okay, what have you told them?' Lou eyeballed Josh, and walked over to the girls, putting a hand on each of their heads. 'Because either I'm dying, or you've swapped our kids for some better-behaved clones.'

'Mum!' Stella scolded. 'Don't joke about dying.'

'Are you dying?' asked Rita, wide-eyed. 'Like, really?'

'She's dying of love for her family, you two,' Josh jumped in. 'And I've got to go. I was thinking I could make a curry for dinner, what do you reckon?'

Stella and Rita nodded enthusiastically. Rita? Curry?

Lou looked around. The kitchen was clean, the girls' lunches were in progress on the bench.

'This is . . .'

'Bye, babe.' Josh kissed her on the head, did the same to the girls, then headed for the door, his ute, the workshop.

You don't have to do this, she thought. Be on your best behaviour. Then again, she was hardly going to complain about easier mornings.

'Can I play with the iPad, Mum?' They felt like the most uttered words in their house. Usual programming had resumed.

And her reply, as she sat and pulled off her running shoes, felt like the most predictable response. 'No, it's a weekday, eat your breakfast.'

Her birthday week. Since when had a birthday become a week? Lou was going to be thirty-seven on Thursday. It didn't feel like a big-deal kind of birthday, but it was the second time it had been mentioned to her in twenty-four hours.

It's your birthday this week and it's been six months. Time to treat yourself. The text had come in at 11 p.m., with classic 'it's late and I'm lonely' timing. Lou hadn't responded, but the message just sitting there, on her phone by her bed, exposed, made her jumpy.

With some help from Sara the therapist and a little more from Gretchen, Lou had stopped obsessing about the debacle of the Easter camping trip and was instead choosing to focus on the fact that her husband was a man who could lift you out of danger when a storm blew a tree through your window. To focus on the deal she'd made in her head when she wasn't sure if Rita had been hurt.

6. Stay positive. That's what she'd written into her phone at the beginning of the month. *Focus on the good. Stop looking for problems.*

'I'm trying a clean slate, not keeping score,' she'd told Gretchen last Saturday morning. They were standing on the sidelines of a kids' soccer match, watching JoJo pretend to play. Stella and Rita were playing their own game in the sharp morning sun on the other side of the pitch, chasing each other back and forth, tackling and falling into the damp grass.

'Keeping score?' Gretchen looked up from her phone.

'Every couple does it,' said Lou. 'You know, I drop off so you have to pick up. I want to go for a run this morning so you get to go for a beer tonight. I let you lie in last Sunday so it's my turn tomorrow . . .'

'Sounds tiresome,' said Gretchen, putting her phone away and pushing her hands into her pockets. 'One of the things I most enjoy about our conversations about your marriage is how they reaffirm my life choices.'

'Said the woman on the sidelines watching her ex-boyfriend's child playing soccer.' Lou laughed. 'You haven't escaped *all* of this shit.'

'I'm just picking JoJo up to get her hair done,' Gretchen insisted. 'Plus it's time for my new colour, so two birds . . .'

'Keep telling yourself that,' said Lou. 'Anyway, I'm trying not to do it. See, usually, the fact I've brought the girls with me to see you this morning after gymnastics would mean Josh owed me, because he's getting a quiet Saturday morning at home. He's probably got his feet up, reading the paper, music loud.'

'But . . .'

'I'm not going to mention it. I *want* him to be happy. He *wants* me to be happy. I'm working on that.'

'And how's it going?' Lou was sure she could detect an edge of sarcasm in her friend's voice.

'I'm focusing on the positive,' said Lou. 'But I worry we're stressing the kids out. There's a lot of tension in the house, I think, with us treading so carefully all the time. They're either melting down or Stepford children at the moment.'

She looked at her girls. They were charging about in the wet grass, jumping on each other like puppies. Stella was usually a bit too cool for this kind of rumbling with her little sister these days. It made Lou happy to see. But maybe . . . was Stella regressing?

Shut up, stupid Mum guilt.

'You should talk to JoJo about it,' Gretchen suggested. 'She lived through her parents' divorce. She can tell you how it felt being a kid in the middle of all that.'

'I couldn't do that!'

'Why not? Adults should ask kids for their opinions more often, if you ask me,' Gretchen said. 'JoJo's not an idiot.'

'You think adults should ask kids for their opinions more often because you're not bloody raising any,' Lou said, still watching her girls. 'Kids have plenty of opinions, believe me, and they're not generally backwards about expressing them.'

'I'm serious. Take her for a coffee before our hair thing.'

Lou looked at her friend. 'A *coffee*? Really?'

'She's a Sydney private-school girl,' said Gretchen. 'She's been on the lattes since she was eight. I'll take your two shopping. It's an aunty's job to treat them.'

'Gretch, you have your own –'

'Shush. Just do it.'

And Lou had to admit that maybe it wasn't a terrible idea . . .

Lou had been remembering it while she was running that morning: the bizarre moment she found herself seeking advice from JoJo, a supremely confident and articulate almost-thirteen-year-old.

As soon as the ten-dollar cakes and elaborate coffees were set down before them in a chi-chi Double Bay cafe, the girl had asked, 'Why are we doing this? Is Gretchen doing something she doesn't want me to know about? Is she surprising me? Am I allowed to look at my phone?'

Lou had leaped straight in. 'Gretchen told me to ask you for advice about something.'

JoJo's hand had already been sneaking towards her iPhone, lying on the table between them in its bedazzled case, but now she stopped. 'What?' she asked.

Knowing that flattery was the way to get any teen to do anything, Lou continued, 'Gretchen said that you have a lot of very insightful things to say about divorce, and I need some advice to help a kid I'm teaching. I can't tell you details, because –' Lou cast about for an excuse '– teachers' code.'

'Insightful?' JoJo took a bite of the huge profiterole-looking thing Lou had bought for her. 'She said that?'

'Helpful, thoughtful, useful.' Lou threw the words out. 'I'm worried about this kid, and since you're close to the experience . . .'

What am I doing?

'You want me to talk to you about divorce.'

'I do.'

There was a moment when Lou thought JoJo was going to laugh at her, and she should.

But the teenager instead took another bite of her profiterole and chewed it slowly. The silence stretched out interminably, then: 'I was glad when he left,' the girl said suddenly. 'I hated the feeling of us living in the same house together.'

Lou raised her eyebrows and arranged her face in what she hoped was a sympathetic expression. She nodded encouragingly.

'It was like we didn't have to pretend we were normal anymore, when we weren't. And anyway' – JoJo pushed her fringe off her forehead – 'most of my friends live with their mums.'

'But don't you miss your dad?'

'I see him,' JoJo said. 'And now when I do, Mum's not there making me feel bad for being nice to him or telling him off for buying me things.'

Lou didn't know what to say. She looked at the latest-model iPhone and JoJo's Apple Watch.

JoJo had another bite of cake. 'He doesn't really tell me off at all,' she said through a mouth full of custard – a rare moment when she did actually look like a kid. 'And Mum knows that if she does, I'll go to his place. Or Gretchen's.'

Lou had never met JoJo's mum, but she'd seen pictures of her – a classic eastern suburbs blonde with long slender limbs in skinny cargos, a shiny, shoulder-grazing bob and a perfect pert nose.

'Why do you like hanging out with Gretchen so much?' she asked.

'Because she likes me,' said JoJo immediately. 'And for the same reason you do: she's awesome.'

'She really is,' Lou agreed.

'She doesn't lie.' For a moment Lou wondered if there was some-thing pointed about that comment, but then JoJo added, 'I think you should tell your kid that it will be better when it's done.'

Now, in her post-run shower, Lou recalled her own girls' smiles over their supremely organised breakfast. Could they sense the tension in the house? Were they feeling, these little people, like they were part of the problem? Were they trying to make themselves unobjectionable so things would be calmer?

Or am I massively overthinking this?

Focus on the positive, Lou, she told herself. At least Josh and I aren't shouting at each other in the kitchen anymore. Josh was always either hiding in the guitar room, or trying to prove himself as Dad of the Year. He was smiling more, but she knew he was tense. Anxious.

Remember why you started this, Lou told herself, and what you want to fix. Remember Christmas. Remember New Year. Remember what brought you to be sitting across from a tweenager, asking for advice about your life.

Lou looked at herself in the bathroom mirror, her familiar face settling into itself. Thirty-seven. No age at all. Still plenty of time to do anything.

Josh

JUNE
Stay positive

My *marriage has six months to live*, Josh typed.

The letters began to roll out on the screen in front of him.

Why six months?

My wife has a deadline.

A deadline?

Yes.

Tell me about that.

It had taken some time for Josh to convince himself he should pay $199 for a one-on-one virtual session with Eva Bernard. Since he'd been watching her videos on YouTube these last few months, information about her personal counselling sessions kept popping up in his email or in his Facebook feed, where Josh was usually only served ads for power tools and guitar workshops. The spiel went:

> *Eva's intimate individualized chat space will allow you to be completely open and honest about your relationship, and get the kind of specifically tailored advice usually reserved for her A-list clients — advice that will only work for you.*

Josh had been concerned about the typing. He wasn't super-quick on the keyboard, and the session was strictly forty minutes. Why couldn't it be a video call?

The FAQ section on Eva's website was very specific about that.

This text-only approach allows for a greater sense of intimacy not colored by preconceptions about appearance. It also means a lower-technology requirement, making Eva's wisdom available to everyone, regardless of their internet speed and data allowance.

Riiiight, thought Josh. Or it allows for there to be anyone at all on the other end of the counselling session. He wasn't an idiot.

They'd thought of that, too.

At the beginning of your personalized session, Eva will appear briefly in your chat window to say hello and reassure you that you're getting the highest-quality professional advice, directly from Eva Bernard herself. Then the camera will drop out to leave you to the privacy of your personal session with Eva, right there on your device of choice.

Josh's device of choice was his battered old laptop, balanced on his knee in the guitar room. Because Eva was in the US – he'd actually thought she was in Europe, but there you go – the timing was tricky. The slot Josh was allocated after all his deliberation was 3 a.m. on a Wednesday. The day before Lou's birthday, no less. He couldn't set an alarm in bed next to Lou to make that time, so he'd told her he was going to sleep in the guitar room that night, for some thinking space, and she had been much less interested in this information than he'd hoped.

*

It was Lou's birthday tomorrow. He wanted to make it special but, also, he was so fucking angry with her he could hardly breathe.

Josh was doing all the things he knew she wanted him to do. Helping out more. Being proactive with the girls. Not disappearing for hours to play guitar. Noticing. Complimenting. Supporting. He looked at the shoebox by his feet. Clearly he'd bought Lou such a disastrous Christmas present it had led her to consider divorce, but he'd nailed it this time, he was sure. Good boy. Good husband.

He'd told the girls that they needed to try extra hard not to upset Mummy at the moment, because Mummy was tired. Tired of him, he added in his head.

These last few days, things between them had been better. They'd made each other laugh dissecting Stella's ridiculous NAPLAN preparation homework.

'I chose you as my life partner specifically so you could help with this moment,' Josh told Lou as he tidied up the small mountain of kids' books on the kitchen table after dinner. 'The one when my eight-year-old needed to explain the oriented narrative of a text.'

'And I chose you for your arms,' she said, smiling.

For a few moments there, it felt like the days before he knew he was on a performance review. Before he knew the clock was ticking.

But when he'd gone to put the arms she loved around her, she'd performed a neat duck and spin away and back to the sink.

Tick. Tick.

*

Tell me about that.

Josh wriggled his fingers then typed: *She decided to give our marriage a year. In January. She told me.*

Eva: *That seems a little aggressive.*

Yes, thought Josh, it does, doesn't it? Thank God someone else thinks so.

I'm trying to work out what to do, he typed.

I can't tell you what to do, the words came back.

Then what have I paid for? he thought. She hadn't finished, though.

But you need to consider why your wife feels that way. And then you need to . . .

The tension of watching the messages come through was torturous. Still, he had seen Eva with his own eyes at the beginning of this session, attractive and authoritative and professional-looking in a silk shirt with her hair swept back, waving at the camera and saying only, 'Let's get started,' before disappearing.

. . . take some responsibility for how these next few months are going to go. What do you want?

I don't want her to go. I want her. I want my family, he replied.

And do you show her that, every day, Simon?

Who was Simon?

Who's Simon? he typed. *I'm Josh.*

There was a second's pause before the reply: *Sorry, Josh, slip of the tongue.*

Tongue?

You need to honor your wife and your marriage vows. You need to show her she's the most important person in your life. You Can Do It!!!!!

It was 3 a.m. Josh was exhausted, but he didn't think Eva Bernard would put five exclamation marks at the end of her statements. She was usually pretty dry, intelligent, serious in her advice.

You show her she'd be crazy to leave you. This was punctuated with a smiley-face tongue-out emoji.

I'm crazy for doing this, Josh thought. One more try.

Can couples move on from their past? he typed.

The typing bubbles popped up again.

A few seconds later: *Cutting out carbs together can be a healthy joint project.*

Huh? Past. Not pasta.

You're a fake, he wrote. *I want my money back.*

Again, there was a bubble pause.

If you talk to your wife like that, I'm not surprised she's leaving you.

This is bullshit, Josh typed, banging the keys hard with one finger now. *I'm going to complain.*

Calm down, robot Eva typed back. *These are hard conversations. Change is difficult.*

That bit was true.

Then: *Anyway* . . . Pause. *What did you do?*

Josh pushed the keyboard away. Put his head in his hands. He was so tired.

To make her want to leave you? What did you do?

He pulled the keyboard back towards him.

We've both done some pretty terrible things, he wrote.

And robot Eva sent him a frowny-face emoji.

Lou

10 September, 2015

Through a drowsy haze of day-sleep anaesthetic, Lou was dreaming of Josh.

Grabs of him were sliding in and out of her consciousness like a Facebook Memories slide show.

His tall, lanky frame waiting for her outside the kebab shop, before she knew his name. His arms around her on the rug at Redfern. Smiling into her eyes as she shuddered with orgasm in the room above the pub in Broken Hill. His tear-streaked, laughing face when he saw Stella for the first time.

She was sure she said his name as she opened her eyes, but who would she ask? As her mind slid back into her body and she remembered where she was, she looked around to see a nurse's white-uniformed back at a machine in the corner. A sign above the blue door reminding everyone to treat the staff with respect. Her own toes, with their chipped blue nail polish.

A hunger pang and a dull ache deep in her belly.

That's right.

She'd just had an abortion.

*

There was almost a year there, after Rita was born, when everything seemed good.

Motherhood wasn't easier, exactly, the second time around, but it was less of a brutal shock. She knew, this time, that babies didn't sleep when you wanted them to, no matter how much you jiggled, patted and studied books of complex timetables. That breastfeeding was a punish. That if she didn't get to the cot within the first twenty seconds of her baby's whimper, her precious bundle wouldn't explode.

She left more to Josh this time, more confident that, really, he couldn't break the baby, even if he never remembered to repack the nappy bag or to take a spare onesie with him. Josh seemed happier, like he was visibly growing with the responsibility of getting Rita to sleep, giving her a night feed, taking the girls out for a walk early on weekend mornings so Lou could 'sleep in'. Rita pleasingly ticked the clichéd box of the 'easy' second baby, a better sleeper, a good eater, a chubby, glowing, gurgling delight.

Josh had seemed to stop sulking about the house – perhaps even to enjoy it, as he slowly began to take over the room that was going to be Stella's one day with his guitars and his stereo and his band paraphernalia. He'd played a few acoustic gigs with some of his old friends at a new brewery bar down the road, and he was getting more interesting jobs and plenty of them since he'd started specialising in heritage renovations. He seemed happier than he'd been in the first year at Botany, when Lou was sure he was just going to walk out one day and return, like a homing pigeon, to a dingy room in a house in the inner west, where he would never complain about bad coffee again.

There was a day – a single afternoon, perhaps – that Lou remembered as being almost perfect. It was deep spring. Rita was six months old, sitting in her bouncer, chewing on a rubber giraffe. Stella was in her knickers, running through a sprinkler on the turf they'd rolled out in the tiny backyard space, shrieking with laughter. And Lou and Josh were sitting on dining chairs on the deck that Josh had built with his own hands, sharing a cold beer and laughing at themselves – together.

'Look at us,' Josh had said, pushing some hair out of Lou's eyes and smiling. 'Just look at us.'

And Lou had felt deep-down happy. In her bones. In her stomach.

Her funny, kind, handsome husband. Her healthy, happy girls. Her lovely home. The job she loved that she would be going back to in just a few weeks.

This was enough. This was everything.

How long was it after the perfect afternoon that Lou saw the two lines on the pregnancy test in the downstairs bathroom on a Saturday morning? Maybe a whole year, she thought.

She was back at work and enjoying it. When she'd first returned after Stella it had been hard; she was job-sharing with another teacher and she could never shake the feeling she wasn't doing enough for either the kids in class, who would have to remind her all the time of where they were up to, or Stella at home, who was adjusting to day care.

But this time, things felt different. She'd started back in a new role as a learning-support teacher, moving between classes – and although she missed having a class of her own, it suited her right now because it was only designed to be four days, and the marking and lesson-planning was minimal. She could go in and do her job, and then by the time she got home Josh had picked up the girls and was often making dinner. It felt as if they had struck a better balance. Like maybe, just maybe, they'd cracked the code. On a good day, at least.

She wasn't ready for the two lines on the pregnancy test. It wasn't in the plan. But at that moment, she was ready to go with it. Three beautiful kids instead of two? It seemed ridiculous to object to abundance, when many friends around her were struggling to have just one baby.

So Josh's first reaction had surprised her. She had expected shock. She had expected him to need a minute. She had expected him to grab his hair with his hands and get that panicked look he got when things seemed overwhelming. But then she expected him to return from a sulk and pull her into a hug and tell her they'd work it out. That they always did.

He didn't. He just looked stricken, and said, 'Do we really want to do this?'

'Do what?' she asked, perhaps stupidly. 'It's done.'

'It's not done, Lou,' Josh said. 'You know that.'

Of course she did. Lou had had a termination when she was seventeen. No-one knew, except for her high school boyfriend, his dad (who'd put up the money) and Josh, because in the early days of their relationship they'd told each other everything. It was also the reason she knew that he and his ex, Sinead, had done the same thing at some point in their messy history.

Lou had felt almost nothing about her own teenage experience. At the time, the idea that she might have a child with this boy she barely knew, that she might tie herself to him and to the responsibility of a baby, was almost laughable. Ridiculous. The procedure itself, the clinic and the professionals and the bleeding and the aftermath, well, it had been frightening, and keeping the secret from her family had been difficult, if necessary. But she never for a moment doubted how right it was.

'This is different,' Lou said to Josh. 'This . . . inside me, it's going to be a Stella or a Rita one day.'

'But it's not that yet, Lou,' Josh said. 'It's not our baby yet.'

'So you're sure two is the right number for us?' We never discussed this, thought Lou. We've never actually discussed this.

'Two is enough for me.' Josh's voice was quiet as he said it. 'We've replaced ourselves. It should be enough.'

'Yes, but sometimes life throws you a surprise.' Lou grabbed Josh's arm, trying to sound upbeat. 'This is our adventure, after all. And there's something about a big family . . .'

'Not for me, Lou.' There was a pause, then he swallowed. 'I'm serious.'

Lou looked at him in surprise. 'So, hang on a moment,' she said. 'You're saying . . .'

'Let's think about this,' Josh jumped in. 'We don't have to be passengers in our own lives, Lou. We don't have to just *roll with it*.'

It had been their first conversation on the subject, and Lou decided to cut it short. 'Let it sink in,' she told him. 'It's a big shock to both of us. Let's just let it all settle.'

But Josh had surprised her again. 'Lou,' he said, 'I don't think I can do it again.' And his face was absolutely serious.

*

'I had no idea,' Lou said to Gretchen two days later, 'how fucking miserable he's been.'

'Really?' Gretchen raised an eyebrow at her friend. 'I think we've covered off a few of Josh's dark moods in recent conversation.'

'No, Gretch, I mean *really*. We were in this fog there, for a while, with the babies, and the house, and his work, and money . . .'

'Oh, nothing big, then,' Gretchen smirked. 'Just the small stuff.' They were driving. Gretchen had picked Lou up from school and they were going for an early dinner at this Japanese-y place that one of Gretchen's friends had opened. The guy she was seeing, Barton, was meeting them there. Lou had never felt less like making small talk with Gretchen's obnoxious boyfriend, so she was willing the car journey to go on and on.

'What I'm saying is that things have been better.' She looked out of the window at the chintzy shops of Woollahra. 'They say having a baby is like throwing a grenade into a relationship. I feel like the smoke has cleared.'

'And you want to chuck another grenade in?'

'I would.' Lou nodded. 'Because there's something gorgeous about all the chaos it creates.'

'Maybe not for Josh.' Gretchen was scanning for a park. Bugger, thought Lou, we must be nearly there. 'But it's up to you, Lou. It's your body.'

'Josh says he wants a say, some control over his life.' Lou was going to cry. 'He thinks I railroad him. On the house, on having Rita so soon after Stella . . .'

'And do you railroad him?'

Lou's throat was burning and she gulped through the tears that were threatening to come. 'Women are the ones who make things happen,' she gasped. 'Aren't we?'

'But are they the things you both want to happen?' Gretchen looked back over her shoulder as she prepared to reverse-park. She must have caught a look at Lou's face, because she put her hand on Lou's. 'Whatever you do, I'll help,' said Gretchen. 'As much as I can.'

'Do we have to go to dinner?' Lou cried. 'Can we cancel?'

'No, Lou-Lou, we can't,' her friend said. 'As much as I am always here for you, my love, not everything is about you. And you need to spend some time with Barton. He needs to get to know you better.'

'Like this?' Lou gestured to her red and tear-streaked face.

'Well, we'll give that a minute,' said Gretchen, and she reached around for her bag and a tissue.

What Lou couldn't find the words to explain to her friend was the weight of this decision. It could be everything, or it could be barely anything at all. She hadn't considered for a moment that the pregnancy she'd terminated at seventeen was a 'baby', not really. The morning sickness was an inconvenience, the heavy, sore boobs an irritation. And then later, with Stella, it was so different. She'd felt so connected to this person inside her, every little symptom and sign was treasured, recorded, analysed. What she wanted to say to Gretchen was that the difference between Life and Not Life, really, was the mother's feelings on the matter. She couldn't say that out loud; it felt traitorous, somehow. But she knew it was the case, down to her bones. She could lean out of the car window right now and shout that she was seven weeks pregnant and strangers would congratulate her. But, equally, it was entirely possible and acceptable to wipe this away, pretend it never existed. No matter what any doctrine thought about where it all began, Lou still knew that if this baby was one hundred per cent wanted, she would consider that their entwined story had already begun.

'I just don't know what to do, Gretch.'

'I think,' Gretchen said, holding Lou's hand, 'you should do what *you* want to do. It will be you who lives with the consequences either way. Women always bear the brunt. And that's why,' she squeezed Lou's hand tight, 'no matter how lovely your girls are – and they are – I am never, ever having any bloody babies.'

'But you really like Barton's daughter.' Lou sniffed, wiping angrily at the smudged mascara under her eyes. 'JoJo.'

'Other people's children are plenty enough,' Gretchen said. 'I can love them to bits and then get on with my life.'

*

When Lou walked out of the recovery room, Josh was sitting in the clinic's reception, waiting to take her home. He didn't see her straight away and Lou stood and watched him for few moments. He looked pale, serious, and was staring intently at something straight ahead. Lou followed his eye line to the waiting room's fish tank, where goldfish chased each other around, memories allegedly wiped on every turn.

'Hello,' Lou said.

Josh turned to look at her and smiled a tight line of support as their eyes met. He stood up, came over. 'Hello. Are you okay?'

There was another couple in the waiting room, and two other women on their own. No-one was making eye contact. The receptionist motioned for Lou to come and sign a form and Josh held her elbow as she turned to the counter.

'Don't do that,' she said. 'I'm fine.'

'Are you?' he asked. 'Are you really?'

Fuck you, Lou thought. Fuck you, Josh. She remembered the conversation they'd had last night. When he'd said, 'Are you going to hate me for this? Because we can't do it if you're going to hate me for it. It has to be our choice. Your choice.'

And Lou had thought, What choice? If I don't do it, you'll resent me. And we'll both resent a baby who hasn't asked for any of this. What choice, Josh? You've told me that you'll be miserable and trapped and your fragile mental health will suffer. You've told me all of that yet you want this to be my choice? A choice between my husband, the father of my children, and a not-yet-baby I haven't even met?

Fuck you.

'I'm fine,' she said. 'Let's just go home.'

'The girls will be pleased to see you,' Josh said. 'Gretch is with them.'

Lou signed the paperwork and they turned to leave.

'They should really clear out that fish tank,' Josh said to her, as they walked past. And he pointed to something bobbing white in the water. 'There's a dead fish in there.'

And of course Lou had to look. And then that was all she could see, riding home in the passenger side of Josh's ute. A bloated, dead fish floating just below the surface, as its tank-mates flashed gold all around it.

Josh

A few months later

'**S**nooping only leads to finding out things that you don't want to know,' Emma was shouting after Josh as he carried a box from her Surry Hills apartment.

'Is that right, Mum?' He put the box down next to the others on the balcony walkway and stepped back through the open door. His mother's home already had the strangely stale smell of an empty house, even though she hadn't quite moved out yet. 'Better to be blissfully ignorant, you reckon?'

'Sometimes, yes,' Emma said. 'I could have saved myself a lot of pain that way. It did me no good to torture myself with details.'

Josh looked around his mum's flat. It was almost done, a lot of life all tucked away now in neatly labelled flat-pack boxes.

'I wasn't snooping,' Josh said, irritated. 'I told you: I just happened to see Lou's diary.'

'And why were you looking in her diary?'

'I was looking for Lou, Mum. I didn't know where she was.'

'A woman's diary is sacred, Josh,' Emma insisted, hands on hips in the doorway to her bedroom, now just an empty space with faded carpet and striped wallpaper. 'I thought I'd taught you better than that.'

Emma was moving out of the city. It was the end of something, he knew. Ever since they'd moved from down the coast, she'd lived in apartments around Surry Hills and Waterloo, always finding a way to make a dingy few rooms into something homey and distinctly her. Cheap prints of paintings she loved in frames from the two-dollar shop; pretty fabric throws over tatty, second-hand couches; Art Deco lamps found in trash and treasure stores. She'd been in this apartment, on the border of Redfern, for almost ten years. She knew all the neighbours, even the ones no-one else wanted to know. Turned a blind eye to the badness that bloomed in the corridors at night. Clucked her tongue at messes no-one wanted to clean up.

'Not everyone's as lucky as you,' she used to say to Josh every time he expressed concern about his ageing mum living in a crumbling inner-city block. 'There's community here. That's why I like it.'

And that part was true. All day, neighbours had been coming by to lend a hand with heavy boxes and to say goodbye to Aunty Emma, who'd minded a lot of their kids when no-one else could, who'd occasionally slipped a tenner to a mum who needed to get to payday, who was always the first to write an angry letter about a broken window that hadn't been fixed or a lift that never seemed to be in working order or a playground whose gate had been pulled off its hinges.

'I don't know how you've lived here so long, Mum,' Josh said, looking around the empty living room. 'I really don't.'

Emma laughed. 'Says you, over there in your suburban pile, wishing you were back here.'

'No, I don't,' said Josh. 'Not anymore. I can see Lou was right about that now. The girls are so happy.'

'It's not a house that makes you happy,' Emma said quickly. 'It's a home.'

Josh snorted. 'You should get that embroidered on a cushion.'

'Shut up and check the kitchen for me, you.' Emma batted him on the bum.

'I think you'll be bored up the coast, Mum,' he said, as he opened and closed cupboards that she'd long since emptied and scrubbed. 'Not really sure why you're going back there.' His mum was almost seventy now, but there was nothing old about her; not yet.

'No reason not to anymore,' Emma said. 'It's time for me to have a bit of peace.' She made a face. 'Far away from all you lot.'

'Very nice,' Josh said sarcastically. 'Anika and I appreciate your grandmotherly support.'

There was nothing more to do. The place really was empty. 'I think we're done here, Mum,' he said. 'Shall we go?'

'In a minute,' Emma said, disappearing into the bathroom. 'Got to check the cabinet.'

For the fourteenth time, thought Josh.

'Anyway,' Emma called out to him, her voice echoing in the tiled room, 'where was she?'

'Where was who?'

'Lou! When you snooped. Where was she?'

*

It was about three months after the termination that Lou stopped coming home in the evenings.

Sometimes, he'd get a text: *Staying back for staff meeting. Please do bedtime.*

Often not.

Are you home for dinner? he'd text.

Silence.

The girls didn't seem troubled by it, at first. They were used to Mummy in the mornings and Daddy in the evenings; most of their neighbours had a similar kind of tag-team arrangement. And Rita was still so little, anyway.

Lou would come home eventually – either just in time to kiss Stella goodnight, or hours later, when Josh was almost asleep. She would shower and come to bed, and he'd put an arm out to pull her close, as he had for years and years, but she would shrug it off. She wouldn't be mean about it, she wouldn't say anything, she'd just shudder a little.

He knew she wasn't sleeping much, because sometimes he would wake in the night and he could sense her alertness, her conscious breathing, her eyes to the window.

'You okay?' he'd ask, and she'd say yes, and that would be that.

He didn't blame her for being angry with him about the baby.

Not the baby, he'd correct himself. It wasn't a baby.

He was angry with himself, too. Fucking furious, in fact. Angry for letting it happen in the first place. Angry for not being man enough to lift his wife into his arms at some unexpected news and tell her that it was all fine, it didn't matter how many little mouths there were to feed, that he would always have enough love for their family. Angry at himself for being a man with limitations, with fears.

But he was that man. And somewhere, underneath the anger, as he lay on the mattress next to his sleepless wife, there was a sliver of pride. Because he had stuck up for himself. He had, in the words of his woo-woo sister Maya, stood in his truth. He had said no to something that mattered.

'Of course, she'll never forgive you for it,' Gretchen had said to him that day, when he'd brought Lou home from the clinic. 'I think you were right, for what it's worth. But she'll never forgive you.'

'I didn't make her do it!' he'd hissed at Gretchen, as he found her jacket on the hooks by the door and Lou hugged the girls. 'I couldn't make Lou do anything.'

But Gretchen had just raised an eyebrow, patted him on the arm and left. 'Good luck,' she whispered as she pulled the door closed.

Lou had turned to him from where she was crouched on the floor, tickling Stella, and given him a weak smile, and he'd decided that Gretchen was wrong. It was going to be okay. It was the sensible decision, caught early. Things were going to get back to normal. Better than normal.

But then Lou had stopped coming home.

The night he looked at her diary was not the night he'd found out what was really going on.

The diary night, Stella was feverish and weak and she missed her mummy. The house was the usual evening chaos, and he'd done baked beans on toast for dinner because he was out of ideas and Stella, who was almost five, could usually be counted on to eat beans above almost anything else. But that night she'd pushed them around her plate and seemed to turn pale in front of him. Afterwards, she'd shivered in the warm bathwater, and Rita was tumbling around the place in the nude, yelling at a very specific volume that seemed to worm into his ears and stick knitting needles into his patience.

Where was she?

Josh had wrapped Stella in a big fluffy towel and laid her down on her bed. 'I'm just going to find some medicine, Stell-star,' he'd whispered, and grabbed a running Rita as she stumbled past him. 'Come downstairs with me, you,' he said, as sternly as he could muster. 'I'll put Peppa on while we sort this out.'

'Peppa, Peppa, Peppa!' Rita yelled. 'Peppa naughty!'

'Yup,' Josh muttered, 'just like her biggest fan.'

He plonked her in front of the TV in the living room and fumbled around with the remote until *Peppa Pig* was located, and then he went into the kitchen to find the kids' Panadol. Here's hoping we've got some, he was thinking, as he rummaged through the kitchen cupboard. They didn't.

Josh called Lou's phone, again. She didn't answer, again.

He texted: *Stella sick. Can you grab Panadol on way home?* And resisted adding, *Where the fuck are you, anyway?*

And then he'd seen Lou's Book of Shit on the sideboard, near the landline.

It was quaint, really, in the age of synced calendars, that Lou was still bonded to her ten-year-old Filofax. She said that she liked having everything there, where she could see it: the days she was doing what with which classes at school; the girls' various appointments and activities. Work Shit and Family Shit, as she called it – her Book of Shit.

It was unusual that she'd left it behind today. And Josh felt like a creepy cliché, staring at it, weighing up whether to open it. Wondering whether it would actually tell him anything about where his wife was and what she thought these days and why she'd stopped coming home to their house with the tree.

'Daddy!' Stella called from upstairs. 'Daddy! I don't feel good.'

'Peppa's so naughty, Daddy,' Rita joined in from next door. 'She's made a mess on the carpet.'

Josh knew it wasn't Peppa Pig who'd made a mess on the carpet.

'Hold on, girls,' he shouted. 'I'll be there in just a minute!'

And he flipped open the red-leather-covered book. Flicked the pages to this week, this day, scanned quickly, guiltily; if his eyes didn't linger, it was like he wasn't really looking at all.

Stage one staff meeting, in Lou's loopy, large writing, *5 p.m.*

Josh's eyes went to the clock on the oven. Seven fifteen.

The only other thing written in the space reserved for that day was a *T* scrawled in the corner.

He looked at the other days on the week's spread. *T. T.* Twice this week.

He flicked back. *T.* Once last week, on Thursday, right after *Stella – dentist*. Josh had thought about last Thursday, how Lou had asked him to take the girls to Stella's dentist appointment, because she'd be home late.

The week before. Two *T*s.

His phone rang. Lou's name flashed up on it, and Josh slammed the diary closed with some force.

'Hi,' he said. 'Where are you?'

'Stella's sick?' Lou's voice. That voice. Even when it was tense, like now, it was the voice of home to him.

'She's got a fever, we're out of Panadol. She wants you. Where are you?'

'I think there's some under the sink in the downstairs bathroom,' Lou said. She sounded like she was in the car.

'Okay.' Again, 'Where are you?'

'I'll pick some up from the late-night chemist anyway. I'll be home in fifteen minutes.'

'Good. But where are you?'

Lou had hung up.

'Daddy, Peppa's made a *big* mess!' Rita yelled.

Let's just get through tonight, Josh thought, as he grabbed a cloth from the draining board.

*

The journey between Emma's new bungalow on the coast – her 'happy ending' as she called it with trademark dark humour – and

Josh and Lou's house took two hours down the tree-lined highway if the traffic was light.

The night he drove home after delivering his mum and all her boxes into the hands of a cheery property manager and Anika, who was staying to get Emma settled in, the road was eerily empty. It was well past rush hour by then, and he was going against the commuter traffic anyway. He played music, turning it up louder than he ever could if Lou or the kids or even Mick was in the car, and he sang along.

Happy, are we? he heard Lou saying in his head. *What have you got to be so happy about?*

What, indeed.

I'm compartmentalising, he said to himself. Things might be rough at home, but my mum's in the place she's always deserved, and I'm driving, alone, listening to Radiohead at an unreasonable volume. Small pleasures.

But the phone rang.

And he didn't answer it, because he was doing one hundred and ten on the highway and he wasn't an idiot, but he saw Lou's name flash up and his stomach clenched. Because it was a week since the diary. When his mum asked what he'd found he'd only said, 'She was at a staff meeting,' but actually, that night, when Stella had fallen into a medicated sleep and Rita had finally run out of energy and collapsed into her bed in a sweaty tangle, he had found Lou in the kitchen and asked her, 'What's T?'

She had gone quiet, looked up at him and said, 'Not now.' And her voice, that voice again, had struck him down somehow.

Because here he was, with a wife who wasn't coming home and a mysterious repeated letter in her diary that you'd have to be an idiot not to think was the name of a lover. But still, it was he who bore all the guilt. Lou's eyes were accusing *him* when she avoided the question.

Josh knew there was a toilet stop coming up on the left, before the Brooklyn Bridge across the Hawkesbury River. He'd stopped there hundreds of times before, as a Little Boy Josh travelling between his father and his mother, and as a Young Bloke Josh on his way up the coast with a mate and an untouched surfboard, as a Dad Josh, ushering a little girl in for a wee before an accident soiled the back seat. On the way home from his dad's funeral, for fuck's sake, with Lou breastfeeding in the back seat of the station wagon and him clearing the windscreen of an unreasonable number of dead bugs. So when he reached it, he pulled in. Sat in the ute for a moment, bathed in the blistering noise of the stereo. Then he shut off the music, picked up his phone from the cup holder and climbed out of the cab. He sat on the kerb. There wasn't anyone around, it was dark, except for the yellow headlights coming towards him in groups and the red tail-lights pouring away from him on the other side of the highway. It was warm, cicadas were loud. He pressed the button to call Lou.

She didn't say hello.

She said, 'I've been having an affair.'

'For fuck's sake, Lou,' Josh said. 'Who says that?' He rubbed his brow, kept his hand there, head lowered, phone to his ear.

'Me.' Her voice was quiet, but matter-of-fact. 'I'm furious with you. And I've been having an affair.'

Josh wasn't sure what he was meant to say next. His mouth was suddenly watery, like right before you vomited. His stomach clenched. His chest suddenly felt tight, as if someone was squeezing him from behind. His body knew what it was doing.

'Josh?' Lou said, still quiet. She was in the kitchen, he could tell. He pictured the kids' plastic dishes on the draining board. The faint splatter of baked bean juice on the inside of the microwave door. Empty water glasses still on the wooden table he'd made for them all. A discarded kid's shoe near the back door. A little red jumper tossed over a chair. A couple of empty bottles next to the bin. He could hear the sudden silence their house took on when the girls were asleep, when you tiptoed down the stairs and exhaled.

'Josh?'

He shook his head, as if to shake the kitchen out of it.

'Are you leaving me?' he asked.

Lou didn't say anything.

Josh squeezed his eyes closed and held his breath.

'No,' she said. 'I don't want to.'

He exhaled, opened his eyes. The traffic on the highway kept going. Headlights. Pause. Tail-lights.

'Good.'

'Aren't you going to ask me about it?' Lou asked. 'Don't you want to know?'

'I do not want to know,' Josh said, fast. It was something he was certain of.

'But . . .'

'Not yet, Lou,' Josh said.

'But I feel like I need to explain . . .'

'Is it over?' He held his breath as he waited for the reply.

There was a pause, then, 'Yes. It's over.'

A bright red car pulled in behind the ute and two young men got out. Ignoring the toilet block right in front of them, they walked over to the trees behind and pissed in unison. One of them threw Josh, sitting on the kerb outside the lit-up dunnies, a suspicious look.

'Where are you?' Lou asked.

'I'm driving,' he said. 'I pulled over.'

'Are you coming home?'

Josh breathed in, out. 'Yes, I'm coming home.'

He sat there on the kerb with the phone to his ear, Lou with the phone to hers in their kitchen, for a long minute.

'I think we need to see someone,' said Lou eventually. 'To help us through this.'

A mosquito buzzed at Josh's ear. The night suddenly felt heavy around him.

'I just need to see you,' he said. 'I'm going to get back in the car and drive home now.'

There was another long moment.

Then Lou said, 'Okay. I'll see you soon.'

Lou

JULY
Trial separation

'**F**ive months.'

While he was still inside her, Josh had said into Lou's ear, 'How long have we got now?'

They were pushed up against the bedroom window, Lou's bum on the sill, Josh's arms on either side of the glass.

It was sex with her husband like she couldn't remember, not in Sex Month, not in years. Lou felt every part of it, like she was covered in Josh's firm fingerprints, like his lips and teeth were branding marks into her skin.

The night was black outside, there were no lights on in the bedroom. The lopsided tree still shielded the window. It felt like they were invisible. Like it was just the two of them again, the pair who had eaten under the covers on the floor in Redfern.

They stayed there, in the window, afterwards. Holding on to each other, her face in his neck, his in her hair. 'We should know better,' Lou said into his skin. 'We're middle-aged.'

'You are nowhere near the middle of your age,' Josh replied. 'I won't hear of it.'

Lou laughed. Breathed him in, the smell of him like no-one else, so familiar, so warm. 'You smell like wood,' she said. 'You always smell like wood.'

She knew that neither one of them wanted to turn the light on and change everything.

'That really was some breakthrough today,' Lou said. 'I think Sara's proud of us.'

'We're her star fucking pupils,' said Josh.

And he kissed her again.

*

That afternoon, Lou had been running late to the appointment with the therapist because she'd been offered a new job.

'Well,' she was saying to Rob on the phone as she walked to the car, 'I've been asked to *apply* for a new job.'

'Is that how it works?'

'That's how it works. No headhunting in public education – just an invitation to come and tangle with the red tape.' Lou was trying to sound light. She didn't feel light. Her heart was racing too quickly and she couldn't quite hold a thought in her head.

'Do you want it?' Rob asked.

'I've wanted it for my whole career,' she said. 'It's just . . . there's a lot going on. This might not be the right time.'

'I thought you were thinking about leaving that school,' Rob said. 'Something about one of your workmates.'

'No, brother, you obviously weren't listening; I really like it here.'

'Oh, maybe it was something Gretchen said. Forget it.'

'You've seen Gretch?'

'We bump into each other out sometimes,' he said. 'You know, the gay mafia and all that. Have you seen that girl she's dating? She has more than a hundred thousand Instagram followers.'

'Stop it, Rob, you sound twelve,' Lou scolded. 'How are you, anyway? It seems like it's been ages.'

'Sad, alone and forty.' His voice was light, but Lou knew he wasn't joking. Rob had broken up with Toby, his first long-term boyfriend since he'd split with Peter four years ago, and he was struggling.

All of our siblings are single now, thought Lou. Is that a sign?

'Is there any chance you and Toby will . . .'

'Stop it, nope.'

'Oh, Dr Rob, I'm sorry.'

'We all know who isn't sorry, right?' Rob said. He sounded like he was walking somewhere quickly, just like her. 'Mum. She's stoked.'

'She thinks maybe you'll grow out of this lifelong gay phase of yours.' Lou gave a dry laugh. 'Finally get it out of your system in midlife.'

'She'll be pleased about your job, Lou. The last time I saw her happy was at the opening of my practice.'

'Come on, Rob, you know she doesn't care about my job, only yours.'

Bitching about our mother is the activity that most bonds us, thought Lou. 'What will we talk about when we can't talk about how terrible Mum is anymore?' she asked.

'We'll talk about how terrible she *was*,' Rob said, quick as anything. 'You know it.'

'I imagine that's accurate.' Lou climbed into the car. 'I have to go, Rob, I'm late for an appointment.'

'How's Josh? Gretch pulled a face when I asked her.'

Bloody Gretchen.

'Not great, to be honest,' Lou said eventually. 'But we're trying to fix it.'

'Of course you are,' Rob said, and she could hear his smile. 'Just as well; the family can't handle any more splits at the moment. Thank God you two have been together for a hundred years.'

Lou suddenly felt like crying. You have no idea, she thought. And it's my fault you have no idea.

'Yes.' Lou paused. 'I really have to go.'

'See you Sunday at Mum's birthday lunch,' said Rob. 'Fucking kill me now.'

'Bye, brother.'

*

'I think we should separate.' It was the first time she'd said that out loud, and she was saying it to Sara the therapist, in the blindingly bright office, with Josh sitting next to her on the couch.

Another release.

It was what she'd written into her phone today, her pulse racing, after her interview with Gabbie, the school principal: *7. Trial separation. Let's see what happens when we have some space to breathe. To think. To see.*

Josh didn't respond.

'Not forever,' Lou said. 'But to give ourselves some room. See what changes.'

He still didn't respond.

Over the past month, things in the house had moved from the brightness of the try-hard, best-behaviour phase into an almost icy, punishing silence. The turning point for Lou had been her birthday, when she'd opened her present from Josh. She could tell straight away that it was a shoebox and realised, with a rush of pleasure, that it was a new pair of running shoes.

But it wasn't. It was a pair of stunning strappy heels, gold with crystal-studded straps. The kind she never wore and had never owned.

'I bought them to take you out on a date,' Josh said.

259

Lou had tried so hard to look delighted, but she wasn't delighted. She didn't want date nights to places she could wear heels. That wasn't what was going to fix this.

Of course, Josh read it in her face in a heartbeat. 'You hate them,' he said, when the girls were out of earshot. 'You really hate them.'

'I don't,' she said, but she knew it sounded like she did. 'I just . . . I don't think I can walk in heels!' She tried to laugh, but it sounded like a strangled yelp. 'Thank you,' she said. 'Thank you for trying.'

But it seemed as if this small thing, the wrong pair of shoes, had pushed Josh into a darker place. A place of resignation. A place of sleeping in the guitar room.

Now Sara was looking at Josh, who was looking at the floor.

'We're clearly not making each other happy,' Lou said, addressing the therapist. 'And I don't want to be responsible for his unhappiness. I'm responsible for enough already.'

Sara's eyes went back to Lou. 'What do you mean by that?'

'Well . . .' she inhaled. 'I'm responsible for a whole classroom full of children and all their parents' expectations. I'm responsible for our daughters – where they go, what they do, who they're with, what they eat . . .'

Josh stirred, and looked across at her. 'Hey,' he said. 'That's not on. I do a lot more for the girls than –'

'Than most of your mates do,' Lou finished his sentence. 'That's true, Josh. But, still, you execute, you don't organise. You're there, but you don't know what snacks they'll eat and how much Vegemite is too much Vegemite on Rita's toast – which is why she never eats your toast, by the way – and you don't know that Stella's friend Amelie is really a little pain and you don't know that their six-month dental check-ups are due next week, or that Rita's been falling asleep in kindy class and that Stella is struggling a bit with her reading and could do with some extra support and that it's their class teacher's birthday next week and we're doing a whip-round for some flowers because she's just lost her mum and that we're out of those organic fucking crispbread things I've been trying to buy instead of rice crackers because of the environment and . . .' Lou realised she was ranting at almost the same moment that Sara cut her off.

'I think you've made your point, Lou,' the therapist said, nodding. 'And it's a good one.'

'Hold on,' said Lou, holding up a hand. 'And there's the house. Do you think you live in a lovely, clean home by accident? Do you think it magically remakes itself like that every fucking night when you disappear into your guitar room – which is *not* your guitar room, by the way – for your precious you time?'

'Okay . . .'

'Not finished, Sara, sorry. And did you know that I bought your sister Maya a birthday present yesterday, because you never would –'

'Maya wouldn't care if –'

'Yes she would, Josh! She gets something from *you* every birthday, wherever she is in the world, and you probably don't even know that, but it makes her feel anchored. And then there's my mum, who I've been disappointing my whole fucking life, and my dad, who's really not well, and Rob, who's lonely as fuck since he broke up with Toby, and –'

'Lou, really,' Sara said, still gentle, but firm.

'And *you*, Josh! I love you, but I've been dragging you around for fourteen years, pulling you forward, bolstering you, cheering you on . . . It's *exhausting*.' Lou was crying now. 'I'm *exhausted*.'

'Enough, Lou,' Sara said. 'You've said your piece.'

Lou felt like she might hyperventilate; she was dizzy, gasping for air, and she couldn't stop the tears. She didn't want to be sobbing in front of Sara. In front of Josh, who was infuriating her with his silence. Snot was bubbling from her nose, her shoulders were heaving.

'Josh,' Sara said, 'it's okay for you to respond, you know. You have your own truth, too.'

The room was quiet again. Apart from the gasps of her own breath, all Lou could hear was the whir of the air-con in the bright, freezing space.

'She doesn't make me unhappy,' Josh said finally. And Lou looked up at him as he pulled back his shoulders and spoke to her directly. 'You don't make me unhappy. You make my life immeasurably better, and you have since I met you. But if you've fallen out of love with me, I want you to go. Because what's crushing me is seeing you unhappy. And that's the fucking truth. Even if . . .'

'What?'

'You're fucking someone else.'

'I'm . . . not.' Lou felt sick, knew her tear-smeared face would be red.

He gave her a long look, and then looked down again. 'Whatever. Everything you said is true. And I adore you, and I hate seeing you so miserable. So, if you want a separation, that's what we should do.'

'What do *you* want, Josh?' Sara asked him, as Lou stared at her husband, the way he had leaned back in his seat, looking like he'd released something.

'People keep asking me that,' Josh said. 'I want what I've always wanted. I want Lou. I want my girls. I want to play the guitar. I swear to God I am not more complicated than that. Maybe . . .'

'Maybe?'

'Maybe that's the problem. I don't want more.' And Josh exhaled. 'I wish Lou was happy with what we have, too. But she's not.'

'I . . . was.'

'Yes, exactly.'

Josh and Lou were sitting maybe a foot apart on the couch, and suddenly, she could feel how close he was. To Lou, Josh looked like he had just been revived after a period of sedation. He was almost . . . smiling.

Turning back to face Sara, Lou realised that Sara was staring at them.

'That was . . . very insightful,' she said. 'Of both of you.'

Josh was still looking at Lou; she could feel it on the side of her head, like a warm light shining on the hair just above her ear.

'A very productive session,' Sara said. 'With a lot for you to think about.'

'But what happens now?' asked Lou. 'After we just . . . said all that?'

'Nothing *has* to happen,' said Sara. 'But I hope it's given you a lot to talk about.'

'But I said –'

'– that you want to separate,' Josh finished her sentence.

'I didn't say I *wanted* to . . .'

'Lou is allowed to express her opinion out loud, Josh, as you are yours. Nothing has to be acted on immediately. Give yourselves time to think about what's been aired here today.'

'We've been in therapy for months now,' Lou said, she wasn't sure whether to Josh or Sara. 'Surely something's supposed to happen.'

'Some people are in therapy for years,' Sara said. 'Drastic action isn't essential. Acceptance and appreciation are more important.'

'Oh.' Lou thought about what she'd said just a few minutes ago. *I think we should separate.* And she looked at Josh again.

He was smiling at her.

'Stop it,' she said. But she felt kind of silly, because she was smiling too.

*

'My bum's cold,' Lou said, and broke the spell.

They'd travelled home from the therapist's office in separate cars. Lou had gone to pick up the girls from after-school care, and by the time they got home, Josh was there, making pasta sauce.

Stella went up to Josh and hugged him from behind.

'I missed you today, Daddy,' Stella said, and Lou saw Josh gulp with emotion, stirring the sauce at the stove.

'I missed you too, sweetheart,' he said. 'I always do.'

'Everything okay, Stell?' Lou asked. She'd put money on that little Amelie being a pest again.

'Yeah, okay.' And she came to stand close to Lou, too, who gave her eldest a tight hug.

'My girls,' said Lou. 'How lucky am I?'

'Soooooooooo lucky!' called Rita, and kicked a shoe across the kitchen floor.

Lou was careful not to catch Josh's eye as she laid the table, persuaded Stella and Rita to unpack their schoolbags and wash their hands.

She and Josh had continued to move around each other as they ate dinner then Lou took the girls up for their bath while Josh did the dishes. It was like every night, the monotony of domesticity. Depending on Lou's mood, she could find it intoxicating or suffocating. Today, after everything she'd said in the therapy session, it was intoxicating; she was looking almost in wonder at what she and Josh had managed to create from a chance meeting in a dingy Newtown pub the night she found out her boyfriend was cheating on her.

Then they'd both been in the girls' room, reading stories and tucking in.

It was cold outside: winter was beginning to settle. The girls wanted an extra blanket. Then a drink of water. Then Rita needed the toilet. Instead of disappearing into the guitar room, Josh loitered as the bedtime tasks tailed off. He and Lou still weren't looking at each other.

Finally, the girls' room was quiet and dark. Lou left, pulling the door to, and found Josh right outside. Now he did look at her, and her stomach flipped in such a clichéd way it made her giggle.

'What?' she asked him.

'What?' he said.

'What are you doing?'

And he moved in on her, her husband did. And he took her face in both his big hands and he bent to kiss her but instead, he stopped just before their lips met.

'You are so fucking sexy,' he said.

And Lou, who was wearing the sensible dress she'd been wearing all day, who hadn't brushed her hair or checked her face since she ran out the door this morning, knew her husband was right. She could see it in the way his eyes were looking at her. She could see herself as he saw her.

He bent again and bit her bottom lip, gently, firmly. And then he'd kissed her, and run his hands down her body and around her waist, lifted her feet off the floor and carried her down the hallway and into the bedroom, bumping the door closed behind him, and he took her over to the window.

But now her bum was cold, and her legs were aching, her back fat was a little bit stuck to the window. She gently pushed Josh away and went over to their bed. She watched Josh watching her as she gathered the doona around her, sitting up near the pillows and looking back at him, her husband, naked, their crumpled clothes scattered around the room.

They weren't invisible. They weren't the only two people in the world. She wasn't a sexy goddess. All their history was still there, even in the dark.

'Well,' she said.

'Five months,' he said. 'I've got five months?'

Lou shook her head. 'I don't think so.'

Josh's face broke into a smile. 'What do you mean?'

'That was so weirdly beautiful,' Lou said, and she meant it. 'What you said at Sara's about me. And you and me.'

'Well, it's true,' he said, sitting on the end of the bed, facing her. 'It's all I want.'

A pang of irritation. 'I don't think that's true,' she said. 'I mean, I know you love me – I know that bit's true – but I think you want lots of other things outside these four walls. I think that's why you didn't want another baby.'

Josh's face immediately fell. 'Are we back there?' he said. 'Three fucking years ago? Let's have another fucking baby!'

Lou flinched. 'Shut up, Josh. That's not what this is about.'

Whatever had happened in the therapist office that afternoon, it had released something. Between them, but also in her. She knew what she was going to say was not what Josh wanted to hear, that it was hard to do and it would ruin this beautiful moment and many more after it. She knew that the words could not be put back in the bottle once she'd said them, but maybe some words had been in bottles for too long.

'You just made it about this,' he whisper-shouted. 'You've been punishing me for years. Funny how that hasn't come up at Sara's office.'

There you go, thought Lou. There it is.

'And I'm the bad guy,' he went on. 'I'm the one who's disappointing you so very much. But what about me? I gave up a lot for *this*.' He gestured around the room. 'My music, my life. You think I want to be building someone else's dream house? You think I like being the oldest tradie at the timber yard? You don't think *you* have anything to do with that?'

Lou watched him from the bed, his face twisting as he almost spat the words at her. It almost felt good to have them flung at her. Like, at last, it wasn't just her.

'And you,' Josh said. 'You act like this is all about me and the abortion, and nothing to do with you . . . *betraying* me.'

With that, Josh had run out of steam. He sat down on the edge of the bed, his back to her, and pushed his hands through his hair.

'See?' said Lou, after a moment. 'I'm not all you want.'

His shoulders rose and fell in an exaggerated shrug.

'It's a mess,' Lou said. 'I think all our shit has become so tangled up we can't see where it starts and where it stops and which bit's me and which bit's you and what either of us wants anymore.'

'Lou, we just . . .' Josh was gulping as he spoke.

'So I think we should try to pull it apart a bit, and see what's there.'

'What the fuck does that mean?' He turned to face her.

Lou sucked in some cold air. 'A trial separation.'

'You're serious?'

'You know I am.'

'But what about . . .' Josh gestured to the windowsill. 'What about *that*?'

'Well, that's something that's there, right?' Lou pushed on. She was beginning to feel sick. More so whenever she looked at Josh. 'Something we have.'

'The girls?' His voice was thick now. 'Are they in the *have* column?'

'Of course they are,' Lou said, trying not to cry at the thought of them. 'But this is terrible for them. They will be happier in a calmer home. Until we make a call.'

'They'll be happier without one of us around? And what do you mean, "a call"?'

'On staying together or being apart.' Lou tried to reach out to Josh but he pulled his arm away. 'Today was a reason to stay,' she said.

'But it doesn't rub out all the other things. It doesn't make everything better.'

'Then I have no idea what will.' Josh stood up. 'What's your deadline this time?'

When Lou looked at Josh, her nerve faded, so she looked away again, kept her eyes on the daisy pattern on the faded doona.

'Five months, still,' she said. 'Let's give our separation five months.'

Josh

JULY

Trial separation

'I t's called bird nesting,' Josh said to Anika. 'The kids stay in one place, but we fly in and out.'

'Sounds like wishful thinking.' Anika was pouring them each a very large glass of wine under the heater at the wooden table in her back garden. It was a heavy red, suited to the cold air. 'You're both going to want your own space.'

'It's only till Christmas,' said Josh. 'We're giving it four more months.'

Anika made a noise that was almost certainly 'pfft'.

'Don't fucking "pfft" me, Anika,' he said. And thought, We're not you and Ed.

'Sorry, Joshy.' She raised her glass to him. 'Here we all are, hey? Who would have thought we'd all be such losers in love. Oh, wait . . . everyone. Did you meet our parents?'

Josh didn't raise his glass. He just looked at the contents. Then took a huge gulp.

'Speaking of which,' his sister said, 'when are you going to tell Mum?'

'I'm not.' He took another swig.

His sister raised an eyebrow at him. 'Come on, mate. You two are tight. How are you going to manage that?'

'I'm not telling anyone anything until Lou and I know what we're doing,' he said. Also, he thought, she knows too much already.

'You told me,' Anika said. 'Because I've been there?'

'Because I need your couch.'

'Lovely.'

Anika was sitting cross-legged in her outsized egg chair, cradling her balloon of wine. She was so thin these days, Josh saw, in her yoga leggings with a blanket around her shoulders and her bare feet resting on her thighs. But rather than it giving her an air of fragility, it gave her an aura of toughness. Sunken cheeks and sinewy biceps tell a story of their own in a woman of Anika's age, he thought. They say, 'I'll show the bastard.' Which was what Anika was doing.

She still lived in the family home in Kensington, which was what she'd always wanted, although Josh had no idea why. If things were really over with Lou, he would never want to set foot in that house again, it would be so tainted by all their tiny failures.

'Why did you stay here?' he asked. 'You could have afforded something else with the settlement, right?'

'It's their home.' Anika motioned to the boys, who, Josh could see through the sliding glass doors into the house, were lying at two ends of a lounge playing Xbox and eating popcorn. Henry and Wilson. Lou always used to say to Josh, 'It's like one person's name, split between two.' He smiled at that.

'And I always loved this house. You should see Ed's new place. I only have from the outside, of course, but it's the exact opposite – shiny and modern. All sharp angles and glass.'

They'd had a traditional set-up, Anika and Ed. He'd earned the cash doing something Josh didn't understand in a skyscraper in the city, and Anika had held the home front and tried a handful of the kind of careers you could dabble in if you didn't really need the money. She'd opened a book cafe with an old friend for a while, but the hours were a killer. She'd trained to be a florist and did weddings and parties for a bit, but when the boys came along she couldn't commit to all those weekends. She styled houses for sale for a company that specialised in facelifts, because she'd always had a bloody good eye. Now she did need the money, and she was a yoga teacher. Josh admired both his sisters' abilities to change direction, not to get stuck somewhere they didn't want to be. They were bigger risk-takers than him. Why was that?

'Do you hate him?' Josh asked, surprising himself. And then he looked down at his empty wineglass and added, 'Because I do.'

'That's very loyal of you, thank you.' She smiled. 'Yeah, I do too.'

Ed had left in a particularly brutal way, Josh and Lou had agreed. One minute he was all in, or so it seemed, and the next, while Anika and the boys were visiting Emma up the coast one weekend, he'd packed up all his stuff and left. Anika had come home to empty wardrobes and a note that said he wasn't coming back. *Sorry.* After almost fifteen years.

Two weeks before Anika had turned up sobbing at their door, Josh and Lou had been at Anika and Ed's and he'd been exactly as usual: talking a lot, grabbing his wife around the waist and kissing her head, boasting about the school they were going to send the boys to next year, their big dream trip to Europe.

'Do you think he had a breakdown?' Lou asked Josh, more than once.

'No, I think he's a cock,' Josh would answer. But of course, even he knew there was more to it than that.

He reached for the wine. 'Do you still love him?'

'Maybe,' Anika said. 'But the hate is stronger right now. What I hate is what he did to Hen and Wil and me with so little thought. A decision like that changes lives forever. Changes people's stories, their sense of themselves. Every damn thing. You know it. That's why you're in denial. But he just fucking did it.'

'I am not in denial,' Josh said, passing her the bottle.

'That's what people in denial say.' Anika smiled, splashed a little more wine into her glass.

'This is a rough patch, it's not the end,' said Josh.

'Okay.'

Josh tried not to let his irritation at his sister's tone overwhelm him as they sat in silence for a moment.

'Also, I miss him.'

'You really shouldn't. He's a cock.'

Anika laughed out loud. 'Yep.'

She stretched out her legs and wiggled her toes. 'Anyway, what about Lou's family? Does the lovely Annabelle know?'

*

Two weeks before, Josh had had his own Ed moment, play-acting at a barbecue at Annabelle and Brian's, and making a disastrous mess of it.

It was only a few days after the night he and Lou had sex in the window.

Josh had spent that night at the workshop, not sleeping under a pile of drop sheets on a saggy old couch. It was dramatic, he could see, to walk out like that, but as soon as Lou had said those words to him he needed to leave. He couldn't be in the house anymore, he couldn't be in the guitar room, listening to Lou move around on the other side of a door. He couldn't bear to think about her tapping away at her phone, talking to God knows who, making plans for God knows what. He couldn't think about the girls, sleeping a few walls away, about to wake up to a new reality.

The workshop was freezing and bleak, and Josh lay there on the lumpy couch staring at the beams across the ceiling and thinking about how the hell he was going to walk around tomorrow with all this toxic fury whirring around his body, making him twitch. He understood why people punched things. He felt the urge to destroy something, anything, and his fists kept clenching and unclenching, clenching and unclenching.

He wanted to talk to his dad. It might have been the first time he'd ever actively wanted to do that.

Weak light started to creep in under the door and Josh knew he needed to get his shit together before Tyler or Mick arrived. He needed to have a shower and get over to the music producer's house in Camperdown and lose himself in planing a fucking pool deck with his headphones in.

His phone beeped in the pocket of the jeans he'd been wearing all night. The ones that had been on the floor of the bedroom, the ones Lou had yanked off him with force before he'd carried her over to the window.

It was Lou.

Are you okay?

Will you come home today?

Can you still pick up the girls?

He didn't answer the first question. He couldn't. To the others he replied:

Sure.

Yes.

Lou wrote back:

Because we need to talk about how all this will work.

All night, a particular image had been pushing other thoughts out of Josh's head: the man at the school fundraising concert, leaning down to talk into Lou's ear.

He tapped out:

Who are you fucking?

And then deleted it.

Is it the same person? Or a new one?

And then deleted it.

I'll see you at 5.

He sent that one.

A response came back almost immediately:

Are you okay though?

Josh pushed the phone back into his pocket. If he got to Camperdown early enough he could shower there.

Just get on with it, mate, he told himself. You're a big boy.

And that's exactly what he'd done: he'd got on with it. He went to work, left on time, picked up the girls, took them home.

When Lou arrived, he tried not to look at her directly, as if she were the sun. She bustled, and he moved out of her way.

He lay on Stella's bed with a daughter under each arm and read *The Gruffalo* for the two hundred and fiftieth time, with voices. He could hear Lou downstairs putting away the dinner dishes.

Rita fell asleep with her head on his shoulder and he told himself that none of this was real, and he'd have every night with his girls, just like this one.

And then he went downstairs and Lou had the wall calendar laid out on the kitchen table he'd built and she was talking to him about how they could divide their time over the next few months. He felt like he was sleepwalking, tuning in and out.

'This Sunday, I've got to be at Mum's birthday lunch. You could come late and take the girls home and stay for two nights. No-one will think that's weird if I tell them I'm meeting Gretch for drinks, and then I'll go sleep at hers . . .'

How long have you been hatching these plans? he wondered.

'Why can't I just sleep in the spare room?' he heard himself asking. 'Save us all the cloak and dagger.'

'Because that's not separating,' she said, and Josh thought she sounded impatient. 'We need to not see each other. To miss each other. To reset. I've been reading about it . . .'

When? When have you been reading about it?

'So the kids stay here but we come and go. It's called bird nesting. The idea is that we establish this structure and then we meet regularly to check in. I'm going to call Sara to talk her through it, see if the meetings should be at her office.'

You're so busy with all this.

Josh picked up his keys. 'Just tell me where you need me to be and when,' he said. 'I'll do whatever.'

Lou put down the pen she was using to write on the calendar. Softened her voice. 'You can't even look at me, can you?'

'Not today,' said Josh. 'Not today, Lou.'

And on the Sunday, just as he'd been instructed, Josh stood on Brian and Annabelle's doorstep, just as he had fourteen years before. He remembered his first encounter with Annabelle, who had probably liked him more that day than any day since, because she didn't know him.

'Come in and have a beer, Josh!' Rob had seen him through the open front door.

So Josh walked down the hall and into the backyard. Part of him felt like that guy of fourteen years ago, a stranger in a strange land. But also, now he could read every dynamic in the place.

Annabelle was sitting at the glass-topped table, nursing a Pimms, which seemed very optimistic in July. The sun was bright and strong overhead right now, but as soon as it dropped below the fence line they'd all be freezing. She was talking to Lou, and seeing his wife there gave Josh a little jolt. She was wearing a dress with buttons down the front and the top few were undone. From where Josh stood, he could see her maroon bra strap. He tried not to think about that.

Brian was at the barbecue, blankly cleaning the plate next to a pile of cooked sausages. Hiding from company with a busy-job.

Rob, who'd welcomed him so warmly, was trying hard to be cheerful, pretending that everything was great, handing Josh his beer and asking how his Sunday had been so far.

There were a few of Annabelle and Brian's friends milling around, golf types.

Stella and Rita had come flying to Josh's legs and hugged him tightly. If anyone thought it was strange that his daughters were so pleased to see him, they didn't let on.

Lou looked up at Josh and smiled. 'There he is!' she said to Anna-belle, as if she was delighted to see her husband. Annabelle looked up too, gave Josh a tight nod.

Lou stood up and came over to Josh, kissed him on the cheek. He could smell her clean hair as she brushed against him. 'Hi,' she whispered. 'Thanks for doing this.'

Josh took a sip of his beer. 'Can I take the girls now?'

'It would be good if you could hang around a little bit,' said Lou. 'More convincing.'

'Sure.'

'Isn't it good news, Josh?' Annabelle shouted from the table.

He was sure that for a moment he must have looked stricken, the bottle pausing halfway to his lips.

'Lou's job!' Annabelle said. 'Her promotion! Aren't you proud?' And from the way his mother-in-law's mouth tightened back into a straight line, the way she cocked her head and narrowed her eyes, Josh could tell that pride wasn't what she was feeling. That, actually, she was sensing that something had shifted.

'Mum, it's not official yet,' Lou called back, and she nudged Josh in the ribs and said to him, 'Just go with it, okay?'

Josh had never wanted to go with it less. 'Please tell me when I don't have to make an effort with these people anymore,' he hissed. 'Put me out of my misery.'

'What are you talking about?' Lou whispered back. 'They're your family.'

'They're not,' he said. And he called to the girls, 'Stell, Reets, we're going to leave in five. Have you got everything?'

Lou frowned. 'I thought you were staying for a while.'

Josh could see Annabelle preparing to get up and head over for a chat. 'What does your new guy do?' he asked Lou.

'What?'

'The guy you've been fucking – what does he do?'

The look on Lou's face, like he'd just spat at her, gave Josh a sharp moment of satisfaction.

'Maybe Annabelle will get the son-in-law she's been after the second time around,' he said.

Lou was swallowing quickly and her neck was red. It looked like she was trying not to cry.

Good, he thought.

Then he saw Lou trying to compose herself as her mother walked their way, saw Annabelle reading her in the ten steps it took to get from the table to here, Pimms in hand.

Not good, Josh thought. I don't want Lou to hate me. I don't want to make her suffer in front of her mother. I don't.

So he put an arm around his wife and pulled her quickly to him as Annabelle bore down.

'I'm so proud of her, Annabelle,' he said, so firmly and loudly that Brian looked up from the barbecue. 'She's amazing, isn't she? You made a brilliant daughter.'

*

'I'm going to get those two into bed before I get wobbly,' Josh's sister said, unfurling herself from the egg chair and heading towards the sliding glass doors. 'If I don't come back, it means I've fallen asleep myself.'

As she walked behind him, she kissed Josh's head. It felt good.

'You know where the blankets and towels are, little brother,' Anika said, putting a hand on his head where the kiss had been planted. 'You'll be okay.'

'Thanks, Ani,' he said. 'Thank you.'

He watched his brave sister head into the family room, grab Henry's foot and give it a shake, reach over for the video game controller in Wilson's hands.

I'm sorry, sister, Josh thought as he watched her deftly haul her boys up from the couch. This isn't what I want. I am not as strong as you.

Lou

13 February, 2016

Lou was working hard on forgiving Josh.

Lou knew Josh was working hard on forgiving her.

'We're so busy trying not to go to bed angry, we barely sleep,' she told Gretchen over takeaway coffees, sitting on a concrete step at the edge of a playground, a place about as far from her friend's preferred habitat as it was possible to get.

'Sounds exhausting.'

'Oh, it is.' She watched as Rita lurched in front of the swings, only narrowly missing being hit by a bigger kid's outstretched Crocs. 'Stella! Can you get Rita, please?'

'And your . . . thing?' Gretchen asked. 'Is it really over?'

'It really is.' Lou took the top off her coffee cup, licked chocolate-powdered froth.

'But you still see him every day, right?'

She pushed the lid back down. 'Well, often. But we just . . . don't.'

'How is that possible?' Gretchen asked, as Lou's eyes tracked Stella and Rita, heading away from the swings and towards the round-abouts, hand in hand.

'It was only ever physical,' Lou said. 'You know how it is. You end things all the time.'

'Yes, but I'm not you, Mrs Relationship,' said Gretchen. 'Even at uni you had to fall in love with anyone who gave you good head.'

Lou looked around quickly, checking none of her mum-friends were in close proximity.

'I did not!'

'Hmmmm.' Gretchen rolled her eyes. 'Anyway, when I end things, I like the other person to disappear. I prefer to imagine that anyone I'm involved with only exists if I can see them.'

'Nothing narcissistic about that at all,' said Lou. 'Look, it's okay. I can honestly say that it was nothing more than sex. I was working stuff out of my system. It was like punching something at the gym.'

Gretchen laughed. 'I'm sorry, but that sounds really, really hot.'

'Yes, well, it's done. Hotness needs to go back home.'

Rita was beaming, sitting on the edge of a roundabout that Stella was spinning slowly, carefully, ushering away other kids who came close and wanted to leap on and go fast. 'Look at that,' she said, nudging Gretchen in the ribs. 'How cute are they?'

'Very,' said Gretchen. 'You two make good kids, I'll give you that.' She looked around the playground. It was a hot Saturday morning and the place was packed with parents hovering around their children, clutching giant coffees and colourful water bottles. 'I wonder how many of these good people are cheating on each other?' she asked.

'I am not cheating,' said Lou. 'It was a blip. A glitch. A reaction to an action.'

'Okay . . .' Gretchen paused and they both watched as Stella helped Rita off the roundabout and directed a triumphant smile at them. 'So what does Josh think about you seeing this guy every day?'

'He doesn't know.'

'What?'

'He doesn't want to know anything about it.' Lou rummaged in her bag for a hat for Rita. 'He says that if I say it's over, he believes me, and if he knows the details it will torture him. To be honest, he's already feeling pretty tortured about David Bowie dying.' A wry smile.

'How is that possible?' Gretchen's voice was loud now, and some heads turned in their direction. 'How could he not want to know?'

'Shhhh, Gretch!' The girls were heading back in their direction. 'You know Josh – he keeps things very . . . closed. I actually think he's afraid of what he might do.'

'But there's an imminent threat.'

'No, there isn't.'

'But it's not like this was a random guy you met at the pub . . .'

'When was the last time I met a random guy at a pub?'

'Exactly,' said Gretchen. 'You shat where you eat. Every damn workday.'

'That's lovely.'

Stella and Rita arrived, babbling at Lou about snacks and when were they going home and five more minutes.

'He has nothing to worry about,' she said to her friend as she pulled on Rita's hat and handed Stella her water. 'Yes, five more minutes, Stell . . . It doesn't matter that he doesn't know. In fact, it's better that he doesn't. It's over. And I don't want to find a new job. So let's choose to support Josh's choice.'

'Like he supported yours?'

'Shut up, Gretch.'

'At least tell me you guys are in counselling about all this.'

'I am. He won't.'

'Healthy. I assume you're supporting that choice, too?'

'Shut up, Gretch.'

*

'We can't do this anymore,' Lou had said down the phone, at ten thirty on a Tuesday night.

'Really? Because that's what people say in movies when they want to be talked out of it,' Theo had answered.

'That's a dick thing to say,' said Lou. 'I don't want you to talk me out of it. I know what I want – and I want it to stop.'

When she first had sex with the deputy principal, it had been over a decade since any lips other than Josh's, any hands other than Josh's, had touched her body.

If men had flirted with her in that time, she hadn't really noticed. First, because she was thinking only about Josh. Then because she had other priorities. Like getting through the day with a baby strapped to her front. Holding down a job. Not being crushed under a mountain of unfolded washing.

She found she just stopped noticing men that way. Josh never seemed to lose his desire to have sex with her, no matter how tired she was, or how alien her body felt to her. Whether there was a baby inside it, or milk in her breasts, whether there was more or less of her in general. His desire seemed to be set at a constant thrum, while hers came and went, surging at unexpected times, like late in her pregnancy with Stella, disappearing at others, like throughout her whole pregnancy with Rita.

But on her first day at Bayside Primary, Lou had noticed Theo. She was coming in as a special support teacher, Rita was a baby, Lou was training for a half-marathon, loving being back running again. She was, she could see now, at a Moment of Change.

The staffroom was like any she'd ever been in. Cluttered and comfy, home to cracked mugs and biscuit barrels (gluten and gluten-free, labelled). It had its own particular political structure, its own set of unwritten rules, as well as the written ones on a notice pinned up in the kitchenette about personal teabags and showing 'respect' by washing cups thoroughly.

Lou had been given a buddy in the head of stage one, Beth, who was smiley and no-nonsense, and had introduced her around the room to varying levels of welcome and interest.

'This is Theo, he's our new deputy head,' Beth said, as a mountain of a man filled the staffroom doorway. Tall and broad and dark, with a smile that took up his whole face, Lou doubted that anyone forgot his name or got him mixed up with anyone else. When he shook her hand and grinned at her, his hand was huge and it made her laugh to imagine telling Stella about the man with the big-bear hands.

'Great to meet you, Louise,' he said, looking into her eyes intently in a way that suggested he'd taken a course in how to make friends and influence people. 'We're really excited about having the extra support on hand. Can't wait to watch you add value.'

Add value? Lou had been in enough staffrooms to know that here was a guy whose departure from a room would be followed by the other teachers' eye-rolls and fingers-down-the-throat gestures.

'It's Lou,' Lou said, and he nodded quickly and moved past her to the tea mugs, asking the room at large, 'Hey, how's everyone on this fine first day?'

Lou was almost certain she would have very little to do with Deputy Theo, who seemed, here in the staffroom, like a literally giant fish in a small pond.

But it hadn't turned out that way. Lou found out later in her first week that additional learning support fell into Theo's 'bucket', as he called it. 'And I have fortnightly WIPs with everyone in my bucket.'

'WIPs?'

'Work in Progress sessions.' Theo smiled. 'Sorry, I was in the corporate world before I came to teaching. Some habits from that world are hard to break . . . and some are still useful.'

He didn't look old enough to have had a pre-teaching life, Lou thought, but whatever.

In the WIPs they discussed the progress of the program, monitoring individual kids' results – 'accountability is everything' – and keeping an eye on the waiting list for kids who could slot in next.

In those meetings, Theo was a talker. While Lou twitchily watched the clock, counting down to day care pick-up or the bedtime deadline, he was exceptionally comfortable filling time by explaining why he thought the way he thought.

As he talked about himself, Lou learned Theo had a fiancée back in Melbourne. That he was a rugby man. That he thought teachers should think more like managers, principals more like CEOs. He had a tattoo on his collarbone that was sometimes visible but impossible to make out. As he talked at her, she pondered what it might be. A wing of some sort.

Lou could tell that Theo liked that she was 'new', too, although he was a term ahead of her. She could tell that Gabbie, the head, was well liked but steady, by-the-book, and that's not what Theo was.

'Theo freaks me out a little bit,' she'd said to Beth in her third week. 'He's so . . . in your face. It's weird for a teacher, don't you think?'

'He's not a teacher,' Beth said, tucking strands of her sensible brown bob behind an ear. 'He's a deputy head. He's a politician, and he's trying to recruit you to his faction. You should stay a little bit freaked out.'

But if the staffroom was divided, as so many classrooms were, between the idealistic and the resigned, Lou had made a decision early in her career to stay in the idealistic camp for as long as she possibly could. She mightn't have her own class and classroom right now, but every day she was away from her own kids, she wanted to feel like it was worth it. So there was a part of her that admired Theo's gung-ho attitude and energy, as much as there was another part of her that thought he was an egomaniac with zero self-awareness.

'I caught him doing chin-ups in the male bathroom the other day,' whispered PE head Greg in the staffroom.

'I saw him telling Jared Soave to shave – and Jared's only eleven,' said Amity, who taught year six.

Beth laughed. 'He's called his project group Growth Mindset – they're six!'

But everything about the meetings Lou and Theo shared changed after she had her termination.

'I find it really hard to explain,' Lou said to the counsellor she'd been sent to by her GP, 'because I'm completely fine, and I know my family is completely fine, I know in so many ways that Josh was right, but I feel so . . .'

'Sad? Do you feel like you're grieving?' the woman asked, tilting her head in a figurative 'aw'.

'No,' Lou said. 'I feel angry. Really, really angry. I finally understand the phrase "eaten up by anger" now, because I wake up every day with this drop of fury in my stomach. Most days it starts out small, but by lunchtime it's like a football in my tummy, and by the time I get home it's like beach ball. And it's like it can't be contained; it just shoots out of me. Everything Josh does annoys me: the way he looks at me, the way he picks up a cup, the way he eats, the way he coughs, the way he does anything for the girls. He does what he's supposed to, but everything's ten per cent off. Like, he makes Stella's snack, but he doesn't peel the apple, which means she won't eat it. And he says, "I cut it up!", but the point is he didn't *peel* it. It makes me furious. Wouldn't that make you furious?'

The counsellor, who clearly wasn't living with preschoolers, nodded her head very slowly, looking blank.

At the same time, Lou's meetings with Theo went from friendly to combative. She found a reason to have a problem with the results he was asking her to report. She disagreed almost as a matter of course with his views on the progress of any particular child. She wanted changes made to the plans for next term, even though they were already locked down.

'It's like I know he can take it,' she'd said to Gretchen, after she ditched the counsellor. 'He's someone I know I can push back on.'

'But he's your boss?'

'Well, he's not directly my boss, but . . .'

'It seems weird to me that this one work relationship is such a focus,' Gretchen said. 'Are you sure there's nothing more here?'

To which Lou had punched her in the arm. 'Euuw.'

And to Beth, at school, Lou said, 'Theo really is a dick.'

'Yep,' said Beth. 'He really is. Get yourself out of those meetings.'

But Lou didn't. Instead, she requested an extra one, about three months after the termination. And that day, she'd looked at herself in the mirror in the morning, at her thirty-something face staring back at her, tired-looking, a little drawn. She'd put on one of the 'good' sets of underwear she hadn't worn for months, possibly years, and she wore a pair of shoes that had something like a heel.

All day that day, Lou felt sick. The meeting was at 4 p.m. in Theo's tiny office next to Gabbie's. Often they held their meetings in the staffroom, sometimes alone, sometimes with other additional-needs staff. But not that day.

She knew that what she was doing was high-risk. She knew it was against all school rules, against her own personal ethics, a betrayal of her husband, but she felt, then, like she was living in an orderless world. The fury pounding at her all the time was exhausting and exhilarating at once. She was barely eating, running on adrenaline fuelled by toxic energy. She knew all this. She knew she wasn't in a place to make sound decisions.

Lou sat down opposite Theo at his desk and she said, 'I'd like to ask you a question, and I'd appreciate your discretion.'

Theo looked worried, as any man would. 'Lou, if you are going to declare anything about another staff member, it might be smart of us to get Beth in here, and possibly Gabbie. Although, I think she's left for the day . . .'

'No, no.' Lou shook her head. 'It is inappropriate, what I want to say, but it's about me.' Her hands, she realised, were shaking, and she suddenly felt slightly ridiculous and embarrassed. Still.

'I wondered – and you can certainly say no . . .' Shut up, shut up. 'Would you like to have sex? You and me?'

'You did NOT say that!' Gretchen had shrieked after the fact, when Lou finally told her friend the details.

'I did. I have no idea how I did, but I did.'

'I can't believe it.' Gretchen's face had been a mixture of excitement and concern. 'What the fuck did he say?'

'Well, he looked really, really shocked, but only for a moment . . .'

Theo had seemed momentarily terrified, actually, looking around the room as if there was a hidden camera or a recorder somewhere, and this was a sting or an elaborate joke.

But then he said, 'What makes you ask me that?'

And something about the look on his face – a little bit fearful but also interested – told Lou she was right. 'I just really need to have sex,' she said, twisting her wedding ring. 'With someone who isn't my husband.'

'I didn't think you . . . liked me, Lou,' he said, with the suggestion of a sly smile. The fear fading, he looked like a man who was getting what he wanted. Smug, even.

He was sitting down on the other side of the desk, but Lou knew that as long as she could convince Theo she wasn't trying to ruin him, it would happen. Bottom line was, she knew Theo was getting hard, sitting there at his tidy desk; she could just tell.

'I don't want an affair, or to split up with Jo– . . . my husband, and I certainly don't want you to split up with . . . your fiancée. I just thought, you might be lonely up here in Sydney and it's something I need to do, and I think we have quite good chemistry, and . . .'

'Did he just pull you over the desk and take you?' asked Gretchen, disbelieving. 'I still can't believe you did that, Lou.'

And Lou nodded. 'Yes, pretty much.'

It had been a little clumsier than that, she had to admit. There had to be a fake exit, to make sure that the office next door and outside had been vacated. There was a fumble in her bag for a condom, from a packet she'd bought specifically. There had been a wrestle to try to get Theo's belt off; it had this weird clip thing . . .

'And was it incredible?' Gretchen asked, almost shuddering with excitement.

'It was' – Lou remembered how quick it was, that first time in the office, how desperate – 'exactly what I needed.'

They never did it in the office again. Theo was a cautious man when it came to his career. He wasn't going down for this.

At their next meeting, he had asked Lou, very matter-of-factly, if she wanted to continue this arrangement. She had nodded, and they drew up a list of rules. 'Do we have to have WIPs to make sure we're sticking to the rules?' asked Lou, only half joking.

'We'll check in,' Theo said, straight-faced, 'to keep ourselves honest.'

Rules
1. *All school communication to be strictly professional.*
2. *No fraternising on school grounds.*
3. *Protected sex only.*
4. *No discussion of partners or relationships.*

5. Either party can call the project off without notice and there will be no negative repercussions, professional or otherwise.

6. NO DISCUSSION WITH ANY THIRD PARTY at any stage.

Logistics weren't easy. Theo lived in Bondi then, which was too far from the school for it to be practical. And he had housemates, old rugby buddies.

But Theo also knew the guy who ran a gym nearby. This guy owed him a favour from old times. He could get Theo the keys to the upstairs storeroom. It was hardly ever used. They could go in the back door, go up the stairs, lock the door, go out the same way.

And so it was that at least once a week for three months, Lou and Theo would have sex between dumbbells and yoga mats, broken spin bikes and foam rollers. It was an almost brutal, aggressive, masculine, uncomfortable space. It was absolutely perfect for what Lou was after.

'I'm invoking rule five,' Lou said down the phone that Tuesday night, just after she'd spoken to Josh on the highway.

And Theo had made a 'huh' noise. 'Well, then, I will respect the integrity of that decision,' he said. 'Until you change your mind.'

Theo's tattoo was a wedge-tailed eagle. Of course it was.

*

'The thing about it is,' she told Gretchen as she packed up the kids' things at the playground, 'I didn't ever really *like* him. I still don't.'

'But are you still attracted to him?'

Lou thought about it. His thick, long fingers and his broad shoulders and his firm hands. And his self-satisfied smirk and the triumphant grunt he gave when he came, and his complete absence of natural curiosity.

'I've got it out of my system,' she said. 'I want to focus on Josh. On rebuilding.'

'Well,' said Gretchen, 'good luck with that, when the bad man's down the hall.'

'All our meetings are in the staffroom now,' said Lou. 'It will be fine.'

And she strapped Rita into the stroller and began to push towards home.

Josh

Later that year

I haven't thought about it for a whole day.

Josh had got to 7 p.m. on 25 November when he realised he had gone a whole thirteen conscious hours without thinking about the imaginary man who'd been screwing his wife.

It's only taken me eleven months, he thought, to get this far through a day without picturing it. Without wondering if Lou was thinking about him. Without seeing them together.

Happy birthday to me, he thought, bumping along in Mick's giant, shiny new ute. Josh was heading home after having a celebratory beer. It was early, but they'd knocked off a few hours ago, and he knew Lou was making him dinner and they were going to sit out the back and drink a bottle of wine on the deck. It was spring, the evening was warm and the jasmine was out.

He was almost tempted to tell Lou about this milestone, but he knew that would be weird. He also knew that after three beers his tone would be unreliable – he couldn't be counted on to not say something that would turn this positive into a negative at speed.

That was the thing about a marriage 'in recovery', he thought. It was fragile, and the winds that rattled it were fierce and unpredictable.

'Mate, here you go.' Mick was dropping him off, since Josh had had a few drinks. 'Home for dinner.'

'Good man, Mick.' He climbed out of the truck. But Mick didn't pull away. And he could have sworn that was Simon's truck over there – Simon who'd just been at the pub with them. And was that Rob's hybrid Toyota?

Oh, right.

Josh had a moment to prepare before he pushed open the front door.

He ran his hands back through his hair, wiped them down the front of his short-sleeved shirt. The one that, come to think of it, Lou had shoved into his bag this morning, in a way that she rarely did. 'You're going out tonight, you don't want to wear your shitty T-shirt,' she'd said. And he hadn't thought anything of it, even though it was a bit strange that Mick had asked him if he was getting changed before they left the workshop to go to the local. 'Since when do you care?' he'd asked.

When he did open the door, it was a straight three–two–one countdown to the scream of 'SURPRISE!' and the light flicking on to reveal a crowd around Lou and the girls in the hallway, fairy lights dangling from the bannister, the sound of a champagne cork popping, music pumping.

'Oh, whoa,' he said, louder than he might usually. 'You've got to be kidding me!'

And Rita started to cry so he went to her and scooped her up in one arm, pulling Lou to him with the other, and motioned for Stella to join the group hug. 'Thank you so much,' he said to the top of Lou's head. 'I had no idea.'

His mum was there. So were Anika and Ed, Henry and Wilson, even Maya. Mick was behind him, Gretchen and Barton, Annabelle,

Brian, Rob and his boyfriend Toby, and a scattering of workmates and parents from day care.

'Well,' said Lou into his ear, 'you're almost forty. We thought we should celebrate before you get too old. Also' – and he could have sworn she swallowed just a little before she said it – 'because we love you.'

'I'm going to kill you later,' he muttered to her. 'But I love you too.'

There was, at the end of 2016, much to celebrate.

His wife, after all, was no longer sleeping with the man of his imagination.

*

He had told precisely one person about what had happened between him and Lou: his mum.

Adult children, Josh knew, needed to believe that their parents didn't know them at all. That they were completely independent entities, complicated mysteries whom the people that raised them would never truly understand.

But becoming a dad to his daughters had changed Josh's view on that. How could it possibly be that someone who had obsessed about every little part of your personality and your wellbeing for so long – who considered the impact of how and when you learned to walk, talk, eat, sleep, love, laugh – didn't know you? Emma knew him to his bones. She was the one who was there, after all, when as an adolescent Josh found his way in a new fatherless world in a strange city. She was the one who nudged him upright when he fell over, literally and figuratively, and she was the one who knew, better than anyone, what kept him down and what lifted him up.

He fully expected her to tell him to leave Lou, which he had already decided he was not going to do. He expected Emma, who was finding her feet in her new home in her newly created estate by the beach, fringed by leafy gums and dotted with things old people liked – coffee shops that didn't serve chewy sourdough, greengrocers where you could buy a single tomato if you wanted, a golf club that also offered tai chi classes, affordable drinks in small glasses and a cheap Tuesday fish-and-chip special – to tell him not to be a mug.

But she didn't. 'You should write a song about this, son,' she said first. 'It might make you a million dollars.'

'Not quite how it works, Mum,' he replied. He was putting together an outdoor table and chairs set that had come flat-packed from the nearby SupaCenta. It was flimsy and cheap, and he was feeling guilty for not making her something sturdier himself.

'The hardest thing you'll ever do in your life,' Emma said, 'is forgive someone for hurting you.'

Josh grimaced, because he hadn't told Emma about what had gone on before the affair. She wasn't holding all the facts, if he was honest. Still. This was surprising.

'But how do you do it?' he asked. 'Like, practically – how do you do it?'

His mum was standing at the back door of her unit, watching him work in her small back garden. She was leaning on the doorframe. He'd expected her to be livid on his behalf, but, actually, she didn't seem shocked; actually, she looked as happy as he'd ever seen her.

'You just do it, Josh,' she said. 'It's a choice. Like everything. Whenever you feel that anger and injustice, you let yourself feel it, but then you let it go. If you can't, you're not forgiving, so don't pretend you can, and move on.'

'When did you become so Zen, Mum?' He looked back to the chair in hand.

She laughed. 'A very, very long time ago. No choice.'

'Hmmm.' Josh turned the chair over, wiggled it to see if it was sturdy. 'And you think I should forgive, right?'

'I can't answer that for you,' said Emma. 'But I'd say that a family is full of secrets and mistakes. You know that. At the end of the day, you just have to be able to live with yourself.' She paused. 'And so does Lou.'

'How long does forgiveness take?'

'Depends how much you dwell,' she said. 'Decide what you need to know, Josh, that's my advice. Not more. Not less.' And she turned and headed into the kitchen to put the kettle on.

He smiled to himself, perhaps for the first time in a long while, because all these years he'd thought he was pushing his father's rage down inside him, but it turned out he really was his mother's son.

'One chair down,' he said as his mother returned to the doorway. And then, 'You don't seem surprised.'

'She's a woman who wants,' said Emma. 'She always has been. She thinks she's so different from her mother, but she's not – not really. She wants things.'

'Fuck.' Josh started on the next chair. 'That is depressing. Lou would hate it if she heard you say that.'

'What's wrong with wanting?' asked Emma. 'It's human. Your wife is human. And she's lucky to have an anchor like you.'

Josh wanted to hug her, this small, slight woman with her soft, lined skin and her non-grey hair. But he had a crappy table to build.

Don't ever die, Mum, he found himself thinking. Don't ever leave me.

*

Emma held him hard on the deck in the backyard as the birthday party rolled on around them. 'Happy birthday, Josh,' she said into his chest. 'Love you.'

'Love you, Mum,' he said, and he knew his voice was thick as he said it. Must be the beer.

'Happy you didn't throw all this away?' she asked him, motioning to the back garden, where Lou and Gretchen were now dancing with the girls, who should have been in bed hours ago and would be feral tomorrow.

'Shush, Mum, not now,' he said, but he put his arm around her and pulled her close to him. Yes, he thought. And I'm glad it wasn't taken from me.

'Anika wants to talk about Christmas and Maya's avoiding her,' Emma said. 'You might need to go try some peace-making.'

'Sure.' But Josh was watching Lou, laughing with Gretchen. She was wearing a blue-and-white sundress that he knew she'd bought in the sales last week because she'd shown it to him and asked him if he liked it, saying it was for the school Christmas picnic, the liar. Her hair was down and she looked happy. Actually happy. Maybe things were going to be okay after all.

Josh looked around, his mum still tucked under his arm.

He could see Rob, Lou's brother, talking to Mick about the renovation he was planning for his new house in Paddington. Rob was thinking about starting his own practice and converting his house with a surgery downstairs and a two-storey home upstairs. Josh knew Mick would be seeing dollar signs in his eyes about that one.

He could hear, behind him, his brother-in-law Ed, talking about trees. About how one of his wealthy finance clients had just paid someone to poison a row of gums that stood between his new house and a harbour view. How now the council had strung up a huge sign between the dying trees, calling out poisoners, and Ed's rich mate had to look at it from his balcony every day. 'As if he gives a fuck,' Ed was saying. 'He knows the sign will be gone one day and he's tripled the value of his property.'

Brian, his father-in-law, had mercifully stopped talking about Brexit and was now complaining to one of the school dads about the plans for the new light rail. 'Why we all have to pay for public transport whether we use it or not, I'll never know,' he was saying loudly. 'I'll never set foot on the thing, but my tax dollars are being handed over to some bloody foreign company to build it, aren't they?'

Sydney conversations, thought Josh.

Emma slipped away to find Anika, and Josh's eyes went back to Lou, spinning around with Stella, hair flying, their heads back in a laugh. This is one of those rare moments, he thought. When they come, you're meant to remember them. He should go and join them.

'You know, all of this is despite you,' a voice said at his shoulder. The accent was unmistakably Annabelle's. 'Not because of you.'

He looked around and his mother-in-law was standing close behind him. She had a glass in her hand, and the way she was holding it, gripping it tightly around the sticky-finger-marked bowl, made him think she must have had several of them. 'Hello, Annabelle.'

'Happy birthday, Joshua,' she said.

'I don't think I heard what you were saying before,' he said. 'But I hope you're having a good time.'

'This house . . .' She gestured with her glass, the white wine sloshing slightly. 'This family. Lou's done it all. With our help, obviously.' And she coughed a dry laugh that didn't sound like a laugh at all. 'Women are the builders, Josh, no matter how many tables you make.'

Josh nodded. 'That's true, Annabelle.'

'I'm glad you know it is,' she said. 'You are a lucky, lucky man, marrying my daughter.'

'You should tell her that,' Josh sighed. He suddenly felt exhausted, heavy, his buoyant mood of seconds ago evaporated. How were they here now? He looked over to Lou, hoping to signal for help, but she was still lost in her dance. He looked around for Rob, but he was still deep in conversation with Mick. 'She'd like to hear it from you.'

'Don't tell me about my daughter,' Annabelle hissed. 'One day she's going to realise how much you hold her back.'

'Excuse me, Annabelle.' Josh turned to walk away but Annabelle grabbed his sleeve.

'You know it's true.'

'I'm going to find my sister, Annabelle, thank you.'

He had only gone a few steps when she called after him, 'It's not too late for her to realise this lovely home might be lovelier without you in it.'

She'd said it just loud enough to cause heads to turn, including Lou's.

Josh kept walking. But Annabelle wasn't finished.

'That's if she hasn't realised already!'

The music clicked off. The evening suddenly felt chilly, and Josh, heading for the stairs at his surprise birthday party, could sense people around him going quiet. He could hear his wife saying to her mother, 'Mum! Stop it! Dad, help me!'

'She knew you'd never be enough for her,' Annabelle called to Josh's back. 'We all knew it!'

Lou

AUGUST
Be the very best
you can be

Ryan Harcourt had started hanging back at lunchtimes, kicking his feet on the linoleum floor to make an infuriating squeak as he sidled up to Lou at her desk.

Squeak, squeak, squeak.

'Need anything, Ryan?' she'd ask him, half smiling, half stern. 'What can I help you with?'

'Nothing, miss,' he'd say. But then he'd find a reason to linger. 'I don't think I got that numbers thing today, miss,' he'd say. 'I'm too dumb for it.'

And Lou would look at Ryan's pout and tell him no, of course he wasn't too dumb for it, and of course she'd go over it again with him.

When the bell went at 3 p.m., Ryan Harcourt never wanted to be the first one on the playground. He knew his mum wouldn't be there early, and that he hadn't been signed up for after-school care like some of the other kids, and he had no desire to be the last one standing by Lou's side as the suburb's pick-up parents watched on.

Often, he just hung back near the door, but today Lou had taken the class out and stood nodding and smiling through all the collections, all the parents who, ignoring the stern emailed warnings that this was not the time to talk, asked for 'a quick chat'. At some point, she turned around and realised she'd lost Ryan. That he'd never left the classroom.

Squeak, squeak, squeak. She heard him before she reached the door.

'What's going on, Ryan?' she asked as she entered the classroom. 'Why aren't you outside?'

'Is my mum there?' he asked, looking at his feet.

'Not yet, Ryan, but we can wait together. She'll come – she always does.'

And she always did. But Ryan Harcourt's mum worked as a cleaner at the local club, and if they'd had a big morning function, like the seniors' bingo, she'd be stuck sorting it out way past lunchtime, and there was no way she could tell her boss she needed to leave early.

Lou had learned all this holding Ryan Harcourt's hand as they waited for pick-up on many days this year. She had also figured out that if she put him far from Andrea Frick and next to Jose Taos, who was quiet but tough as nails, Ryan would be less likely to erupt and that would buy her some time to deal with Amber Lin, who'd just had her ADHD medication changed and was impossible to keep still after lunchtime, or Daniel Olsson who was so anxious about maths that every time a number flashed up on the interactive board he'd start to cry.

As she and Ryan sat in the playground this afternoon, Lou was assessing her campaign to get some flexible after-school care places funded by the P&C for kids like Ryan.

His mum finally turned up, her face pinched with stress, gushing her apologies while avoiding eye contact, in case Ryan's teacher should look disapproving.

I'm not judging you, lady, Lou thought. You should see the mess my life is in right now.

There was a staff meeting scheduled for 4 p.m., and she was going to bring up the after-care places again. Not, as Gretchen suggested, purely as a distraction from thinking about the trial separation, but because it was something she could control. And getting life back under control was part of Lou's new plan.

8. Be the very best you can be, she'd written in her notes app. *Stay strong for your girls. Test your limits.*

She'd signed up to train for a marathon, something she had never done before, and had stepped up her running training on nights she didn't have the girls. Reacquainted herself with the local athletics field, assigned herself some achievable goals. It's what all the self-optimisation experts advised.

'Self-optimisation?' Gretchen had asked as she cleared the spare room so that Lou could stay there when it wasn't her turn in the nest. 'That sounds inhuman.'

'It's the more positive version of self-help,' Lou told her. She'd been reading a lot of blogs. 'Needing "help" makes you sound like a victim. Optimisation says you know you're already pretty excellent, you just need some strategic upgrades.'

'This version of you is killing me,' Gretchen told her, with arms full of shoeboxes. 'It's like living with fucking Oprah. If you post an inspirational quote on Instagram next, we're done.'

'I'm just trying to keep my shit together,' Lou said. 'Bit of support might be nice, Gretch.'

Support was also what she was looking for at the staff meeting. But instead, there was Theo. Rumours were swirling that Theo was leaving, but since Lou still had him blocked on her phone, and was making an extreme effort not to talk to him about anything personal at all, she didn't know if this was true.

She slipped in late to the meeting and stood near the door, her back against the wall, trying not to make eye contact with him.

A lot had changed for Theo since their 'thing' almost three years ago. His Melbourne fiancée never had moved to Sydney, and they had split. He'd bought a house near the school, to show his commitment to the area and was supposedly dating a local councillor with a special interest in local education. He was still 'holding on' for Gabbie's job, since if the grapevine was to be believed she had been tapped to head up a new state-of-the-art public school in the eastern suburbs. He was trying hard not to be bitter about *that*.

Theo was almost as cocky as he had been when they first met, but his bravado was sagging a little at the seams, around his chin, his waistline. He didn't do fortnightly WIPs with everyone in his bucket anymore; he just stuck to the staffroom meetings, like everyone else did. He'd stopped telling people they 'added value'. No-one had seen him doing chin-ups in the male toilets for some time.

'Hi, Lou!' he called across the room loudly as she came in, as he did to everyone individually. 'Good day?'

She nodded and smiled politely, seeking out Beth to talk to about Ryan Harcourt. But then Theo was there, next to her. 'Have you heard about your job yet?' he asked.

'No,' Lou answered. Theo knew that was the answer, of course he did. As deputy principal, he would know if she'd been made head of the year before she would.

'I'm sure you're a shoo-in,' he said. 'Just waiting for the rubber stamp.'

Lou nodded. 'Thanks.'

'You should probably ease off on this after-care project though,' he added quietly. 'Not core school business. Probably won't help in the selection.'

'That's not why I'm doing it,' she answered.

'Oh.' Theo looked genuinely confused. 'Then why are you?'

Lou shook her head, turned back to the room, just as Gabbie was coming in to start the meeting.

'Have you been working out?' Theo whispered. 'You look great.'

Lou pushed off the wall and moved away to stand near Beth.

*

'JoJo's pissed that you're taking *her* room,' Gretchen said that evening as Lou, tired from the long day – she wasn't used to the commute – walked down the hall to the spare room to dump her coat and bag.

'I won't be here that often.' Every time Lou thought about it, staying here while her girls slept forty minutes away in a house without her in it, she wanted to cry.

'I think she's reconsidered that divorce advice she gave you.' Gretchen lounged against the doorframe. 'Smart kid's figured that bit out.'

'I can't believe I did that.' Lou slipped off her shoes and sat on the bed. 'Pumped a teenager for marriage advice.' She smoothed the linen bedcover with her hand. Staying at Gretch's place was a little like staying at a fancy resort. Someone had clearly ironed these sheets, and Lou doubted it was her friend.

'Any regrets?'

Lou shook her head, but her shoulders were slumped. 'We've got to figure it out,' she said. 'Sooner or later.'

'Well, you can stay here as long as you want,' said Gretchen. 'But as much as it's like old times, I hope it's not for too long. I'm rooting for you two to get back together. It's not about you – it's about me. I need a functional role-model relationship in my life.'

'For you and Kim?' Gretchen and Kim were planning a trip together, which counted as a major commitment for Gretchen.

'And for JoJo,' Gretchen said. 'She needs to see that not everything has to go to shit. Even though it usually does.'

'Have you spoken to Josh?' Lou looked up at Gretchen, who grabbed her hands to pull her off the bed.

'No, I don't need that kind of negativity in my life.'

'That's not fair, Gretch.'

'He's sad, Lou. You can't pretend he isn't.'

Lou hadn't spoken to him either, other than to talk logistics about who needed to be where with what to deal with the girls at any one time. They were meant to be confining any more communication than that to Sara's office. They had an appointment next week and Lou was almost looking forward to it, which was not what she was expecting.

'Come on, Gwyneth, you're not self-optimising sitting there looking like someone stole the olive out of your martini. Let's go.'

'Where?'

'Gym and Japanese. Come on.'

'Theo asked me today if I'd been working out,' Lou said.

'Blatant come-on. No-one has ever asked anyone if they've been working out if they didn't want to see them naked.'

'Well, technically, he already has . . .'

'I know that. I don't want to talk about him, Lou. You're not thinking of going back there, are you?' Gretchen was looking as seriously disapproving as it was possible to look in day-glo active-wear. 'I mean, I know you could *technically* be dating at the moment. But there are less troublesome options for sex, my friend, I'm sure of it.'

Lou didn't say anything. She wasn't thinking of it. She really wasn't. But there was just a tiny piece of her, the same one that had sat behind the red car in the car park with her keys in the ignition, that thought, Why not? It might make you feel better.

No, no, no. What will make you feel better is discipline. Eating vegetables, staying positive, working towards your goal, being a good mum, steps clocked up on the running track, helping Ryan Harcourt to overcome his dread of the school bell. *Come on.*

Josh

AUGUST
Be the very best
you can be

I will not be sad today, Josh thought, as he parked his car in the underground car park.

I will not be sad today, he said to himself, as he pushed the parking ticket into the back pocket of his jeans and pushed the button for the lift.

'I will not be sad today,' he whispered almost silently as he bounced in place, watching the numbers move up through the floors, all the way to the therapist's office.

The lift doors opened and he immediately saw the back of his wife disappearing through the door at the end of the hall that led to Sara's office. His heart rose at the familiar sight of Lou. In that momentary glimpse, he'd seen she was wearing school clothes – a shirt dress, a denim jacket, those trainers Gretchen had brought back from New York that she said were smart enough for class. That bag over her shoulder was the one her mum had told her she needed to replace because it had scuffs, and Lou had laughed and told her that leather looked better battered and the kids had laughed at the way that sounded. Her hair was down, which meant she'd washed it this morning. In their shower at home, with the kids not putting on their shoes downstairs after breakfast. Lou's was the most familiar back in his life. Heading into their marriage counsellor's office.

No. I won't be sad today, Josh told himself. It's not bloody helping, sitting here stewing, begrudging.

It had been six weeks. Almost six weeks since he'd had sex with his wife and then left to sleep in the workshop. Six weeks of waking up and working out which hat he was wearing today – was he his sister's house guest, trying not to make her life harder, rubbing along with the teenage boys, filling time he wasn't used to having? Or was he Single Dad, racing to pick-up and trying to remember whether it was gymnastics day or choir day or whether there was a birthday party or a teachers' meeting?

It was impossibly sad being in the house without Lou, but also, his girls were there. So it was this weird mixture of abundance and absence, and . . . No. I will not be sad today.

'Hi, Lou.'

She was sitting on a straight-backed chair in the waiting room when he walked through the door, phone in hand.

'Hi.' She looked up quickly, gave a little wave. She was wearing some shiny lip stuff. For him?

'How are the girls?' Such a strange question to ask your wife in this context.

'Rita's got an earache, Stell's scared about a maths test.' Lou was looking at her phone again. 'But they're fine.'

'Are you okay to take time off from school this afternoon?' Josh sat down a couple of seats away from Lou. Next to her would be weird.

'I'm being covered, but I'll have to get straight back. You?'

'We're on a different job this week – shop fit-out in Alexandria. Tyler's on it. It's fine.'

Small talk.

The receptionist acknowledged Josh's presence with a smile. She must see some things in here, he thought.

And here came Sara, all smiles, to usher them into her blindingly bright office.

'Did you ever think of getting some blinds in here?' Lou asked her, before they sat on the couch.

Josh had to stifle a laugh, because that's what she'd always said she was going to ask Sara one day, when she'd stopped being a little bit scared of her. Clearly, that day had come.

'I love the view, the natural light,' said Sara. 'And, you know, sunlight is cleansing. You know what they say, shame can only exist in shadow.' She smiled brightly.

'Oh, that's interesting,' Lou said, apparently disarmed by the answer. She started tapping something into her phone. Josh was certain she was writing, *Shame can only exist in shadow*. Then Lou put her phone into her scuffed leather bag and looked up expectantly. 'Still,' she said, 'it's a bit squinty.'

Josh did actually laugh, and both women looked at him, Lou swallowing a smile, Sara a bit surprised.

'So, we're here to check in on the progress of the trial separation,' Sara said firmly. 'Who'd like to start?'

*

Josh had stopped himself obsessing about whether Lou was sleeping with someone else by sheer force of will.

His mind was too free to go there when he was working so he'd started wearing headphones on the job.

Well, she's done it before . . . Quick, there must be a podcast worth listening to.

That guy at the fundraising concert . . . Turn up the volume on that song you were studying for chord inspiration.

She could do so much better than you . . . Radio National, I am finally old enough for you.

Avoidance, yes. Denial, possibly. But essential if he was to keep moving, to keep from falling into the kind of angry pit that consumed people. Sad men. People like him.

He worked alongside Tyler most days, but Josh couldn't bring himself to talk about his marriage with his workmate, who'd been through all this before. If Tyler suspected anything, he never said so.

'Are you lonely?' Anika had asked Josh when he entered the kitchen one night, having been locked in her garage with his guitar since he got home from work.

'I don't think so, not yet,' he answered, and he meant it. He was writing. He had nothing to do with the songs he was creating, no place to take them, but it felt good to get them out.

'Play me what you've been working on,' his sister suggested.

'No way, they're all break-up songs, sad as hell,' he said, moving around her towards the fridge.

'My kind of thing, then,' Anika had said.

But Josh just shook his head. He wasn't ready.

So life revolved around work, the girls, his sister's house, the guitar. It was small. That was the safest option for now.

*

'It's giving me time to think,' Lou said, in the therapist's office. 'I'm really trying to be present with myself, get myself in the strongest possible place to make good choices.'

Josh looked at her, eyes wide. And she looked at him and raised her eyebrows, like, *What?*

'Why are you talking like you've swallowed a self-help book?' he asked Lou, a smile tugging at his lips.

'That's a bit aggressive, Josh,' Sara said. 'Remember, this is not an adversarial space.'

'It's not self-help,' said Lou. Josh could have sworn that she too was trying not to laugh. 'It's self-optimisation.'

'It's what, now?'

'Lou's choice to work on herself is perfectly valid, Josh,' Sara scolded. 'We don't mock in here.'

'I'm growing,' Lou said firmly. Her mouth was definitely twitching. 'I've set goals and I want to achieve them. I'm taking a very disciplined, wide-awake approach.'

'Oh, good for you.' Josh slapped his knee.

'This is excellent, Lou. You can't possibly make informed decisions about your relationship and family unit unless you are dealing with your own happiness first.' Sara seemed truly delighted. She looked at Josh. 'It's that whole "put your own mask on first before helping others" idea – you know, from the flight safety instructions.'

'Oh, right.' Josh felt an overwhelming urge to giggle. He had no idea why he was finding it so funny that Lou appeared to have had a personality transplant, when usually he would find it intensely irritating. Perhaps it was because she didn't appear to be taking it particularly seriously herself.

Lou turned to him. 'Maybe you could handle some self-optimisation yourself. I have some books you can borrow.'

'Now, Lou, don't push Josh to follow you down this path,' said Sara. 'Remember, it's not uncommon for one half of a couple to feel threatened by the other's personal growth.'

Josh spoke across Sara. 'That would be great, Lou. I'm sure some books on how to be less of a loser would really help.' His words were harsh, but he wasn't upset, and he could tell Lou wasn't either.

The therapist looked at them, appearing a little confused. 'Are you two aware that eighty per cent of communication is non-verbal?' she asked. 'Many experts think that *what* you say is not actually as important as *how* you say it.'

'Really?' Lou and Josh chorused, then exchanged looks out of the corners of their eyes.

'And right now, you two appear to be disagreeing about something, but the energy is really quite different.' Sara looked up from her notes. 'I'd say this is a very positive sign.'

'Hear that, Lou?' Josh asked. 'We're getting better at fighting with each other in our therapist's office. That's progress.'

I will not be sad today, he said to himself, in the pool of bright light on the couch.

And I'm not.

Lou

11 November, 2017

'**Y**ou are welcome in our house, Mum,' Lou said. 'Under strict conditions. And the main one is that you are decent to my husband, your son-in-law, the father of my children.'

Lou was inviting her parents over for a dinner to celebrate her and Josh's anniversary. Nine years. It was a thing in their family, she'd decided, to make a big deal out of the unremarkable milestones. So, a big party for your thirty-ninth, not your fortieth; a family dinner for the ninth wedding anniversary, not the tenth. 'You're just trying to be different for the sake of it,' her mother had told her sniffily, when the invitation was first proffered. 'Honestly, BB, there's a reason for traditions, you know.'

But if Annabelle was going to come, sniffiness must be put aside. And if she was going to come, a year of tentative avoidance had to be broached.

'It's not like I haven't seen him in a year,' she said. 'And it's not like I haven't apologised.'

'I know, Mum, but you've seen him in passing, at family things. This is a sit-down dinner at our *house*. It's different. And I need to know it's going to be okay.'

'It's going to be okay,' Annabelle said.

'And it wasn't much of an apology,' Lou muttered. 'I'm going to find Dad.'

November was a big month in the Poole house, with Josh's birthday and their wedding anniversary. And almost a year ago, after Annabelle had said what she said at the surprise party, it looked like family celebrations wouldn't be on the calendar again any time soon.

But Josh was more forgiving than most – as Lou knew too well, she thought, then pushed the thought away – and Annabelle had her excuses ready.

'I'm on some new blood-pressure medication,' she'd said to Josh, when Lou had forced them together to talk it out. 'And I should not have drunk a sip of alcohol, never mind all that champagne. It sent me completely doolally; I can barely recall anything I said.'

'I can,' said Josh. 'But let's move on. We've all said things we shouldn't after a few too many.'

It was gracious, but it wasn't game-changing. Josh didn't rush to spend time with Lou's family, and Annabelle wasn't rushing to reverse the perception that she thought her son-in-law could do a better job of providing for his family.

Today, Lou was at her mum and dad's place to collect the kids. They'd spent the afternoon there while she'd sorted things out for tonight. Collected a cake, cleaned the house. Why did family gatherings always land on her plate? She knew the answer. Josh would be happy not to have them, and if she wanted them, she had to make them happen.

She found Brian with Stella and Rita in his shed. It was a space that couldn't be more different from Josh's equivalents – the workshop and his guitar room, both of which were chaotic, while this was an impeccably organised area of calm. Brian had been an engineer for his entire working life, and order, structure and detail were what made his world turn.

He had the girls organising nails into various sizes in a large plastic tray divided into satisfyingly proportional spaces. They were engrossed.

'Um, Dad,' Lou said, after she'd doled out kisses to all, 'Rita's three. Is playing with nails an appropriate activity?'

'The girls are having a marvellous time, darling,' said Brian, going back to dusting his hanging tools. 'She's learned not to spike herself – responsibility. And children love order too, you see?'

You wouldn't think so if you saw our house, Lou thought, but she knew better than to say so. She needed to get going; there were still twenty-five jobs that needed doing before she could have people in her home tonight.

'I'm worried about Mum and Josh at the dinner tonight,' she said. 'Should I be?'

Brian looked pointedly at the girls, then took Lou's elbow and guided her back out through the shed's door.

'Your mother hasn't been herself lately,' he said. 'She's worried about me.'

'Dad, that was a year ago, never mind lately.' Lou looked at him suspiciously. 'And what's wrong with you?'

'Nothing, nothing.' He glanced back at the shed. 'I'm just getting a bit forgetful, which is completely natural at my age, but I think your mother finds it a bit confronting. You know . . . Life, death. Et cetera.'

'Okay.' Lou couldn't tell if her dad was fobbing her off. 'Life, death et cetera sounds serious.' She pushed the thought away. She had enough to worry about already. 'But what about tonight?'

'I want to tell you something about your mother,' Brian said.

He put his hands on Lou's shoulders and pulled her close to him, looking directly into her eyes. This was highly unusual.

'You are everything to her, BB. You and Robert, and me, and the girls. She has no family. You have to remember that.'

'She had Nana Belmore . . .' Lou vaguely remembered a child-hood visit from her grandmother who smelled of toast.

'No. She left all her people behind.' Brian shook Lou, ever so gently. 'Her childhood was hard, and she cut her ties. It creates a siege mentality, darling, being rootless.'

'Rootless?'

'You're not listening. I'm trying to tell you' – he kissed her on the forehead, something she couldn't ever remember him doing – 'your mother's love is stronger than anything. But it's exclusive. She sees everyone from outside as a threat. Even your husband.'

Lou looked at Brian. It was a Saturday afternoon in November, her young children were playing with deadly DIY equipment on a shed floor, and her father had just delivered one of the truth-bombs of her life. Her mother trusted no-one. Everyone was the enemy. The neighbours. The teachers at school. Their friends. Their partners. Everyone but them. She couldn't remember her father ever talking quite so eloquently about anything as intangible as emotions before.

'Dad,' she said, 'that was *profound*.'

He let go of her shoulders, turned back towards the shed. 'Be kind to your mother. There are advantages to that kind of thinking, you know, even if it might seem harsh. Her loyalty is unshakable. I am a lucky man in that regard.'

Lou felt that comment as a little jab to the kidneys, although she knew he couldn't possibly have meant it that way. 'You are, Dad,' she said. 'Thank you.'

She called to the girls to leave the organising and come. And back in the car, with Stella and Rita strapped in, she called Josh.

'Babe,' she said, 'I've just found out why my mum is such a red-hot bitch to you.'

'Oh good,' said Josh. 'Now can you work out how to turn it off?'

Josh

Later that month

Josh had made Lou a picture frame for their wedding anniversary. It was long and slender, made from the slats of their old bed, his obsession with never wasting wood at an all-time high.

'Are you telling me,' Lou asked, as she looked at the frame, which had been divided into a series of smaller frames, containing pictures of the two of them, the girls, their family, 'that we've basically had sex on this picture frame? Like, lots?'

It was the kind of thing Lou said when she was in a good mood, and he laughed.

'Yes, it's a celebration sex-frame,' he said, leaning in to kiss her. 'Nine years, and we're still here.'

Josh always thought of his father on his wedding anniversary.

It was a shitty memory among a whole host of beautiful ones of that day. His old man walking away with Christine and that crappy little leather holdall. He'd gone over it in his mind any number of times, wondering if there had been another way to play that moment, but he always came up blank. It was what it was, as Maya would say.

That morning, he brought Lou the frame in bed, with a cup of tea and his kiss. It was a Monday, and everyone had to go to work. The girls were already banging around downstairs; there was no time for sentimentality.

'Happy anniversary, Lou,' he said. 'Thank you for organising that family dinner where no-one insulted anyone to death.'

'Pleasure,' said Lou. 'May there be many more family gatherings with no blood spilled.'

And she lay back to look at the frame as Josh turned to head downstairs.

'Wait,' Lou called. 'There's someone missing from these pictures.'

'Who?'

'Your father,' she said. 'He should be here. Especially today.'

And she looked at him, and for a moment, Josh suddenly felt like he was about to cry.

'He might have been a bit of a prick,' Lou said, with a gentle smile, 'but he made you. He's part of us. I'll put in one of the pics of him and baby Stella when I get home tonight.'

Josh came back to the bed and took the frame from her hands, lay it down on the bed and hugged her hard. So hard.

'Thank you,' he said. 'I love you.'

'Happy anniversary,' said Lou, her voice muffled in his shoulder. 'Nine years. We're fucking insufferable right now.'

In that moment, from their bed in Botany, Josh could see that other insufferable moment, on the banks of the river in the Snowys. They never had moved to New York. Or Arnhem Land. He had never built them a house in a tropical rainforest, and Lou still hadn't written a play. Their life had been smaller than the one they'd imagined.

But he knew, like he'd known on that day nine years before. He'd found someone to help him be strong in the face of the shit that made him weak.

And they were still standing. Just.

Lou

I give my separation four months.

The weirdest thing, Lou tapped into her phone, *is the silence.*

One minute I'm at home, with all the noise and mess and the hundreds of tiny eruptions of chaos that kids bring every day.

And then I'm here. And there's no mess. And there's no noise. And there's only order. And it's . . .

What was it? Lou looked around Gretchen's apartment, where Gretchen wasn't. It was beautiful, and white, and relentlessly clean. She had settled into the guest room, complete with TV and Netflix and a gift from Gretchen – a still-boxed vibrator in the bedside drawer.

. . . it's not home. It's like a holiday from my life.

Which made it sound nice. Look, don't be ungrateful, Lou told herself, it *is* nice. For a few days, it felt like a lifted weight, like a rediscovery of herself. But three nights in a row was enough.

Too much.

Lou had a list of reasons why this separation continued to be a Good Idea. She had specifically written it to read in moments of doubt. She read it every fucking night she was at Gretchen's.

9. Try the single life.
Pros:
1. SPACE to think.
2. SPACE to not get on each other's nerves while we think.
3. A test of what life would really be like if we split.
4. A chance to miss each other – or not.
5. A chance to assess whether external influences (this was a euphemism and Lou wasn't sure why she was bothering to use it on her own password-protected phone) *are truly significant, or just distracting.*
6. A chance to test the impact on the girls of zero family time.
7. Opportunity for therapy to do its work.

Of course, it was still 'separation lite'. Life was still being funded by two wages going into a joint account; she wasn't living in one of those flats she'd been looking at on her Rent app for months. And, crucially, hardly anyone knew.

Hardly anyone.

'Is it true you're leaving?' Lou had asked Theo. She had gone to his office, knocking on the door with her heart pounding, feeling foolish about feeling foolish for talking to him.

'Why?' he asked her. 'You haven't given me any sense you give a shit lately.' He was sitting at his desk, which was messier than it used to be but still looked too small for him, his jacket on the back of the chair, his shirt sleeves rolled up.

'Well, I don't, not really,' she said. 'But there are some things we need to clear up.'

'I am leaving,' he said. 'I'm going back to Melbourne. I can't keep waiting for Gabbie to die.'

Lou raised an eyebrow.

'Figure of speech,' he said, and gave a short, barking laugh. 'Turns out she doesn't want that other job.'

It's funny talking to people you've had sex with, Lou found herself thinking. People who you're not having sex with anymore. Even when you've stopped wanting them, you've always got the context that once you did. And you know more about them than you're comfortable with. Like what face they make when they come.

Of course, they know that about you, too. Lou found herself doing up her top shirt button as she stood there.

'Okay.' She shifted her weight from one foot to the other. Why did she feel weird saying this? 'I feel like all year I've been giving you mixed messages.'

'No shit!' Theo said, a little too loudly. 'The year got off to such a promising start. And then . . .' He mimed an explosion, making the whistling noise of a plane going down.

What a dick. Honestly.

'Well, what I wanted to say, and I should have said this a long time ago, is that it's really definitely over. It was. It should have been in the first place. January should never have happened. We should have left it when we left it. I want to draw a line. Stop any confusion.'

'You mean the confusion of you messaging and not messaging me, blocking me and unblocking me?' Theo's voice was mocking now. 'Were you genuinely confused? Or do you just like to tease?'

'Don't be . . .' Lou pulled a face.

'What? Don't be what?'

'Gross,' Lou said. She lowered her voice. 'I'm not a teenager, and this isn't the place for this conversation, Theo.'

'Well, you walked in and started having it, Lou,' Theo said, his fingers drumming on his desk. 'Just like you were the one who started this thing, all that time ago. And you were the one who invited me over to your house on New Year's Day. *You*, not me.'

'Alright, well . . .' Lou was feeling embarrassed, more than a little uncomfortable about his version of events. 'There's no need to be a dick about it.'

'Don't worry about it, Lou,' he said. 'I got bored of this little game of yours a long time ago. And I'm out of this ridiculous, old-fashioned school before the end of term four. So you can stop looking so tortured.'

'I'm not tortured,' Lou said. 'I just know that if I were to be with anyone who wasn't my husband, it wouldn't be you. It might have taken me longer than it should have to see that clearly, but I have.'

It was time to go. Lou turned.

'I hear he's moved out,' Theo called after her. 'You'd better get on the dating apps, Lou. That's where all the action is. If you've got the guts for it.'

'Fuck off,' Lou said, to his face, before she turned again. This time, she left.

*

Not my finest moment, Lou reflected. Where was the witty comeback when you needed one?

Must focus on the positives, she wrote, then padded into Gretchen's kitchen, wearing nothing but an oversized T-shirt and those expensive midlife slippers they were always trying to sell you on Facebook. Her brother had bought them for her birthday in June, with much sarcasm.

Gretchen was away on a trip with Kim. An all-expenses-paid trip to some island location with overwater bungalows and vegan orchids on your pillows. 'I can work anywhere these days, Lou, so

I am succumbing to being a trailing spouse for a while,' she'd said as she packed. 'My house is your house, as it always has been. Text me if you need me.'

'Do they even have reception in paradise?'

'Of course they fucking do,' Gretchen said, shoving more shoes into her bulging bag. 'Their whole business model is based on making people who have to be constantly connected feel like they're disconnected. Their wifi's better than you've got at school.'

'That wouldn't be difficult.'

It really wasn't so bad, this weird in-between life, Lou told herself again. Three days at Gretchen's, four days at home, then swap. Four days at Gretchen's, three days at home, then swap. Half frazzled homemaker, half single-woman-at-leisure.

The handful of mum-friends who knew what was going on told her they were jealous. She'd had to confide in a few for pick-up/drop-off help on 'her' days; she didn't want Josh picking the girls up from school then – it didn't feel right for her to get home and him to be there and then leave.

'Oh my God, three days kid-free, you're so lucky!'

'Not having to worry about your husband! Heaven, he's like my third fucking child.'

'A whole weekend without the girls! Are you going to go *wild*?'

Lou wanted to punch these women in the face. *It feels like a holiday from my life* was true, but it didn't look like the brochure.

Sometimes, if she let the silence wash over her as she lay on Gretchen's lounge, she was consumed by panic. What was Stella doing right now? What was Rita eating? Josh never remembered to lock the front door. Every night they'd lived there she'd be checking those locks before they went to sleep. Sometimes he'd nod off without remembering to close the sliding doors at the back. Anything could happen.

Breathe.

And what if Rita just wanted to go and find the cute puppy from next door and the front door was open?

Breathe.

What if they were having a better time with him than they did with her? (They definitely would be; Josh had never been very good at putting his foot down.)

Breathe.

What if they didn't miss her at all? What if they hated her for doing this to their lives?

Fucking breathe, Lou, she told herself.

So she couldn't let the silence get to her, and filled her non-girls days with as much busy-business as was possible.

In the last month, she'd gone out for drinks with the new young teachers at work more than she ever had previously.

She'd binge-watched seasons one to five of *Mad Men*, and resolved to buy more turtlenecks and silk shirts.

She'd caught up with old friends she'd barely seen since uni days, suddenly feeling the need to 'reach out' on Facebook to people entirely irrelevant to her existence. One of those catch-ups had led to a memorable night in Kings Cross, a place she'd forgotten existed, where she was almost certain she had been propositioned by a football player, and had definitely spent twenty-two dollars on one martini. One of many.

Before Gretchen went away, she'd been taking her to Barre Body classes to try to focus Lou on something positive that involved neither rekindling ill-advised affairs, martinis or panic attacks. And Lou had never felt so old or lumpy as she had when standing next to her friend (who was exactly the same age) on one leg, trying to grab at a rubber band around her ankle.

Running was a more reliable proposition, an old friend who wouldn't take her out and get her drunk.

And then there was her mother.

Annabelle did not know about her and Josh's separation, but ever since Josh's devastatingly shit play-acting at her birthday barbecue, she could smell trouble.

Annabelle had taken to calling Lou at unusual times, just to ask, 'Where are you?' and, 'What's Josh doing?' and, 'Can I pop around and see the girls?'

'Don't pop around now, Mum, the house is a state, but Saturday would be good. Or Thursday night, but not Tuesday. No, a surprise visit really wouldn't be good . . .'

This holiday from her real life was very complicated.

*

In Gretchen's beautiful kitchen, Lou opened one of the apps everyone was telling her to try.

The single mums at school – 'Sex on tap, not much else.' Gretchen – 'Absolutely no-one meets anyone the way you and Josh met these days.' The non-single mothers at school – 'Oh, I'd love to have a play, it's like online shopping!' Fucking Theo.

She'd downloaded it just to look.

Swipe. There was a guy with bulging muscles, no shirt and a hunting dog. Swipe. There was a junior teacher from the girls' school. Swipe. There was a man wearing a *Make Australia Great Again* T-shirt. Swipe. There was a man with a warm smile whose description said, 'No fatties.' Swipe. Was that . . . Anika's ex-husband, Ed?

Yuck.

Lou put the phone back on the bench. Time to go for a run. Sex was not a priority. Dating was unthinkable until she and Josh had worked out what the hell they were doing.

Josh. Josh smiling on the therapist couch. Josh looking at her the way he looked at her.

What if *he* was ready? What if she swiped and saw her husband?

Lou picked the phone back up, held her finger on the app and deleted it.

Not. Now.

Josh

SEPTEMBER
Try the
single life

The sound of a chainsaw woke Josh up.

'No.'

He swung his legs off the edge of the bed and ran to the window. 'No!'

He was fumbling with the slatted blind. With Lou gone, he'd been closing it at night, something she'd never do. 'I like to see the light change,' she'd said, a hundred times, in the years he'd known her.

Then the window lock. 'NO!' He was shouting now.

'What is it, Daddy?' Stella was at the bedroom door, in her rainbow pyjamas, hair standing up at angles.

'Wait, baby.'

Finally, he clicked off the window lock and pushed it open, leaned out, looked down to the base of the tree.

No-one there.

Lycra Aiden from across the road, coming back from his morning bike ride, took off his helmet and looked up. 'You okay, Josh?'

Josh realised he was bare-chested, leaning out the window, red in the face, breathing hard.

'Yes, mate, sorry,' he called down. 'I thought I heard . . . never mind.'

Josh looked down the street. Nothing – just that woman who always watered her hedge before work, and Ahmed walking out to his motorbike. No chainsaw. No tree man.

Jesus.

'Daddy?'

'I'm sorry, baby, I must have had a bad dream,' said Josh. 'Let's go and make pancakes.'

'It's Wednesday, Daddy,' Stella said, her face very serious. 'We can't have pancakes on Wednesday.'

'Really? Oh, I guess not.' Josh pulled the window back down, flicked the lock. 'Let me get some clothes on. Is Rita still asleep? What time is it anyway?'

That fucking tree.

*

The school gate was weirder than the dreams Josh had been having.

Neither Lou nor Josh were meant to be telling anyone that they were separated, but word seemed to have got around, because Josh suddenly seemed to be the focus of some distinctly different attention.

Women who were friends of Lou's smiled from a distance and raised a cautious hand but did not approach. The sort of small talk they'd once shared while waiting for the girls was now clearly considered some sort of betrayal.

Strangers were more likely to come up and ask him outright – 'Is it true that you and Stella's mum have broken up?' The second time it happened, Josh, who didn't want his sister to say the words out loud, never mind a pitying acquaintance, just shook his head and walked away.

By the time a woman he'd never met before came up and offered to drop off a lasagne, Josh knew he was going to have to start waiting in the car. Lasagne, after all, was the internationally recognised dish of pity.

The day the lasagne offer happened, he went home and looked at himself in the mirror for a long time. Did he look terrible? Heartbroken, wasting away, unkempt? He couldn't tell. Certainly he looked tired. Sleeping was hard at the moment.

But mostly he was pissed off that word was out. Because how was the word going to go in again when they sorted all this shit out and got back together?

He suspected Dana.

A few weeks into the new arrangement, he'd inadvertently had coffee with Dana. Meaning, he was waiting for Rita to get out of gymnastics at the sports and rec centre, nursing a long black in the cafeteria and poking at his phone to try to extricate himself from his Eva Bernard membership, when Dana had sat down next to him.

'I heard Lou's moved out,' she said, by way of a hello.

'Not true,' said Josh, straight away.

'Has kicked you out then,' Dana said.

'Nope,' he said, looking pointedly at his phone which, in his rush to flick away from the screen that said, *Are you really ready to unsubscribe from the advice that could save your marriage?*, had ended up on the backup screen, the lyrics to 'Here Comes the Sun', which he'd been optimistically picking at late last night.

'Break-up song,' Dana said, pointing at his phone. She was certainly close enough to see it.

'You're insane,' said Josh. 'And anyway, no it's not. It's a love song. Everyone knows that.'

'Nooooo,' said Dana, sitting down next to him at the cafe table. 'He's pining for a better day.'

'It's the happiest song ever written!' Josh pushed his phone into his back pocket. 'Anyway, got to go get Rita. Bye.'

'Gymnastics doesn't finish for another twenty minutes, Josh, chill out.'

'Are you stalking me?' Josh asked, and Dana spat out her latte in a show of shock.

'We have kids the same age, you idiot, don't flatter yourself,' she said. 'I know when gymnastics is.'

And so Josh had sat back down. He wasn't really sure why. He knew that if Lou saw him, or even heard that he and Dana had been talking, she would hate it. But, then again, why should he care about that, when she was almost certainly sleeping with someone else, maybe someone called T? Damn it. He hadn't pushed the thought away, and it caused him to have a physical reaction, a pain in his stomach. Thinking about that was what stopped him from sleeping.

So he sat back down and changed the subject. He found himself telling Dana about the music producer he was working for in Camperdown. About how interesting it was to see her studio loading in, about how he'd googled her, and the list of the people she'd worked with was incredible. How on the two occasions he'd spoken to her, she was generous and interesting. He told Dana that when he'd started that job, he'd felt bitter and resentful and jealous, but now he felt impressed and maybe . . . if it didn't make him sound like a total dick . . . inspired.

'That's awesome,' said Dana. 'She's unbelievable. And you're working with her?'

'Um. No, I'm planing her pool deck.'

'But it's destiny! Anyone could be planing her pool deck.' Dana grabbed Josh's hand, and he immediately pulled it away, but she kept staring. 'You have to give her a song.'

'And I repeat, Dana, you're crazy.'

'I am not. I know you think so. But I need to tell you again: all that camping stuff was nuts. It was not me.'

'It looked like you,' Josh said. 'Sounded like you.'

'Marco has left,' she said. 'And to be honest, it's for the best. Nothing has been good between us for ages. I can't *stand* him, actually, although I know you're not supposed to say that. And I have no idea how I ended up married to someone I can't stand.'

Josh shifted uncomfortably on his stool. 'I'm sorry.'

'Don't be. I just worry about the kids. You must, too.'

Josh still couldn't tell her what she clearly already knew.

'Anyway, I know that was a bad scene, down the coast. I promise you, I just want to be friends.'

Josh was sure he must look dubious, but he repeated, 'Friends?'

'And a friend would tell you to give that music producer a song!' Dana whacked the Formica table with the palm of her hand.

'I am her middle-aged carpenter,' Josh said firmly. 'Do you have any idea how many idiots come up to people like her every day and give them songs or ask for a favour? I'm not that guy.'

'Clearly not,' said Dana, and she looked at Josh in a way that said this was not a Good Thing.

As he walked away, she called after him. Loudly. 'Lou's mad to give up on you!'

So yes, he blamed Dana for the lasagnes.

And for the fact that now, every time he caught a glimpse of the music producer onsite at the Camperdown warehouse, he felt a twinge of panicky excitement.

*

This morning, he was making the girls Vegemite sandwiches for their lunchboxes after he'd made them Vegemite toast for their breakfast.

One minor upside of Lou not being around was freedom from the Vegemite police, he told himself.

He was running late for his morning start, but on the days he had the girls, he always was. He'd told Mick he'd happily make up the time elsewhere, but Lou's new job had changed and she couldn't drop off every day at the moment. His old friend had looked at him through narrowed eyes and muttered about Camperdown's looming deadline. The irony, Josh knew, was that if he told Mick the truth, his friend would happily change the whole shape of the job to help.

'More Vegemite than butter, please Dad,' said Stella as she came to stand in the kitchen doorway, already dressed in her school uniform.

'More butter than Vegemite, Dad!' said Rita, behind her, still in her pyjamas with her hair standing on end.

'Reets! You're not ready – we've got to go!'

'I am ready,' said Rita. 'I've got my school shoes on.' And she proudly stuck out a foot to show that, along with her unicorn pyjama shorts, she was wearing knee-high white socks and shiny black sandals.

Josh looked up at the kitchen clock. Almost eight. By rights, he should have been at work half an hour ago. Shit.

'Come on, Reets, let's make that top half match the bottom half,' said Josh, and he grabbed her hand and headed for the stairs. 'Stella, can you finish those sandwiches off?' he called.

'Me?' His oldest daughter, so like him around the eyes, looked genuinely horrified. 'I can't pack my own lunch, Dad!'

'I think you can, Stell, I really do.'

At the top of the stairs he looked into the girls' room and saw the jumble on the floor where Rita had clearly been attempting to find her school clothes by pulling every last piece of clothing she owned out of her drawers and throwing them behind her. 'Shit.'

He scrambled around for her school polo shirt and skirt and threw them at her while he attempted to get the pile back where it had come from. Tonight was handover time; Lou would be bringing the girls home and he was heading back to Anika's. He couldn't have her coming back to this.

Josh didn't ever want Lou to walk back into the house and throw up her hands in disgust. If she was brooding about him in his absence, he refused to let it be because he made her life messier, harder. Not anymore. He wanted her to be brooding because she missed him.

That was his plan. If he exhausted her with his presence, he didn't want his absence to do the same damn thing. On his nights at home with the girls, he had come to realise the full impact of the evening shit show, the million tiny jobs that kept you busy till 10 p.m., from bath time to the endless bedtime rituals, tidying up from dinner and prepping for the morning, the bottomless washing. Alone, it was a lot. How much of this had Lou just got on with, while he'd been patting himself on the back for being an 'involved' dad? All this picking up and putting down and reordering chaos – it's what Lou was taking care of when he was in the guitar room. Gently re-righting the ship, every damn night.

He went to help Rita, who had her shirt on, but inside out. 'Clearly, we do too much for you girls, if you don't even know how to pack a sandwich or put your shirt on right,' he muttered, and Rita gave him a big sloppy kiss for his trouble. As he straightened up, Josh saw a note pasted to Rita's bedhead behind his daughter's mess of curly black hair, which he was about to attempt to tame.

Mummy loves you more than chocolate. Even when she can't be with you. Lou's writing, accompanied by texta-drawn love hearts and chocolate bars.

Josh stared at it for a moment, wondering why he hadn't noticed it before. A rush of emotion caught in his throat.

Truth was, every time Josh walked into the house and Lou wasn't there, it knocked the breath out of him.

The place felt so much colder without her in it. He missed the shape of her in the spaces she always inhabited: standing by the kitchen bench; sitting with her legs outstretched on the sofa; bending down to one of the girls ('Just one more hug, Mum'); reading in bed beside him; curled in a comma, sleeping.

'I miss Mummy,' Rita said, as if the little five-year-old could read his mind. 'And I miss you.'

And Josh had to turn his head so he could control the tears that he was sure were going to come. Today, clearly, was not a day he could pretend not to be sad.

'Come on, Reets, let's brush this mop,' he said, clearing his throat.

'Daddy, it's not a mop,' said his daughter. 'Mummy says it's *your* hair. I've got your hair.'

'You do, baby.' He nodded.

'She says that's why she can never be angry with it,' Rita went on, tolerating him tugging her this way and that way with the brush. 'Even when it ruins her morning.'

And Josh struggled to breathe again.

Downstairs, Stella, clearly proud that she'd pushed the lunch-boxes into schoolbags, was standing by the door. 'You won't be *too* late, Daddy,' she said to him, and the tight look around her mouth gave him a painful jolt. His eldest was working hard to keep things even, he saw; to smooth this weird situation over. She, like him, didn't want to be another problem.

He pulled her to him and kissed her on the head. 'You're my star, Stell,' he told her.

Lou

OCTOBER
Put the
girls first

'**M**um?'

'Yes, Stell?'

'Are we going back to normal soon?'

Lou was driving Stella and Rita to a birthday party on a sunny Saturday morning. The traffic was as bumper-to-bumper bad as rush hour on a Tuesday afternoon. 'What do you mean, normal?'

'Me and you and Dad? In our house?'

Lou swallowed. Paused. 'I don't know, darling.'

'How come you don't know?' Rita asked. 'You know everything, Mum.'

'Not everything, Reets.'

'But you must know this one!' Rita said. 'This one's easy!'

'It's complicated, grown-up stuff,' Lou said. She knew she was fobbing them off, she knew she needed to come up with some better answers. That *they* needed better answers. 'All I do know, for absolute sure is that –'

'Mummy and Daddy love us very much,' said Stella. 'Right?'

'Stell . . .' Lou looked in the rear-view mirror, could see her

334

older daughter's face hardening. 'We say it all the time because it's true.'

'Right.'

10. Put the girls first. Lou sat with her phone in the car, catching her breath for a moment, as the girls ran off towards the balloon-strewn picnic table in the suburban park. *What's best for them is best for you.*

*

It had been a month of difficult questions.

'Do you want to be his fucking mother?' Ryan Harcourt's mum had asked her loudly, as she'd grabbed Ryan's hand. 'Because he's already got one of those. And I'm doing my best.'

This was after telling Lou to stay the fuck out of her business after Lou had worked out a way to get Ryan into after-care two days a week for free.

'Sorry, I didn't mean to suggest . . .'

'We don't need your bleeding heart,' Ryan's mum shouted as she walked off.

'Thanks, though,' called Ryan, as he was being pulled away, and Lou gave him a little down-low wave.

'Overstepping,' said Theo, who, of course, happened to be passing. 'Told you.'

'Piss off,' she hissed under her breath.

*

'Why did you lie to me about that whole divorce advice thing?'

At Gretchen's place, JoJo was staying for some of the school holidays and was mortified that she was in the *spare* spare room, instead of the guest room where Lou had taken up residence.

'I didn't . . .' But she did.

'If you hadn't tricked me into telling you to leave,' JoJo had said to Lou, 'I wouldn't be watching *Riverdale* on my *laptop*.'

'JoJo, that's just not true.'

'Sure it isn't! Such a *teacher*!' JoJo flounced off, slamming the door of the spare spare room behind her.

*

'So, why are you separated?'

Lou and Rob were in a beige hipster cafe near Rob's Paddington place. The menu was full of plant-based goodness but they had both ordered desserts. It seemed like that kind of day, the kind of conversation they were finally having. Giant coffees, bigger cakes.

'It's a good question today, since I'm not making anyone happy,' Lou said to her brother. 'I've fucked absolutely everything.'

'I can't believe you've been faking it all this time,' Rob said, forkful of chocolate mush halfway to his mouth. 'Why didn't you tell me?'

'You have enough going on,' Lou said. 'And Mum can't know. Not yet.'

'Well, now I'm offended. Why would I tell Mum?'

'It might . . . slip out. The more people in her world who know, the greater the risk.'

'Like Mum and I are having all the fireside chats.' Rob rolled his eyes. 'So, tell me why.'

Lou wanted to put her head on the table. She felt so far from that choice, now. How to explain it?

'Fourteen years happened,' she said. 'And I didn't know if I wanted to play the role of being Josh's wife for another fourteen years. And maybe another fourteen years after that. All this crap builds up, all these things that you've done to each other. It takes you so far from where you started, you can barely even see each other anymore. Who is this person I'm doing all this work for, taking care of every day? Is this what we signed up for? What *I* signed up for? And . . . do we even like each other after all of this *shit*?'

'I always thought you and Josh seemed to really like each other,' Rob said, chewing. 'More than most married couples I know.'

Lou actually did put her head on the cafe table for a moment. Then lifted it up, pulled a 'yuck' face at her big brother. 'I sound so spoilt, don't I?'

'No, you don't. But you look sad, Lou.' Rob reached across the table for her hand. 'What can I do?'

'You can tell me I'm not the world's worst person for doing this to my girls.'

'Of course you're not, Lou. Kids need a happy home, not just any old home.' Rob lifted Lou's chin. 'And you're an excellent mother.'

'Thank you, Rob.' Lou grabbed his hand, kissed it, shoved it back at him. 'And I gave myself a deadline – it's the end of the year.'

'Well, we're nearly there. But if the suspense is killing you . . .' Rob said. 'I'm sure it's moveable.'

*

'What do you want from your career, Lou?'

Two days later, on a strangely hot spring afternoon, Lou found out that she'd got the job.

When she went back to work after the summer school holidays, she would be the head of year one at Bayside. She would still have a class of her own, but there would be a lot of extra duties, a pay rise, and a chance to try to change things that had been frustrating her for years.

Gabbie Scott had told Lou the news and congratulated her. 'I'm delighted you're open to this possibility, Lou. I've always thought

you were a very intuitive teacher, with buckets of leadership poten-
tial. I'm only sorry it's taken this long for you to make this move.'

'That's very kind of you to say,' Lou had said. 'You really don't
have to.'

'I do,' Gabbie said. 'We can't let the shouty people get all the
attention.'

'Well, no,' Lou said, smiling. 'That's true.' They both knew who
they were talking about.

And then Gabbie asked her: 'What do you want from your career,
Lou?'

Lou didn't know what to say. When was the last time anyone had
asked her that question? Had they *ever* asked her that question? Or
had they assumed that a teacher was a teacher, labouring under the
quaint illusion that it was a great job for a mother because the hours
were school hours (ha!) and the holidays were long? *What do you want
from your career, Lou?* Had she assumed the same thing about herself?

Annabelle had always wanted Lou to marry a principal. But if
Lou was honest, wasn't she much more interested in *being* a principal?

'I want to make a difference,' she said. But she knew that sounded
empty, clichéd. That Gabbie was already looking down at the notes
for her next meeting. 'I wouldn't mind your job one day, now my
kids are getting older.'

Gabbie looked up, smiled. 'Well, Lou, I'm confident you'll get
there, if that's what you really want.'

*

'Do you want to meet me at therapy?' Another question. From Josh,
on the phone. They didn't have an appointment scheduled. Lou had
assumed he'd be calling to organise the girls' trick-or-treating. 'There
are some things I want us to talk about.'

Interesting. They'd been avoiding each other as much as possible, avoiding the confusion of being in the same space for too long. 'Is it a therapy conversation? Not a kitchen conversation?'

Josh laughed softly. 'Not a kitchen conversation. Let's get the next available.'

'Okay, I'll call Sara.'

'It's okay,' said Josh. 'I'll call her.'

Josh

OCTOBER
Put the
girls first

The house at Camperdown was finally finished. It had been one of the longest jobs Josh had ever worked on for Mick, and he and Tyler had delivered a beautiful result if he said so himself, which he didn't.

Pearl Hass had put on drinks for the tradies to mark the house's completion. Most likely she wasn't going to be there, Josh had thought, as he'd changed out of his work shirt in the ute, and the long-suffering foreman would be the one offering up the tinnies around the newly filled pool.

But she was there, along with her girlfriend and their tiny newborn son in a sling. And there were no tinnies. Just big timber buckets of icy-cold bottles of craft beer, kombucha and green juice (which mostly went untouched), and trays and trays of meat and vegan sliders, tacos and artisan pies. He hadn't been to a party like it.

Josh had hung back with Tyler and watched Pearl and her family diligently go around and speak individually to the army of (mostly) men who'd transformed the giant warehouse space, some of whose roles had finished weeks or months before.

'She's a class act,' Tyler said, motioning his bottle towards Pearl. 'You've got all that money, you don't need to be this nice to people.' And Josh had to agree.

The resentment he'd felt when he'd started the job still raised its toxic little flags sometimes. He'd told Lou and anyone who'd listen that he was a simple man who loved his life, but this . . . well, this was an alternative he really wouldn't have minded.

He was by the beer bucket, looking for a lite one, when it was his turn for an audience.

'You're one of the carpenters, right?' he heard Pearl say at his shoulder. 'You and your mate did the deck we're standing on.'

'Yes,' said Josh, suddenly feeling nervous, turning around to look down at Pearl, a tiny, neat person in overalls that looked expensive, a blunt-looking mohawk and almost certainly vegan trainers. 'And the stairs, and the mezz.'

'It's exactly how we imagined it,' said Pearl. 'We didn't want it to look new, and it doesn't. It's beautiful work, with soul. You guys are artists.'

It was the perfect compliment, and an opportunity. Was he going to take it?

'I am an artist,' Josh found himself saying quickly, cringing about how boastful it sounded. It was a sentence he'd never used before in his life. Here we go, here we go . . .

'I know. It shows in your work.' Pearl nodded and gestured to the oval edges of the pool deck, which had been fucking difficult to pull off, actually, thought Josh, and he hoped they were going to re-sand after all these idiots in greasy work boots had trampled all over it.

But he said, 'No, I mean I'm also a musician.'

And just as he'd feared, Pearl Hass's face fell, just a little. 'Oh, great,' she said, but she also looked left and right for a saviour, and he knew one would be coming. People like Pearl had minders at hand for moments like this.

'I'm sorry,' he said. 'I know you must get that all the time.'

'Yes, I do,' she said. 'But, you know, there are worse things.'

'Oh? Like what?'

'Everyone in LA,' Pearl Hass said, rolling her eyes. 'It's why we want to spend more time at home. Fewer grasping fuckwits.'

And Josh laughed a little; she was warmer than he'd thought. 'Apologies for upping the grasping fuckwit quota of Sydney. What do you say to all the musicians who come up to you with a song?'

'I say send me something,' she said. 'And then I get someone else to listen to it. Or . . . not.'

Honesty. Admirable. Josh nodded.

Then Pearl added, 'You're not the usual demographic for that approach.'

'Too old?'

She held her thumb and forefinger close together, up near her face. 'Li'l bit.'

'Yeah.' Josh was rolling the cold beer bottle between in his hands. 'Well, look, this party is great. Most people don't give a fuck, so, thank you for the . . . tacos.' Shut up, you idiot.

'I appreciate all this skill,' Pearl Hass said, as her saviour, in the form of her partner and the baby sling, arrived at her side. 'Char, this is . . .'

'My name's Josh.' And Josh wiped a cold, wet hand on his pants and offered it to the beautiful Indian supermodel. 'I'm a chippie.'

'He's an artist,' Pearl corrected, and she smiled at him as Char accepted the handshake.

'Good luck with the baby,' Josh said, still feeling like a dick, but one who'd been granted more time than he should have been allowed. 'This early bit is hard, but it's like falling in love turned up to a million.'

Char and Pearl both beamed and looked at the little bump in the sling, whose crop of black hair was just sticking out of the folds of fabric. Their faces were glowing, Char's eyes looked exhausted. They were just parents, like he and Lou were, once.

'Any parenting advice?' Char asked.

'Share it,' he said, before he could stop to think about it. 'As much as you can. Share it.'

The beautiful new mum raised her eyebrows at Pearl. 'Easier said than done with this one,' she said. 'She's kind of busy.'

'Sure,' said Josh, feeling foolish. His time was up, the magical couple was preparing to move on to the next person who'd played a part in building them this dreamy inner-city palace. He realised, possibly for the first time, that almost all the natural light sources in the building came from above. The roof was almost entirely glass, and the exterior walls were three-bricks solid. It was a fortress. A haven.

Pearl and Char began to drift away, stroking the baby's head.

But then Pearl turned around. 'You should still send your stuff,' she called back to him. 'They always do tell me if it's good.'

'Or not,' he said, although he wasn't sure why.

'Or not,' she agreed, and they disappeared into the crowd.

*

'Are you joking?' Mick asked Josh on the way home. He'd turned up late to the Camperdown party, drunk too many beers to drive home, had bummed a lift from Josh. Typical boss Mick behaviour, Josh thought. 'You're going to send her some music?'

'Yeah, why not? If I've realised anything lately, mate, it's to go for what's important to you.' Josh sounded more confident than he felt, but still, Dana's advice hadn't turned out to be the worst ever. He looked at his phone. He must tell her about it.

'What's going on with you?' Mick, just this side of slurring, punched Josh in the arm.

'Mate, I'm driving!'

'Come on, you haven't been yourself lately, even for a quiet prick like you.'

The way Australian men talk to each other, Josh thought. I've been conditioned to do it my whole life. Mate.

The roads were quiet, dark. Josh had taken a detour through some Newtown backstreets, enjoying cruising his old stomping ground with his old mate, old music in the speakers. He'd been feeling nostalgic lately.

'Remember when we lived in that place?' he asked Mick, slowing right down and pointing to the old share house they'd been in when he'd met Lou. It used to be a shambolic terrace with a lounge on the porch. Now it was a renovated middle-class family home, a security door across the front, windows glowing behind tasteful French shutters.

'What are we doing back here?' asked Mick, glancing up briefly. 'I thought you were taking me home. And anyway, you haven't answered the question.'

'Lou and I are separated,' Josh said, and he hated saying the words out loud.

'No!' Mick punched him again.

'Hey!'

'No, no, no! That can't fucking be!' Mick grabbed his head dramatically.

'This is an unexpected overreaction, mate,' Josh said, sliding the car back into drive and moving off. 'I mean, *I* feel like that, but *you* need to calm down.'

'I was your best fucking man!'

'I know, mate, I know.'

'You two are the best couple I know!'

Josh didn't know what to say. Part of him was soothed by Mick's reaction. It was a disaster, and it was nice not to be the only one who seemed to realise this. But part of him was irritated. It was a disaster, and didn't Mick think he knew that?

'You have to fix it,' Mick said, too loud. 'Whatever it is, whatever you did, you need to fix it.'

'I'm working on it,' was all Josh could bring himself to say. And it was true. He *was* working on it.

'How the hell did you end up separated? You two? Of all the crappy couples I know?'

Mick. Mate. 'It's a long story. But I'm done putting myself and my girls through this shit. It's time to sort it out.'

Lou

25 December, 2018

Lou was woken up with a small knee to the eye.

'*Santa's been! Santa's been!*' Rita was screaming what felt like three centimetres from her ear.

'Ah!'

She rolled over, with Rita still attached, and opened her good eye. Next to her, Josh was asleep. How was that possible?

She was looking almost directly into Josh's open, snoring mouth when he was suddenly eclipsed by the weight of their flying elder daughter, landing pretty squarely onto his head.

'Dad! Dad, Dad, Dad, Dad! Wake *up!*' Stella was yelling.

'Argh.'

Lou looked at the blinking time on her phone by the bed: 5.30 a.m. It was going to be a long day.

'Girls, we said six o'clock,' she said sternly. 'We talked about this.'

A barely awake Josh wrapped his arms around Stella and rocked. 'Happy Christmas, hooligans,' he said.

'It's not six yet,' Lou said, aware of the edge of annoyance in her voice.

'Oh well,' said Josh. 'We can't ruin Christmas over thirty minutes, can we?'

If we start presents now, Lou thought, it'll all be over by 7 a.m. It's all cooking and drinking and fighting from there.

'Small presents at six,' she said to the girls firmly. 'Tree presents when Grandma and Uncle Rob get here.'

'When's that?' Stella asked.

'Later,' said Lou quickly. And then she caught Josh's eye, his irritation at her irritation obvious.

'Can we just have a nice day?' Josh whisper-hissed. 'It's Christmas.'

'Spoken like a man who doesn't have to spend all day making salads and whipping cream,' Lou said, and immediately felt bad about it.

'I'll whip cream for you, baby,' Josh said in his comedy-Elvis voice, and it made the girls fall around laughing and it made Lou want to slap him.

Just got to get through today, thought Lou, as she gave the girls a guilty hug and pushed them gently out of the door to go and find their stockings.

An angry Annabelle. An anxious Rob. A distracted Brian. Josh trying to pretend everything was okay again.

'Happy Christmas, Lou,' Josh said from the bed, where he was stretching awake. 'Another one!'

'Yes, another one,' said Lou. 'Merry Christmas and get your arse out of bed to police those girls around the chocolate.' And she threw him a smile, which he appeared to accept gratefully.

'Let's do it!' Josh yelled, and swung himself out of bed.

*

Lou had read that every long-standing couple only has one fight. They just have it over and over until they divorce or die.

She thought that if her and Josh's one fight had a title, it would be Why Can't You Be Better?

She had friends whose fight titles would be Why Do I Have To Do Everything Around Here? or Would It Kill You To Appreciate Me, Just A Bit? And she knew backup titles for her and Josh's fight could be Why Don't We Have Another Baby? And Why Did You Sleep With That Guy? But, really, they all boiled back down to the original, and the best (worst): Why Can't You Be Better?

And the basic script of the fight would be her frustrated, and him defensive, and if there was a cheerleader for Lou in this fight it would be Annabelle, her mother, whether she was present or not. And if there was someone with the bucket and towels on the sidelines, it would be Gretchen, who was selfishly away this Christmas, but who could always be counted on for moral support and sustenance. And if there was an audience, well, she really didn't want it to be their kids.

Especially not on Christmas Day.

So Lou took deep breaths at eight, applied a dab of rescue remedy to her pulse points at nine (a gift from Gretchen, who had offered Valium, but been refused) and looked at a positive affirmation on her phone at nine thirty. *You Are Enough. You Are Enough. You Are Enough.*

By then, the girls had ripped open most of their presents and examined everything for ten seconds before deciding which of the mountain of gifts that Lou had spent months planning and saving for were worthy, and which ones were 'sad'. She tried not to think that her beautiful daughters were ungrateful as they barely looked at the books she'd chosen so carefully and on whose flyleaf she'd written personalised messages. She'd made them all their favourite Christmas breakfast – chocolate-chip pancakes in Santa shapes for the girls, BLTs with a festive bit of holly sticking out of the top for her and Josh – and wondered why the hell she bothered as she watched them wolf it all down with barely a glance in her direction. She fixed Josh a buck's fizz – and pretended to fix herself one too, but really she just stuck some fizzy water in her OJ, fearing what she might do if her inhibitions were loosened with booze at this early stage of the day.

'Tell me what you want me to do to help!' Josh said brightly, draining his drink.

In the version of Why Can't You Be Better playing out in Lou's head, she said, 'Why do I have to tell you what to do? That's just another thing for me to do.'

But . . . Christmas, so what she said was, 'Just take the girls out with their new stuff for an hour so I can get on with everything.'

And so, by 10 a.m. on Christmas Day, Lou was alone in her lovely little house surrounded by breakfast washing-up, mountains of torn wrapping paper and a carpet of homeless plastic toys.

*

By 2 p.m., Lou's mother was crying in the kitchen.

'It's just getting harder and harder to deal with him,' Annabelle was saying. 'He barely says anything anymore.'

'He's barely said anything forever, Mum,' said Lou, simultaneously chopping parsley and stirring raspberry syrup. 'I always thought that was one of the reasons you got on so well.' She glanced at her mum's prosecco glass. 'Have you had a lot of those, or . . .'

'No, Louise, he's not just being quiet. He's sick.' Annabelle grabbed Lou's wrist, which was not at all convenient in that moment. 'Forgetting things, saying words that don't make sense. Sometimes I look at his eyes and he's not . . . there.'

Lou stopped stirring for a moment and thought about that. A ping of recognition. She couldn't remember having a proper conversation with her dad for months. 'Shit,' she said, and wiped her hands on the tea towel draped over her shoulder. 'What does Rob say?'

'I haven't mentioned it to him yet.' Annabelle emptied her glass, and Lou took it from her and put it down.

'Well, why not? He's a doctor. He's probably already noticed himself.' He's a doctor, but of course you're talking to me about it, she thought but didn't say.

'It just makes it all so real, doesn't it?'

'Mum!' Lou scolded. 'You've got to advocate for Dad. If what's happening is what you're thinking is happening, he needs you to champion him.'

Annabelle was quiet. 'You could,' she said quietly.

'I could what?'

'Advocate for him, whatever that means.'

'Mum, I have a full-time job and two small children . . .'

'Three children, with that husband of yours.'

'Do not start that today, Mum – this is Josh's house,' Lou said, turning from the stove. 'And no-one here has forgotten what happened at that surprise party. You're lucky we still let you in . . . so not too many more bubblies, please.'

'Josh's house,' Annabelle scoffed. 'As if.'

'That is exactly what I mean,' said Lou. 'This is his house as much as mine and it's our family home. Be nice.'

And as she grabbed a tray of roasted potatoes out of the oven, she added a note to herself: You too, Lou.

*

By 4 p.m., the girls were flying loud and high on sugar and Lou's brother Rob was fighting with his boyfriend Toby in the driveway.

'Do you think I should go and say something?' Annabelle asked Lou from her position at the window.

'Like what?' asked Lou, who was the only one sitting at the kitchen table, still spread with much of the food she'd spent days making. Stella and Rita were screaming at each other over their Christmas toys in the back garden, Josh was over at the bench making some complicated and messy festive cocktail that he insisted Rob would love, and Brian had fallen asleep on the lounge. Or he was pretending to have fallen asleep on the lounge.

'Like, it's Christmas, so stop making a show of yourselves in front of the neighbours,' Annabelle said. She never sounded closer to her northern English roots than when she was drunk.

'You would never say that to Rob,' Lou said.

'I don't know why he's here, anyway, that man,' Annabelle said, motioning to Toby. 'Did you even invite him?'

Lou sighed. 'Of course I did – he's my brother's partner. They've been together for three years.'

'Nonsense,' said Annabelle. 'Partner! Nonsense.'

'Mum, just . . .'

'What have I done now? Seems I can't do anything right around you, Louise.'

Lou stood up and started clearing, just as Josh came over carrying almost-overflowing martini glasses filled with brown goo and topped with cherries.

'Oh, Lou, are you tidying?' he asked, looking around. 'What about Christmas pudding?'

'What about Christmas pudding?' she asked. 'We had pavlova and chocolate cake.'

'Oh.' Josh's face fell a little. 'I thought . . .'

'She didn't do Christmas pudding, Joshua,' said Annabelle from the window. 'I know. It's not Christmas without pudding, really, is it?'

Breathe, Lou. Rescue remedy. Gin. Whatever.

Her face as she walked past Josh with the plates must have said enough, because he put the glasses down and started back-pedalling. 'No-one really likes Christmas pudding, of course,' he said. 'You could just have a fake one on the table, couldn't you?'

'Don't be so ridiculous, Joshua,' snapped Annabelle.

The door slammed and Rob was back inside, alone, trying to compose his face into any expression other than devastated.

'Where's Toby?' asked Josh. 'I've made him a humdinger. And you, Rob.'

'Great,' said Rob flatly. He walked over, took the glass of chocolate mess and downed it. 'Ugh.'

'Guess this one's mine then,' said Josh, taking a glug of the second glass.

'Why don't you ever pay attention to anything going on around you?' hissed Lou from behind him, feeling her frustration at absolutely everything tumbling inside her.

'What?' asked Josh.

'Daddy! Daddy! Will you come and jump on the trampoline with us?' Lou dodged a running Rita, narrowly avoiding dropping the plates on the kitchen floor.

'Hey, Rita, slow down!' she snapped.

'Oh, Reets is just excited, aren't you, Reets?' yelled Josh. 'Yes, I will!'

'Is that a good idea?' asked Lou. 'You just drank half a bottle of Baileys in that thing.'

'Of course it is!' Josh said. 'It's always a good idea to jump, isn't it, Reets?'

'You're forty-one!' Annabelle called sharply. 'You'll put your back out and then you'll really be useless!' And she giggled to herself.

Lou shushed her mum but silently agreed with her. And then all this mess will be mine, she thought silently. Oh, wait, it already is.

Rob was staring at the table, stone-faced. 'You're well rid, son,' said Annabelle. 'Don't think another thing about it.'

'Shut up, Mum,' said Rob. He looked up at Lou. 'I've got to go after him. Do you mind?'

Lou looked around at the crap all over the table; at her mum, keening for a fight with someone; her dad, seemingly passed out. The girls, manically leaping with their drunk dad.

'Of course not,' she said. 'Go!'

'But Mary and Pat aren't here yet!' Annabelle cried.

'Who the hell are Mary and Pat?' asked Rob.

Good question, thought Lou. But Rob was already closing the front door behind him.

'Your dad's cousin Mary – you've met her a thousand times. She and Pat are down from Mooloolaba. We've plenty of dessert for them, haven't we, Louise? I told them cake and champagne.'

Suddenly Brian stirred on the couch, sat up and looked around, his eyes terrifyingly empty.

'Where the fuck am I?' he shouted, as loud as Lou had ever heard him.

*

By 9 p.m., Lou was lying on her bed, in the dark, alone.

She was fairly certain that Stella and Rita were still awake and downstairs, mindlessly staring at *The Christmas Chronicles* and eating chocolate.

She could hear Josh playing music in his guitar room, talking loudly to someone, probably Ahmed from down the road. He'd somehow appeared at some point and been press-ganged into joining Josh and Mick, who'd also arrived unannounced, and drinking a 'Christmas port', despite neither Christmas nor port being of any interest to him.

This is normal, Lou told herself. This is probably the most normal Christmas anyone has ever had.

So why couldn't she stop sobbing?

An hour earlier, she'd been standing in the middle of her living room, lost. She'd managed to get her parents into a taxi, against Brian's strong objections, and she'd messaged Rob about an appointment for their dad as soon as humanly possible.

She'd cleared up as much as she could face. She'd comforted Rita who had, of course, gone flying off the trampoline and split her lip. She'd fed everyone who'd come through the front door. She'd smiled politely at her 'cousin' Pat's awful, misogynistic Me Too jokes. She'd arranged her face in a 'pleased to see you' smile when Mick walked through the front door with a six-pack and a mate she'd never seen before.

It was all normal.

But in all that chaos, she'd been searching for Josh. He was there, in the house, but he certainly wasn't at her back. Did he see her, doing all she did? Did he think to hug her, to bolster, to offer to help? Did he let her know she wasn't alone in this emotional family mess, in this mundane slog of manual labour that was supposedly a gift to be able to give to your family?

Or did he actually see her, and it was just that he didn't care? Because this was what she deserved, still: penance, for a selfish act.

Shut up, you're a whiner, Lou told herself. But also: Is this it? Is this really all there is now?

For a moment, lying there in the dark, the tree tapping gently at the window, Lou felt as if she lifted up and drifted ahead, looking into the next ten, fifteen years of raising these girls, these remarkable little humans. And then they'd be gone, off to have their own adventures. Just like she had left, barely looking back.

But would they also find themselves, after years of freedom and being told they could do anything they wanted, wiping spills and messes and tears and blood and snot, the one who was working double-time to please everyone? Would they be the only person in their family without a present under the tree, because they were the ones who bought all the gifts?

And when her girls left her, would this relationship and Lou's own career be enough? Teaching and lying next to Josh every night, hoping his hand wouldn't stray across the bed?

The room was still but the house's noises snaked in under the door – one of the girls was crying, guitar music, laughter, clinking bottles.

She lay there, trying to stop sobbing.

Get your shit together, Lou.

Next year, she thought. Next year has to be the year this changes.

Big deep breaths. Someone has to go and make those girls sleep.

Another deep breath. Come on, calm down.

Lou sat up in the dark and swung her legs to the floor.

And then her phone lit up next to her.

Weirdly, the text message said, *I'm thinking about you on Christmas night. And I like it. After all this time . . .*

Josh

New Year's Eve, 2018

At 9 a.m., Josh was hastily wrapping Lou's Christmas present in his guitar room.

You complete idiot, he was saying to himself. What were you thinking, not buying Lou a present?

He didn't notice, on the day. But he had noticed the next day, and the next, that she was very quiet. Quiet in a way he hadn't seen for a while.

Yes, a certain distance blew through their relationship regularly since they'd pieced things back together, but silence was never a good sign.

Idiot, idiot, idiot.

'Are we doing presents this year?' he was sure he'd asked, some weeks ago.

And Lou, he was almost certain, had shrugged. 'If you want.'

And then the end of the year had happened, in a whirl of preschool graduation (because that was a thing now), carol concerts, Lou working overtime to finish up the school year, Josh out on last-minute jobs for people who thought their holidays would be perfect if only they had a Balinese door fitted on the pool house.

It was a stinking hot December; every end-of-year concert was steamier than the last. They both came home drained, wrung out.

He hadn't thought about presents again until Christmas Eve, when, after the kids had gone giddily to bed, a mound of wrapped and unwrapped gifts appeared on the living room floor, and he was handed a beer, a roll of sticky-tape and some wrapping paper.

'Where the hell do you hide all this stuff?' Josh had asked Lou as she, like a magician making coins appear from assorted ears, came holding another toy, another book, another ball.

And under the tree the next day there was a present he hadn't wrapped. It was for him, from Lou, and it was a guitar strap he'd been lusting after. Leather, American, the brand once used by Johnny Cash, for God's sake.

She did all that, and he didn't have time to buy her a present? Idiot, idiot, idiot.

Maybe that's why she was so quiet.

Now, it was New Year's Eve and at 10 a.m., after getting distracted by an email newsletter from Guitar Nerds United (terrible name, deeply informative newsletter), Josh went to give her his present.

He could hear the girls splashing outside in the oversized paddling pool they'd got for Christmas that had taken him a day to blow up. He knew Lou would be near, and she was, out in the kitchen at the back door, folding washing with her headphones on, one eye on the girls and the water, one on the mountain of underwear and T-shirts.

'I got you something,' Josh said, coming up behind her.

She didn't react.

'I got you something!' he said, louder.

The girls stopped splashing and turned to watch.

'I GOT YOU SOMETHING!' Josh yelled, and he leaned forward to pull one of Lou's earbuds out. Reactively, she slapped his hand away.

'Don't do that!' she shouted, like he was the most annoying creature to have entered her orbit in a very long time.

'Sorry.' He held out the small, hastily wrapped parcel. 'It's your Christmas present.'

Lou pulled out the earbuds. 'What?'

'It's your Christmas present.'

'It's New Year's Eve.'

'I know. New tradition,' he said, a little bit pleased with himself.

'When did you buy it?'

'What do you mean?'

'When did you buy this?'

'Does it matter?'

'Yes, if you bought it yesterday.'

Josh shrugged. 'Just open it.'

Lou turned over the present and peeled back the sticky tape.

Josh waited for her reaction. It was a necklace. He'd bought it at the hippie shop over in Newtown. When they were first dating, she'd loved that shop, buying up cheap rings that turned her fingers green, weighing up the pros and cons (mostly cons, let's be honest) of tie-dyed rainbow fisherman's pants.

The necklace was silver and had a stone that looked something like an opal, pale with bits of colour in it, kind of sparkly, and there were twiddly bits around the outside.

She held it up.

'Do you like it?'

'She doesn't wear silver anymore, Dad!' Stella said, in a tone of voice that reminded Josh of Lou's when he'd done something wrong. 'She likes rose gold now.'

'Shush, Stell – it's lovely,' said Lou. And she looked at it again, turning it around.

'And she hates opals!'

'I don't think it's really an opal . . .' Josh started, but he could see this wasn't going well.

'Thank you, it's lovely,' Lou repeated, and she put it back in the box and closed the paper around it. 'Very thoughtful.'

'It's from that shop in Newtown,' Josh pushed on. 'You know – the one you like. In fact, girls' – he turned to Stella and Rita – 'it's just a few doors down from where I met your mum for the very first time.'

'In a pub,' said five-year-old Rita.

'That was a long time ago,' said Lou. And she put the box on the kitchen counter and turned back to the washing.

'It won't turn your neck green!' he went on, even as he knew he should stop. 'It wasn't that cheap.'

And for the first time, Josh noticed that Stella was looking at him like he was an idiot.

'What?' he said to her, and she shook her head at him.

'I want to go to that party tonight,' Lou suddenly said, from the washing basket. 'The one Beth from school's having.'

That was the last thing Josh was expecting Lou to say. 'On New Year's Eve?'

'People go out on New Year's Eve, Josh.'

'Not people with kids,' said Josh. 'We haven't been out on New Year's Eve for nine years.' And he poked his tongue out at Stella, who was still fixing him with a withering look. 'You really cramped our style, Stell.'

'What style?'

'Ha. Anyway, I thought we were just having a few people round.'

'Exactly,' said Lou, still not looking at him. 'I don't want to have a few people round. I want to go out and have a few drinks, and not have to organise, and entertain, and clear up tomorrow.'

'Well, I could . . .' Josh was about to say that he would help with all that, but he knew he was on dangerous ground. 'Okay,' he said cautiously.

'I thought Maya could babysit.'

'My sister Maya?'

'Yes, your sister Maya,' said Lou. 'She's back from your mum's and she always says she hates Sydney on New Year's. Ask her.'

'It's a bit short notice.'

'When was the last time she babysat? Lay a guilt-trip on her, Josh – she'll do it.'

Josh was running out of excuses.

'I'm driving up to Mum's tomorrow, remember?'

'So what? I'm not suggesting we stay out till dawn.'

*

By 5 p.m., Josh was settling Maya in with the girls and Lou was getting ready upstairs.

Josh felt heavy, and irritated. He hated house parties, and going out on New Year's Eve. He hated the drama of getting to where you were going, never mind getting home. He hated the idea of making small talk with Lou's colleagues and school friends, whom he barely knew. He hated that he was also currently having to make small talk with his sister, whom he hadn't seen enough of over the last couple of years, meaning their interactions required the kind of effortful politeness usually reserved for acquaintances, albeit one who was very comfortable doling out the insults.

'You've been in Chile?'

'No, Josh, I've been in Gili.'

'Where the hell's that?'

'Islands in Indonesia. For fuck's sake, Josh, do you listen to anything anyone tells you?'

Fair enough. But he wasn't ready for Maya's sudden change of topic.

'You two alright?' she was asking. 'Lou seems a bit . . .'

'We're fine,' Josh said, too quickly. 'Don't worry about us. Help yourself to whatever you want, and I've made up the sofa bed in the guitar . . . in the spare room. Don't touch anything in there, though.'

'Why would I?'

'I don't know . . . You guys strum guitars around the campfire, right?'

Maya, with her cheesecloth shirt and her baggy purple shorts and her dollar-shop thongs, rolled her eyes. 'You're a dick.'

Stella and Rita were delighted by the idea of a night of unlimited treats ahead with Maya in charge.

'Daddy, can we have ice cream?'

'Ask Aunty Maya. She has to deal with you afterwards.'

'Can we play on the iPad?'

'Up to your aunty.'

'Movie night? Popcorn?'

'Again, ask Maya . . .'

And Lou came downstairs looking bloody gorgeous in a rusty-red dress he didn't remember seeing before.

'Wow. Is that new?'

'No, it's old. Just haven't worn it for ages.'

'You look amazing.'

Lou smiled, and he knew she was pleased he'd told her that. He really must remember to compliment his wife more often. She always liked it.

They kissed everyone goodbye at about 6 p.m. and got in an Uber to travel across two suburbs to Lou's work friend Beth's place.

Josh bit his tongue about the price of cabs on New Year's Eve. He bit his tongue about the route the driver took them, and he bit his tongue about how early they were, and how they were definitely going to be the first ones there. Let's not have a fight, he kept thinking, let's not have a fight . . .

'You'll be alright at this thing tonight, won't you?' Lou asked, and she took his hand in the back of the car, which gave him a surge of hope. 'You won't feel too left out of all the teacher talk?'

'No, I'll be fine,' he assured her.

'I'm sure there'll be people there you can talk to, and Beth has great taste in music, so you'll like that . . .'

'Sure. Lou, it will be fine.'

'Just don't drink too much because you're nervous.'

'Come on, Lou, I'm not a child,' he said, and he squeezed her hand. 'I won't embarrass you in front of your friends.'

*

By 9 p.m., Josh was definitely drunk.

I am definitely drunk, he thought, as he pulled up his fly after peeing on Beth's back fence, just out of reach of the light streaming from the house. I could just hide out here for a while.

He looked back towards the crowd through the yard, and he wondered, as he always did at parties, at the ease with which all these people were talking to each other. Laughing out loud and touching each other on the arm and passing each other drinks and putting their hands on each other's backs. Josh thought there was a handful of people in the world he was that comfortable with. Not whole rooms of them.

'That's why you're not a fucking rock star,' he muttered to himself. 'You didn't go to enough parties.' Then he laughed, because even he knew that wasn't true. Shit, he was a bit drunk.

He could see Lou, in her hot dress, talking to Beth and some other teachers from school he vaguely knew by sight but couldn't have named with a gun to his head.

He'd been in that circle a couple of hours ago, and he could hear grabs of conversation floating up from that group and the others, over the shit music – was that really Dido? – that sounded to him exactly the same as all the other conversations in every other little circle in the kitchen and backyard.

It was the sound of what teachers talked about.

'No, please, let's have another meeting about that . . .'

'Yes, Mrs Gabbet, of course it's on the curriculum . . .'

'Only a can of Coke in his lunchbox . . .'

'Fucking Trump . . .'

'I want to go live in a cave . . .'

'Is it too late to retrain?'

That's why I'm drunk, he thought. I didn't know what to say so I just kept drinking, and going to get another beer, and another beer, mostly to avoid standing in one of these circles like an idiot. And I hardly ever drink that much anymore. I thought it would be okay, but I think I might be wrong.

He'd already busied himself checking out Beth's music collection, which was nowhere near as good as Lou had led him to believe. He'd spent quite a long time in the inside toilet, playing on his music trivia app, but people kept knocking on the door. He'd offered to help with the barbecue, but was ushered away.

He knew Lou would be pissed off with him if her friends saw that he was drunk, so now he was kind of hiding. Beth had a big, bushy backyard, with a chicken coop and a vegie patch, so sitting here on a tree stump for a while, pretending to be looking at something important on his phone, might buy him another hour. Did they really have to stay till midnight?

'Hello there.'

Shit. Someone had found him. Josh turned towards the voice that had greeted him and saw another man doing up his flies. Thank God.

He was huge, this guy. Taller even than Josh, and about twice as broad. He had what Josh would describe as a private-school-boy haircut – neat, but a bit floppy on top – and he was wearing chinos. He didn't really look like one of the male teachers, who on a night like this were all more likely to be wearing ironic band T-shirts and beards.

'Oh, hi. I was just checking out the vegie garden. We're thinking of . . . getting one.'

'Right.' The guy looked around for the vegie garden.

'It's here.' Josh pointed to the wooden bed next to him. 'These are tomatoes.'

'Right.' The guy nodded. 'Yes, I can see the appeal. You must get a sense of achievement, eating something you've grown.'

'As opposed to smoking something you've grown, right?' Josh laughed, and then immediately felt terrible. That was a stupid joke to make to chino man, who was probably important. Where did it even come from? It's not like he'd even smoked weed in the last ten years.

The guy didn't walk away, though. He was looking at Josh's face like he was trying to work something out.

'I'm Josh,' said Josh, hoping he didn't sound as out of it as he felt. 'I'm here with my wife. She's . . . a teacher. With Beth.'

'Oh, right!' Chino man's face seemed to change. It was like something had clicked with him, like he knew where to file Josh now. He smiled and stuck out his enormous mitt of a hand. 'I'm Theo. I work with Lou at Bayside, too.'

'Oh, I see.' What to ask? What to say? 'You're a teacher too, then?'

'I'm the deputy principal,' Theo said. He had this big, bouncy voice. 'I think Lou's just fantastic.' His smile grew bigger.

'Good, good,' said Josh. 'So do I.' Why did he say that?

'She's one of the best teachers we've got,' the man said. 'I think she's going to have an amazing career now that, you know, her children are . . . your children are . . .'

Are what?

'Older.'

'That's nice,' said Josh. Again, why? 'I mean, um, that you know about our kids. Our girls. They are . . . getting bigger.'

Please go away, big man, thought Josh. I don't want to keep talking to you. You're important and I will get Lou in trouble, I know I will.

Theo looked at the chicken coop, then back at Josh. 'Are you alright out here? You coming back in?'

Not with you, thought Josh.

'Yes, sure, in a moment, I just need to . . .' Josh remembered he was holding his phone. 'Make a call. Check in with the babysitter. I mean, my sister. She's the . . . babysitter.'

'Well, okay.' This guy was looking at Josh with more interest than he'd expect from a chino man, or maybe Josh was imagining it. 'I'll see you in there.'

'Yep, right.'

He turned to walk inside, finally, and Josh felt a quick rush of embarrassment. He needed to get himself together and go find Lou.

But the big man stopped and turned around. 'You're a lucky man, Josh,' he said. 'Happy New Year.'

And Josh wasn't sure if the guy meant he was lucky because he was hiding in the garden and not inside the party, or if he . . . did he mean because his sister was babysitting? Babysitters were expensive on New Year's Eve.

'Yeah, I am, thanks. You too,' Josh said. And he watched the guy walk back towards the light and over to the circle with Lou in it, and she looked up at him and said hello and the guy pecked her cheek and Josh sat down on the tree stump and threw up on his shoes.

*

By 11.30 p.m. they were back in a surge-charging Uber on their way home.

'I really would have liked to stay until midnight,' Lou said. Her hand was very far from holding his. 'That's kind of the point of New Year's Eve.'

'I'm sorry, Lou, I am.' Josh's head felt thick, his tongue felt thick, his head was already pulsing. 'Must have been something I ate.'

'I don't think it was something you ate, Josh,' Lou said sharply.

'Well' – Josh couldn't be sure if he'd already said this, but it seemed reasonable – 'you could have hung out with me more. I wouldn't have felt like such a spare fucking part.'

'I don't want to babysit you, Josh, you're a grown man. I should be able to take you to a party.'

'You know I hate parties. Especially teacher parties.'

'But you could do it for me, right? Once a year? Or are we way past doing nice things for each other?'

Josh put his head between his hands, holding on to it to stop it spinning. 'Here we go. Let's count the ways I'm such a disappointment to you.' And he knew that was a gateway line to a fight they'd had many times – but this time, Lou didn't bite.

After a beat, he looked over at her, and he could see, even in the dark of the car, that she was crying.

Shit.

'I'll be out of your hair tomorrow,' he said sulkily. 'I'm going to Mum's.'

'Good,' said Lou.

Josh coughed.

'One hundred and fifty dollars if you're sick in the back,' said the Uber driver.

'Happy New Year to you too, mate,' said Josh. He looked at Lou again.

She was still crying.

Lou

NOVEMBER

Confess

I *give my separation six weeks.*

Bold. Underlined.

I give my separation six weeks.

Six weeks to decision day.

Lou had written it in her notes as she sat in the car outside Sara's office.

The office wasn't so bright today. The city was shrouded in smoke haze.

It was the first time Lou hadn't wished for blinds to soften the light in the room, and it felt like the end of the world.

All anyone could talk about was how unsettling it was that Sydney was circled by fires and choking with smoke, and compare their degrees of separation from the places that were in flames.

The sense of anxiety was palpable, but Lou couldn't stop looking at Josh.

He was wearing a shirt she'd never seen before. It was navy blue, which was a colour she'd always told him was great for his eyes. The number of navy things she'd bought him over the years that sat in the back of wardrobes, or got worn but washed until they disintegrated.

Lou was trying to picture Josh deciding he needed to buy a new shirt, planning to go to a shop, travelling there, picking it out, trying it on, buying it. Choosing to wear it today, on the day he'd booked the appointment.

'Is that a new shirt?' she asked Josh, who was sitting forward on the lounge with his hands on his knees, as if he was ready for something to happen and wanted to give it his full attention.

Josh shrugged. 'I guess,' he said.

It was deeply strange, trying to unknow someone you knew better than anyone.

Sara looked up from her notes, ready to start. 'The smoke's terrible today, isn't it?' she said.

'The kids can't play outside,' said Lou. 'School's like a madhouse.' Then, to Josh, 'I think Rita's getting asthma.'

'She's not,' Josh said. 'She just has a cough.'

'Who doesn't?' asked Sara, and they both looked at her, a little shocked. Nope, she doesn't have kids, thought Lou.

'So,' said Sara brightly. 'It's been four months, and I'm really interested to see how you are both feeling about where you are in this trial.'

Lou sucked in her breath. She didn't want to go first, not today.

She didn't have to. 'There are some things I want to say,' Josh said.

Lou and Sara looked at him, surprised.

'I wanted to say, Lou, that you are right,' Josh said, in the weird sinister glow of the therapist's office. 'About almost everything.'

Lou had to stop herself from laughing. She instantly thought of all the women she knew who would die to hear those words, which was, actually, every woman she knew.

'What?' she said, but Sara held up a hand that said, *Let the man talk.*

'You're right: you have been dragging my arse around for fourteen years. It's not your fault that I have let my passions . . .' he still couldn't actually say that word without a sarcastic tone, Lou was reassured to see, but still, '. . . slide and sometimes blamed you and the family for it. I can be passive, and I can be boring to live with, and I adore you but I don't appreciate you enough, all the things you do for me, and all the ways you make my life better. I just don't.

'I don't support you enough, I don't see all the work you do, I didn't deliver you the kind of life your mother wanted for you. All of that. You're right about all that.'

As Josh stopped speaking, Lou was expecting a 'but'. He was sitting there, her husband, in his new shirt, looking at the floor.

Then he drew a breath and said, 'And I know we have another month of the trial separation to go, but I hate it and I think you hate it and I'm fairly certain the kids hate it, too.'

Please stop talking, Josh, Lou was thinking. I can't hear this. Six weeks. We have six weeks.

'But' – here it was – 'I am wrong and you've been wrong, too. You took your anger at me and you used it to do something that made everything so much worse. The "stuff" we told Sara about when we first came here, it's still hanging over our heads. I'm pretty certain that's why we're sitting here in this – excuse me, Sara – fishbowl that we can't afford. And we tiptoe around it, because you think the point of coming here is for me to understand what an imperfect partner I am and all the ways I've let you down. Fair cop. But I've accepted my punishment for long enough, really, Lou. I think it's time for you to come clean.'

Lou wondered if she would ever not feel nauseous again. She had been feeling that way for months, she realised.

She could feel Sara's eyes on her.

'Come clean?' she managed.

'Talk about the elephant taking a shit in the middle of the room,' said Josh, irritated. 'I know we're doing all our non-logistical communication only in this office at the moment, so that's why I'm saying this here. I think you have to tell Sara – and me – the truth about your affair.'

'Excuse me, Josh, I just have to jump in.' The therapist was tapping her notebook with her pen. 'Lou doesn't *have* to tell me anything. She has the agency here.'

'Apologies, Sara, I understand your point and your role.' Lou couldn't remember when she'd seen Josh so confident, and so . . . certain. 'What I meant to say was, I am ready to hear it all, here, now, and maybe I wasn't, for a long time. If I'm going to stop being a deadweight, we've got to get it all out . . . The truth will set us free and all that.'

Sara looked at Lou. Lou looked at Josh. She heard herself go immediately on the defensive. 'Oh, so *now*, because you're ready to hear it, I'm meant to be ready to –'

And Josh stood up, ran his palms down his jeans. 'I know it's bad form to walk out of therapy,' he said. 'But I'm just saying, if we can't be honest, when the stakes are so . . . so very high, for us, the kids, our families, then . . . I want you to call me back when we can.'

And he walked to the door, opened it, and left.

Lou stared after him. She knew she was going to cry. She couldn't cry in front of Sara. She awkwardly started gathering her jacket and bag.

'You know, Lou, you don't have to take that on,' said Sara. 'You don't need to be told off. You just need to think about whether or not you're prepared to give what he's asking. It's not right or wrong.'

'Thanks,' said Lou, fighting back rising tears. 'I know. It's just . . . a lot at the moment.'

'And you stayed in the room,' Sara added. 'He didn't.'

'Thank you.' Lou was trying to put her jacket on, but the sleeve was half inside out and she spent what felt like a long minute wrestling with it. 'I appreciate it.'

'I'm not trying to make you feel better,' Sara the therapist said. 'That's not my job.'

'Sure, right.' Lou finally made it to the end of the sleeve. She wanted to run after him, almost overwhelmingly. But she wasn't sure what she'd do if she caught up with him. 'I should run after him, right?' she said to Sara from the door.

'This isn't a movie, Lou,' the therapist said, but she sounded kind.

*

Lou didn't run after Josh.

Instead, she messaged Gretchen, who was now in bloody Iceland, pushing her tilt at being a digital nomad to the extreme. *Can we talk?*

But the time difference was clearly off, or Gretchen was caught halfway up some photogenic glacier, because there was no response. Maybe it was just as well, Lou thought, putting her phone away. Gretchen couldn't clean up every single one of her messes. Maybe that's why she was in Iceland in the first place.

So Lou went back to work. She'd left at three for the appointment, and when Josh stalked off he was presumably heading for the girls' school, since it was his night at home. She could go and sort out the classroom, get a jump towards the end of year reports, avoid thinking about Josh's ultimatum.

Driving through the smoky gloom of Matraville to Bayside, she realised that wouldn't be possible. Whichever way she looked at it, she knew what the last item on the list had to be:

11. Confess. All of it.

Back in the classroom, Lou looked around at the mess she'd left behind after a day of up-cycling rubbish into solar systems. The room was a sea of plastic bottles, scourers and toilet rolls. On every desk sat the results of the kids' efforts, paint bubbles popping and glue drying. She was focusing on tidying when she heard a familiar clearing of a throat and looked up to see Theo's frame filling the doorway.

'Congratulations, Ms Winton,' he said cheerfully. 'I heard your promotion is official.'

'What are you doing here?' Lou asked, her stomach contracting.

'It's my last day,' said Theo. 'I came to say goodbye.'

He'd had his leaving drinks with the staff. Lou had found an excuse not to be there. The last thing she needed was to spend any more time with Theo than was absolutely necessary. Especially this week.

'Missed you at my farewell.'

'Yeah, well, I was busy.' But, again, what are you doing here?

Theo sat on the edge of one of the kids' tiny desks. It was Ryan Harcourt's. Despite her misstep with his mum, Ryan had come a long way this year. Sometimes now he sat still for as long as twenty minutes at a time, and today he'd put an enormous effort into the order of his dish-sponge planets, painting them just the right colours, a look of concentration on his face. Now Theo's arrogant arse was centimetres from squashing it.

'There's something I haven't told you,' Theo said. 'On New Year's Eve, the day before you called me, I met your husband at Beth's party. He was drunk, in the garden, talking to the chickens.'

Really? Lou felt a stab of panic. 'I don't think that's . . .'

'That's what he was doing.'

'Let's not talk about this here, Theo,' Lou said, looking over to the open door. 'I think you should go.'

'I had never seen him before then,' Theo went on.

'Good.'

'Of course, I've seen him since. At the concert. He's a handsome guy.' That was the kind of thing Theo said about other men. Words like 'handsome'. Big manly words, big manly compliments.

'So what?' Lou was feeling a bit sick.

'He was also fucking miserable.'

'You don't know anything about him, Theo,' Lou said.

'I know that he made a fool of himself that night and the very next day you called me to come over to your house and fuck you,' Theo said, and he pushed off Ryan Harcourt's desk, sending a tiny spongy Pluto flying from his night sky, and walked towards her.

In three years, he had never spoken words like that to Lou inside the walls of the school. It made her feel unsafe. This was the kind of risky behaviour they'd avoided for years, dancing around each other with exaggerated politeness.

But who was she kidding? A guy who screwed a workmate in a public gym and sexted her when he knew she was home with her family? Who turned up at an event when he knew her husband would be there? That wasn't risk-averse behaviour. Gretchen was right.

'That was a mistake,' she said. 'I was in a bad place.'

'Such bullshit,' Theo said, smiling a little. 'A *bad place.*'

'Theo, I want you to leave, please.'

'Your home is lovely, Lou,' Theo said, and he was walking towards her, stopping an arm's length away. 'I spent six months hoping you'd call me over there again.'

'Theo, we've already been over this. It was a mistake. It's done.'

'Don't worry about it,' he said. 'I have other distractions. I just needed to tell you that.'

Lou looked again to the open door. She could just walk out. There were people around. It was okay.

'And something else. After observing what I observed – and I am a good observer, a people person, you know that – you're just going to end up back there again, Lou, no matter what you think.'

'I don't know what you're talking about,' Lou said. 'Please, Theo just *piss off*.'

'Even if you choose to keep your husband and your happy little home with its pretty yellow tree,' Theo said, his voice quiet, steady, 'you'll still be back. I've met him, now. And I know you'll be back there again one day. You'll be sitting across from some other guy, saying, *I need to have sex with someone who isn't my husband*' – Theo gave her a high, whiny, desperate voice – 'and starting all kinds of trouble.'

For a split second, Lou imagined punching Theo in the face. Or flying at him, whirling, pulling and scratching. In that instant she pictured a crash, a commotion, a scene.

No. She wasn't going to do that.

She was aware of the sounds of voices and scraping chairs in the corridor down the hall.

Lou clenched her fists and said, 'You're pathetic, Theo. I find it very hard to believe I ever thought otherwise. Actually, I don't think I ever did. I think I was just *unwell*.'

He sneered. 'Sure you were, Lou. All those times.'

'You . . .' Lou stepped towards Theo, not away from him. It was hard to look up at him, he was so tall, but she wanted to be clear. 'You don't know anything about my husband. You don't know a thing about my marriage, or my family, or my home, whatever you think. I never gave anything of myself to you. You' – check the door again, Lou, she thought – 'were a *fuck*. And your fragile little ego can't deal with it.'

I hope no-one heard that, was Lou's first thought, as she finally did push Theo, who looked like he'd been slapped, towards the door.

'Now get the fuck out of my classroom,' she said.

Lou was shaking; she knew she was flushed from her neck to her scalp, and her voice was cracking. This is what fury feels like, she thought. This is what fury looks like. Don't cry. Don't cry. Don't cry.

Theo looked like he was wrestling with fury, too. He was ridiculous, this giant man in this colourful room of tiny furniture, standing there, wondering where to go.

'Does he know you slept with me in his bed?' he asked, as he started a slow walk towards the door. 'Was that just a *fuck*?'

And just before he stepped out into the corridor he turned and gave her a little wave. 'Good luck, Lou.'

Josh

NOVEMBER

Confess

'**D**id she like the shirt?' asked Dana, leaning across the pub table to flatten a spring of Josh's hair.

'Don't do that,' said Josh, with a little duck of his head, and Dana pulled a face at him. 'She noticed it, didn't offer an opinion.'

'Do you feel better?' she asked. 'Taking a stand?'

'I feel' – Josh looked into his beer – 'like I'm in limbo.'

'Write that down,' said Dana, pushing Josh's phone towards him.

'I just . . . I need to force the issue. The girls are suffering, we're suffering. We just need to get on with it.'

How did this happen? Josh wondered. How had Dana become his confidante? And then he pulled himself up. He knew how it had happened. Intentionally. Like a whole lot of shit that he was trying to do at the moment. On purpose.

They were at a pub together because they'd come to see a band. Josh felt like he'd travelled back in time, sitting in the Annandale Hotel in the inner west, waiting to see an old friend play. When was the last time he and Lou had done this? Would Lou maybe still like to do this sometimes? Did she ever like it?

Every other pub in Sydney might have moved on to espresso martinis on tap and crab sliders, but the Annandale seemed reassuringly unchanged. The carpet was still a touch sticky, the beer was still served in unreconstructed schooner glasses and the clientele generally had jeans that went all their way to their shoes. I really am an old bastard now, thought Josh.

'You know this isn't a date, right?' he said to Dana. 'You're just the only person I know who might not hate this.'

'Sure,' she said. 'We're both still married, after all.' But she was smiling as she said it, and Josh knew that he was probably being a bit of a dick, encouraging this. But fuck it – he was allowed to go to a gig with a female friend. Right?

The writing was going well. It was helping him feel less . . . wretched. Once a week for the last few weeks, he and Dana had met in the garage of her house, him with his guitar, her with her keyboard, and thrown a few ideas around. The kids were inside the house, entertained by iPad or asleep, as they'd play a few songs they both knew, and then he'd show her what he'd been working on, and she'd critique.

He knew it couldn't go on forever, that the words said through the camping truth serum of whisky were still floating around out there somewhere, and that Dana was an unreliable narrator of the reality of either her own or his marriage, but he enjoyed it; it felt like a bright spot in his life. He was thinking of asking one of his old muso mates, Bob Oslo, if he could play in his band sometimes.

Which was why there were here tonight. It was not a date.

'I think you seem lighter lately,' said Dana, shouting slightly over the music. 'How's Lou?'

'She seems fine,' he said, sipping his drink. I can't talk about Lou with you, he thought, that's not what this is. But the trouble was, in between the writing and the playing, little slivers of actual companionship had slipped into this strange arrangement, and he had found himself telling Dana things he never intended. His sister Anika didn't know what went on in the therapist's office, but Dana had encouraged Josh to stand up for himself, even if she didn't know all the details. No-one did.

Except Mum. At the thought of Emma, Josh automatically looked at his phone. He, like most of Sydney, had downloaded an app called Fires Near Me. Josh had plugged in Emma's address up the coast. So far, nothing had come too close to the blond-brick retirement community, but there were fires above and below, and he'd been arguing with Anika and Maya about going up to get her before the threat got any more serious.

'She won't want to leave,' Maya had insisted. 'It's her home now.'

'She doesn't have to leave,' Josh had said. 'She just needs to take a little break in the city.'

'Where in the city?' Anika asked. 'The two of you are pretty much homeless and my couch is booked out. Let's wait to see if it's necessary.'

Tonight, the fire app didn't show anything more alarming than the new normal: little blue diamond markers covering the state's coastline. But blue didn't signify an emergency.

The crowd began to shuffle and clap, as Josh's old friend Bob climbed onto the stage, guitar in hand, to start the show.

'I approve of your therapy breakthrough giving you something to write about for Pearl Hass,' Dana shouted. 'Since I appear to be your agent these days.'

*

After the show, Josh added an extra stop to the Uber and dropped Dana at her house.

Pulling up outside in the dark, the night mercifully still after the gusting hot winds that had been fanning the fires all week, Dana didn't open the car door. 'You should come in,' she said. 'Have one more drink.'

'Not a chance,' he said, but he hoped he said it kindly.

'You're messing with me,' Dana said. 'It's not nice.'

He looked at her. Could he imagine being with Dana, either for one night or many? He liked her honesty, her humour. He liked how he looked through her eyes. He liked that she liked his music. All of that was flattering. And he liked the way she moved in these tight jeans and this T-shirt that stopped just in time to show a little stripe of stomach when she raised her arms. And her swinging ponytail. He liked all that. But he also knew this was about the most complicated rebound sex he could choose. It would be like an act of war.

'I thought we were friends,' he said. But even as he did, he knew she was right. It was not nice.

'Then come in as a friend,' she said, nodding towards the house. 'There's only a teenage babysitter to pay in there, and then it's all quiet.'

Josh looked at her, feeling the Uber driver's irritation at this lengthy pause. 'I . . .'

She leaned into him again, like she had that night when they were camping, and stopped with her lips a couple of centimetres from his mouth, looking into his eyes.

'Come on, guys,' said the Uber driver. 'Is there another stop or not?'

'No,' said Dana. 'Is there, Josh?'

She was about to kiss him when his phone rang.

'Don't look at it,' Dana said, pulling back and putting a hand on his crotch. 'Don't look at it.'

'I'm . . . a dad,' he managed. 'I'm looking at it.'

It was Lou. 'Oh,' he said.

'Don't answer it.'

He pressed the green button. 'Lou?'

Dana took her hand off his jeans and sighed loudly.

'I need to see you now,' she said. Her voice was thick from crying.

Josh looked at the time on the Uber dash: 12.30 a.m. 'Is everything okay? The girls – are they okay?'

'They're fine,' she gasped. 'It's me. I'm not okay. Can you come?'

Josh didn't even think about it. 'Yes,' he said. He pressed the red button to end the call, looked back at Dana.

'Ridiculous,' she said. 'Fucking ridiculous. I don't know if there's a word anymore that you're allowed to use for "cock-tease", but that's what you are, you spineless, cruel prick.'

As Dana climbed out of the car, Josh said to the driver, 'Sorry, there's going to be another stop.'

*

Lou was sitting under the tree.

When Josh climbed out of the Uber he saw her there, on the grass, in a big white shirt he recognised as his, one of the rare collared shirts he owned. Lou had bought it for him for her friend's wedding; they'd had a row about him having to wear it. She looks good in it, he thought. She always looks good.

Lou didn't look up to acknowledge his arrival. He walked over to her and crouched down, put a finger under her chin and lifted her face until she met his eyes.

Lou's eyes. He'd looked into them every day for fourteen years. He knew everything about them. Tonight they were full, and they were so, so sad.

'You're going to get grass stains on my shirt,' he said to her, still holding her chin.

She attempted a smile. 'You never wore this shirt,' she said.

'I might want to now,' he said. 'I might have to go on dates.'

And she almost laughed. 'Yeah,' she said. 'You'll be terrible at that.'

He let go of her chin and sat beside her. Both of their backs were against the tree trunk.

'I hate the fires,' said Lou. 'I feel sick all the time. I'm worried about your mum.'

'Me too,' said Josh. 'I'm thinking about going to get her.'

'Everything is trashed. The world terrifies me.'

Josh said nothing. They sat there. The street was quiet. Just street-lamps and a few cats, some lights still on in a sprinkling of houses, the flicker of a TV screen in the window of one of the flats across the road. The slightest breeze in the tree's leaves above them. One a.m. in the suburbs.

'I'm ready to tell you,' Lou said. 'That's why I called.'

'What about Sara's office? What about four weeks?'

'I need to tell you.'

Okay. Josh took a big gulp of night air into his lungs, held his breath for a moment. He could taste smoke and beer, and the hot chips he and Dana had eaten when they'd left the pub. He reached for Lou's hand and held it.

'Go on.'

'He's called Theo,' Lou said. 'The guy from years ago. The guy from this year. He's called Theo.'

T.

'He was the deputy head at school.'

What Josh felt then was like a thud. It took a second, just a second, for his mind to fill with images of the days – all the days that Lou had gone off to work, in her dresses and her jeans and with her hair up and her hair down. Day after day. He was the deputy head at school. That rang a bell somehow.

'Go on.'

'Back then, I was so angry. You know that. And I wanted to hurt you, and I wanted to feel something other than empty and bruised.'

Josh closed his eyes and rested his head back against the tree trunk.

'And I ended it. When I told you that I ended it, I ended it.'

'But . . .' And Josh found it hard to talk, like the sound had to be hauled out from somewhere really deep inside him. 'He still worked there. You still worked there.'

'Yes.' Lou held on tight to his hand. 'But it was over.'

Josh opened his eyes, looked at Lou, but she wasn't looking at him. She was looking straight ahead. There were tears on her cheeks. 'And then, this year.'

He pulled his hand away. He couldn't help it. He couldn't bear to be touching her. He put his hands over his eyes.

'I slept with him again on New Year's Day.' She paused, took a breath, and whispered, 'Here.'

Josh, his hands still over his eyes, thought about New Year's Day. He'd had a hangover. He was up at Mum's with the girls. They'd seen a stingray at the beach. He'd come home to a cheerful but tired Lou in the house, assumed she'd been cleaning all night. That awful New Year's. That party.

'Have I ever met this person?' he asked suddenly.

'He says he met you at Beth's party, in the garden.'

Yes. That guy. That was the guy. Chinos. Enormous. Huge hands.

'And he was at the concert.'

The guy leaning down, talking into Lou's ear. Fuck. Fuck. Fuck.

'I decided to give us a year,' said Lou. 'I felt shit about what had happened, but also, well, you know, angry, confused about what was happening with us. I never slept with him again, I promise. I thought about it sometimes, but I promise you, this year, it's been all about us.'

Josh took his hands from his eyes. He turned back to look at Lou and she was looking at him. She tried to take his hand again, but he pulled it away.

'At the school concert. You lied about it.'

'Yes.'

'He was calling you.'

'Yes.'

'The fucking Sex Month.'

'Yes.'

'All this year when I've been trying . . . so fucking hard . . . to please you, to look for answers . . . every day, you'd go to work, and he'd be there.'

'Yes.'

Josh didn't know what to say now. There isn't anything to say now, he thought. Everything was worse. Even worse.

'Josh, I don't work with him anymore. He's gone.'

Josh felt the mossy tree trunk sticking to his shirt. The night was still warm, the air still had the acrid taste of smoke.

'You asked me to tell you everything so we can make decisions in the light,' Lou said. 'I have always known that if you knew about this, you couldn't live with it. You always chose not to know.'

'I didn't choose any of this, Lou,' he said. And the anger began to seep in. It started with a taste in his mouth that was worse than the smoke. Went to his stomach, his chest. His hands, twitching into fists. He had to move. Now.

Josh stood up. He ducked a little to step out of the reach of the tree branches, still long, still everywhere.

'Josh,' Lou said, still on the ground, 'I promise that's everything. I promise that's true. I've genuinely been trying to save our family this year, to save us. That's what it's all been about.'

'I have to go,' said Josh. 'I have to go now.'

'Not like this Josh,' said Lou, standing up too, now. Bare feet on the grass, chipped orange polish on her toenails. He looked into her face. She was still crying, but she wasn't trying to reach him. He felt like he hated her face. Pathetic, pitying. 'Please. You said you wanted to know.'

'Now I know.' He started to walk away.

'Where are you going? You don't have your car. It's late. Josh!' Lou called after him. 'You said you wanted to know.'

Josh started walking down the road, and then he started to run. A middle-aged man, in jeans and a nice blue shirt, running down a dark, suburban street in the middle of the night.

Lou

DECEMBER

Let go

Lou had looked up at the sound of a door closing in the corridor. Waited a moment.

It wasn't him. It hadn't been him the last time, either. Or the time before.

'That's it then,' she said to Sara.

Josh wasn't going to come. He wasn't going to forgive her. He wasn't even going to fight about it.

'I think he's given me the answer to my question.'

'What was the question?' asked Sara, her voice just a little less businesslike than usual.

'Has he given up on us?'

'That wasn't your question, Lou,' Sara said. 'You're rewriting history. You came here to see if this marriage was still viable. If it was still alive.'

It was the last therapy session of the year. Sitting there waiting for Josh, high up in the choking haze, Lou had told Sara what happened that night. What she'd told Josh.

'You know,' she said, 'I was *so* angry with him. But I can't conjure that feeling now. I can't even really remember it, how it felt, that fury.

Now, I can't imagine our family any other shape than it is. Me, Josh, Stella, Rita. I don't . . . feel a space where anyone else should be.'

Lou put her hands on her stomach, like she had done every time she thought about that day, for years. She felt nothing.

'Lou,' Sara said, 'have you ever thought that, rather than punishing Josh, you were punishing yourself?'

Lou looked up.

'You didn't do anything wrong, Lou,' Sara said. 'You need to forgive yourself.'

Lou felt like she might cry again. 'I slept with my boss, Sara,' she managed.

And the therapist smiled, just a little. 'Yeah. That bit wasn't ideal.'

*

It was ten days until Christmas, and she and Josh still hadn't spoken.

If Lou texted, he didn't answer. If she called, he didn't pick up. The only thing that would elicit a response was a question about the girls.

Are you picking them up today?

Yes.

Are you okay?

Nothing.

It was childish. It was infuriating. It was heartbreaking.

Lou had gone to the house when she knew he was there, but she couldn't bring herself to go in. Standing in the twilight near the side window like a stalker, like a ghost, looking in at her husband serving the girls sausages, the house lit up with glimmering fairy lights that Lou had wobbled on a stepladder to string up.

He'd added to them, she noticed, in the high-up places that she couldn't reach. A string of golden stars across the top of the kitchen cupboards. An angel at the very top of the tree that Rob had helped her with. A string of solar icicles along the roof of the back deck.

He did that for the girls. He wanted to make them happy, still. It was just her he couldn't talk to. Just Lou he couldn't see.

In their kitchen, he was smiling at Stella and Rita, laughing. And they were laughing with him. It was late. They should be in bed. It was nearly Christmas.

And Lou realised how ridiculous it was, *she* was, being locked out of her home, watching on, and she left, cursing herself.

12. Let go, she typed into her phone in the car outside her own home. *Just let the hell go.*

'What you must not do here,' Gretchen counselled her, back in her white kitchen over a large glass of wine, no sausages in sight, 'is make the mistake of transferring the power of this to Josh, just because you're feeling guilty and he's the one holding you at arm's length. Remember how all this started. Remember what you want.'

'But I don't know what I want,' said Lou.

'It's time to decide,' her friend said firmly.

'We have a couple of weeks left.'

Gretchen rolled her eyes. 'It's time to drop the game, Lou. The clock doesn't matter. The date doesn't matter. You need to make a fucking decision and go with it. A week here or there is bullshit, and all of this makes me think there can only be one reason why you're delaying it.'

'What's that?' Lou was smarting, but she knew Gretchen was right.

'Because it's very painful to end a marriage,' said Gretchen. 'And you're putting it off.'

'I don't know if it's my decision to make,' said Lou. 'Not anymore.'

It had been a grim run-in to Christmas. As the smoke lowered, Lou's father Brian was getting worse, and Rob had organised for a live-in carer to help Annabelle. Annabelle hated having someone in her home, and was on the phone to Lou constantly, usually with a few wines under her belt, complaining about all the things the nurse did wrong. Which was nothing, as far as Lou could tell.

Meanwhile, as the term finished up, Lou prepared to say goodbye to her class. To Ryan Harcourt and Amber Lin, to the tears and the messes and the tiny breakthroughs. All these years as a teacher and she always, always got emotional at the end of term. This year, her emotions were closer to the surface.

Thankfully, Theo was gone and she hadn't heard a thing from him. Their last encounter made her furious every time she thought about it. How had she let that man in? How had she missed all the signs – glaring now in hindsight – that he had become so reckless?

That night at the school concert, when he'd appeared from nowhere and begun whispering to her in front of her friends, in front of Josh.

'Meet me outside . . . This is driving me crazy . . . Why are you making me suffer?'

She'd dismissed it, thought he was playing games, turning up the drama for effect. How had she somehow overlooked his anger? She knew why, really, if she was honest. Theo was never a real person to her, and she didn't really care about him. He was just a thing she was doing to distract herself.

Let go, she told herself again. *Let all that go.*

*

Lou packed up her last pile of drawings for the kids to take home, and headed out to her car.

It was her last night away from the girls before Christmas. She'd heard via Anika that Josh was preparing to go up and see his mum, hopefully to bring her back to the city. The fires in Emma's neighbourhood had died down, Lou knew from her constant checking, but no-one could be sure for how long. Josh wouldn't be back until the twenty-third; he was doing a job on the way up the coast. A last bit of extra Christmas money for the girls' presents, Lou knew he'd be thinking.

How the hell are we going to do Christmas like this? You need to talk to me, Josh.

That's what was running through her head when Lou saw the woman standing next to her car.

It took her a minute.

Dana.

Dana was standing there, in denim shorts and a striped T-shirt and red sandals, her hair in a ponytail, sunglasses pushed back on her head. She'd been looking at her phone, but glancing up every few minutes, and when she saw Lou, she put the phone into her bag and smiled at her.

'Dana?' Lou said. It was a question. A question that meant, *What the fuck are you doing here?*

'Hi, Lou. Sorry for the very random visit.'

'I'm . . . going home.'

'I know, I know – and I know this is weird, I do. I just . . . need to talk to you about something.'

Every single bit of Lou wanted to run away. She had this over-whelming sense that whatever Dana was going to tell her, she didn't want to hear it, that her life would be better if she didn't. 'Dana, I don't think . . .' She jangled the car keys in her hand. 'I don't think I want to talk to you.'

'I know, it's *really* weird.' Dana looked down, seeming embarrassed. Then she looked back up at Lou. 'But I saw Josh today.'

You did? Why did you? Lou started to feel a bit sick. She didn't say anything.

'Marco's gone,' Dana went on, which seemed unrelated. Or maybe not. 'He left. I'm glad.'

This was getting worse.

'And I've been lonely, and I've been an idiot.' Dana was always like this, Lou remembered, just blurting out brutally honest, inappropriate things. If absolutely everything in their circumstances were different, they might actually be friends.

'But, to be honest, Josh hasn't been entirely . . . fair with me, either.'

Not friends. Definitely not friends.

'Dana, I'm sorry, I don't know what you know, but like I said, I don't want to talk about this with you,' Lou said, and she went to step around her.

'Lou, he's so devastated,' Dana said, reaching out for Lou's arm. 'And I've been a dick, but really, I would never, ever want to be with anyone who was so clearly madly in love with someone else.'

The smoke haze was in Lou's eyes. The cicadas were started to chirrup.

Madly in love. Not the words you still thought about after fourteen years.

'I just had to come here and tell you that,' said Dana. 'Because he hasn't told me anything about what's going on with you two, but . . . Look, I was really angry with him because I thought he was free, or at least on his way to being free. And I thought he was rejecting me. But he wasn't free at all. And he's not going to be.'

Lou blinked again. She still couldn't think of anything to say. What did one say in this situation?

'I just wanted to tell you.' Dana let go of her arm.

They both stood there, looking at each other for a moment, the strange summer evening settling around them.

'I've got to go and pick up the kids,' Dana said eventually.

'Yeah,' was all Lou could manage. 'Thank you.'

Dana looked around before she turned away, at the old building and the green gums of Bayside. 'Nice school,' she said. 'You should send the girls here.'

Lou shrugged. 'I'm here,' she said, for some reason.

'Yeah,' said Dana. 'They might like that.'

And she turned and, this time, walked away towards her car, her sandals flip-flopping as she went.

Josh

DECEMBER

Let go

There was no-one on the road going the way Josh was going.

The traffic was bumper to bumper heading towards Sydney and the safety of the high-rises and the concrete, but the road heading north was empty.

But the journey north was fine, once you were used to driving slowly with your headlights glaring through the ever-present smoke, and passing the occasional smouldering stump. The road was open, the truck stop was still serving terrible coffee, everything was as it was.

Except that it was almost Christmas and Josh had no idea what his family was going to look like by then, or on Boxing Day, or on New Year's Eve. He hadn't felt so untethered since he was a teen, travelling up and down this highway in his dad's Beemer, breathing in cigarette smoke with a constant soundtrack of racing commentary.

Josh thought about that as he took the Newcastle turn-off.

Emma was safe for now; the fires had backed away from the fringes of her estate. She didn't want Josh to come up, but of course he was ignoring her wishes. He needed to know that his mum was okay and still with him while everything else was floating in space. He needed to bring her home.

But first, he had something else to do.

Josh found a seat at the back of the old, dingy pub, facing the door. He felt awkward, being here in the middle of the day, alone. He looked around at the men who didn't feel awkward, the day drinkers and the shiftworkers and the people who hadn't yet been shamed into moderation. He played with a middy, wondered what the hell he was doing.

It's your turn to have a midlife crisis, he thought. Questioning everything, looking for answers.

The night Lou had told him the truth about Theo, something had shifted in Josh. He had run until he was exhausted, and then he'd flagged down a taxi and asked the driver to take him to the beach. He had no idea why, but he needed to sit there, at the edge of things, and breathe in some air that wasn't thick with toxic dust and wonder how the fuck he'd let this happen to his life.

He was almost embarrassed to think of it now, but Josh had jumped into the ocean pool at Coogee surf club at two in the morning and floated there, in the black, among the burnt twigs and the singed leaves and the seaweed. And he knew what he had to do. But he had no idea how.

He had to stop hiding.

How the hell had he avoided that name, that detail, for so long? That night, in the cool, dirty water, it felt as if Lou's confession had changed everything he knew about his wife and what she was capable of. That night, he actually hated her.

He'd climbed out of the pool, after what seemed like a long time, and pulled on his black jeans and his new blue shirt, and he'd walked to the other end of the beach and up onto the headland, and sat on the clifftop. A bedraggled middle-aged man having some sort of clichéd epiphany in the face of the sunrise.

Time to face things, Josh, he'd told himself.

And here he was, waiting for the door to swing open and reveal some answers.

There was a small commotion, and there she was. Christine. The woman who'd been by his dad's side when he was breathing his last. The woman Josh had barred from his wedding. The woman Len had been fighting with when a car hit him.

She was loud, Christine, and she called out in her broad Irish accent as she came in – to the barman, to the day drinkers and then, when she saw him, to Josh. She was older, and slower, but just as loud.

'Hey there!' she said. 'I never thought I'd see you again!'

Josh stood, and she hugged him, and she was short, her face pushing into his chest. 'Buy an old duck a drink, won't you?'

They sat there, at the back table, and Christine talked. About where she was living now – with her eldest, but she didn't get on with his missus so that was never going to last – and about the little dog she wanted to buy when she got herself settled with her own place one day. And about Josh's dad, and how much she missed him.

'Such a stupid old bugger,' she said. 'Such a temper. Always bloody right.'

'Yeah.' Josh drank the last mouthful of his middy, flat on his tongue now. 'That sounds like him.'

'Miss him, though. I bet you do, too.'

Josh shrugged. 'I didn't see him much.'

'Still,' Christine said, looking out the window, 'you don't have to see someone to miss them. At least you knew they were there, hey?'

That was true.

Josh had come here to ask Christine something specific, but now it seemed grossly inappropriate, in the face of this tired, tipsy woman, someone just looking for a bed and a puppy, as she had been now for years.

She was still talking – about a friend who had made her fortune on eBay – when Josh interrupted to ask what he'd come to ask.

'Did my dad step in front of that car, Christine?'

And she stopped, mid-sentence, and turned to look at Josh properly. 'Of course he didn't!' she said. 'Why would he do that?'

'I don't know,' said Josh, and he dropped his head to his hands. 'I'm still thinking about his last minutes, all these years later, and it's just something I need to know, for me.'

Christine cocked her head. 'You having a hard time, love?' she asked.

'I am a bit, if I'm honest,' said Josh. 'It's not been a great year.'

'Well, we should definitely have another drink then, love, because misery loves company,' said Christine. 'But first, let me tell you something about your dad that you need to know.'

Josh waited while Christine seemed to think about what it was, this thing.

'Your sister called him, you know, about the baby,' said Christine. 'I remember it.'

'Stella?'

'Must be. Anyway, he was so delighted, Len, he was carrying on, so pleased. And your sister got all upset on the phone because he was so excited. Because you were his son, you know; he had a special bond with you.'

'He did?'

'He did,' said Christine, tapping out a smoke from a battered packet and tucking it behind her ear. 'And I couldn't stop him from coming down there to see you, even though I knew his knee was dicky and he shouldn't be driving. It was his knee that folded on him that night, you know, when he didn't get out of the way of the car.'

'His knee,' Josh repeated. Really?

'It was his bloody knee. We had a blue, but he was just being dramatic, stomping across the road, and he turned to yell something at me.' Christine looked like she was almost enjoying this awful story. 'And his knee, it just went, and there was a car, and . . .' She looked back at her hands, fell quiet.

Josh swallowed. Waited.

'Anyway . . .' This time Christine reached over and took his hands. 'He couldn't be stopped. And he loved you, your dad, in his own way. He was all about wetting that baby's head, even that night. He loved you, but he couldn't really tell you. That wasn't his way.'

There it was.

Josh felt better. And worse. His dad was not so bereft and lonely that he'd ended it all. Also, his dad had loved him, and never bloody showed it.

'I don't think that's your problem, is it?' asked Christine.

'What?'

'Not showing people you love them.'

Josh considered this for a moment. 'No, I don't think that is my problem.'

Christine smiled. 'Buy me another?'

*

Josh spent that night at a motel near the highway. He wanted to be alone, in some space, before he drove on to pick up Emma.

He lay on the cheap floral bedspread and drank a beer, clicked through the TV's digital channels, and he thought how easy it would be for him to keep hiding now, to keep moving, keep drinking, keep dodging the difficult parts. Like his old man.

And he thought about how, yesterday, he'd gone to find Dana to apologise to her for the night in the cab. How hard that had been, and how much simpler it would have felt to avoid it.

'I'm sorry,' he said at her front door, with the noise of the kids fighting deep in the house. 'I think I led you on.'

'Such a quaint phrase,' Dana said. 'But I suppose it's possible I didn't want to hear what you were telling me.'

It had felt good, afterwards, as he walked down the path to her front gate. It felt good to have dealt with something.

Was that how Lou had felt after she'd told him absolutely everything under the tree that night? She'd given their marriage a year, and now it was in pieces. Didn't you have to believe in something to hold it together?

His phone beeped. It was Lou. What timing. Maya would say she must have known he was brooding about her.

Are you safe up there?

He turned his phone over. Not now, Lou. Now it's me who needs a bit more time.

It buzzed again, and he ignored it.

That giant man at that awful party and Lou in her red-rust dress.

The phone kept buzzing.

His girls and their beautiful eyes, and Lou and her laugh.

Buzz, buzz.

Her face when she'd watched him leave, that night under the tree.

Zzzzz. Zzzzz.

He reached out and grabbed the phone, ready to turn it off. But it was Emma calling.

'Joshy,' she said, 'they say the fires are coming back. Maybe you should come and get me after all.'

Lou

24 December, 2019

I give my marriage a week.
   Bold. Underlined.
   <u>I give my marriage a week.</u>
   If I still have a marriage.
   Lou was at the kitchen table, surrounded by the brightly coloured chaos of Christmas. Mince pies and panettone – food that no-one would eat at any other time of year – and more chocolate than her girls would have set eyes on in the past twelve months. Bottles and bottles. Rolls of cheap wrapping paper, cards received and not returned.
   It doesn't matter what else is happening on Christmas Eve, Lou wrote. *If you have kids, the show must go on.*
   She could hear Annabelle and Gretchen next door in the living room, helping wrap the last of the presents in front of the TV. This was always Josh's job, wrestling to find the end of the sticky tape after a couple too many beers. But Lou's mother and her oldest friend were not going to let her be alone tonight after her giddy girls finally fell asleep.

Clearly, if Gretchen and Annabelle could form an alliance, things were bad.

And they were.

Josh was cut off two hours north. He and Emma had been told it was too late to leave, the fires had closed in and the roads were locked down. Phone signal and wifi were out. All Lou knew came from the TV and her fucking fires app, and that seemed to be flashing more emergency red diamonds at her every time she looked. The last she had heard, they were safe. They must be safe.

It seemed unthinkable, here in suburban Sydney, where the worst of the smoke had cleared days ago and the summer holidays were attempting to unfold as usual, with beach days and pretty young people drinking in short dresses and manic prawn shopping and late-afternoon meltdowns from tired kids. It seemed unthinkable that beyond this bubble, everything was burning. People had died, lost their homes. People were isolated, alone, terrified.

Pebbly Beach, their honeymoon place, was burning.

Get it together, Lou told herself at the table. Put the phone down. Go and help Gretchen.

It's not like Josh would be *here* if he wasn't there.

He still hadn't spoken to her since her confession under the tree. She'd seen him once since Dana's bizarre visit, when he came to say goodbye to the girls before he went to pick up Emma, but he still couldn't look at her. His face was pinched closed, his eyes lowered to Stella and Rita height. She'd tried to reach out and touch his arm, to get him to talk, but he wouldn't. He shook her off with a shrug and kept moving.

Madly in love? Really?

Lou couldn't cry. She'd cried a hell of a lot that night under the tree, in Josh's white shirt, and plenty since. It was all gone. And somehow it felt self-indulgent, when a collective dread was creeping across the whole country, to be focusing on the mess splattered on the walls of her own, still-standing home.

Before communications were cut, Josh had sent Lou a message.

They're closing the roads, he wrote. *I don't want the girls to worry. I'm with Mum. Stuck but safe. Might lose phone reception.*

Lou had wanted to write: *Are you still angry?* But that seemed trite. *I love you.* But that seemed too small. *Can you forgive me?* But that seemed unfair.

Get home safe x was what she'd gone with. There had been no response.

Get it together, Lou. Put the phone down. Go and help Gretchen. Come *on.*

Gretchen was still tanned from Iceland. How was that a thing? She looked clear-eyed and light on the floor of Lou's lounge, even as she tried to work out how to wrap a pair of rollerblades in brown paper. Annabelle was sitting in an armchair with a glass of white wine, offering directions.

'You have no skills in this area, do you, love?' she was saying. 'You're wrapping as if you have no thumbs.'

'Not something I've had to focus on, Annabelle, to be honest,' Gretchen replied. 'Rollerblades haven't featured much in my life since the *Boogie Nights* fetish blew through my teens.'

Annabelle gave a tight-lipped smile, took a sip of wine, looked up at her daughter.

'Any word, Louise?' she asked.

'No, Mum. Looks like phone reception is still out.'

'Typical of Joshua, really,' Annabelle muttered. 'If anyone's going to get stuck . . .'

'Mum, don't,' said Lou sharply.

'Look on the bright side,' said Gretchen, triumphantly sticking down the last corner of the rollerblade parcel. 'Closed highways mean I can't go to visit my dad tomorrow, which is good news for everyone. Including you, because you're stuck with me.'

'What about Kim? Where will she be?'

'You mean the love of my life? The song in my heart?' Gretchen really was working hard to lighten the mood.

'Honestly, Gretchen,' huffed Annabelle. 'Pick a side.'

'Mum!'

'It's okay, Lou.' Gretchen laughed. 'My dad's just as confused as you, Annabelle. I may have finally chosen – I'm pretty mad about Kim. But she's in Aspen. Back before New Year.'

'Aspen sounds like the place,' said Lou, bending to pick up bags and boxes. 'Cold. Snow. Phone reception. God, she lives the life.'

'You know, since she's been tagging me as her girlfriend, my Insta following's up by five thousand.' Gretchen was looking around for something else to wrap, so Lou threw her a mini-football.

'What are you going to do with all those eyeballs?'

'Feed my insatiable ego.'

'I have no idea what either of you are talking about,' said Annabelle. And then she took a look at the flames filling the TV screen. 'Christ almighty,' she said. 'This country.'

Lou walked over to the television and snapped it off.

'I can't watch anymore,' she said. 'I'm going to check on the girls, get the stockings.'

She climbed up the stairs and went to Stella and Rita's room.

Stockings hung at the end of their beds, covers kicked off in the heat. Lou took off her fancy slippers and climbed into bed next to Stella.

She stroked her daughter's hair and watched her sleep. She could honestly say that, to her, there was nothing more beautiful in art or nature than her daughters' faces. She felt breathless with it, the perfection in every dent and curve and freckle and mole.

'I know, you know,' said a soft voice behind her, and it was her mother.

Lou didn't say anything, just rolled over on her side to face Annabelle, hands together under her head like she was sleeping.

'I know you and Josh are living apart,' she went on in a whisper, as the girls' soft snores punctuated the silence. 'And I'm hurt you didn't tell me.'

'How could I tell you, Mum?' said Lou, her voice equally soft. 'You'd only gloat. Please don't gloat.'

'I won't gloat,' she said. 'But you will understand, as your girls get older.'

'Understand what?'

'How much you want to protect them. From struggle and heartbreak and sorrow. And themselves.'

'But you can't.'

'No, you can't.' Annabelle nodded. 'But you'll die trying.'

Lou uncurled herself from Stella's bed, picked up the stockings and walked to the door, to her mum. She gave her a hug and, after a long minute, they both stepped into the hall.

'I think it might be over, Mum,' said Lou.

'Maybe,' said Annabelle. 'And if it is, you'll survive. You and your brother have a very strong sense of self. You get it from me.'

Lou almost laughed.

'But it might not be as over as you think,' Annabelle said, as Lou followed her down the stairs.

'I don't know what you're talking about, Mum. I'd think you were the last person who'd be looking for the Hail Mary save.'

'I'm talking about men with honour, Lou. It's an old-fashioned word, but it means someone who will always do the right thing by you, at the end of the day, whatever comes. Someone who loves their family and shows it, someone who respects you and what you've built together . . .' Annabelle drifted off a little, her voice cracking, then came back. 'I have my troubles with Joshua . . .'

'You have been bloody awful to him!' Lou couldn't help herself. 'And I've never really got it, Mum, not really. It's not like Dad is the master of the universe.'

'I know, Lou.' And Annabelle almost looked embarrassed. 'I have always worried he wasn't enough for you. I have always known you wanted a *life*, just like I did. But even I have to admit Josh has honour. Look at where he is right now. He's with his mother. And I have never for one moment doubted that he loved you more than life. Your dad, quiet achiever that he is, is also such a man. And watching him slip away is making me absolutely . . .' Annabelle raised her eyes to the ceiling. 'Absolutely fucking furious with the world and all of you who are still fully in it.'

Lou was stunned. The wisdom, the generosity . . . the swearing. 'Mum, are you feeling alright?'

'I'm just saying,' she concluded, as they went back into the lounge room, where Gretchen was wrapping a giant cuddly taco for Rita, 'that it might not be as over as you think.'

Gretchen looked up at Lou, smiled.

'I need him to be safe,' said Lou.

Josh

28 December, 2019

The evacuation centre was surprisingly calm, Josh thought.

For all the national talk of panic, no-one had really appeared to be panicking in the old golf club, the one with the pokies, the million-dollar view and the ring of exhausted firefighters protecting it. Rather, the people gathered there seemed to understand that there were things worth railing against. Patronising politicians, forgotten internet passwords, fourteen types of milk. And there was this. Nature. Catastrophe. Getting through the night.

Timing was everything, thought Josh. He had arrived at his mum's door in time to load her things into the back of his ute and drive off with her in the passenger seat beside him, only to be told a few hundred metres down the road that no, you're too late, the fire is coming in fast. You're going nowhere. Turn around and stay put.

The man who'd delivered this news to Josh was young, wearing hi-vis yellow streaked with dust and mud and reeking of smoke, like everything else.

'I just drove up from Sydney yesterday,' Josh said. 'I got through fine.'

There had been smoke and fire and devastation all around, he added silently, but he'd got through fine.

'Mate, it's too late to leave,' the young man said, exhaustion audible in his voice, visible behind his eyes. 'The highway is closed. You need to get to a safe place.'

It's too late to leave were the words no-one wanted to hear in the summer of 2019, and people up and down the country were being told exactly that.

'Joshy,' Emma said beside him, unreasonably calm, 'listen to the man. Let's go where we're told to go and hold on. We'll be fine.'

'This,' said Josh, throwing the ute into reverse, 'would not be happening if you'd stayed in your bloody high-rise. Nice and safe there with the inner-city gangs. Didn't have to worry about you then, did I?'

Even as he joked to Emma, Josh's head was pounding. I must tell Lou, he thought. I must stop with the silence and tell Lou to tell the girls not to worry.

As they turned around, Josh considered the sky – which was a pale grey – and judged they just had enough time to go back to Emma's to fill the ute with as much food and water as they could; he could see others around them doing the same.

But by the time he was throwing blankets over the boxes and bags in the ute's tray, the sky had darkened almost to black. It was 2 p.m. and Josh couldn't see a metre ahead through a thick black-red haze. When he hurried around to slip into the driver's seat, he saw the passenger side, where he had asked his mum to sit and wait, was empty.

'Mum!' he shouted, his lungs immediately filling with the acrid air. He spun around, peering through the dark. He could see no-one. '*Mum!*'

And then there she was, coming out of the house, holding something to her body with both hands.

'Get in, Mum! What are you doing?'

'I'm here, Josh,' Emma said, her voice still remarkably calm. She didn't comment on the gloom, or the smoke, or the fact that the horizon appeared to be glowing an orange-red. 'I've got what I need now.'

Five minutes later, the ash-covered ute was one of hundreds of ash-covered vehicles trying to get into the golf club car park, being directed by more tired people in yellow vests. 'There's no time for this queue,' Josh decided out loud, and he turned again, driving the ute up onto the median strip and pulling into the adjacent park. 'Let's walk, Mum. I'll come back for everything when I can.' And Josh picked up as many bags as he could manage in one hand, and took Emma's free hand in the other.

'What have you got, Mum? What was so important you had to give me a heart attack?'

And, in the dark, with the sound of sirens and the roar of a deadly wind and the lights of the tired, old golf club up ahead, she showed him.

A photo, of course. It was faded, in an old frame, but it was a picture he'd never seen before. There was Emma, young, smiling, and Len, his dad, unsmiling, smoking. He, Josh, was there, just a toddler in shorts and no shirt, Maya a baby in his mum's arms, Anika standing to one side in knee socks.

'Why?' he asked, as they walked past the queuing cars and joined the stream of people heading towards the golf club on foot, many pushing wheelchairs, prams and shopping trolleys full of supplies. 'Why would you save that picture, of all the pictures?'

'It's a moment in time,' she said. And she squeezed Josh's hand. 'No regrets.'

'Jesus, Mum, even in a crisis you're like bloody Yoda.' He squeezed her hand back. 'What are you talking about?'

'Your dad had his flaws, but what he gave me was everything.' Emma sounded like she was wheezing, ever so slightly. 'And I know you worry that you're like him, and you are – but only in the best ways.'

'Save your breath, Mum, we're nearly there.'

'I can't see you giving up on your family,' Emma said, ignoring him. 'You have his passion, but it's in the right place.'

*

Now, four days later, Josh was standing outside his own house, in the garden, looking at his tree.

The power and communications had dropped out as soon as they got into the golf club. As soon as he'd got his message to Lou.

The fire had passed through, picking and choosing where to aim its most destructive powers seemingly at random, reducing some homes to dust and leaving others untouched.

He'd spent one terrible night in the eye of that storm, holding Emma while she slept, fitfully, on blankets heaped on the luridly patterned carpet, thinking that the future was entirely unknowable. He knew everyone there was thinking the same. And in the middle of that night, even with his mother in his arms, he'd had to physically stop himself from getting up and driving hundreds of burning kilometres through the smoke and flames and poisonous ash to get back to one place. This place.

It was the only thing that mattered. Everything else had seemed ridiculous, irrelevant and frivolous.

And now he was here.

Light had returned to the sky the next morning to expose the fire's aftermath. Of course, it wasn't really over – it had just moved on to another community, another golf club – but for the moment this place could breathe again. The losses had been slight. They were the lucky ones.

But the highway remained closed, the power remained out, there was no fuel to buy, no food on the shop shelves. The days called Christmas and Boxing by name were really just hours to get through with nothing to do, little to eat, and too much time to think. In those hours Josh had scribbled lines and words to songs to follow what he had already sent to Pearl Hass before the world ended. The email with the link to the songs was titled: *I know you'll never hear these – or not*.

And now, standing outside his house, all the intensity of the last few days seemed so far away already, and he was desperately holding on to the clarity he'd felt in the middle of that night.

'Daddy!'

Rita – glowing, messy, loud – came flying through the front door as it banged open. And suddenly, as she wrapped herself around his legs, there were people, so many people.

Stella, of course – beautiful, tall, strong girl – with her arms around his waist. But also Annabelle, with an unfamiliar grin on her face, holding Brian's hand. And Rob, with a bear hug. And Gretchen, jumping up and down like a pogo stick and clapping, next to a teenage girl he assumed was JoJo, wearing the smirk of a kid too cool to grin.

And lastly Lou, hanging at the back of the crowd, but with a smile on her mouth and in her eyes.

'Wow,' said Josh, gasping for breath. 'You know I didn't fight any fires, right?'

'We were just so worried about you and Nana, Daddy,' Stella said. 'Where *is* Nana?'

'I dropped her with Anika and Maya,' he said. 'She's tired, but she's okay.'

'She's coming,' Lou said from the back. 'I called. They're all coming. We're going to do Christmas again.'

'We are?' Josh looked at her. 'Great.'

'Did you bring us our presents?' asked Rita. 'Daddy? Did our presents get burned in the fire?'

And Josh laughed and mouthed 'shit' at Lou, because the Christmas presents he'd bought them were at Anika's, under her tree.

'I might have to make a couple of calls to Santa about that,' he said to Rita. 'See if he's dealing with bushfire delays.'

'Of course he is,' said Rita. 'Come on, Daddy.'

And she took Josh's hand and led him into the house.

*

It was evening and Josh and Lou were at the kitchen sink.

A Christmas dinner calamity had exploded across the counters. The dishwasher was overflowing. Josh was washing, she was drying.

Lou had told him about her new job and he had told her he was proud of her.

'Lou, this is your time,' he said, soaping the potato pan, scrubbing at the little welded-on crusty bits. 'I don't think anything can stop you now.'

'It would be more hours,' she said, looking sideways at him. 'I'd need support.'

'It's time you got that,' said Josh. He didn't look up. 'You more than deserve it.'

They wiped in silence for another minute.

'Theo's really gone, you know,' Lou said.

Josh had been prepared to flinch when he heard that name, but its power had vanished. Theo, Theo, Theo.

'That's good,' he said.

They could hear everyone – and really, it was everyone – in other parts of the house. Rob and Annabelle arguing about climate change out on the back deck, an open bottle between them, Brian nodding along, holding his wife's hand. The girls shrieking as JoJo beat them on their new Nintendos upstairs in the guitar room. Maya reading tarot cards for Anika and Gretchen next door in the living room. Emma, Josh knew, was asleep on Stella's bed, exhausted.

As was he.

'I should take Mum home soon,' he said, putting down the last dish.

'Where's home?' asked Lou, wiping her hands on the tea towel.

'Here,' he said immediately. 'But not tonight.'

'Why not tonight?' Lou asked.

Surprised, he looked across at her.

'Because everything has changed, Lou,' he said. 'I know what's important to me. I always have, but now it's the loudest thing in my head. I can't keep auditioning for the part of your husband.'

'And I,' Lou said, and she took a deep breath, 'can't put this off any longer.'

He kept looking at her. He pictured her when they'd first met, when he picked her up from the floor of the pub. Lou was smaller then, she was wilder, she was exactly the same. Now she pushed her hair back off her forehead, just as she had that night, and he dreaded what she was going to say next, but he knew he had to hear it.

'I want to give my marriage another year,' Lou said.

And Josh almost laughed, but he couldn't. He couldn't do this, not again. He knew what he wanted, he'd felt it and seen it that night, in the tired old golf club with his indomitable mum sleeping next to him.

'Lou, I just can't,' he said. 'I really can't.'

'And another one,' Lou said, as if he hadn't spoken, and her smile turned into a big, broad grin. 'And another, and another, and another, and another . . .'

And Josh dropped his dishcloth and took his wife into his arms, and kissed her.

Lou's arms reached up around his neck and she pushed her hands into his hair as she pulled him into her.

'I thought there were four more days,' he said through the kiss.

'Fuck the date, fuck the clock,' Lou said, pulling back just enough to speak.

'So a year at a time?' he asked, looking down at Lou's face, his daughters' face, his history's face, his future's face.

'A year at a time,' she said. 'I'm thinking . . . fifty of them.'

Josh and Lou

New Year's Eve, 2019

L ou and Josh were in bed. The blind was up, the sun was already casting rays across the sheets through the tree's leaves. Lou's head was resting in the crook of Josh's neck. They'd thrown technology at the girls to buy an extra thirty minutes of peace.

Josh had his guitar across his body, he was playing Lou one of the songs he'd sent to Pearl Hass.

I chose some words to tell our story

And not one of them is big enough for you . . .

'She told me it's clearly not for her – it was for you,' Josh said. 'Which might be a pretty way of rejecting me, but she also said she liked a few of them.'

'I can't believe you did it,' Lou said. 'It's like you needed to get rid of me to do it.'

'Please,' said Josh. 'You got rid of *me*. Mostly to decide you're going to run the world.'

'Um . . . or a school someday?'

'Same, same. You need a very supportive husband to do either.'

'Which is why I had to get you back.'

'*That's* why.'

They lay there for a long moment, the guitar silent, grinning at each other like idiots. Insufferable idiots.

'Lying here, looking at you, I've just realised something,' Josh said.

Lou smiled encouragingly.

'Something bad.'

'Go on . . .' Her smile froze, just a little.

'I forgot to buy you a fucking Christmas present.'

'Again?'

'Again.'

Lou laughed and, with her head on his shoulder, stared at the window and the tree's waving yellow leaves. 'Play it again,' she said.

And Josh started singing up the next part of their story.

Acknowledgements

Thank you to every woman I know who has ever talked to me about love. Which is to say, every woman I know.

Actually, that's trite, and untrue. Everyone wants to share the beginnings of a love story. Everyone wants to sell you their version of an ending. But that long road in the middle? No-one wants to talk about that.

Even though – whatever our relationships look like – that's where most of us are, most of the time.

My wise writer friend Andrew Daddo told me to be careful writing a book about a marriage that was fighting for its life. He thought it might brush up too closely against my own relationship. That a few too many intimate truths might spark out of the story and scald us.

Those words stuck with me, and I am happy to report that at the time of publication, no serious fires have been started between myself and the man who needs the biggest thanks for anything I get to do, Brent McKean. For your support, belief, love, humour, loyalty and ridiculous footwear, I love you, Brent. You are the heart of our family and the soul of my real life.

But in conversations on love and marriage and friendship and motherhood and daughterhood and moving through an imperfect world as imperfect people, it is my unruly band of female friends who have all the best insight.

A special mention to my great mate and cheerleader Penny Kaleta, whose love, loyalty and generosity of spirit keeps a whole army of girlfriends afloat, myself included.

And just so many thank yous to all my favourite conversationalist mates: Miranda Herron, Karen Graham, Rachel Corbett, Leigh Campbell, Claire Isaac, Lee Christian, Dave Christian, Sally Godfrey, Helen Campbell, Angie McMenamin, Kate De Brito, Jacqueline Lunn, Katie Denton, Tara Flannery, Mark Brandon, Lucy Walker, Mel Thomas, Nick Bhasin. Oh, and to Clive Phillips, for the carpentry tips.

Big appreciation to Mel Ware and Sam Marshall and Leanne McLaughlin and Rebecca Rodwell for all your hilarious, heart-lifting honesty. And camping.

And to Monique Bowley and Lucy Ormonde, my ridiculously talented and clever mates who always, always give me the best advice about books and whether to write them.

And to Mia Freedman and Jessie Stephens, who are the best people to talk to and with about absolutely everything, all of the time. Thank you to all the Outlouders who listen to podcasts and consider us friends to share with and trust their stories to. And Mia, obviously, gets all the extra snaps for giving me the confidence to have confidence in my ideas.

And thank you to Claire Kingston for making me an author in the first place.

Thanks to some of the remarkable women I've met through Mamamia this past year, who have helped me get better at perspective and writing in general: Kate Fisher, Annabelle Chauncey, Gabbie Stroud, Sally Hepworth. Thank you also to the lovely Tess Woods, for writerly introductions and sound advice.

And thanks to my family, because when do you ever get to thank your family and they are far away and c'mon, this is my moment, please: My parents, Judith and Jeffrey Wainwright, who are the people with all the books. My brother Tom Wainwright, his partner Emilie Powles, the no longer small nieces and nephews, Lila, Louie, Poppy and Henry.

To Shaun McKean and Kieran Fox and to Jessie Friedrich for all the distraction of small people at crucial moments.

To my soulmate Lindsay Frankel and her Ian McLeish. Because just thank you, always.

And thank you to my publisher Cate Paterson and editor Brianne Collins at Pan Macmillan for all your enthusiasm for this story, and for making this a much better book.

This footnote is being written in June, 2020, and we're halfway through the strangest year any of us have lived yet. God knows how Lou and Josh's marriage would have worked out if this was the year Lou had started her clandestine experiment and they had to survive lockdown homeschool. Which brings me to Matilda and Billy, who are the kids unfortunate enough to have been cooped up with me as I worked and edited and shouted and stared into the fridge for unfeasibly long periods of time. You two are the very best reason to do anything.

MORE FICTION AVAILABLE FROM PAN MACMILLAN

Nine Perfect Strangers
Liane Moriarty

Can a health retreat really change your life forever?

From the no. 1 bestselling author of *The Husband's Secret* and *Big Little Lies*.

The retreat at health and wellness resort Tranquillum House promises total transformation. Nine stressed city dwellers are keen to drop their literal and mental baggage, and absorb the meditative ambience while enjoying their hot stone massages.

Watching over them is the resort's director, a woman on a mission to reinvigorate their tired bodies and minds.

These nine perfect strangers have no idea what is about to hit them.

With her wit, compassion, and uncanny understanding of human behaviour, Liane Moriarty explores the depth of connection that can be formed when people are thrown together in . . . unconventional circumstances.

The Mother-in-Law
Sally Hepworth

Bestselling author of *The Family Next Door*

Everyone in this family is hiding something . . .

Someone once told me that you have two families in your life – the one you are born into and the one you choose. Yes, you may get to choose your partner, but you don't choose your mother-in-law. The cackling mercenaries of fate determine it all.

From the moment Lucy met Diana, she was kept at arm's length. Diana was exquisitely polite, but Lucy knew, even after marrying Oliver, that they'd never have the closeness she'd been hoping for.

But who could fault Diana? She was a pillar of the community, an advocate for social justice, the matriarch of a loving family. Lucy had wanted so much to please her new mother-in-law.

That was ten years ago. Now, Diana has been found dead, leaving a suicide note. But the autopsy reveals evidence of suffocation. And everyone in the family is hiding something . . .

From the bestselling author of *The Family Next Door* comes a new page-turner about that trickiest of relationships.

The Best Kind of Beautiful
Frances Whiting

A warm-hearted novel from the author of *Walking on Trampolines* about music, grief, relationships, gardens, love, laughter and family.

Florence Saint Claire is a loner. Albert Flowers is a social butterfly. Good friends who think they know each other.

But, somewhere between who they are, and who people think they are, lies *The Best Kind of Beautiful*.

Award-winning journalist and author Frances Whiting brings her renowned warmth and empathy to this witty and gentle novel about bringing out the best in each other.